Andre

MW01487625

Princess of Dorsa

by Eliza Andrews

AuthorElizaAndrews.com

COPYRIGHT NOTICE

Cover credit:
Thank you Clarissa Yeo of YoClaDesigns.com.

Other books by Eliza Andrews:

To Have Loved & Lost: A new adult lesbian romance
https://www.amazon.com/dp/B01M7YF05A

Anika takes the long way home up soul mountain
https://www.amazon.com/dp/B074L7NJYX

Reverie
https://www.amazon.com/dp/B078WCN762

Paradise: A (short) lesbian romance
https://www.amazon.com/dp/B07212Z4GD

FREE SHORT STORY:
http://authorelizaandrews.com/readersclub

Learn more about Eliza:
http://authorelizaandrews.com

For LT.
As Snape would say… "Always."

Part I:

The Princess Natasia of House Dorsa

"As a child, the Princess showed no particular exceptional promise or talent; she was known more for her tendencies towards petulance, stubbornness, and disobedience than for excellence. In fact, there was nothing in her childhood or early education to suggest that she would be anything more than ordinary. How surprised the Wise Men who educated her would have been, had they lived to see the woman she became! How surprised her father, the Emperor Andreth, would have been to know that her name would one day overshadow his own."

— Wise Man Tellorin, *The Updated Histories of House Dorsa*

1

The dawn light didn't wake Tasia from slumber; the birds did. She was accustomed to the morning song of the birds. In childhood, they woke her nearly every morning with their musical chittering, their high voices like crystal chimes blowing in a gentle wind. Birdsong was followed by the matching chatter of her mother, cooing to them as they cooed to her while she sprinkled their breakfast of seeds and grains across the red brick of the inner courtyard. Tasia, not quite five yet, would go to the window, stand on tiptoes on her trunk in order to peer through the muslin drapes and into the courtyard below.

Even then, her mother had seemed more angel than human, her long blue sleeping gown hiding her feet so that she didn't walk across the courtyard so much as she glided, her little white birds with their bright yellow tails following along behind her, singing out their morning joy, waking the royal family one by one.

But the palace birds imported from her mother's Northeastern homeland were not the birds that woke Tasia now. There was nothing magical or musical or joyful about this birdsong; it was the rough

"CAW, CAW!"

of city crows that roused her from sleep, that reminded her she wasn't at home.

She woke from the dream of her mother with a shallow gasp — disoriented, eyes wide and searching for light in the dark, stuffy room. She stifled an annoyed groan when she realized where she was, disentangling herself from the heavy bare arm and heavy bare leg draped over her. She hadn't meant to fall asleep. What time was it?

She stood from the bed, nearly tripping on a sheet that had wound itself around her ankle like a constricting snake, then began groping blindly for her discarded clothes. Moonlight filtered in through the high open window, which meant she had somehow managed to wake herself before dawn.

Well, the city crows had woken her, actually.

Gods be thanked for those damnable birds, she thought, shaking an undergarment loose from another tangled sheet. She pulled it on hastily even as the man in the bed grunted and seemed to half-wake.

Where had she dropped that ugly brown shift she'd had her handmaid borrow from the cook's daughter?

"Tasia?" said the man in the bed groggily. He lifted himself up on one elbow, combing long brown hair from his face with his other hand. "Are you leaving?"

"It's the middle of the night, Markas," Tasia said. "Close to dawn, really — the crows woke me."

Markas's brown eyes grew large. "Did we fall asleep?"

Tasia almost snapped, *Of course we did, you idiot!,* but

managed to contain her irritation. It wasn't his fault she had fallen asleep; he always fell asleep after sex. That was the time when she generally dressed and slipped out, just as the city guard called out eleven-of-the-clock. But last night he had begged her to stay with him a while longer, and Tasia, with her thoughts drifting to other topics, other worries, other lovers, had foolishly allowed herself to fall into the welcome oblivion of unconsciousness.

"Yes," Tasia said, pulling on the shift she'd finally found. "We fell asleep."

Markas sat up, sheets falling away from his bare chest. With moonlight glinting off the well-defined planes of his body, Tasia momentarily remembered why she still found herself in his apartments once or twice per week.

"There's no point in you leaving now," he said. "If it's almost dawn, the cart merchants will be setting up outside anyway. They'll see you. You should stay."

Tasia shook her head. "It's not *that* close to dawn. The moon is still out. I have time."

He reached for her wrist, but she took a quick step backwards.

"Stay," Markas implored.

"No," she said curtly. "We've talked about this before. It is risky enough for me to be doing this as it is. You know what would happen if my father found us out."

"I'm not afraid of your father," Markas said, but his eyes gave him away.

She let out a half-laugh, not bothering to humor him with a response. "Until we meet again," she said, bending forward to kiss his brow.

She slipped her shoes on, pulled the navy blue cloak with the heavy hood around herself, and picked up the basket of bread she'd left next to the door — her usual prop for these visits. Anyone on the street who saw a hunched and hooded girl with a basket of bread would just assume she was a baker's girl, finishing a late night delivery to the Ambassador Quarter.

Late night delivery, maybe, but pre-dawn delivery…? No one with respectable business would be leaving the quarter at this hour.

Tasia continued to chastise herself as she hastened down the back stairs from Markas's apartments, fabricating an excuse in her head in case she had the misfortune to arrive at the palace during the changing of the guard.

Which was why she didn't see the shadow slip onto the street a few paces behind her as she hurried up the hill that paralleled the Royal Canal.

She had an arrangement with the guardsmen of Sunfall Gate, the palace gate most commoners referred to as Westgate — two silver pennies for each man on guard when she quietly slipped away, one penny on her way out, the second penny on her way back in. She'd bought their silence, it was true, and as her father was wont to say, *Loyalty paid for is no loyalty at all.* Which was why she'd also taken care to learn each of their names, their wives' names, their children's names. On the nights when she had the time for it, she traded bawdy jokes with them, shared the leftover pastries from her baker's girl's basket.

The night guardsmen of Westgate were her friends, inasmuch as a princess can make friends with common soldiers. But the morning guard — that was a different story. The night belonged to Tasia; the morning belonged to her father, the Emperor. No quantity of pennies or dirty jokes would stop the morning guard from turning her in. And so she walked as fast as she could without running, panting and perspiring up the hill, determined to make the gate before the guard changed.

Later it would almost amuse her that her most pressing concern that night was not getting caught by the morning guard.

Tasia was so focused on making the hill's crest that the first touch of the hand behind her did nothing to dilute her focus. It wasn't until the same hand tightened around the arm that held her bread basket that Tasia noticed it at all.

The man acted too quickly for the Princess to call for help. In one swift sweep of his arm, he swung her towards him with such force that Tasia lost her balance, feet tangling together beneath her. On instinct, she opened her mouth to scream, but he slapped his other hand against her mouth.

"I will make it hurt more if you scream," he hissed, yellowed teeth mere inches from Tasia's face. He was taller than her, but not by much, with black hair cut in a severe ring around his head, shaved to his scalp below the black fringe. He wore heavy robes, grey and plain and cinched at his waist with a white rope.

He's a Wise Man, Tasia thought with a shock of

incredulity.

But that made no sense. She knew every Wise Man in the city, and she'd never seen this man's face before.

He pulled an iron knife from somewhere within his robes, its blade as black as his hair.

Not just any Wise Man. A Wise Man who intended to kill her.

Something about the realization brought the world into focus for her. Regaining her balance, Tasia struck out with one foot, hard and low against his shin.

The first kick in a fight should always be low. She'd learned that from the night guardsmen's bragging, boisterous tales of their barroom brawls and misadventures.

The Wise Man's grip on her arm loosened — not much, but just enough for Tasia to take a half-step backwards. She drove her knee upward, hard and swift. She'd aimed for his groin but missed somehow, and felt her knee crack against the bottom of his ribcage. It was good enough — he grunted and let go. Tasia sprinted up the hill, knowing if she could just out-pace him by a hundred yards, she'd be able to call out for help, and her friends of the Westgate guard would recognize her voice in the night.

But she could not out-pace him. He was on her again in an instant, before she'd managed to evade him by so much as a yard. This time he grabbed the back of the cloak, yanking hard so that the leather tie in the front dug into her throat.

"You're only making it harder on yourself, Princess," he said as she stumbled backward into him. He threw her roughly to the ground, her chin smacking against the cobblestones before the rest of her.

He planted a knee in her back, pinning her. He leaned closer to roll Tasia over, but she was ready for him, grabbing the wrist that held the knife, trying to wrest it from his hand.

"No!" she screamed at him, unable to find any other words. "No, no, *no!*"

The Wise Man tried to extract his wrist, but she had the wrist with both hands now, refusing to let go. He used his free hand to slap her hard against the face — once, then twice.

"No!" Tasia yelled again, still stubborn and fighting despite the pain blossoming in her chin, her cheeks, the scraped palms and bruised knees where she'd hit the pavement. But he was far stronger than she, far heavier, and she knew she would lose this battle.

And that was the worst part about it — knowing that she would lose before the end actually came.

2

He pulled his wrist loose at last, and the knife arced up, its black blade refusing to reflect the moonlight. Tasia closed her eyes on instinct, body tightening in anticipation of the final blow.

But then there was a series of shouts, a muffled cry, and the weight pressing her into the cobblestones mercifully disappeared.

Tasia opened her eyes in time to see two men in city guard uniforms sling the Wise Man face-first into the middle of the street. One guard yelled obscenities, his short sword's blade pressed to the Wise Man's throat; the other guard busied himself tying the would-be-assassin's hands behind his back with a length of twine.

Dazed, Tasia made her way to her to her knees, gathering the scattered contents of her bread basket from the pavement. On instinct, she picked up the Wise Man's black iron knife as well, dropping it into the basket with the bread.

Fortunately, the ring with the royal crest of the House of Dorsa was still in its hiding place inside a loaf of bread. She pulled it out hastily and put it on her finger, rotating it so that the crest faced down instead of up. She would only reveal her identity if she had to.

One of the guards looked over at her. "Girl? Are you alright?"

"Yes. Thank you." She tugged her hood down a little lower, avoided his gaze, and went back to gathering her fallen bread.

But she could feel the guard's eyes on her.

"Awfully late for a bread delivery," he said with obvious skepticism. He took a few steps closer to her.

Tasia decided the best course of action was to not respond. That was what a humble, lowly baker's girl would do if approached by the city guard, wasn't it? So she only nodded and brushed dirt from a loaf.

"Where are you going?" asked the guard.

Through the shadows cast by her cloak's hood, she glanced at the guard, then her attacker. The Wise Man on the ground appeared to be unconscious now; a starburst of blood painted his temple red and trickled down his cheek.

Like it or not, Tasia had the full attention of both guards. One of them was huge, with wiry black hair and a black beard that protruded out from beneath his leather cap and spilled halfway down his chest like a plant that had overgrown its pot. The other, the one who'd suggested it was too late for a bread delivery, was average-sized but looked puny next to the big man. He wore no leather cap, and he wore his oiled hair slicked back behind his ears. Both guards inspected her with open curiosity. It was indeed the wrong time and the wrong place to find a baker's girl alone on the street.

"I'm going home," Tasia replied. She made her voice

soft, timid, the way a baker's girl's would be. She looked away from the guards, keeping her face hidden within the hood.

"We'll escort you," said the guard with the slicked-back hair.

"No."

Tasia said it too firmly, too quickly, realizing as soon as the word escaped her lips that a baker's girl wouldn't speak in such a contrarian tone to a member of the city guard. Especially not a frightened baker's girl who'd just been attacked.

She tried to correct herself but instead made a second blunder: "I'm close to home. I know the way."

The big guard with the wild black hair stood up, straddling the fallen Wise Man. He was even bigger on his feet, looming over the unconscious man.

"Close to home?" said the bear-sized man. "You're in the *Ambassador* Quarter."

The shorter guard took another step closer. He cocked his head like a cat, narrowing his eyes at Tasia.

Feign confusion, instinct told Tasia.

She straightened, turned her gaze away from the guards, rubbed the tender spot on the back of her head with imagined absent-mindedness as she rotated in a slow circle. Behind her, dark water gently lapped at the bank of the Royal Canal.

"But isn't that the canal?" she asked.

"It is."

She paused. "The Merchant Canal?"

"No," said the big guard. "The Royal Canal."

She spun on her heel back towards the guards. "The *Royal* Canal? How... where am I? Did you say this is the Ambassador Quarter?"

The guards exchanged a glance, and the one with the slicked-back hair chuckled. "I think you must've hit your head harder than you thought, girl. You'd better let us walk you home."

Tasia didn't respond.

"But wait, Mack," said the big bearded one. "How's we gonna walk her home, eh? What're we goin' t'do wit' *him?*" He toed the body of the unconscious Wise Man.

The slick-haired guard — Mack — considered this for a second. "Take him to the guard station and wait for the shift change. You can handle him on your own as long as he's tied up, can't you? I can walk her home."

The big guard grinned. "Sure, Mack. *You* get the girl to yourself. *I* get stuck with the murderous Wise Man."

"Just take him. I'll be back soon enough."

The big guard grumbled, but he bent down anyway, hefting the Wise Man and slinging him over one huge shoulder, like an over-large sack of potatoes.

"You're only making me carry him because you don't have the strength t'do it yourself," the guard told Mack.

Mack huffed in irritation. "I've met highborn daughters who whine less than you, Dawk. Get going. We'll settle who's stronger later."

"You hain't known any highborn daughters," the big one shot back. But he turned away from them and headed across the street with his burden anyway.

Tasia let out a tense breath of relief to see her would-be assassin move away from her on the shoulder of the guard. But conflict brewed inside. She wasn't sure if the Wise Man's receding form was a good thing or a bad thing.

It was good, because she was out of danger for the moment. But it was bad, because she did not know his identity, and that meant he might return — or worse, he would find his way back to whomever else he was working with or working for and strengthen his position before making a second attempt on her life. Letting the guard take him away might be a mistake.

"A friend is someone you can let out of your sight for a short while," her father's voice said in her head. *"An enemy is someone you never allow out of your field of vision."*

The Wise Man was almost out of her field of vision already. It would be much better if the guards took the assassin to the palace, where he could be properly interrogated by the Emperor's men.

She drew in a breath, about to call out to the big guard to bring him back, but instinct stopped her again.

They will not heed your words, instinct said. *You've made them believe you're a baker's girl. The only way to make them obey is to reveal that you are the Princess. And what will happen once they know that? The wheels of your fate will begin to roll. If they believe you — if — then they will take you back to the palace along with the Wise Man. The palace guard will wake your father. You will have to explain why you've been found outside the walls — again — in the dress of a baker's girl.*

She weighed both options. Nearly losing her life was deeply disconcerting. But explaining to her father why she was leaving Markas's apartments at four-of-the-clock... That was even more disconcerting.

She held her tongue — and realized the guard named Mack was watching her.

He smiled unconvincingly. "So, girl," he said. "Which way towards home?"

She turned, facing the palace. The gate was only a few hundred yards up the hill, the gently glowing torchlight visible even from here. Once she made it to the privacy of her own quarters, she would figure out what to do about what happened tonight.

"Girl?"

"Sorry, sir," Tasia said. She let out a giggle that she hoped sounded jittery and nervous. "I think I'm still a little shaken up."

"I don't have all night. Which way are we going?"

Tasia pointed up the hill. "North," she said. "Past the palace."

#

They marched up the hill in silence, the occasional hanging lantern wavering in the breeze and casting eerie yellow patterns against the canal's black water. Tasia stared straight ahead of her, mind busy with the task of deciding how she would lose Mack and make it to Sunfall Gate without him.

"I hope the Wise Man at least paid you for your troubles before he attacked you," Mack said, words breaking into Tasia's contemplations.

"Beg pardon?"

"I said, I hope he at least paid you."

"Paid me for what, sir?" Tasia asked, genuinely confused.

Mack chuckled, tucking a long strand of hair behind one ear. "Come on, girl. You might've fooled my mate Dawkin back there into thinking you're just an errant baker's girl out past your bedtime, but you didn't fool me."

Fool him?

And then understanding struck Tasia all at once: *Mother Moon, he thinks I'm a prostitute!*

"I *am* a baker's girl," Tasia said, tone brooking no room for disagreement. "The baker I work for has several clients in the Ambassador Quarter, one of them with a tendency to entertain guests late into the night, which sometimes requires late night replenishment."

"Replenishment? Is that what they call it when you visit?" Mack gave her a smug smirk. "I can tell just from the way you talk you're no baker's girl." He eyed her, inspecting her up and down. "I bet you're from one of them high-class brothels, eh? Where they teach you to read and play the lute and all the other pig shite so rich men can pretend you're highborn."

Tasia turned her gaze away from him, kept her eyes

fixed firmly ahead of her. "I am *not* what you imply, sir. I am a baker's girl far from home, nothing more."

"Which baker?"

"He's not — his shop is new," Tasia sputtered. "I doubt you'd recognize the name."

Mack's hand snaked out, and for the second time in one evening a coarse man grabbed the Princess's wrist. He jerked her toward him.

"Don't lie to me, now, girl." He was so close to Tasia that she could smell the fish and ale on his breath. "Half the brothels in Port Lorsin are under the protection of the city guard; surely you know that. And you wouldn't want your mistress finding out you lied to a kindly guardsman who only tried to walk you home. *After* saving your life."

The palace was so close. If she could only get away from him, she might be able to outrun him to the gate. Or at least come close enough that the Sunfall guards would hear her shouting for help.

Composing her face into a mask of cold neutrality, Tasia looked down at the rough hand around her wrist.

"Neither would my mistress be pleased to hear that a guardsman bruised one of her chattel," she said cooly.

He let her go, wide grin revealing a missing tooth. "Ha! I knew it! You should've just said what you are to begin with, girl."

Tasia straightened her cloak, resumed her trek up the hill. "It would have been unbecoming for a woman like me to state her true occupation to a member of the city guard."

"So it would, so it would," Mack mused with a light

chuckle, clearly pleased that his infinite intelligence had revealed the truth about Tasia.

A few seconds later, the same hand that had grabbed her wrist goosed her bottom. Tasia jumped, barely managing to repress a startled yelp before it escaped her throat.

Mack laughed. "And do you think your mistress would allow a humble city guardsman a few minutes on the house as thanks for saving one of her girls?" He wrapped an arm around Tasia's narrow waist and pulled her into him. Before Tasia had a chance to react, a stubble-coated chin pressed against the side of her neck and a tongue slipped into her ear.

"Sir!"

He let her go, but only after he'd buried his nose in her hair and taken a crude, dog-like sniff of her. "Strawberry-blonde curls, green eyes, and smelling of perfume. You're every poor man's fantasy of a rich girl." He fingered the collar of her cloak. "So what do you say, girl, eh? Indulge a poor man with a few minutes of fantasy when we get back to your mistress?"

Tasia glanced from Mack to the Sunfall Gate, a series of quick calculations running through her mind.

She swung her basket of bread at the guard's face, hitched up her cloak and the shift beneath it, and sprinted for the gate as fast as her feet would carry her.

Behind her, Mack cursed loudly and pursued her, the soles of his leather boots slapping the cobblestones, short sword jangling against the metal studs riveted into his leather tunic.

"Help!" Tasia shouted as she approached the gate. Mack was only steps behind her now. "Help! Tedric, Tomkin, Grizzle, hel — "

But it was too late; he caught her. A fist wound itself into her hair, yanked her backward roughly, and she collided into his chest with a soft grunt.

"You ungrateful little whore!" Mack spat, wheeling her around to face him. "I'll teach you some manners! No wonder the last man tried to kill — "

The protesting whine of a door hinge interrupted him, and he dropped his hand as three guards emerged from the small side door beside the main Sunfall Gate. One of the guards held a sword in one hand, a lantern in the other.

"Princess?" he said. His unshaven face was as rough as Mack's was, but where Mack's stubble retained its color, the half-grown beard on the palace guard's face was pure white. He glanced from Mack to Tasia.

Tasia straightened her cloak, shook loose the tangles in her hair.

"Grizzle," Tasia said, mixing the name of the night shift's captain with a deep a sigh of relief.

"Princess Natasia," Grizzle said, dipping his chin respectfully. Tasia could smell the booze on his breath even from where she stood; she hoped he wasn't drunk enough to be over-powered. "We expected you home much earlier. The lads and I were beginning to worry." Grizzle turned in Mack's direction, holding up his lantern and squinting at the other man. "But I see you found a member of the city guard to walk you home. That's good — when we heard you shouting, we thought something was wrong."

Mack's eyes widened. With what Tasia could only assume was mounting horror, he looked from Grizzle, to Tasia, back to Grizzle again.

"Princess... Natasia...?" he mumbled to himself.

Tasia adjusted the ring on her finger, rotating it so that the royal crest of her family faced outward. The silver eagle inlaid in obsidian glittered in the lamp light.

She sighed heavily, because she knew what she must do, even if was distasteful to her. Revealing what had happened tonight to her father was no longer a choice to be deliberated over but something unavoidable.

Servant of the Empire before servant of my desire, she recited to herself. It was probably for the best. If there was someone who knew her movements well enough to attempt an assassination tonight, then her father needed to know.

"This man is no ordinary city guardsman," she said to Grizzle.

Mack began to protest, panic filling his face, but Tasia silenced him with a single raised finger.

"This man — and his patrol mate — are heroes, because tonight..." She paused for effect, glancing at the face of each of the three guards. "They stopped an assassin who tried to take my life."

Grizzle's face registered shock. "My Princess! Are you alright? Should I wake one of the Wise Men?"

"No, no," Tasia said immediately. The palace's Wise Men would be involved in this debacle soon enough, but she could delay it for now. "I'm not hurt. Mack — that's what you're called, isn't it?" she said, turning to the guard.

He hesitated, then nodded, shrinking back a step.

"Mack and his patrol mate saw to it that no harm came to me. I did scrape my chin when I fell, but that is the worst of my injuries." Tasia took a breath. "I do, however, need you to rouse my father. Send someone ahead to wake him, and let him know that we will meet him in his offices." She glanced sideways at Mack, whose mouth remained half open. "And arrange for another one of your men to escort us there."

"Yes, Highness."

3

Mack the city guardsman was silent as he trailed behind Tasia and Tedric, one of the younger Sunfall guards, to the Emperor's private offices. Tasia gave Mack a subtle backward glance at one point, and could see clearly from his gawking at the lamplit silk tapestries hanging from the walls that he'd probably never seen the interior of anything finer than a city guard outpost in his entire life.

She hid a smile.

Mack had nearly assaulted the daughter of the Emperor, the Princess of the Four Realms. Tasia could have had him put to death with a few words if she'd wanted to, and surely he knew it. He had to be wondering if she still would. But she didn't plan on doing that. Just as she'd learned that it was useful to have some allies at the Sunfall Gate, she might eventually find a use for a city guardsman who owed her a favor, too.

More than a favor. He owed her his life at this point. If Tasia were anyone else, saving her from the assassin would have made them even. But she wasn't anyone else. She was the Princess. Stupid as Mack seemed to be, Tasia was sure he understood this.

The Emperor was already in his main office when Tasia entered with Mack and Tedric. Her father paced restlessly behind the heavy cedar desk in the center of the room, night clothes fluttering behind his massive frame like a cape. Even if he hadn't carried the title "Emperor of the Four Realms," Andreth the Just of House Dorsa would still be an intimidating man. Taller than all the other men in the room by at least a head, he had a broad chest, log-thick limbs, and a beard that made him look like a giant from a child's tale. Above the beard was a large and crooked nose, with a scar across it that suggested violence. His skin was ruddy and pock-marked; his eyes were as black as his beard. The total effect was a man who looked more ogre than Emperor — cold, shrewd, and prepared to give an early grave to any man who crossed him.

He stopped pacing when his daughter entered, studying first her, then Tedric, then Mack .

Three other members of the palace guard were also in the room — the two men who always guarded the Emperor's chambers at night, along with Cole of Easthook, the head of the palace guard and the Emperor's long-time personal guard. Cole was seated in a plush chair to the side of the Emperor's desk, rubbing his bad leg absentmindedly as he regarded Tasia with an appraising look.

Cole didn't look like a man who'd been woken from sleep. As always, his face was fresh and alert.

The Emperor flicked his hand at the door, and all the guards, with the exception of Cole, bowed and exited quietly. Mack, still in a state of obvious shock, also bowed and began backpedaling.

"No, not you," the Emperor said. "You stay. Sit." He

pointed at a divan upholstered in red velvet, trimmed with ornately carved golden wood, and draped with a large white doily.

Mack hesitated, glancing between the divan and its small wooden footstool. After a moment, he settled onto the footstool, knees jutting upward uncomfortably.

Good choice, Tasia thought as she settled onto the divan next to him.

Cole continued to study her from across the room. She busied herself with straightening her hair, but her baker's girl disguise practically burned her skin beneath Cole's steady gaze.

"An assassin?" said her father.

He widened his stance behind the desk, crossing his arms against his broad chest like a statue of a stern god. His stomach had rounded over the years, but his beard showed no grey. Dinner plate-sized hands were clenched into fists, and Tasia could see the muscles twitching in his forearms as he repeatedly squeezed and relaxed his hands — the only outward sign of tension he would allow himself to show.

Tasia cleared her throat. She met his eyes, intending to hold his gaze, but she couldn't. She looked down at her own hands instead, folded and lady-like in her lap.

"Yes," she said.

"Where?"

"The Ambassador Quarter. Not far from the Royal Canal."

"Visiting Markas of House Boling again, I take it," the

Emperor grumbled. "I'm growing rather tired of this behavior, Natasia."

"I know, Father," she said, letting her gaze fall to the rug patterned with vines and flowers below. "I'm sorry. After tonight, it won't — "

"I don't need your false promises," said the Emperor. "But tonight *is* the end of your foolishness, even if I have to lock you in your quarters each night and hang any guard who lets you out."

Tasia opened her mouth to protest, but Cole spoke before she could.

"Did you recognize him? The assassin?" The Commander of the palace guard's gravelly voice was unhurried, seemingly unconcerned. Almost lazy, like they were discussing the unseasonably warm weather instead of an assassination attempt on the Princess. Tasia's father often lost his temper, but Cole never did. The man was smoother than the silk of her finest gowns.

"No," Tasia answered, "but he was a Wise Man — or at the very least, he was dressed as one."

Tasia felt her father's eyes on her, and she looked up, willing herself not to look away this time.

"Much the way *you* are dressed as a common servant?" he said.

She wouldn't look away. She wouldn't. "Yes."

A noise emerged from the back of his throat; it sounded like an animal's low growl.

Years ago, when Tasia was still just a girl, circus performers had been permitted to perform a series of shows at the palace. Tasia thought now of the lion the troupe kept caged in the inner courtyard for over a week. The creature paced between the iron bars day and night, snarling at anyone who came too close, giving Tasia nightmares when she imagined what he would do if he had somehow gotten out.

That was what the Emperor reminded Tasia of now — the caged lion, waiting for his opportunity to escape.

He turned on his heel, paced two steps, turned again, paced back to his original spot. A meaty finger jabbed at Mack.

"And you. My daughter says you stopped this would-be killer?"

Mack didn't have the same determination as Tasia; his eyes fell away from the Emperor's immediately. "Y-yes, Your… Emperor — Highness. Your Highness."

"Tell me what you saw."

"Me an' my mate — uh, my patrol partner I mean, Dawkin is his name — we was finishing up our supper in the guard post in the Ambassador Quarter, the one just west of — "

Cole interrupted. "Get to the point, guard."

Mack turned on the wooden footstool towards Cole, seeming to notice him for the first time. Tasia could understand how he'd missed the head of the palace guard; the Emperor did tend to take up all the attention in a room, after all. Cole, on the other hand, had a way of making himself unseen. If the Emperor was a lion on display for all to see, Cole was a crafty tomcat, hiding in the bushes and waiting for prey to come to him.

Mack took in the criss-cross of scars across the Commander's face, the scraggly dark blond hair, and seemed to grow a shade paler. He swallowed, Adam's apple bobbing visibly.

"Yes — yes, sir," Mack said. He stared at an indefinite point on the floor as he described running from the guard post to find a Wise Man with his knife raised high above what appeared to be a baker's girl.

"And where is this man now?" said the Emperor.

"Dawkin took him back to the post, your... Emperor... ship."

Cole turned to the Emperor. "It is the standard procedure of the city guard that when patrol pairs come upon a drunk or a rogue in the night, they hold them in their local post until the change of guard, when they can escort them to a magistrate's for safekeeping until sentencing."

The Emperor nodded at Cole. "Go rouse some of your men — ones you trust to be discreet — and have them bring this supposed Wise Man here. You know where they should take him."

Cole dipped his chin deferentially, rose from his seat. "Yes, Majesty."

"And Cole... come back once you've woken your men. I have something else I wish to discuss with you."

"Yes, Majesty," Cole said, and cat-like as ever, he slipped soundlessly from the room.

"As for you," the Emperor said, walking around his desk to address Mack, "you've done the Empire a great service tonight, you and your patrol partner. You saved the life of the future Empress, who will one day sit beside a husband who rules the Four Realms in the name of the House of Dorsa." He stood a few inches from Mack, who still balanced precariously on the footstool, leaning slightly away from the most important man in the known world. "Many will say that the strength of an Empire comes from its Emperor, but in truth, we are only as strong as a single common soldier's sword, only as rich as a single fruit merchant's success. Do you understand, guardsman?"

Mack ventured a gaze in the Emperor's direction before dropping his eyes to the floor again. "Yes, your Emperorship."

The Emperor hovered above him for a moment, turned back towards his desk with a sigh. "It doesn't matter whether you understand the point or not, guardsman. Your actions were enough for tonight. Go, now. Wait outside for Cole to return."

Tasia offered Mack an appropriately gracious, regal smile, but he was too busy bowing and shuffling his way out of the Emperor's office to notice her.

The Emperor waited for Mack to close the door behind him before addressing Tasia. He placed both palms on his desk, leaned over it before hissing, "Leaving the Ambassador Quarter mere *hours* before dawn? Even for you..." He pursed his lips, shook his head. "You leave me at a loss for words. And if two half-drunken, feckless city guardsman hadn't happened upon you, you would've left me at a loss for a blood heir, too."

"You have a third child yet alive," Tasia said. There was bitterness in her voice, but she said it without lifting her eyes to the Emperor.

"Adela is a twelve year-old girl who prefers ponies and pageantries to politics."

"And you think *I* prefer politics?" Tasia countered.

"I think that you remind me of your grandmother. At least you have the potential to make the clever wife of an Emperor. Your sister is too much like your mother. Bewitched by birds and flowers."

Tasia bristled. "Do not speak of the dead that way. Or of Adela, for that matter. As if she is nothing."

The Emperor slammed his fist against the desk, rattling the lanterns, vase of roses, and ink bottles upon it. Tasia flinched without meaning to.

"And do *not* speak to your father, the Emperor, that way!" he bellowed. "You want to know who is nothing, Natasia? *You.* You are nothing without that royal crest you wear so easily upon your ring. You are nothing without the name of the House of Dorsa to bolster you. Without that name, you are nothing more than another spoiled and arrogant highborn girl. And despite being born with so much, you seem content to throw it away — an entire Empire — for the sake of another night with some *Ambassador's* son!"

Tasia knew her father well enough to know when to hold her tongue. She was also similar enough to her father that she failed to hold her tongue most of the time. But now, miraculously, she managed to stay quiet.

Her father turned from the desk, paced again, running his hands through his hair.

"You are the strongest of my children. You always have been. Nikhost was weak, insecure. He never would've been able to command the respect of even the ambassadors, let alone the lords."

Hearing her brother's name sent a stab of pain through Tasia's heart, as if the assassin had succeeded and his black blade was still lodged between her ribs. First her mother. Now her brother. Her father seemed determined to resurrect ghosts tonight.

"Nik wasn't 'weak,'" she said. "He was thirteen."

"He was *weak,* Tasia, and you know it. Your mother saw to that."

"Stop speaking ill of those who are not here to defend themselves," Tasia snapped. "Maybe Nik wouldn't have been so insecure if his father didn't always look at him as if he was a disappointment. If I'm strong, it's only because you ignored me. You've always had more important things to take up your time than your daughters."

The Emperor stopped pacing, pinned Tasia against the divan with his black eyes.

Angry, she held his gaze with defiance. Several seconds passed before Tasia realized she was holding her breath. She exhaled, and her eyes broke away from her father's at the same time.

"You think you know so much," the Emperor said. "But your actions reveal that you are hardly more than a child. A *foolish* child, at that, who nearly got herself killed tonight. For *nothing.*" He practically spat the final word, then lowered himself in the chair behind his desk with a heavy sigh. "If two city guardsmen know that the Princess was found leaving the Ambassador Quarter before dawn, it won't be long before word spreads and people begin to talk. I cannot wait any longer, Tasia. It's time you accept a husband."

He might as well have doused her in ice water. She sucked in a breath as her chest tightened. "No. I'm not ready. There's no one who — "

"Natasia. You're nineteen. It's been over a year and a half since you came of age. And you've rejected every proposal I've offered so far."

"Which is my right," she said.

"Which is your *privilege,*" he corrected. "But while you remain unmarried, the Empire remains vulnerable. I need an heir to mold while I am still in my prime."

She said nothing.

"You're old enough to remember the Western Rebellion," her father went on. "Or the end of it, at least. We barely held the Four Realms together. Don't fool yourself into thinking that every taproot of those weeds have been pulled. The Empire cannot survive another rebellion in my lifetime, not while we fight a war in the East and wait for one to erupt in the south."

Tasia said nothing for a moment. She said she didn't care for politics, but that wasn't to say she didn't understand them. And although she might not want to marry some pliable Lord's son with ambitions for the

Emperor's crown, she didn't want the Empire fall into chaos and disarray due to her own foolish selfishness, either.

"I'm sorry, father," she said, sincere for the first time. "I didn't mean to... take my duty for granted."

He sighed. "At the moment, I'm simply glad you came home to me alive. I prefer planning royal weddings to royal funerals. You think I care nothing for my daughters, that I ignore you both. That is not true," he said. The words were as close to an expression of affection as Tasia could hope for. "Well. I may not have a wedding or a funeral to plan quite yet, but as long as Cole's men bring your assassin back alive, it seems I *do* still have an interrogation to plan."

And as if he was some kind of spirit, summonable by the whisper of his name, the Commander of the palace guard reentered the room and closed the door softly behind him.

The Emperor met Cole's eye, an unspoken question on his face.

Cole nodded. "It is underway, Majesty. The assassin will be in the dungeons before the sun rises."

"And the city guardsmen?" the Emperor asked.

Cole gave a sly grin. "They will enjoy a healthy addition to their salaries, provided the girl who was attacked remains simply a..." He glanced at Tasia. "Baker's girl."

The Emperor nodded. "Good. We shall see how long they can hold their tongues."

"They'll keep quiet," Cole said. "I made it very clear what would happen if they did not. I'm afraid I made quite the impression on young Mack."

The Emperor stroked his beard. "Very well. Speaking of guards, Cole. There is the other matter I wanted to address." He sat up straighter, regarded Tasia with his bottomless black eyes for a long few seconds. "Since someone seems to know my daughter's movements better than I do, and is bold enough to send an assassin, she requires a bodyguard of her own."

Tasia opened her mouth to protest, but Cole spoke before she could.

"That is easy enough to arrange, your Majesty," he said. "I can think of several good men in the palace guard who would be suitable — men I trained myself."

The Emperor nodded. "Good. We can discuss them. Whomever we choose is to stay at her side every hour of the clock."

Tasia cleared her throat. "Father, Cole — I appreciate your concern for my well-being, but... Someone with me at every hour of the clock? Even in my personal apartments?"

"Every hour means every hour," her father said.

Thank Mother Moon. They'd given her a loophole to this house arrest without realizing it. "But while I remain unmarried," Tasia said innocently, "it is unlawful for a man to be in the apartments of a princess without her father's supervision or the supervision of a trusted male chaperone."

"It is unlawful for a man to be in your apartments with you *alone*," Cole corrected. "Your handmaid — what is her name again? — she would be there, as well."

"Lady Mylla, of House Harthing," Tasia supplied. "But that's where you misunderstand. Mylla isn't with me continuously. She leaves on errands, or to fetch my meals, or goes into the city for parcels. And three times per year, she leaves the palace for a week to visit her family in the West."

Tasia was careful not to let the triumph show on her face. As frightening as the assassination attempt had been, she refused to allow her father to foist a babysitter upon her.

The Emperor and Cole were both quiet, appearing to contemplate their dilemma. Tasia felt her hopes rise.

"Well?" the Emperor said to Cole after a moment's silence.

Cole nodded slowly. "It does complicate matters, but… I believe I may have a solution, Majesty. May I speak to you about this again tomorrow, after the noontide meal?"

The Emperor nodded his agreement, then rose from the chair behind his desk. He waved a hand at Tasia and Cole. "Very well. We sleep for now. Tomorrow we turn our attention to this assassin. In the meantime, Cole…"

Cole got to his feet. "I will increase the number of guards around the royal family's wing," he said. "Especially the guards around Princess Natasia's apartments."

Cole gave a quick bow to each of them and left the

room as quietly as he'd entered it. Tasia moved to follow him.

"Natasia."

She turned, one hand still on the door knob before her. "Yes, father?"

"Sit a moment longer."

She closed the door reluctantly, returned to the divan.

"I know you think I do not understand you. That I do not know how the name of 'Dorsa' weighs you down," he said. "But I understand that weight better than anyone. You think that when I was Prince I did not long to escape my fate? You think I had any say in choosing your mother as my wife?"

Tasia looked down, saying nothing.

"You've learned, just as I learned at your age, that the name we carry on our backs shackles us as much as it elevates us," the Emperor said. "It is fate, daughter. But you can find happiness in your fate once you stop fighting it."

"You say you understand, but you don't," Tasia said. "The fate of a prince is not the fate of a princess. At least your fate was to rule. My fate is to be some lordling's broodmare while you teach *him* to rule."

His bushy brows knitted together, the first sign of his ire. "Mind to whom you speak. And you will be more than a 'broodmare,' as you so crudely choose to phrase it. You will be an important support and confidante to your husband."

"I'm sorry, Father," Tasia said. She knew she should

stop at the apology, but she didn't. "I don't want to be a sycophantic lordling's confidante. He'll only marry me for your crown, or because his own father forces him into it."

"You don't know that."

"I *do,*" she said emphatically. "That's how every suitor you've brought before me has been. You know I speak the truth." When her father's brows furrowed a second time, she took a deep breath and reined in her temper. "It's just that… the duty of a princess is to smile and charm and make the lords feel good about themselves. The only difference between an unmarried princess and a married one is that a married one is also expected to bear children."

Instead of arguing with her this time, the Emperor gazed at her thoughtfully, stroking his beard. "There are Empresses who were considered leaders in their own right, even during their lifetimes. The Empress Adela, for whom your sister is named, comes to mind."

Tasia scoffed. *"One* Empress who was named her father's heir. In the thousand-year history of the House of Dorsa."

"There were others."

"Who?" Tasia demanded.

"Their names escape me."

Tasia barked out a short laugh. "As I said: *one* girl-child named heir in our thousand-year history."

The Emperor frowned. "Sometimes, it seems you wish for us all to believe that your tongue is sharper than your mind." He pushed up from his desk with a hefty sigh. "The hour is late. Or early, as the case may be. Goodnight,

Tasia."

She echoed his sigh with one of her own. She knew he was right. There was no escaping her fate, and she might as well accept it.

"Goodnight, father."

4

The sky was still a deep blue, but now tinged with pink, by the time Tasia finally entered her apartments. She was exhausted in every sense of the word — physically, mentally, emotionally — and ready to put the night's horror behind her. She closed the inner door softly when she entered her bedchamber, hoping not to wake her handmaid. But Mylla was waiting for her, lying crosswise on Tasia's bed in a thin silk night robe.

The girl rolled onto her side when the door closed, blinking awake and yawning hugely. "You're home rather late." Mylla waggled her eyebrows. "Or early, as the case may be. What time is it?"

"Early. Late. Take your pick." Tasia hung her cloak next to the door, shimmied out of her baker's girl shift and hung it as well. She turned to Mylla wearing only the rough undergarments she'd searched for so desperately at Markas's a few hours earlier. She marveled at how much life could change in the span of three hours, at how heavy a price one could pay for simply oversleeping.

"So? How was he?" Mylla asked, then answered her own question with, "Good, I hope, if he's not sending you home until now."

Tasia blew out a breath, flopped down back-first on the

bed beside the girl who was a year and a half her junior. "Markas is never particularly good — you know that. He's a bore. And he's an arrogant and stupid bore, which is all together the *worst* combination for a man to be."

Mylla ran the tip of her finger down the exposed skin between the bottom of Tasia's brasier and the top of her linen drawers. The Princess shivered.

"Then why do you still visit him every week?" Mylla asked. "When you could have just as much fun here with me, in the comfort of the palace?"

Mylla stuck the tip of a finger beneath the string of the linen drawers, then rubbed the plain white cloth between thumb and forefinger. She made a face.

"And how can you stand to wear these? They're so rough. Don't they *itch* you down there?"

Tasia wrapped her palm around Mylla's thumb and forefinger. "Don't tease me, Myll. Not tonight." She took a deep breath and told Mylla everything, from the beginning, even though she was sure it was something her father would have advised her not to do. *"No matter how close you come to the people around you, even the highborn, never forget that your station is higher still,"* he would say. *"A certain amount of distance between you and them is always necessary."*

But Tasia never kept secrets from Mylla. She couldn't.

Mylla gasped when the Princess finished her story. *"Tasia.* Please tell me you're having me on."

Tasia let out a ragged breath, and she felt the control she'd kept tightly wound in her chest all night begin to unfurl. Mylla was the only one Tasia felt she could be completely herself with.

"How could I joke about this? It was awful, Myll, just awful." She dropped her voice to a whisper despite the fact that it was only the two of them. "The Wise Man... he had this knife with a black iron blade — I still have it in my bread basket — and his eyes were so filled with hate, I couldn't... I've never seen anyone look at me like that, like he'd do anything he could to wipe my existence into the waste bin of eternity."

Tears pricked at Tasia's eyes, and she felt one of them roll out of one corner and down across her temple.

It must've been the sight of her mistress's tears that made Mylla's own eyes water. "Oh, Tasia," she said. She bent over the Princess's face, gently kissing her forehead and stroking back the hair from Tasia's face. "I can't lose you. What would I do without you?"

"Go home to Harthing and marry some rich lord, most like," Tasia said in her best Port Lorsin accent.

Both girls laughed wetly.

Mylla sniffled, wiping both eyes with the heel of her palm before going back to stroking Tasia's face. "Well, that's going to happen eventually, anyway," she said. "But unlike someone *else* in this bed, *I'm* not quite of age to marry yet, so you're still saddled with me. For a while. Even if you'd rather be rid of me for Markas."

"Don't say so. You know I'd choose you a thousand times over Markas."

Mylla gave Tasia a devious smile, leaned down, fit her

lips against Tasia's. The girl's dark hair fell in a curtain around Tasia, blotting out the rest of the bedchamber and what little light there was coming from the low-burning candles still flickering in the window. Tasia closed her eyes, letting the blackness become complete, disappearing for a sweet moment into a world where there was no Empire, no Markas, no assassin, no Cole, no Father, no Mack or Dawkin or Grizzle. Disappearing into the world which contained only her — her, and Mylla.

The world where she wanted to live forever.

Mylla broke the kiss too soon, pulling back and sweeping her long hair to one side. She grinned at Tasia. "If you'd choose me a thousand times over Markas, why'd you pick his bed instead of mine tonight?"

Because you would choose Markas over me, if given the chance, Tasia thought bitterly.

But rather than say it, she said to her handmaid, *"Your* bed? Are you forgetting your station, Lady Mylla?"

Mylla huffed. "Fine, then. *Your* bed. I would sleep in mine occasionally if *someone* would remember to tell the chambermaid to replace the mattress. It's far too lumpy to get a good night's sleep in."

Tasia rolled over swiftly, knocking Mylla off-balance and pushing her onto her back. "Maybe that's *exactly* why it keeps slipping someone's mind," she said, pinning Mylla's wrists beside her head. "Maybe I'm afraid you'd stop climbing into bed with me in the middle of the night." She slipped a hand beneath the opening of Mylla's robe, running it up the girl's ribs until she found a bare breast.

She cupped it, then gave the nipple a gentle pinch.

Mylla smiled, watching Tasia's face. "Markas. An assassin. Your father. Six-of-the-clock already, with the sun about to rise. And yet you still have energy enough for me?"

"I will *always* have energy enough for you."

"And what if I said no? If I told you it was more important for you to sleep — to let *me* sleep?" Mylla asked.

"You've never said no before."

"But if I did?"

Tasia took her hand out from its spot beneath Mylla's robe and tugged at the loosely tied sash around the girl's waist. It gave way easily, and Tasia pushed both sides of the robe apart, admiring Mylla's smooth, unblemished skin under the warm glow of candlelight.

"If you said no," she said quietly to Mylla, "I would be forced to remind you that I am your princess, and you are my handmaid, serving at my pleasure."

"And where is it written that handmaids cannot tell their princesses 'no'?"

Tasia ran her hands lightly down Mylla's sides, stopping on the curves of her hips. "It does not need to be written. It is something everyone knows."

"Maybe I'll say no anyway, just to see what you will do."

Tasia reached between Mylla's legs. "You wouldn't." But then she gave Mylla a quizzical look and removed her hand. "Are you really saying no? I hope you know I would never force you to do anything you don't want."

"I know."

"Good," Tasia said, and her hand caressed the inside of Mylla's thigh again.

Mylla grabbed the wrist disappearing between her legs. "Tasia, stop a moment."

Tasia laughed. *"Now* you're saying no? I thought you just said yes."

"I did. But now I'm saying no. Temporarily." Mylla sat up, crawled on hands and knees to the other side of the bed.

Tasia's brow furrowed. Sometimes she feared Mylla actually *did* acquiesce to her wishes simply because Tasia was her superior. It was another one of those consequences of being royal — always wondering if one's friends were *actually* one's friends, or mere sycophants.

Always wondering if one's love truly loved one back.

Mylla reached beneath the bed, grunting as she fished for something.

"Mylla?"

"Give me a moment, Tazy… I know I put it between the mattresses somewhere around — ah!"

Mylla sat up, holding something triumphantly above her head. Tasia squinted at it, but couldn't make out what the dark shape was.

"I picked something up for us today while I was out," Mylla said, walking back to Tasia on her knees across the mattress. "Look."

She held the object out, and Tasia took it from her automatically. It was leather, she saw, cylindrical and a few inches in diameter, but curved. One end was attached to what appeared to be a complicated belt of some sort.

"What is it?" Tasia asked, turning the leather thing and its straps over in her hands.

Mylla gave a delighted laugh. *"You're* the naughty princess who sneaks out at night to rendezvous with boys who catch your fancy only to nearly get yourself killed, and yet you're asking *me* what this is?"

"Mylla, that's not funny. I thought I might never make it home to you tonight."

Mylla took the mystery object from Tasia's hand and bent down, untying Tasia's linen underwear at both hips before tossing it aside. She busied herself with the leather straps, wrapping them around Tasia's waist.

"I know, Princess. I would have been heartbroken if you'd left me without so much as a warning. But you didn't. So I say that's reason enough to celebrate," she said, cinching tight one of the leather straps now encircling Tasia's thighs. She tilted her head up. "Is that too tight?"

Tasia shook her head. "No, but — *oh.*" She gave a soft gasp, forgot completely what she'd planned on saying as Mylla reached between her legs and pressed something soft just inside her. She looked down, assuming Mylla was teasing her with a finger, but Mylla's hands were both adjusting the leather cylinder.

Mylla sat back on her heels, letting the silk fabric of her night robe flap open. "There," she said, sounding satisfied. She looked down at Tasia with the slyest of grins.

"What have you... what in the name of all the Gods is

that?" Tasia said. The curved leather cylinder jutted up from her crotch, and as she sat halfway up to get a better view, it bobbed slightly, like a dog's wagging tail.

Still grinning, Mylla inched forward on her knees. She put a hand around the curved leather cylinder, stroked down the thing suggestively. When she reached its base, she pressed lightly, and whatever was inside Tasia dipped in a little further.

Tasia shuddered.

"Haven't you ever wondered," Mylla whispered, positioning herself so that the leather cylinder's tip tickled between her thighs, "what it would have been like if you had been born with one of *these* between your legs?" She reached around Tasia's back with both hands, untying her brazier. "Markas would never think he stood a chance with you; guardsmen would never mistake you for a cheap and willing whore; and your father wouldn't be nearly so concerned with marrying you off."

Slowly, Mylla pulled the brazier up and over Tasia's head. Once it had joined Tasia's rough linen drawers on the rug, Mylla lowered her mouth to one of Tasia's nipples and sucked, then teased it with her teeth. Her thighs rubbed against the leather at the same time, and every bit of pressure she put on it resulted in a corresponding pressure against Tasia.

"Never," Tasia breathed. "I've never wanted a boy's appendage between my legs. Though if I had one, maybe you'd never leave me for some rich Western ambassador. Maybe I would marry you, make you my Empress."

Mylla laughed musically, rolling off Tasia and laying back onto the pillow. She grasped Tasia's hands and pulled her forward. The Princess placed her hands on either side of Mylla's face, gazing down at the most beautiful creature she knew.

"I would never marry you if you were a man, Tasia," Mylla said. "You would grow up to be a self-involved, spoiled little brat. Your father would've seen to that. You wouldn't have been worth the trouble, not even to be your Empress. Or your mistress." She flicked the tip of the leather dildo. "That's the best thing about this, you know. When we finish, it goes back between the mattresses, and you go back to being my lovely, sweet princess." Mylla spread her legs wide, hooked her heels around the backs of Tasia's thighs. "Now take me. Show me what you would do with me if you'd been born Nathaniel instead of Natasia."

Tasia lowered her hips towards Mylla. The tip of the dildo seemed to hesitate as if uncertain, floating half an inch above the handmaid's sex.

"But I can't feel it when it touches you," Tasia said. "What if I hurt — "

But Mylla silenced her by taking the leather shaft with both hands and guiding it inside, letting out a small moan as she did. The sound seemed to erase the last of Tasia's hesitancy, and she thrust down and forward, driving the dildo deeper inside her handmaid. At the same time, as if a reward for good work, the smaller piece of the device inside Tasia dug in, sending an undulating ripple of pleasure down her hips and thighs, up her spine. Encouraged, she thrust again harder, and again.

She glanced at Mylla, worried her sudden lack of grace might've hurt the girl, but Mylla's eyes were closed — mouth half ajar, head tilted back. The handmaid lifted her feet, locking her ankles together in the small of Tasia's back.

That did it. Tasia gave in to her desire, letting her hips rock up and down in a rhythm all their own as Mylla's hands clenched around fistfuls of sheets. Tasia's hips demanded she go faster, deeper, and she put her hands onto Mylla's shoulders, pushing the girl down even as she continued to thrust up. After a minute or two of this, Tasia felt her own orgasm on its way, just on the edge of its sweet release. Mylla let out a low groan and dug her heels deeper into Tasia's back, her body rocking with a spasm; Tasia's own body followed suit a moment later.

Tasia let out a long and satisfied moan, then collapsed forward onto Mylla's chest, the dildo pulling out at the same time with a tug and a wet squelch.

"Mother *Moon,*" Mylla said between gasps of breath a few moments later. She rolled Tasia off her, wiped the sweat from her brow. "I might retract what I said earlier about refusing to be your mistress had you been born Nathaniel. I still wouldn't have married you, but you would've been good for an occasional roll. You seem like you know how to use one of those things properly. I suppose you should — you've had enough practice on the receiving end, haven't you?"

Tasia laid on her back, said nothing. Like her, Mylla had already enjoyed her share of male lovers. If anything, Mylla's promiscuity was exactly why Tasia had so many men herself. It seemed so easy for Mylla to be callous, casual about what transpired between them alone in Tasia's bedchamber. It seemed so easy for Mylla to make Tasia one of many. So Tasia would be callous, too. She would make Mylla one of many, too. If it was only a game to the handmaid, then it would be nothing more than a game to the Princess.

Tasia held her tongue rather than answer Mylla's question about having plenty of practice. She also swallowed the comment about how no man had ever pleased her the way Mylla did. Tasia stared in silence instead at the moist leather shaft of the dildo jutting upright from her crotch. The candles cast dancing shadows across it, and it looked like a living thing.

Mylla rose, tied her night robe back on, and padded barefoot from the room.

A minute passed, and the handmaid hadn't returned. "Mylla?" Tasia called. "Where'd you go?"

No answer. The girl must have gone out of earshot. "Myll?"

How was it possible, Tasia wondered as she laid alone in the dim bedchamber, for so many wonderful *and* horrible things to happen all in the same night? A meaningless, careless night with Markas that nearly ended in her death. A mad rush towards the Sunfall Gate, escaping a city guardsman who seemed intent on raping her. A tense meeting with her father, followed by the healing touch of Mylla. A peak of pleasure unlike anything she'd ever felt before, only for her lover to walk from the room afterwards without explanation.

Mylla indeed *would* leave her Princess one day, permanently. She would leave without thinking twice, as soon as she came of age six months from now, as soon as an eligible bachelor with the right-sized coin purse who appealed to both Mylla and her father came along. And that would be the end of this nighttime secret they shared. Forever.

"Mylla?" Tasia called, louder this time.

But all remained quiet. The exhaustion Tasia should've felt hours ago finally caught her, and her eyes drifted closed.

"I'm back, Princess," came the handmaid's voice just as sleep took Tasia. "I had to make a run to the garderobe. I picked your delicates up off the floor while I was up... Tasia?"

Tasia forced her eyes back open. "I'm sorry. I think I must've fallen asleep."

"You've had a long night," Mylla said kindly, stroking Tasia's cheek. She glanced down and chuckled. "But your little soldier seems ready to keep going, doesn't he?"

Tasia lifted her head enough to see the upright dildo at her midsection, then laid back onto the pillow. "Let's not call it a 'he,'" she said groggily. "I've had enough men for a lifetime already."

She struggled to stay awake, but her eyes closed on

their own accord while Mylla fiddled with the bridle-like straps around her thighs and waist. The handmaid grunted, tugging it off, then settled down beside Tasia, nestling her face against the Princess's shoulder. Mylla yawned and pulled the bedcovers up around them.

"Whatever you wish, my Princess," she said.

What I wish... Tasia thought. *I wish for an Empire in which I could make you my wife, in which our daughters would be our heirs, in which belonging to a royal house wasn't their prison sentence. What I wish is...*

But she fell asleep still wishing, and dreamed of wishes which could never come true.

5

Sunlight woke Tasia from a heavy slumber some hours later. She blinked sticky eyelids open to find Mylla still breathing deeply beside her. The girl looked innocent and child-like while asleep, more like Tasia's younger sister than a lover.

Before her eyes had opened, she'd dreamed of Nik, of the time they'd played in the farthest palace meadow, exhausting themselves with running and laughing and daring each other to jump from trees before finally falling asleep in a patch of purple flowers.

Nik. Her brother. Her best friend. She felt shame for thinking it, but she missed her brother even more than she missed her mother.

Tasia sat up, pulled her robe around her to block the chill.

The candles in the windowsill from the night before had disappeared, and the round table where she and Mylla usually had their meals was set with fresh pink and white flowers, a carafe with teacups beside it, and two dishes with silver covers over them.

The chambermaids had come and gone, then.

Tasia wondered if the food on the table was the morning meal or, judging from the strength of the sun, the noontide meal. It wasn't unusual for her and Mylla to sleep through the arrival of the morning meal and wake just before noontide, but given that they hadn't gone to bed the night before until nearly dawn, Tasia wouldn't be surprised if they'd slept through both meals.

She stretched, winced when her bare feet touched the cold stone of the floor. She crossed from the bed to the table, lifted the metal cover above her plate. The steamy smell of roasted hen, garlic, and wilted greens struck her nose and made her mouth water.

Definitely the noontide meal.

Tasia replaced the cover and plucked a grape from the bowl between the dishes, popping it into her mouth while she wandered to the window overlooking the courtyard.

It was the same courtyard where her mother had kept the exotic birds she'd brought to the palace when she married the Emperor, and Tasia saw one of them now, its snow-white form flitting from the tree to the cobblestones below. It hopped around, cocking its head. Tasia wondered if it was one of Mother's original birds or its offspring. Did it know that a beautiful woman with golden hair used to glide through the courtyard each morning, spreading seeds for her precious pets? Probably not. Like so many in the Empire, the birds had probably forgotten the Empress Cristianne years ago.

A knock at the bedchamber door startled her out of her musings.

"Princess Natasia?" came a muffled male voice. Whoever it was knocked again, and Mylla stirred with a grumpy groan, rolling over without opening her eyes.

Tasia tightened the robe at her waist, straightened her hair, and walked to the door with an assured step.

"Who is it?" she asked.

"Commander Cole of Easthook. And someone I wish to introduce."

Tasia opened the door.

Cole stood in the doorway, one hand on the hilt of his short sword, scarred face inscrutable as ever. Next to him stood a tallish, serious-looking woman. She was dressed in one of the black and silver uniforms of the palace guard, but Tasia knew there were no women in the guard. She'd heard there were a handful of women in the city guard, along with a few score in the Imperial Army, but there were no women in the palace guard. There never had been.

But there she stood in a palace guard uniform anyway, as if no one had informed her of her mistake, the black padded leather shining and smelling of oil. The silver-pommeled short sword and silver-pommeled dagger hanging from her hips appeared equally clean and new. Like Cole, she rested her hand on the pommel of the sword, but unlike the head guardsman, it was a stance that made her look slightly awkward and uncomfortable.

The woman stood just behind Cole. She took in Tasia with inquisitive eyes the same color as her uniform, eyes that contrasted with her rich bronze-colored skin. Tasia could tell in a single glance that she was an easterner — but not from the Northeastern mountain provinces like her mother, or even the far East where the war was being fought. The tanned skin, the gentle folds around the woman's eyes, the high cheekbones: They all marked her as a nomad of the desert tribes.

Tasia tried to decide which was more surprising — a woman wearing a palace guard uniform or a nomad wearing one. She found herself staring at the woman before her without decorum.

"Good midday to you, Majesty," Cole said with a perfunctory bow.

Tasia tore her attention from the guard to Cole. "Good midday, Commander Cole of Easthook."

Cole indicated the woman. "This is Guard Joslyn of Terinto," he said. "After discussion with your father earlier today, it is decided that she is to be your personal guard from now on."

Of Terinto.

If Tasia had needed any confirmation that the woman was a desert nomad, there it was. The barely conquerable, barely rulable territory stood just east of the Capital Lands, consisting mainly of a vast and empty desert and a sparse scattering of nomadic herders who smelled much like the animals they tended to.

There were a few cities in Terinto, nestled against the coastline. But these were mostly small, dirty places. The kinds of cities that pirates and crooked merchants called home. And Cole hadn't introduced the new guard as being from one of these places — she wasn't Joslyn of Paratheen or Joslyn of Negusto; she was Joslyn of Terinto. To name someone as being "of" an entire, empty territory… only the homeless, tribal people of the desert wastelands were named in such a way.

Tasia's heart sunk.

So. Her father and Cole had found a way around the problem of having a male guard in her private chambers after all. They'd sifted through the bottom dregs of the army's ranks and created themselves a female guard.

Tasia did her best to hide her disappointment. "It is a pleasure to make your acquaintance, Guard Joslyn," she said to the nomad. She held out her hand, palm-down, as a royal or noble-born woman did when meeting a servant for the first time.

Joslyn hesitated. She glanced at Cole for the briefest of moments, but then quickly dropped to one knee, took Tasia's hand, and kissed it stiffly. "It is my honor to serve both you and the Empire, Princess," she said, the words as stiff as the kiss had been.

She rose again.

Behind her, Tasia heard bedsheets rustle, and Joslyn's eyes flitted towards what Tasia assumed was a sleepy, half-awake Mylla. It was not good that they had seen the handmaid in Tasia's bed. But it was unlikely that either of them would draw the correct conclusion about the girl's reason for being their. Handmaids were often close to the royalty they served, and it wasn't that unusual for two close girlfriends to share a bed. The chambermaids might chatter amongst themselves about the frequency with which they found Mylla in Tasia's bed, but even they probably simply thought that Mylla and Tasia were especially close. Which was true.

Nevertheless.

Commander Cole was no chambermaid, and he reported directly to the Emperor. For once, Tasia wished Mylla had slept in her own bed.

"Joslyn is a distinguished infantry veteran who has served the Empire well as we fight to protect our borders in the East," Cole said.

Tasia gave a curt nod.

The Empire's fight to protect (and expand) its borders was never-ending, of course, with war following war for as long as Tasia could remember. Terinto itself was a border territory won through one such a war, its land declared part of the Four Realms when Tasia was a toddler. But although Terinto might be considered a part of the Four Realms by men like Cole and the Emperor Andreth, the desert people were ferociously independent, and some of the more stubborn nomadic tribes still gave the Imperial Army trouble from time to time.

Tasia studied the woman soldier. Had she ever had to fight against her own people? A nomad slaughtering other nomads? But the guard's face remained impassive.

So she was a well-heeled nomad, at least. Domesticated, one might say.

"The Empire appreciates your service," Tasia told the guard.

"She saved General Galter of House Keltior's life as he lay wounded in a battle with the barbarians only a month ago," Cole said.

Joslyn remained still and silent.

"How impressive," Tasia said, though there was no mistaking the mocking edge in her voice.

The muscles of Cole's jaw clenched almost imperceptibly.

"Guard Joslyn is to remain at your side at all times, day and night, by orders of the Emperor," Cole continued. "She will leave your service only upon his order or mine. Or upon death."

"I see." Tasia locked eyes with the guard. Instead of respectfully looking away as a commoner should, the woman held Tasia's stare without so much as flinching, almost as if she was returning Tasia's challenge with one of her own.

Then it seemed she suddenly recalled who it was she stood before, shifted her eyes hastily away.

Good. The guard knew her place. Or could be taught it. There was that, at least.

"The farthest she is permitted to be from you is in your antechamber," Cole said, gesturing behind him. "Which is also where she will be staying. I already had the chambermaid arrange a bed."

"Very well," Tasia said to Cole, resigning herself to her fate.

"Once you determine there is no immediate triumph to be had, you accept your circumstances and begin your probe for other routes to victory," said Wise Man Norix in her head. Tasia's lifelong tutor probably hadn't intended for his lesson to be used this way, or for his royal pupil to manipulate the very person who had been sent to protect her. As the Emperor's senior advisor, Tasia wouldn't be surprised if old Norix himself was partially to blame for this new bodyguard scheme of her father's.

Cole gave a swift bow. "Good day, Princess," he said, and left without further commentary, closing the bedchamber door behind him, leaving Joslyn of Terinto behind to stand awkwardly just inside the doorway.

Although sometimes brusque, the curt, unadorned politeness was the one thing Tasia liked about Cole; he understood his role and seemed to have little or no interest in expanding it. He didn't strive to curry Tasia's favor for his own gain. Nor had she ever seen him strive to curry anyone else's favor, for that matter, not even the Emperor's.

Tasia didn't like him, but she respected him. With any luck, this new hand-picked guard would be like him. If not... Tasia would employ the Wise Man Norix's advice and search for other routes to victory.

Tasia looked the woman up and down. "So," she said. "A female member of the palace guard. You might be the first in the Empire's history."

Joslyn inclined her head. "It's possible, my Lady."

"I am the Princess, not a lady," Tasia corrected. She turned, indicated Mylla, who was sitting up in the bed, holding her night robe closed. "Mylla of House Harthing, my handmaid until she comes of age and marries, *she* is a lady. When you meet a princess, you call her 'Princess' or 'Highness' or 'Majesty.' Not 'Lady.'"

Joslyn said nothing.

Tasia locked eyes with the guard, but for a second time, the woman didn't flinch. She stayed as frozen as a courtyard statue. Tasia found the stillness unnerving.

"Come," Tasia said. Giving commands always helped her disguise unease. "You may as well make formal introductions with Lady Mylla, as she is with me often as not."

Joslyn followed Tasia across the room to the unkempt bed. Too late, Tasia realized the harness end of the dildo was half-visible, sticking out from beneath the sheets. She met Mylla's eyes, glanced quickly at the dildo. Mylla followed her gaze, subtly pushed the leather contraption completely out of sight. If Joslyn saw the exchange, she gave no indication.

The guard gave Mylla a rough, unpracticed bow, and the girl extended her hand in the same manner that Tasia had earlier. Joslyn kneeled and gave it a swift kiss.

"Lady Mylla," said the guard. "I am pleased to make your acquaintance."

"And I am pleased to make yours," Mylla said. She cocked her head to the side. "You're well-spoken. For a nomad."

Tasia thought she saw some kind of emotion flash through Joslyn's dark eyes, but it passed so quickly that she would be hard-pressed to say if it had actually happened or if it had only been her imagination.

"Thank you, my Lady," Joslyn said.

"I hope you understand that I expect you to defend the Lady Mylla's life with the same fervor that you would defend my own, should it ever come to that," Tasia told Joslyn.

The guard gave a single nod.

Mylla giggled. "So *dramatic,* Princess. What would anyone ever want with *my* life?"

Tasia allowed herself a smile. "I just want our new guard to understand that her duty includes you, too. One never knows."

"I suppose one never does," Mylla agreed. "At any rate — shall we eat before our food gets cold?"

They settled in for their meal, both doing their best to pretend the guard was not still in the room as they chattered and laughed.

A guard is just another servant, Tasia reminded herself. And like any other servant, she would be seen and not heard. Until she could find a way to get rid of her, Tasia might as well grow used to having her near.

"Tell me about that boy I caught you with in bed last week," Tasia said. "What was his name again — Lars?"

"Lars?" Mylla repeated, her brow furrowing. "I don't remember a 'Lars.' Which boy do you mean?"

"Which boy?" Tasia laughed. "Just how many of them are there, Mylla?"

The open secret of Mylla's active love life and Tasia's own was the other reason the Princess didn't worry too much about chambermaids and palace guards coming to any scandalous conclusions about Tasia's relationship with Mylla. The men were a smokescreen, in a way, obscuring the place where Tasia kept her true heart hidden.

"You're one to talk," Mylla said. She chewed her lip thoughtfully for a moment. "Lars... oh — do you mean Willem? The son of... Oh, bollocks. *Who* is the Lord from Gart Red?"

"Do you mean Lord Burke of House Gartón?"

"Yes, yes, that's it," Mylla said. "That was definitely Willem. Not Lars."

"Ugh, whatever his name is, I don't know why you bother with that one, Myll. He's terribly dull."

Mylla smirked. "Maybe. But he has a great ass."

"Point taken," Tasia said. "But honestly, House Gartón... those lords and their sons never speak of anything but horses and hunting dogs. How can you take someone so *boring* to bed?"

"It's never stopped *you* before," Mylla countered playfully. "As if you chose Markas for his quick wit!"

Tasia glanced in Joslyn's direction. Open secret or no, she wasn't sure that she wanted the new guard to hear about her various activities with the young men in and around the palace. Who knew what the guard would say to Cole, or what Cole in turn would say to her father.

"Sorry," Mylla said in a low voice, following Tasia's gaze to where the guard stood a few yards away.

"Your Highness, my Lady," the guard said into the silence that had followed Mylla's mumbled apology, "would you prefer that I remain in the antechamber until I am needed?"

Tasia paused a moment. The guard must have been listening to their conversation, which Tasia didn't like. But she had the good sense to offer Tasia and Mylla some modicum of privacy, which Tasia *did* like.

"Yes, actually," Tasia said. "I would prefer that."

The guard turned to go.

"Wait a moment, Joslyn. Have some grapes before you leave." Tasia broke off a handful of grapes and extended them towards the guard. A peace offering. A token of appreciation.

A treat for an animal still being trained.

When Joslyn didn't come any closer to accept the grapes, Tasia said, "They're fresh from the vineyards just outside the city. Probably picked this morning."

Perhaps Joslyn could be won over, just as Tasia had won over the night shift guards at the Sunfall Gate.

Joslyn shook her head. "Thank you, Princess, but I ate with Cole and His Majesty the Emperor at the noontide meal already."

Tasia shrugged. "Suit yourself. But they are here if you change your mind." She smiled at Joslyn and plucked a grape from the stem with her teeth.

#

"You're going to be late, Princess," Mylla said when she finished pinning Tasia's second braid into a neat curl on the top of her head.

"I wouldn't have been, except for the girl who insisted on telling me the entire raunchy adventure between herself and Willem the boring dog boy."

Mylla grinned. "Don't blame me. You asked for the details; I merely fulfilled your wishes. As a good handmaid is meant to do."

Tasia caught Mylla's eye in the mirror of the vanity. "You're so much more than a handmaid to me," she said, no longer teasing the girl. "You know that, don't you?"

Mylla chuckled. "I suppose, Princess." She placed her hands on Tasia's shoulders, leaned forward and pecked her on the cheek. "Now hurry up, or you truly will be late. And I don't want you telling Norix it was my fault again. Last time you were late, he stopped me in a corridor and berated me on 'negligence in my duties' for ten minutes." She rolled her eyes mightily. "And stared at my breasts throughout the entire lecture, I should add."

Tasia laughed. "That sounds like Norix. He's hardly looked me in the eye since my twelfth birthday. Unless my nipples are actually eyes and I didn't realize it."

Mylla gave a mock gasp and covered her mouth. "What would your father say, if he knew?"

"He wouldn't believe it. I don't think my father knows or cares what a nipple is. Or what it's for."

"Mmm, *I* know what it's for," said Mylla, and she leaned around the Princess and dipped her head, biting at Tasia's breast through her gown until the Princess squealed and cuffed her lightly.

"Stop that!" Tasia said through bouts of giggles. "You'll leave a smudge on the dress and then everyone will know."

"No one knows anything," Mylla said tiredly, with the

air of someone who had said the same words many times before. "If they did, I would have been removed from your service ages ago."

She had a point. Tasia didn't know what to call the relationship she had with Mylla, but she knew they'd been something more than friends for at least three years now.

"Do you think that the guard saw the contraption in the bed earlier today?" Tasia asked, keeping her voice low.

"No. And if she did, so what? I doubt nomads have enough imagination to create such a toy, let alone to guess its purpose."

"I hope you're right," Tasia said.

Mylla gave an impatient sigh. "What are you still doing here? You need to get to your lessons already."

"You're right, of course you're right," Tasia said, and she hurried from the bedchamber and into the antechamber. Joslyn stood in the center of the room, alert but still, hand on the pommel of the short sword. "You're to go everywhere that I go, correct, Guard?"

"Yes, Princess," said the guard.

"Then you are about to enjoy your first royal tutoring session. In which we will be discussing the *fascinating* topic of the early history of the Empire. Come along now."

6

The tower room where Tasia attended lessons with Wise Man Norix was at the top of a winding set of spiral stairs, one of the highest points in the entire palace. And because heat rises, and because there was only one window, narrow and high enough that Norix never opened it, the room was perpetually hot. Not the breezy kind of hot that comes from the sun beating on the face while at the beach on a summer's day; the kind of breezeless hot that makes the air feel thick and impossibly hard to breathe. The kind of hot that traps the mingled smells of dust and sweat and old food. And the musk of wet things that had never properly dried.

The kind of hot that makes a person drowsy, that makes a person's eyes want to automatically droop closed, almost as soon as she comes into contact with it.

"…which was when the House of Wisdom was formed, of course," Tasia heard Norix say. His voice sounded distant, as if he were at the opposite end of the room instead of seated across the table from her.

She nodded with a head that felt twice as heavy as it normally did as she tried but failed to piece together what her tutor had just told her.

When the first Emperor came to what was now Port

Lorsin... except he wasn't an Emperor then, just as there was no House of Dorsa then... he was a barbarian... there was a great fight... the legends about the beasts who'd chased the tribe south were only that — legends, tribal myths... and there were two brothers... one thought himself a sorcerer... the one who didn't think himself a sorcerer who killed the one who did... and that was when the House of Wisdom was formed. Of course.

"Princess Natasia," said Norix. "Are you listening to me?"

Tasia's chin, which had been dipping towards her chest, snapped up. "Yes." She cleared her throat. "Yes, I was listening — that was when the House of Wisdom was formed."

He peered at her, clearly displeased with his pupil. "And what were the events immediately leading up to its formation?"

She'd fallen asleep for a moment, hadn't she? Had she heard that part? There were brothers... mythical beasts... a sorcerer... Or had she dreamed that part?

Tasia looked away from Norix, letting her gaze wander the room as if she might find the answer somewhere amongst his dusty floor-to-ceiling shelves of parchment scrolls and books, rodent skulls and maps of the known world, arrays of glass jars filled with milky liquids and who-knew-what inside, half-burned candles and tattered, faded tapestries.

Joslyn stood next to the dusty shelf nearest the door, hand resting on the silver pommel of her short sword as always, and it seemed that she watched Tasia as intently as Norix.

Tasia returned her attention to her tutor. "I'm sorry, Wise Man Norix," she said. This time, at least, honesty might be her best choice. "I think I might not have heard you when you said what conditions led to the formation of the House of Wisdom."

Norix sighed. He sat across from her, looking as old and desiccated as ever, his snow-white hair cut in the Wise Man way — a close-cropped but thinning ring around his head. Despite the neat discipline of his hair, his beard consisted of unkempt, patchy tufts that refused to face any particular direction.

He pushed back the sleeves of his grey robes. "Princess, your father told me about what happened last night. I'm sure you must be shaken — and very tired — from your ordeal."

"I didn't mean to doze off. It's just... it's hot in here, and it makes me sleepy."

"Your father told me earlier today that he intends to make you his true heir," Norix said. "You'll still have to marry, of course, but your father wants *you* to be the one with the power, not your husband."

The unexpected non sequitur jolted her awake. Perhaps Norix had designed it that way.

Tasia sat straighter in the high-backed wooden chair. "Me?"

"Yes," said the old man with a wry grin. "You."

"But... why?"

Norix gave her a kind, if somewhat condescending, smile. "When Emperors only have a daughter, they find a young lord to marry her, and that young lord becomes the adopted son of the House of Dorsa. You know this from our recent studies of the Empire's early history."

Tasia nodded. Of course she knew that. She was the Princess, after all; she didn't need to read the Empire's early histories in a textbook to know that her sex had determined her destiny from the time of her birth.

But it was Norix's way to take his time getting to the point. Everything had to be a lesson with him.

"It hasn't always been this way," Norix continued. "Everyone knows the story of the Empress Adela, who ruled the Empire after her father died in the early days of the House of Dorsa. Few realize there were three more Empresses after her who, directly or indirectly, had been their father's heirs." Wise Man Norix paused, as if choosing his next words carefully. "And I happen to believe that your father's decision is rooted in wisdom. This may be the right time in history — and that you may be the right princess in history — for a woman to rule the Empire again."

Tasia's brow furrowed. She was the right princess to rule the Empire? Norix's sudden proclamation was more than out-of-context and unexpected; it was out-of-character. She was relatively certain that her tutor didn't even *like* her, let alone think her capable of ruling an entire empire.

And besides the fact that he rarely did anything but criticize her — for her work ethic, for her willingness to learn, for her attention to detail — women were simply not heirs. The Empress Adela had been history's one shining exception; the three other Empresses Norix named must have been obscure or had short rules, because Tasia could not think of any of their names. Neither could her father, when they'd discussed Empress Adela the night before.

So why this? Why now?

Slowly, Tasia said, "Wise Man Norix, I respect my father's judgment, and yours, of course — " (a bald-faced lie) " — but why does my father intend to make me heir? And why are you telling me this before he has the chance himself?"

Norix sighed deeply, leaning back in his chair and lacing his hands on the table before him. "Last night's assassination attempt gave us all a fright. My Wise Men have been interrogating the man who tried to kill you, but so far, they have only learned one thing of use: He can resist truth serum."

The revelation hit Tasia with a shock.

The man who almost killed her had resisted the truth serum of the Wise Men. That wasn't possible. To resist the truth serum required years of careful, painstaking training. It required poisoning oneself with the serum in ever-increasing doses, tolerating months of sleepless nights and vomiting until one built up an immunity to it, built up the ability to push back against it. And the fact that the assassin could even get his hands on enough truth serum, over a long enough period of time, to make it through that training...

It meant the assassin really *was* a Wise Man. Which in turn meant he was connected to a noble family.

The other alternative was that he'd been trained by a Wise Man. Which in turn made him part of a noble family. Or extremely close to one.

Which option was more frightening — a traitor amongst the Wise Men, or a traitor amongst the highborn with a Wise Man accomplice?

The thought of it made Tasia's pulse quicken.

"It is clear that someone wants to destabilize the Empire, Princess," Norix said, lowering his voice despite the fact that they were in one of the most remote parts of the entire palace. "That 'someone' has enough resources, influence, and ingenuity that they could be successful. But we do not yet know who they are. What if, in choosing a husband for you, we play right into the conspirator's hands? What if we inadvertently choose — "

"The son of the very lord who tried to have me killed," Tasia said softly.

"Precisely." Norix sat up straighter, shook an arthritic finger at her. "Do you see that, Princess Natasia? When you actually *use* the mind that your father gave you, you are very clever. You think like he does. You have the potential to... to..." His rheumy eyes went distant and he waved one hand in the air before him as he searched for the right words.

But he didn't need to finish his statement, because Tasia already knew what he was thinking.

"I have the potential to carry on my father's legacy,"

she said, "if only I would stop behaving like a foolish girl."

"I would not have phrased it *quite* that way… your Majesty," Norix said.

Another shock. Norix had never called her *your Majesty* or *your Highness*. Other servants did sometimes, but not Norix, her father's senior-most advisor. Her tutor since the age of four. And the Wise Man never said anything he hadn't carefully considered first. Which meant that by using the honorific now, he was sending a signal to her. A signal that implied who she could be. And who *he* could be to her.

"You are many things, Princess. You have a quick mind — though you rarely use it for your studies," he added wryly. "You are savvy when it comes to reading people, both men and women, both highborn and commoner alike. You are capable of manipulating the people around you, and you press on those levers to your advantage." Tasia opened her mouth to protest, but Norix spoke over her. "Like the guards of the Sunfall Gate, for example."

She blanched, snapped her mouth closed.

"Surely you didn't think the Emperor and I were unaware of your nighttime … erm, *meanderings?*" He offered a slight smile — a sly smile, Tasia thought. "I am the palace's chief Wise Man, after all. It is my duty to know the comings and goings of each palace inhabitant. I am not that different from Cole of Easthook in that way; he knows where they each hide their knives." He leaned closer to her, tapping the side of his head. "I know where they keep their minds."

Tasia said nothing, and Norix took her silence as an invitation to continue his lecture. He shook his finger at Tasia.

"You are many things, my dear girl. Impudent, churlish, impulsive, mule-headed — these all describe you well. Still..." he said, almost as if to himself, "they are traits you can learn to temper, should you decide to. Traits you could use, even. As your father has. Statecraft, strategy, the right balance of daring and caution: These are things I can teach you. But loyalty — *ahh,* loyalty cannot be taught. And the one thing I know you are *not* is a traitor. So when your father brought up the idea about making you his heir, I agreed with him. Encouraged him, even." He gave her that sly smile again, but showed more of his yellow teeth this time, giving him a wolfish look. "The trait of loyalty runs strong in the bloodline of the House of Dorsa. And in these precarious times, it is loyalty — to House and to Empire — that the next ruler will need the most. Someone without that loyalty..." He spread his hands wide in a *who-knows-what-will-be* gesture. "There has never been an Empire as mighty as ours. That doesn't mean it is incapable of falling."

The statement sent a chill down Tasia's spine. "So it *was* his idea?" Tasia asked, checking that she understood what the Wise Man had said. "Not yours?"

Norix gave her an incredulous look. "You think that *I* would propose you as his heir?" he said. Before Tasia could react with offense, he added, "It is not suitable for your father's senior Wise Man to suggest an heir. After all, given the absence of your mother, should your father die unexpectedly without an heir who is of age, the role of Regent would pass to me. So yes, Princess. It was your father's idea. I merely agreed."

Tasia stared at him without saying anything. Heir to the throne. Ruler of the Four Realms. *Her.* She remembered their conversation from the night before, when Father brought up the Empress Adela, the warrior-queen who'd saved the nascent Empire after a series of wars that had nearly destroyed it. Adela's father had only the two daughters, and the younger one died before reaching adolescence. Rather than marrying Adela off and turning her husband into the heir, he named Adela the heir and never forced her into marriage.

"Why tell me this?" Tasia asked Norix. "Why tell me before Father does?"

"The Emperor is going to bring it up with you soon," he said. "Probably later today. I didn't want him to take you by surprise. I wanted you to be prepared, to show him the cool head that you are occasionally capable of demonstrating, rather than call into doubt his decision." Norix gave a small shrug. "As advisor to the current Emperor; to his father, the previous Emperor; and possibly to you, the future Empress, I take a certain pride in guarding the continuity and stability of the House of Dorsa. That continuity is critical to the Empire and its long-term health."

"Alright," Tasia said. "Alright. I will respond... appropriately."

"You do realize that being the heir comes with certain responsibilities, I hope?" said Norix. "You'll be expected to attend council meetings, attend ceremonial events, and join in when your father meets with his advisors."

"Yes, I know," Tasia said, remembering how much Nik hated having to accompany his father all the time once he turned thirteen.

Norix cocked one bushy eyebrow. "You'll also need to take your education more seriously."

"I do take it seriously," Tasia argued.

Norix let out a cough that might have been a laugh. Tasia bristled.

"And until we know who tried to have you killed, it's no longer safe for you to leave the palace without a full guard." He lifted his chin, indicating Joslyn, who still stood posted near the door. "Even with your new bodyguard. Even... erm, under the cover of darkness."

Tasia felt her cheeks coloring, and hoped the light in the dusty tower room was too dim for Norix to see it. "I know," she said. She straightened in her chair. "If my father sees fit to name me his heir, then I will not disappoint him." *Or the House of Dorsa,* she added silently. *Or the Empire.*

Not disappointing the Empire. The thought suddenly made Tasia understand the weight of responsibility that her father was about to lay on her shoulders. It was bad enough to be royal; it had never occurred to her that she would also have to carry the burden of making safe and prosperous the lives of over a million souls.

Norix gave Tasia a satisfied nod. He laced his fingers together before him and smiled.

#

The spiral staircase leading down from the Wise Man's tower seemed more dizzying than usual as Tasia left her tutoring session with Norix, and she walked down cautiously, one hand keeping the hem of her gown well above her feet, one hand trailing along the rough stones of the wall beside her. Joslyn walked down the stairs ahead of her, hands free to pull a sword if necessary.

Even when the spiral of steps stopped, the dizzy feeling did not. Her head felt muddled — no doubt the combination of lack of sleep, the previous night's assassination attempt, and Norix's unexpected revelation all conspired to cloud her thoughts.

Her head wasn't the only thing that felt uncomfortable; her stomach ached, too. And not from hunger or from over-indulgence. Instead, it flashed alternately too hot and too cold, knotting and twisting in pulsating time with the images racing through her mind.

Fear: The assassin's black blade arching above her the night before, its downward course interrupted only at the very last moment.

Anticipation: What her father would say when he raised the possibility of her ascendency as heir.

Fantasy: A fleeting image of herself seated in her father's chair at the council table, crown atop her head, gazing out regally into a room full of lords and ambassadors.

How did she feel about such a future? How did she feel about becoming the Empress? How would the lords react? Tasia wasn't sure.

Loss: Imagining herself wearing her father's crown only reminded her that she wasn't supposed to be the one to wear it. It was supposed to be Nikhost.

Nik. Her baby brother. Her best friend.

How she missed him. How she would trade anyone — even Mylla — to have him back, even for a single day. If only so she could tell him goodbye.

Gaze fixed on the heels of Joslyn's boots ahead of her, Tasia followed a few paces behind her new guard without a word, content to let the nomad lead the way back to her apartments while her head and stomach both churned.

Joslyn stopped abruptly to let a chambermaid cross the corridor ahead of them, and Tasia, unprepared, rammed forehead-first into the guard's back.

"Excuse me," she mumbled, rubbing her forehead.

The guard turned, met Tasia's eyes. Joslyn's irises were so dark that it was hard to distinguish iris from pupil. Nonetheless, Tasia thought she saw a look of concern in those dark eyes.

"Are you alright, Princess?"

"Yes. It was only a slight bump."

"That's not what I meant."

Tasia narrowed her eyes. "No? Then what *did* you mean, guard?"

And as if she had been party to Tasia's thoughts, Joslyn said: "The meeting with your tutor took a... turn I don't think you expected. And only last night someone made an attempt on your life. It is quite a lot to stomach. For anyone. So when I asked if you were alright, that was what I meant."

Quite a lot to stomach. An odd coincidence of words, given the fire in Tasia's gut. Unconsciously, she placed a hand across her middle.

"Yes, it is a lot to stomach," Tasia said. Then, remembering that she was trying to train her new servant, she sharpened her tone. "Although I don't see how any of that is a guard's business."

Joslyn nodded. "Apologies, your Majesty." She hesitated a moment. "Princess... if it eases your burden any... I want you to know that no assassin will get near you again. Not while I remain in your service."

"That eases my burden *none,*" Tasia said. "I've known you for all of — what? Four hours of the clock? Five? And as you pointed out, the attempt on my life was only last night. Then you suddenly appear today? For all I know, you are my assassin's accomplice, weaseling your way into the palace to finish the job."

She stalked past Joslyn, continuing down the corridor at a brisk pace. She could hear the guard's boots rapping hard on the flagstones behind her as the guard hurried to catch up. A moment later, Joslyn walked beside Tasia again.

The Princess expected Joslyn to say something in order to defend herself, but she remained silent.

They walked side-by-side the rest of the way to the Princess's private apartments, at which point Joslyn slipped ahead of her and inspected all three chambers — the antechamber, Tasia's bedchamber, the servant's bedchamber. Tasia put on a show of the inspection being superfluous and unnecessary, but secretly she was glad for the guard's diligent caution.

Joslyn returned to the Princess a minute or two later, giving the Princess a single nod and stepping aside to allow her to enter.

Maybe it was the bottomless blackness in the guard's eyes, maybe it was knowing from Cole that she was some kind of war hero, maybe it was her proclamation that no assassin would come near her again — whatever it was, Tasia had to admit to herself that she felt just a little bit safer as she crossed the threshold into her private chambers.

7

It was a long, tedious afternoon, as Tasia had only a short break between her lesson with Norix and her military history lesson with General Remington, her father's senior war advisor.

"You're late," he barked when Tasia and Joslyn came in.

"I'm sorry," Tasia said. "Wise Man Norix kept me behind for a few minutes."

"You're late nonetheless," Remington said. He was a grizzled old soldier who tended to speak to everyone with the same gruff manner, but Tasia liked him anyway. Remington was an uncomplicated man who barely looked at Tasia during their short weekly lesson. Others might have found his indifference offensive, but not Tasia. Compared to Norix, the General's lack of judgment — or even attention — was actually refreshing.

Remington stood from behind his desk, stretched, then clomped over to the table he used for meetings and Tasia's lessons. He lilted oddly to one side as he walked, most likely because one of his legs was nothing but a wooden peg. Some lordling Tasia had kissed a few times had explained with great awe the battle in which the General had lost his leg, but frankly, Tasia hadn't listened to the story very closely and could no longer remember when or how it had happened. It was during the Western Rebellion, she thought, but wasn't quite sure of even that detail.

The General gave Joslyn an inquisitive once-over before seating himself at the table and spreading out the map of the Empire.

"You have a palace guard with you today," the General said to Tasia.

"Yes. My father and Commander Cole assigned a guard to me after..." Tasia paused, wondering how much to reveal. He might already know about the previous night's assassination attempt, but Tasia didn't think she should make that assumption, so she held her tongue.

Fortunately, the General was not an overly curious man. He didn't press Tasia to finish the sentence when she trailed off. He did, however, look Joslyn up and down a second time.

"What's your name, Guard?"

"Joslyn of Terinto, sir."

Remington grunted. "Terinto. I lost good men in Terinto, battling your kind's ragtag fighters." Frown lines showed as he scowled for a moment. "Fierce, though, the nomads. Not a coward amongst them. How did you come to be in service of the palace guard? Don't believe I've ever seen a woman or a nomad in the guard."

Joslyn shifted almost imperceptibly, giving Tasia the smallest hint that the General's line of questioning made her uneasy.

"I was in the Imperial Army, sir," the guard answered.

"My battalion had been rotated out from the front for winter, and we'd come back to the Capital Lands for leave. That was when Commander Cole approached my commandant to see if I would be available to serve the Princess."

"Imperial Army, eh?" said the General, seeming to warm up a bit. "I had a few female soldiers in my time, but most of them worked supply routes. Is that what you did? Supply route guard?"

"No, sir."

"What then?"

"Infantry, sir."

General Remington's eyebrows shot up his forehead. Tasia had rarely seen his face register such surprise. "Well. You are a rarity, Guard." He turned to Tasia. "To our lesson, then. We had been studying the Second Battle of New Tevon, but the Emperor requested me to leave off with that and brief you on the War in the East." He dropped a meaty finger onto the map, tapping the mountain range that marked the eastern edge of the Empire's lands. "So, Princess. Tell me what you know about the war and we will work from there. Causes, milestones, current conditions." He looked past her, lifted his chin in the direction of Joslyn. "Though your guard might be able to speak better to current conditions on the ground and recent developments than myself."

Tasia searched her mind. The War in the East. It had been an ever-expanding project of her father's for nearly half her life. She still remembered attending the celebration in Port Lorsin when the first imperial troops marched eastward; she must have been ten, maybe eleven, and had been instructed by Wise Man Norix to stand very, very still between her father and her brother. Her father gave a rousing speech to the soldiers; Nik fidgeted the whole time, playing with a loose thread on his trousers until Tasia finally slapped his hand away. Norix had not been pleased by their performance later.

If that was the true start of the war, she could say that she remembered it. But as to why it started…?

"Barbarians," she said after a few seconds of silence. "They encroached westward into the Empire's lands, then began raiding the farmlands just on the other side of the mountains. So we sent the Imperial Army in to push them back."

"True — in part. But a vast oversimplification," said the General. "Barbarians began raiding the Empire's farmlands and that triggered our initial dispatch of troops. But as we fought them back… Do you know what a 'proxy war' is, Princess?"

She didn't. She knew what a "proxy" was. She knew what a "war" was. She'd never heard the two put together. Joslyn probably knew. Tasia resisted the urge to look over her shoulder at the guard.

"No," she admitted at last.

"A proxy war is when two nations fight through the medium of a third party," said the General. "A few years ago, we captured a barbarian leader who spoke some of the common tongue. After intense questioning, along with some of the Wise Men's truth serum, the ruffian told us that the mountain tribes had all been retained by..." He unrolled the map further, revealing the lands to the south and east of the mountains. He tapped a finger on a land mass that jutted south into the Adessian Sea. "Here. The Kingdom of Persopos."

"Why?" Tasia asked, surprised. She'd never heard it said before that the Kingdom of Persopos had anything to do with the war. "What quarrel do we have with them?"

"*We* had no quarrel," General Remington said. "The Kingdom is small, secretive. A place that doesn't look kindly upon outsiders and which our Wise Men therefore know very little about. We have tried and failed to plant spies within the upper ranks of the Kingdom; all we have managed to learn is that the current king is rumored to be a madman obsessed with sorcery. *Sorcery,*" he said again, sneering. "He might as well be obsessed with hop-and-fetch."

Tasia nodded. In the Empire, the last of the so-called sorcerers had been expelled by the Wise Men centuries ago. Pockets of commoners here and there probably still engaged in the superstitious practices of old, but for the most part, the Wise Men had debunked the old gods and the "magic" rituals that went with them, replacing primitive superstitions with reason and logic. Tasia wouldn't have been surprised to hear that the barbarians were still practicing their magic, but it did surprise her to hear of a king from a civilized land obsessed with sorcery.

"At any rate," the General continued, "for years, we ˙

wondered how the mountain barbarians had gained the equipment and the organization to carry out sustained attacks in the East. Without doubt, the mountain tribes have been harassing farmers on the border in little raids for the better part of a century. But their attacks were always seasonal, carried out in bands of no more than fifty men, and ended as soon as the first leaf browned and fell. Now we understand they are being financed and trained by the Kingdom of Persopos. We just don't yet know why."

Tasia studied the map. "The Kingdom couldn't be trying to expand their borders into our lands," she said, thinking out-loud. "There must be a thousand miles of independent territories and city-states between their western border and our eastern one."

"A 'border' can be a strange thing, Princess," the General said. "In the Empire, we believe in hard borders — in rivers and mountains and other lines on the map that divide one piece of land from another. But the Kingdom of Persopos… their borders may be smaller than the Empire's on a map, but in practice, they control many lands outside those borders through other means. They fight us through the barbarians, for example, and as you said, the barbarians are a thousand miles from their western border. So perhaps from that point of view, the kingdom is rather bigger than it looks."

"No one ever told me about the Kingdom of Persopos's involvement in the war before," Tasia said.

General Remington's face twisted into a dangerous snarl. "That's because your father's Wise Men refuse to believe that the Kingdom is involved," he said, his words filled with bitterness. "A single captured barbarian who spoke of Persopos over a fifteen year period, they said, does not make a case against them. The Wise Men may know logic, but I know men. The war lingers on because the Empire continues to fight the wrong enemy."

Tasia was startled to hear the General speak so plainly. He was coming dangerously close to disagreeing with the Emperor. At the very least, he was in open disagreement with Norix.

"Recently, however," the General continued, "we've gotten our hands on evidence that even that old twit Norix can't — "

A soft knock came on the door, then it opened a few feet. Joslyn's hand went to the hilt of her sword; General Remington's to the dagger at his waist. But it was just Nathan, one of the Emperor's errand boys.

"Lord Hermant is here, sir," Nathan said. "The Emperor requests your presence in his offices."

Lord Hermant?

Why was Tasia's grandfather here? Lord Hermant of House Farrimont was her mother's father, a man Tasia had interacted with so little over the years that she could probably count each meeting with the fingers of one hand.

"Go ahead of me," Remington said to the boy with a wave of his hand. "Tell the Emperor I will be there shortly." He turned to Tasia. "We will pick this up next week, Princess." He stood from the table, rolling up the map and tying it closed. Then he crossed the room with his odd, hitching gait to his desk, picking up what looked like a letter before heading through the door. He acknowledged Joslyn with a respectful nod on his way out.

Tasia listened to the sound of his peg leg thudding rhythmically down the corridor until it faded to a vague echo.

"Well, Guard," she said to the nomad. "So much for my military history lesson today." She glanced at the candle clock burning in the sconce on the wall of the General's office. "And only four of the clock." She stood from her place at the table. "Let's see what trouble we can get into before the evening meal, shall we?"

But Nathan reappeared in the doorway. "Princess Natasia?"

"Yes?"

"The Emperor requests your presence as well." When Tasia lifted an eyebrow, the boy added, almost apologetically, "I didn't know when I came the first time for the General, your Highness. One of the palace guards stopped me on my way back to his office and sent me back to fetch you."

Tasia made an effort to wipe the surprise from her face and compose her expression into something more dignified. Her father never invited her to meetings with lords or ambassadors or advisors. But neither had he ever asked General Remington to fill her in on the current state of the War in the East.

This, she supposed, must be what it meant to be his heir.

8

Tasia heard the shouting before she ever reached the heavy cedar doors that led into her father's offices, but with the doors closed, the sound was muffled and indecipherable. Palace guards stood on either side of the doors, solemnly erect with black spears in their hands. Nathan walked briskly ahead of the Princess and spoke to the guards as he approached.

"He called for her, mates," he told the silent men at the door, dropping any pretense of formal speech. "And he said to let her guard in, too." Nate melted away down the corridor without waiting to be dismissed.

One of the guards turned his head slightly in the direction of Joslyn. His upper lip curled, twitching into a sneer. "A nomad?" he said under his breath, and added something else Tasia couldn't quite make out. It sounded like a muttered curse.

Granted, Tasia had nearly the same reaction when Cole introduced her to Joslyn a few hours earlier, but she also couldn't allow someone to insult a member of her staff in front of her without repercussions.

"Watch your tongue, Guard," she said sharply. "And open the door."

The guard's jaw clenched. "Apologies, Princess." He

opened the door without another word.

" — which changes everything," Tasia heard her father saying once the door was open.   He sat behind his desk, hands folded in front of him, a placid expression on his face. Norix sat on one side of him; the General sat on the edge of the divan. Cole was in his normal place against the wall.

Her grandfather stood a few feet from the desk. "It changes nothing!" he shouted.

Tasia slipped into the room, Joslyn a step behind her.

"Ah, Princess. You're here," Norix said. He sounded remarkably relaxed, given the fact that Lord Hermant had just shouted at the top of his lungs. He waved at the divan. "Come sit down."

Tasia nodded and settled herself next to General Remington.

Lord Hermant whipped around. He glared at Tasia and Joslyn for a moment before turning back to the Emperor.

"What is *she* doing here?" he demanded.

"Given recent events," said the Emperor, "I've decided to name Natasia as my heir. She is here because she will be present at all of my meetings from now on."

Lord Hermant was the only one whose face registered shock.   General Remington raised both of his bushy eyebrows, glancing at Tasia beside him.

Tasia's stomach clenched, and suddenly she was very glad that Norix had prepared her to hear the unprecedented proclamation her father had just stated with such casual ease.

"Wh — *What?*" the Lord sputtered. In his youth, Lord Hermant's hair and mustache had been a red-blond, much like Tasia's mother and Tasia herself. But he had gone white years earlier, and as his face rapidly reddened in apparent anger and shock, the hair looked somehow even whiter. He pointed behind him without turning around. "She's a woman!"

The Emperor met Tasia's gaze. He held it for a moment, giving her a small nod before looking at the red-faced lord before him. "She is my eldest child."

"She is a woman," Lord Hermant repeated stubbornly. "No — worse than that. She is a *girl.*"

Perhaps emboldened by her father's presence and support, perhaps simply irritated and falling victim to her typical impulsiveness, Tasia spoke up from her place next to the General. "Actually, my Lord, you were correct the first time: I came of age last year. I *am* a woman."

Now her grandfather turned around to look at her. "Adulthood is more than a number, granddaughter. And the whole of the Empire knows you are nothing but a child. A spoiled, impetuous *child.*" He spat the final word.

Tasia opened her mouth to give a sharp retort, but her father beat her to it.

"Hermant, remember whose presence you are in," he growled. "You just insulted my heir. In front of me."

Lord Hermant looked prepared to argue, but he snapped his mouth closed instead.

The office door opened and Wise Man Evrart, Norix's protege, strode in. He crossed quickly and bent to speak quietly into Norix's ear.

Norix turned to the Emperor. "With your leave, Majesty, something has happened with our, erm, new guest which requires my attention."

New guest? Tasia wracked her mind to think of who Norix could be referring to. The spring council meetings would be starting shortly; were there other lords from far afield besides Lord Hermant wandering the palace Tasia hadn't seen yet? Then, with a chill running down her spine, she realized who the "new guest" must be: her assassin. Given the dark circles under Wise Man Evrart's eyes, they'd no doubt been interrogating him — the polite way of putting it — since the night before.

"Attend to it," the Emperor said. "This meeting is over anyway. Cole, see to it that Lord Hermant is escorted from the palace grounds."

Cole stood and took one long step in the older man's direction.

"This conversation is not over, Andreth," said Lord Hermant.

The Emperor rose swiftly from his seat, pressing his fists into the surface of the heavy wooden desk. At his full height, he towered above the older man before him. "I have been patient with you, Lord. More patient than you deserve." His tone was deadly calm. "But if you think the fact that you were, for a while, my father-in-law gives you the right to speak to me with the same casualness as my own father, you are gravely mistaken. I would strongly recommend that you do not speak another word in my presence today. I don't know what kind of *impetuosity* I might be capable of if you do."

Lord Hermant pressed his lips tightly together, as if resisting the temptation to argue. Commander Cole ushered the older man ahead of him, walking him out of the office.

The Emperor let out a heavy sigh once the door closed and lowered himself back to his seat with a grunt. "That went about as well as I expected."

"Does this mean the Lord is withdrawing his financial support for the war effort?" asked General Remington.

"It would seem that way," the Emperor said. He propped an elbow on the arm of his chair and bent his head, rubbing his brow.

Tasia stayed quiet, chewing the inside of her cheek. Her grandfather was more than a stubborn old mule with a propensity for criticizing the Emperor. He was a stubborn *rich* old mule with a propensity for criticizing the Emperor. In particular, he hated the fact that the War in the East still had not been won, despite the fact that it had continued, on and off, for nearly a decade and a half. For the past few years, the silver mines of the House of Farrimont had been a primary source of funding for the war. But it seemed her father would need to find another funding source if the war was to continue. Tasia wondered what the commoners would do if he raised their taxes yet again.

Wise Man Evrart looked down at Norix expectantly.

"Your Majesty..." Norix began.

"Yes, yes, Norix, you have my leave to go," the

Emperor said impatiently, waving his hand at the Wise Man. "What's the problem with our guest?"

"The problem is…" Norix paused, seeming to gather his thoughts. "The man who attacked the Princess last night is dead."

#

"Poison," Tasia said to Mylla, flopping down onto the bed. "Some concoction with bizarre ingredients that Norix tried to describe before Father cut him off."

"At least he's dead," Mylla said. She sat cross-legged near the head of Tasia's bed, filing her nails while she listened to Tasia talk about her day. "But how did he manage to poison himself? Didn't they confiscate everything on him when they brought him into the palace dungeons?"

"He had it hidden in a false tooth," said Tasia. "Norix said it was exceedingly rare and hard to make. Yet another sign that whoever tried to kill me has deep pockets and Wise Men in their service." She yawned. "Gods, it's been a long day. First I get a new bodyguard — " she gestured towards the antechamber where Joslyn was doing whatever she did when outside Tasia's presence " — then Norix tells me my father wants me to be his heir, then my grandfather withdraws his financial support for the war *and* nearly gets himself beheaded at the same time, and now the man who tried to kill me is dead, without giving us so much as a single clue as to who hired him."

Mylla spoke without looking up from her filing. "Are you sure anyone hired him? Maybe he acted alone. Just some Wise Man who went mad."

"Everyone said that's unlikely," Tasia said.

"Who's everyone?"

"Everyone," Tasia said. "Father says he must have known my movements, and that indicated he had an accomplice inside the palace. Norix said he had to have been well-trained to resist truth serum, so that indicated he'd been planning the attempt with someone — 'someone' as in a well-educated Wise Man — for quite some time. And Cole said people who attempt to kill royals are almost always part of a larger coup." Tasia rolled to the side, propping herself on one elbow to grin at Mylla. "Even my new guard had a theory. She spoke without invitation to my father."

Mylla paused for a moment in her filing, looking up. "She *didn't.*" Then she snorted. "But then again, the Terintans are barely civilized, so it's not surprising they don't know how to speak in the presence of an Emperor. What did her vacant nomad's head come up with?"

"It's rich," Tasia said, sitting up and getting off the bed. "I should let her tell you herself." She crossed to the door leading into the antechamber and opened it a few feet. "Joslyn? Come into my bedchamber, please."

The guard entered a few moments later. She was out of her black guard uniform. A cream-colored linen shirt, simple and with no sleeves, hung loosely above a pair of plain brown trousers.

Tasia's grin faded momentarily. She'd never seen arms like that on a woman before, arms where every muscle was defined so clearly. A strange, inexplicable urge to touch them appeared from nowhere.

She shook the feeling away, dispelling it as quickly as it had come like a pesky fly.

"Joslyn, tell Mylla what you told my father," Tasia said, taking a more regal tone than what she'd used with her handmaid. "Tell her about the knife."

The guard hesitated, glancing uncertainly between the two young women.

"Go on," Mylla said. "If you're insubordinate enough — or stupid enough — to speak out of turn to the Emperor about it, surely you can say it to me."

Tasia started to giggle, then stopped herself. She resented the guard being foisted upon her, but it wasn't Joslyn's fault. And she'd been taught to treat those who waited upon her respectfully. One never knew what a commoner could be tempted into, so it was best to keep good relations with them. With her father naming her his heir, she was determined to start behaving with at least a little more decorum.

"The Princess showed her father and his Wise Men the black, iron knife that the traitor used in the attempt to kill her," Joslyn said to Mylla. "In Terinto, it is well-known that such knives are the trademark item of the Cult of Culo."

Mylla put down her nail file, stared wide-eyed at Joslyn. "The Cult of — ?" But she couldn't finish the statement. She doubled over, bursting into laughter. It took her a moment to catch her breath long enough to speak again. "You're saying the Cult of Culo tried to kill Tasia? You might as well say that goblins and faeries tried to kill her!"

Despite her attempt at regal behavior, Tasia couldn't help but join in with Mylla's laughter. Bringing up the Cult of Culo was rather outrageous, and mentioning it in the Emperor's offices showed that Joslyn was both as superstitious as all other nomads and surprisingly dense for speaking out of turn in front of the Emperor.

Mylla continued to laugh uncontrollably, tears rolling down her cheeks as she occasionally exclaimed, "The Cult of Culo!" Joslyn stood stiffly by the door, not seeming to know if she should stay in the bedchamber or excuse herself into the antechamber.

Tasia's own laughter died down, and at the nomad's expression, she felt a pang of guilt. The guard had clearly only been trying to help when she'd brought up the old religious sect that the Wise Men had stamped out centuries ago; she probably hadn't been prepared for the reaction she'd gotten — which was nearly as much laughter from General Remington, Commander Cole, Wise Man Norix, and the Emperor as she was getting from Mylla now. But the Emperor and his advisors had been somewhat more discreet with their amusement, disguising their laughs through snorts and coughs before quickly regaining their composure.

Then Commander Cole had censured her: *"You are*

new at this post, Guard, but in the palace you should be seen but not heard."

After that, Joslyn had simply nodded once and not brought it up again.

Mylla's laughter finally died down. She addressed the nomad, looking her up and down before speaking. "You do realize, don't you, that the Cult of Culo was destroyed by the Wise Men a good two hundred, three hundred years ago? The only people who bring them up are nursemaids and older brothers with a wish to scare small children." She held her hands up and mimed horror, pitching her voice high. "The Cult of Culo! Oh, no! Oh, save us!" Then she broke into giggles again.

Joslyn faced the Princess. "Your Highness, do you require me any further tonight? Or shall I retire to my quarters?"

Her "quarters." It was a rather complimentary way of describing the rice paper screens that separated her small corner of the antechamber from the rest of the room.

Tasia waved a hand. "You're dismissed."

Tasia waited for the door to the antechamber to close before giving Mylla a playful slap. "You're terrible. You made her feel bad."

Mylla wiped the tears from the corners of her eyes. "So? She's a dumb nomad who was dumb enough to think she had been invited to be a part of the conversation about your would-be killer. *And* she brought up the Cult of Culo. You expected me not to laugh?"

"I just didn't think you needed to embarrass her like

that," Tasia said.

Mylla rolled her eyes. "You laughed, too. And besidesI can't believe I'm saying this, but sometimes I think you're far too kind to your servants."

Tasia grinned wickedly and slid a few feet up the bed, positioning herself beside Mylla. She tugged at the collar of the handmaid's dress and kissed her neck. "Too kind? Like this?" She kissed Mylla's ear, tugging on the girl's earlobe with her teeth.

"You'd *better* not be this kind with all your servants," Mylla said.

Tasia kissed the girl's beautiful smile, leaned her back against the pillow.

But Mylla pushed her off. "I can't right now, Tazy," she said. "I think I forgot to tell you — my father's in town. And he's arranged for me to meet some nobleman's son who's interested in my hand tonight."

Tasia sat up, alarmed. "Interested in your hand? But you're not of age to marry yet!"

"No, but you know my father. I'll be eighteen in less than six months. He'll want me married and pregnant in six and a half months."

Tasia flopped back on the bed. "Ugh," she groaned, and in that moment she rather hated Lord Galen of House Harthing, Mylla's father.

House Harthing was small — a minor house, really — but Lord Galen was ambitious. He'd managed to get Mylla named as Tasia's handmaid a few years earlier, doubtless to draw House Harthing a step closer to House Dorsa; now it seemed he'd been quietly working on his eldest daughter's marriage prospects. Actually, Tasia thought, he'd probably been working on them for years.

But she supposed she should be glad for Lord Galen's ambitions. If he didn't have any, Tasia probably never would have met and fallen in love with Mylla.

"When do you have to leave to meet your father?" Tasia asked.

"Seven of the clock," the girl said. "Which gives me less than an hour. You'll help me pick out a dress, won't you?"

Tasia did her best to put on a happy face. "Of course," she said.

Three quarters of an hour later, she walked the handmaid from the bedchamber, through the anteroom, and into the main corridor. Since they were in public, the goodbye kiss Tasia gave to Mylla was cordial, nothing more than the polite peck on the cheek any girl might give to a friend.

"Behave," she told Mylla. "Don't embarrass your father."

"Now that's amusing advice, coming from you."

Tasia glanced around to make sure no one was looking, then goosed the girl's bottom. Mylla let out a short, high-pitched noise of protest.

"That is exactly what I was referring to," Mylla said, shaking a finger at Tasia. "I'll be back in a few hours."

"Alright," Tasia said, knowing that it would probably be much longer than that. She smiled at Mylla, hoping that she was hiding the fact that she felt abandoned and really didn't want to be alone. After all, in the past twenty-four hours, someone had attempted to kill her, she had been named heir to her father's throne, been assigned a new bodyguard, and the man who tried to kill her had managed to poison himself.

She sighed and went back into her antechamber. She needed to find a distraction from her troubles, or else she probably wouldn't sleep that night.

Lamplight flickered behind the rice paper screen that cordoned off Joslyn's corner of the room from the rest. Tasia stopped before the screen, hesitating.

"Guard?" she said quietly.

A shadow moved behind the screen. Joslyn pushed a panel open, gave Tasia a look that bordered on suspicion. Tasia supposed she didn't blame her; the last time they'd spoken it was so Tasia could humiliate Joslyn in front of Mylla over her "Cult of Culo" theory.

"I'm sorry," the Princess said suddenly. "I shouldn't have — I know you were only trying to help when you brought up the Cult of Culo. I wish Mylla hadn't laughed at you the way she did. And me," she added. "I shouldn't have laughed, either."

The apology had come spontaneously, surprising Tasia and probably surprising her new guard, too.

But Joslyn's face softened and she gave Tasia a slight smile. "You shouldn't apologize to a common soldier, Princess."

There was an edge of sarcastic humor in the guard's

voice, just subtle enough to be denied if Tasia called it inappropriate. Tasia opened her mouth to do just that, but then she changed her mind. If she was unkind, Joslyn might deny the request the Princess had in mind for her.

"Do you... do you play Castles and Knights?" she asked the guard.

Joslyn cocked her head to the side, black eyebrows drawing together until a small V appeared at the bridge of her nose. Tasia realized she hadn't noticed how smooth Joslyn's tan skin was until that furrow appeared. Part of her wanted to reach out, wipe the V away with her thumb.

"Castles and Knights?" Joslyn repeated.

Tasia nodded. "It's a game. It's popular here. Well, maybe it's only popular inside the palace. It's not popular amongst soldiers?"

"Soldiers play cards," the guard said.

"Follow me," Tasia said, turning towards her bedchamber. "I'll teach you a much better game than cards."

9

The Princess unfolded her Castles and Knights board, which was a giant map of the Empire, divided into a grid. Then she opened her box of pieces, pulling out the delicately carved figurines and placing the white ones in front of Joslyn.

"You can be white," Tasia said. "I'll be red. Red always goes first, but white starts with a stronger position on the board." She held up a square piece carved to represent a stone tower. "Place your fortifications wherever you want, but keep in mind that you resupply troops from the fortifications, so if your front line gets too far from one, your soldiers get weaker. Oh, and once all your fortifications fall, you lose the game. Mountain fortifications are hardest to conquer, but the mountains also tend to be a fair distance from the front lines."

"What's this piece?" the guard asked. She held up a figurine of a soldier, his standard-issue Imperial Army short sword drawn.

Tasia grinned. "That's you. Those are your foot soldiers." She reached across the board and picked up a carved figure of a man on horseback. "These are cavalry pieces." She put it down and picked up the next one. "And these are your trebuchets. Trebuchets are slow to move, but powerful to attack. Your foot soldiers have the weakest attack, but you also have more of them than any other piece." Tasia tapped the cavalry piece. "And the cavalry pieces are the fastest. They're stronger than the foot soldiers but not as strong as the trebuchets."

The guard listened carefully while the Princess explained the rest of the rules of the game, showing Joslyn how to set up the board, how to move each piece, how fortifications could be attacked, how the game could be won without destroying all the opponent's fortifications by capturing Port Lorsin.

"And these," she said, pulling out a stack of cards from the box, "are the cards of fortune. You draw one at the beginning of each turn. Some have good fortune, some have ill fortune." Tasia turned one of the cards over to show Joslyn. "See this one?" She read it out-loud. "'Your troops grow sick from eating spoiled food. Two foot soldier pieces are immobilized this turn.'"

Joslyn frowned.

"What?" Tasia asked.

"I can't... I'm afraid I don't know how to read," said the guard.

"Oh," Tasia said. She supposed she wasn't that surprised, now that she thought about it. The Emperor before her father — her father's father — had wanted the Empire to be the most educated land in the world, and he started an initiative with a much younger Norix to have Wise Men teach the children of commoners to read. Tasia's grandfather had believed that a literate Empire would be a prosperous Empire. But the region of Terinto hadn't been conquered at that time, so the initiative probably hadn't reached Joslyn's parents. Still, in the years since Terinto became part of the Empire, the House of Wisdom had made special effort to train Wise Men and send them into the region. Some of the Wise Men even traveled with the nomadic tribes, educating the poor herders as they moved their apa-apas from one grazing area to the next.

Tasia voiced that thought to Joslyn. "Were there no Wise Men traveling with your tribe?"

Joslyn shrugged. "Perhaps. But I wouldn't know. My father sold my older sister and I when I was five. I remember very little about my tribe or my parents."

"Your father *sold* you?" Tasia repeated, incredulous.

"It's not uncommon amongst the tribes," Joslyn said, turning a castle piece over in her hand without meeting Tasia's gaze. "Children are hard to feed in the desert. Girl children in particular are sometimes worth more to poor families as slaves than as extra hands."

Girl children in particular... Tasia thought through the implications of what Joslyn had mentioned so casually, and shuddered.

But instead of revealing to Joslyn how much it bothered her, she arched an eyebrow and said, "Well, anyone who intends to be on my personal staff long-term needs to be able to read. I'll read the fortune cards for you tonight, but we will begin your reading lessons tomorrow night."

Joslyn gave a slight smile. "Very well." She paused. "Commander Cole and your father wish for me to teach you to protect yourself. So you can teach me about letters," she said, tapping the fortune card Tasia had turned over, "and I will teach you about self-defense."

"What? Self-defense?" Tasia said, horrified. "No one informed me of this."

"You've had an eventful day, Princess," Joslyn said. "They must have forgotten to mention it."

Tasia was still irritated. She crossed her arms against her chest. "They expect me to... what, exactly? Fight? Learn to use a sword?"

"I think swordplay will come much later," said Joslyn, not reacting to the Princess's sharp tone. "For now, training you in basic escape maneuvers and grappling techniques seems a good starting point. And possibly learning to use a dagger."

Daggers, escape maneuvers, grappling techniques? It was all too much for Tasia. Princesses didn't *fight*.

"Why on Earth would a princess need to learn to defend herself?" Tasia demanded. "If I'm not mistaken, that's what *you're* here for!"

Still looking at the castle piece in her hand instead of the Princess, Joslyn answered, "My understanding is that you have shown a tendency in the past to slip away from the palace on your own for... liaisons with young men. I believe your father and the Commander worry that, despite my best efforts, you and I may become separated somehow."

The Princess blushed fiercely.

"There may come a time when you need to find your

way to safety without me." Joslyn shrugged. "Hopefully that will never happen. But in case it does, they wanted me to prepare you with a rudimentary level of self-defense."

"Fine," Tasia huffed, looking down to hide her reddening face. She didn't mind learning to fight so much as she minded this illiterate ex-slave having so much access to the private details of her life. But perhaps the lamplight was too soft for Joslyn to notice her embarrassment. The Princess took in a breath and focused on controlling her voice. "Alright, Joslyn. You teach me self-defense. I teach you to read. But for tonight, Castles and Knights."

"Castles and Knights," Joslyn repeated with a nod. She smiled, and to Tasia it looked very much like a smirk. Very much like a knowing smile from someone who knew they'd subtly gained the upper hand.

The Princess ground her teeth. Just when she'd started to almost like this guard, Joslyn had proven herself to be just like all other commoners — eager to find a way to show herself to be better than a highborn. Tasia put the insulting self-defense lessons out of her mind and continued her explanation of Castles and Knights.

#

"He smelled of onions," Mylla said for the third time.

They sat together at the small table, sipping tea and sharing the breakfast the chambermaid brought for Tasia. It was just after dawn on the third day of Tasia's new schedule of duties. Two days earlier, Tasia began attending all her father's meetings. So far, that included only private meetings with his close circle of advisors, but today marked the first day of the annual spring council meetings.

And as if the private meetings and council meetings were not enough, Tasia was also expected to keep up with her regular lessons with the Wise Men *and* her new self-defense lessons with Joslyn. Her hands were still sore from the previous day's so-called "self-defense" lesson, in which she had primarily carried rocks up and down the beach while Joslyn stood idly by and watched.

Normally, the busy schedule would irritate Tasia, lead to her complaining to her father that it was all too much. But she was still shaken over being attacked, and the fact that the assassin had managed to kill himself before they got any useful information out of him did nothing to ease her nerves. At least the new schedule, from meetings to lessons to "self-defense" to Mylla's complaints about her latest onion-smelling suitor, all helped her to keep her mind off the fact that whoever wanted her dead was probably still out there, plotting a second attack.

"Onions aren't necessarily a bad thing," Tasia said to Mylla. "They go well with duck and — "

"Tasia. He smelled of onions, he's nearly shorter than I am," Mylla said, ticking off the boy's faults on her fingers, "he's chubby, his teeth are yellow, and he acts as if he has probably never talked to a girl in his whole life."

Tasia giggled. "He probably hasn't." She nibbled on a piece of bacon.

"And he smelled of onions."

"You mentioned that part already. Does all this mean you will refuse to marry him?" Tasia asked. She tried not to sound hopeful.

Mylla made a sour face. She dropped another sugar cube into her tea — her fourth, by Tasia's count — and stirred. "Well," she said with deliberate slowness, "unlike *some* people, *I* don't have the luxury of refusing my father's wishes."

"Actually, you do. By law," Tasia said. "The Emperor Godfrey established that after the Second War of Unification. All highborn girls have right of refusal over their suitors. How do you think I've managed to remain unmarried all this time?" She waggled her eyebrows at the handmaid.

But Mylla clicked her tongue against the roof of her mouth impatiently. "You and the Emperor Godfrey can both go lay an egg," she said. "I'm very happy you've been listening to Norix's history lessons for once, but *I* don't have any right of refusal. I cannot tell my father no. He has already made clear that the fortunes of House Harthing ride upon my marriage."

"How many suitors are you up to now, Myll?" Tasia asked. "There's this onion-boy, before that was horse-face, and freckle-nose, and — "

"I'm so glad you find my misery so amusing," Mylla said drily. "While you go prancing around being the new heir, gloating and refusing your suitors, some of us still have to marry on our eighteenth birthday and be pregnant with our second child by our nineteenth."

The conversation lapsed into an awkward lull.

After a few seconds of silence, Tasia reached across the table, took Mylla's hand in her own. "I'm sorry, my sweet. I wasn't trying to gloat at your misery. Would you like for me to do something? I could get my father to intervene. Lord Galen can tell you what to do, but he can't tell the Emperor what to do."

Mylla withdrew her hand. "No. That would only make things worse," she said, shaking her head and gazing down at the table. "Onion-boy is wealthy. And if he proposes marriage then I have to accept it and that's that."

"What was his name again?"

"Onion-boy."

Tasia laughed. "What's his real name, Myll?"

"Oh, I don't remember," Mylla said, waving a dismissive hand. "Hubert or Herbert or Humphrey or something as boring as he is. I'll end up lying beneath him while he ruts and I'll try to imagine he's you." She got up abruptly, her back to Tasia as she gathered the dirty plates. "So what is your schedule for the day? Lessons with Wise Man Evrart at half-past, then moving rocks up and down the beach with the nomad after that?"

"Not today," Tasia said with a sigh. "Today the spring council meetings begin. Though honestly, I don't know which is worse — the council meetings, listening to Wise Man Evrart go on and on about the way ancient folklore has infiltrated modern literature, or having to run up the beach in boys' trousers carrying rocks. They all seem like varying degrees of torture to me."

"And remind me again what carrying rocks has to do with self-defense?" Mylla asked, brushing crumbs from the table.

"Mother Moon bless us if I know," said Tasia. "Apparently, Joslyn thinks I have to get stronger before I can be trusted with actual self-defense techniques."

"I have no love for the nomad," Mylla said, "but I must admit that I am glad you will be learning to defend yourself. The situation certainly seems unusual, but I would never have recovered if that fake Wise Man had killed you that night."

Tasia grew quiet. Her brush with death wasn't a memory she liked to go back to.

"I'm sorry," Mylla said. She came up behind the Princess and kissed Tasia's bare neck. "I shouldn't have mentioned it."

"It's alright," Tasia said. "I know you only said it because you care for me."

"I care for you more than you'll ever know, Tazy," said the handmaid, and she kissed the Princess's neck again, this time letting her lips linger a moment. "I want you to be safe, no matter what it takes. Even if you have to be shadowed by that woman for the rest of your life."

"Mylla?"

"Yes, sweet Princess?"

"They're still out there," Tasia said. "Whoever wanted me dead, I mean. I can just... I can feel it. I wouldn't be surprised if it's one of the lords who's here for the spring council meetings. Maybe he'll even be in the room tomorrow. Maybe he'll — "

"Stop that," Mylla said. She draped one arm around Tasia's shoulders and sat in the Princess's lap. "You'll give yourself nightmares, talking like that. You'll give *me* nightmares, for that matter."

"You're right, but... why would someone want to kill me? I'm not special."

Mylla threw her head back and laughed. "Not special? You're the eldest child of the Emperor. You're the first female heir to the crown in a thousand years. How can you say you're not special?"

"But I wasn't heir until just a few days ago," Tasia argued. "Hardly anyone outside the palace Wise Men and you even know yet."

"That doesn't matter," Mylla said, shaking her head. "You're still the daughter of the Emperor, and you're his favorite. No, don't argue with me — you are. You always have been, even when Nik was alive. If someone wanted to strike at the Emperor, they would strike at you first."

"Maybe," Tasia said doubtfully. It still didn't make sense that someone would try to kill her. "I wish the assassin hadn't died before we got more information out of him. He gave us absolutely nothing to go by. Unless you count that knife..."

Mylla snorted. "Oh, *don't* tell me you're humoring the nomad's theory?" She waggled her fingers and mocked a menacing face. "Is the Cult of Culo coming after you, my little princess?"

Tasia chose to ignore the jest. "It all just seems so

strange."

"Come on, Tazy. You're a smart girl; can you truly not think of any reasons why someone might try to have you killed?" Mylla said. "To begin with, there is the simple fact that you are the Princess and the eldest child of the Emperor, which makes you a target out of jealousy or vengeance if nothing else. Do you think your father has no enemies?" She paused a moment after the rhetorical question, then answered it herself. "House Harthing allied with your father during the Western Rebellion, but I know — and you know — that there are Western lords who still give the Empire only grudging loyalty. I'm sorry to be the one to say this, sweet princess, but there are definitely lords in the West who would kill you just out of spite, if they thought they could get away with it."

Tasia blanched, but she knew Mylla was right. Living in the palace as she did, with every lord who met her dropping to a knee and kissing her ring sycophantically, it was easy to forget how many of them still probably hated her father for putting down their rebellion. She knew that Norix and General Remington both thought he should have executed more of the Western lords than he did. But Father argued that his mercy was the only thing that kept the Empire together after the rebellion was over. That was why they called him "Andreth the Just" — he was fair instead of cruel after the rebellion ended.

"But that is just spite and vengeance," Mylla went on. "Don't forget there is also political expediency. Who knows what schemes may be afoot to pressure your father through you or through Adela. After all, your father has only two blood heirs." She cocked an eyebrow, looking puzzled. "Though why your father won't simply take another wife and make new heirs is beyond me. I'm sure he could find a highborn woman he found pretty enough to bring his soldier to attention. Then he and his member could simply *make* another son, and he wouldn't have to name a daughter heir to the — "

"Could you please not speak so coarsely?" Tasia said. "They may be just the House of Dorsa to you, but for me, Father and Adela are the only family I have left. Especially if Lord Hermant is cutting ties with Father."

Mylla stopped, genuine remorse showing in her eyes. She leaned down, gave Tasia a gentle kiss on the cheek. "You're right, Tazy. I'm sorry."

She leaned closer and kissed Tasia again — a real kiss this time. Tasia resisted at first, but then relaxed, parting her lips to permit Mylla's tongue to meet her own. They sat there like that for a long few minutes, Mylla with her arms wrapped around Tasia's shoulders, Tasia's hands finding their way beneath Mylla's dress.

A knock sounded on the bedchamber door. Mylla hastily hopped out of Tasia's lap, smoothing down her dress. Tasia tucked back a few errant blonde curls.

"Enter," the Princess called formally.

Joslyn walked into the room and gave a short bow. She was dressed in her palace guard blacks, the leather gleaming with fresh oil. "Are you ready for the council meeting, Princess?"

Tasia rose from the table and walked to her vanity, checking her braid, straightening her necklace. Today everything needed to be perfect.

She turned to Mylla. "Well. Wish me luck."

Mylla put her hands on her hips, smirking. "A princess at the spring council meetings. Some of the older lords will probably die of a heart attack."

Tasia smiled, but her stomach churned.

In just a few minutes, her father would greet the heads of the eighty-one noble Houses in the Empire, or, in some cases, their representatives. Also present would be most of the two hundred forty-three ambassadors, men who were almost always as rich as their local lords, sometimes richer, but due to quirk of birth were not noble. The ambassadors were supposed to represent the wishes of the common people in their region, but often they represented only other rich merchants like themselves. The three weeks of spring council meetings were meant to give everyone in the Empire, highborn and commoner alike, the feeling that they had a say in the governing of the Empire. Technically, the Emperor had final decision-making power over all affairs of state, but he usually at least took the opinions of his council into consideration. Yet another reason they called him "the Just."

For the first time in her life, Tasia would attend the council meeting alongside her father. For the Emperor's heir to attend a council meeting was not unusual at all; her own father attended council meetings from the time he was twelve until his father died when he was nineteen. But there had not been a female heir in living memory, which meant Tasia's appearance at the council would be doubly noteworthy. She was probably the first female to attend the council meeting in generations.

"Princess?" Joslyn said. "Should we go?"

Well, at least Tasia wouldn't be the *only* female there. Joslyn would be there, too, standing inconspicuously behind the Princess. Tasia supposed she should be comforted by that. Especially considering that whoever wanted her dead would probably be somewhere in the audience.

"Princess?" Joslyn said again.

Tasia took a deep breath. "Yes, I'm ready. Let's go."

For once, the Princess was glad for the guard's company.

10

The Emperor, Wise Man Norix, Wise Man Evrart, and two palace guards were waiting when Tasia and Joslyn arrived. The Wise Men were both in their normal grey robes; the Emperor had dressed formally for the first council meeting of the season. He wore rich black silks embroidered with silver moons and the silver eagle of House Dorsa. Atop his head was a slim crown, the steel one with the black pearl in its center.

So. The steel crown. A symbol of strength.

The Wise Men stood on one side of him, two of the palace guards stood on the other.

"Are you ready?" the Emperor asked his daughter.

Tasia gave him a quick curtsy. "Yes."

"This is an important council meeting," the Emperor said. "It's the first meeting of the spring council sessions, and because they know we'll be discussing the War in the East, nearly every lord and every ambassador in all Four Realms has turned up."

Norix, who'd been standing silently next to her father, rocked back on his heels a little before smiling at the Princess. "And we'll be announcing your ascendency today."

"I haven't forgotten." Tasia ran her hands down the

front of her gown, smoothing it.

Norix rested a hand on her shoulder. "Project confidence. Believe that you are the heir and they will also."

Tasia nodded.

The Emperor signaled to the guards, and they walked down the hallway ahead of the Emperor's party, opening the heavy double cedar doors that led into the council room. The doors were carved in relief with the history of the House of Dorsa, showing how Dorsan, son of Zokaz, first led his refugee tribe from the dangerous Unknown Lands in the far north to safety in the south almost two thousand years earlier. According to legend, the half-beast, half-man monsters of the Unknown Lands pursued them all the way to the southern coast, where Dorsan and his kinsmen made a final stand and defeated the monsters at last. Port Lorsin, the Empire's capital city, was founded by the surviving tribe members — "Lorsin" meant "victory" in the old tongue. The palace the House of Dorsa had lived in ever since was originally just a hill fort the tribe had made to protect itself.

The detailed carving that showed the founding of Port Lorsin, complete with a stylized Dorsan and the first Wise Man, Gorak, was the last thing Tasia saw before the doors swung open.

"All stand for the Emperor Andreth the Just of the House of Dorsa, ruler of the Four Realms, Father of the Empire's Children," boomed the guard. The room of lords, lords' sons, ambassadors, Wise Men, and their guards stood automatically. The door guard hesitated for only the slightest moment before adding, "And for his daughter, the Princess Natasia, heir to the crown, future Empress, future Mother of the Empire's Children."

At the mention of the Princess, glances were exchanged, jaws fell, whispers rippled through the crowd.

Apparently this was what Norix had meant by "announcing" her ascendancy. It was a bold move, to be sure, but there was wisdom to it, Tasia supposed. Her new position as heir had been made a simple statement of fact, without giving time for discussion or room for interpretation.

The Emperor strode in, his silk robes billowing behind him like a flag, with Tasia close on his heels. She followed him to the table on the raised dais at the front of the room. A guard pulled out a chair for her to his right, and Tasia settled into it gracefully, as if she'd done it a thousand times, as if her heart wasn't hammering so hard that it threatened to break free from her chest.

Wise Man Norix and Wise Man Evrart took the seats to the Emperor's left. Also at the raised table were General Remington and a handful of her father's other advisors, all of them Wise Men or military men.

Once everyone at the Emperor's table sat, the rest of the room settled back into their own chairs.

Tasia looked out over the crowd, the hairs on the back of her neck prickling. Somewhere amongst these men was most likely at least one who wanted her dead.

Her father had been right: Today's council meeting was

particularly full. With three straight weeks of council meetings each spring, summer, autumn, and winter, not all lords attended every meeting in person. After all, Port Lorsin was many weeks' journey for some of them, and so many sent their sons or Wise Men instead. A few, the ones who had particularly good relationships with their local ambassadors, relied upon the common people's representative to bring back news from the capital. But with the war going poorly in the East, and an imminent spring offensive likely, nearly every Head of House, their heirs, Wise Men, and ambassadors were present.

Tasia kept her expression calm and composed. For once, she was glad for the countless formal functions she'd been forced to attend over her nineteen years; she knew how to fake an emotion for a crowd.

In this case, Tasia faked a warm smile and utter relaxation.

The first third of the council meeting was unremarkable. The Wise Man of Trade and Coffers reported that, despite the ongoing War in the East, the Empire's treasury remained healthy. Grumbles spread through the crowd, however, when he said that an increase in taxes might be necessary in order to fund an "expansion of hostilities".

Following the report from Trade and Coffers, other Wise Men stood at the raised table at the head of the room and gave the council their seasonal reports on agricultural production, infrastructure, and mercantile activities.

Finally, General Remington stood from his seat to give

his report. He was the one the council had been waiting to hear from, and the General knew it. But the old war hero carried himself with a confident presence that still commanded the room's attention, despite the white hair and wooden peg leg making him look like the stitched together remnants of a man.

He cleared his throat and unfurled a parchment. "It is with a heavy heart that I must inform the council that the battalion guarding the outpost at Deerpark Pass — Fox Battalion — was routed a fortnight ago. We received word of this defeat only yesterday. Casualty numbers remain unclear, but at the moment, it appears that approximately four hundred fifty Imperial soldiers are dead or presumed dead, with another twenty to thirty who sustained serious injuries."

"Four hundred and seventy dead, missing, or injured?" asked an ambassador with a long face and even longer black mustache. He wore a cylindrical red hat decorated with golden bands, which marked him as a representative of the Central Steppes. "Do you mean to tell us that only *seventy* men from a battalion of five hundred and forty survived?"

"Yes, Ambassador Lorent. Your arithmetic is correct," General Remington said. "The survivors are recovering at our winter camp. After that they will travel to the capital and enjoy a month's leave before they return to the front."

"A month's leave. What a consolation," muttered another ambassador.

"There is more bad news," the General continued,

ignoring the muttered comment. "Once the barbarians routed the battalion and took the outpost, they poured into the valley below. Several villages of House Druet have been razed. Three have been occupied. Within the occupied villages, all males above the age of ten were executed; all other villagers were presumably taken as slaves."

Concerned whispers ruffled through the council room. Barbarian raids were one thing — they had been commonplace during this long war — but it was atypical for them to overwhelm an entire battalion and then occupy villages. Barbarians were wont to destroy villages; they weren't wont to stay there.

General Remington raised his voice above the low talking. "Given recent events in the East, all of you can understand the absolute necessity of our upcoming spring offensive. I have here — " he lifted the parchment in his hand " — the exact conscript numbers we require from each House. Your new recruits — "

"Hold," said Ambassador Lorent. "We've been fighting the barbarians in the East for more than twelve years now. Many a sheep herder's son from my own province has already died in a faraway land defending the Eastern Realm. And after all these years, what do we have to show for those deaths? We haven't gained any new territory. The Empire certainly isn't *richer* for it." He shrugged and curled his lip, making his long mustache jut up his face. "So we have killed a few barbarians. Well done. But they breed like field mice. Each year there seem to be more of them, and each year there are fewer sheep herder's sons. Now you ask me for more. What makes you so sure the people of the Empire want to continue providing you fodder for this unending war?"

Other ambassadors and lords nodded their ascent. Tasia sensed that the mood of the room might turn against the General at any moment. If it hadn't already.

"Ambassador — " started the General.

"I agree with the ambassador of the Steppes," said a heavyset lord a few places down from Lorent. "The West is sympathetic to the plight of the East, but between the taxes and the conscripts we provide…" He unfolded his hands, held them up in a helpless gesture. "Like the ambassador said, it seems as if this war will never end. All it seems to do is swallow lives and gold."

Tasia glanced at the faces of the other Western lords. Unrest amongst those houses was never good for the Empire. The West was the largest and most populous of the Four Realms, and the lords there had always resented being controlled from Port Lorsin — that was why the Western Rebellion had started in the first place, some twenty years past. Now, with the failure of their rebellion still a wound that had not completely healed, the Western lords were being forced to support a war that seemed to have very little to do with them. After all, they had an entire continent between them and the barbarians; why should they care what happened to the comparatively small and poor East?

"The benefit our fight brings, Lord Wendell," the

Emperor said, his voice rising above the mumbled conversations that had broken out in the council room, "is that it stops the barbarians from occupying the entire East and expanding their raids even further west."

"With all due respect, Emperor," said the fat lord, his jowls quivering as he spoke, "it sounds like a problem that the East should resolve. I don't see why I should drain my own House's coffers to solve *their* mess."

A handful of other lords and ambassadors nodded.

It was a precarious moment. The room seemed to hold its breath, waiting for the Emperor to respond.

This was what she would have to face one day, Tasia realized. Her father had no good choices. He couldn't abandon the East to its fate, but by providing the realm with the resources it required to push back the invaders yet again, he risked alienating powerful and influential lords in other realms. On top of it all, he knew that someone amongst these noble Houses had attempted to kill his daughter. Disagreement over the war had progressed far beyond civil debate.

Tasia surveyed the crowd, her eyes roaming from the fat Lord Wendell on one side of the room to the ambassadors beside him; to the two exotic-looking lords of Terinto; to Mylla's father, Lord Galen of House Harthing; to the young and handsome Lord Simon of House Brundt on the far end of the room.

She'd bedded Lord Simon once, before he'd inherited his father's House. He had been tender with her.

But now an unsettling thought occurred to her: What if

he was the one who tried to have her killed? Simon was a Western lord, after all.

"We are *one* Empire," the Emperor said. "You think what affects the East does not affect the West, but you are wrong. Tell me, Lord Wendell, the last time you garnished your roast with meravin mushrooms, where did those mushrooms come from? And you, Ambassador Lorent, how much coin did your sheep herders earn last year when they exported their wool East?"

No one responded.

"The Empire is a single body," said the Emperor, looking from face to face. "And just as an infection in the foot will eventually poison the blood and sicken the entire body, so allowing an infection of barbarians in the East to remain will eventually sicken the entire Empire."

Murmured conversation filled the room as lords and ambassadors agreed or disagreed amongst themselves.

An exhausted-looking lord with a messy mop of hair and a sparse, grey-blond beard spoke up. "Without the brave citizens of the East acting as a buffer for the rest of the Empire, soon you would be the ones begging the Emperor to come to your aid." The lord was Albert of House Druet, Tasia realized, the Eastern lord whose villages had been sacked. His statement silenced his peers. "What none of you understand, because you are not there, is that the barbarians have been growing stronger these last three years. They've been harder to beat back. They've been killing more of our soldiers. The routing of Fox Battalion at Deerpark Pass... I've been expecting something like that to happen since last winter."

The other council members seemed to weigh his words.

"Your Majesty," said a new voice in a heavy accent. "We in Terinto appreciate your efforts in the East. Our lands are directly to the west, and although the barbarian horde would have to cross our desert first, if the East falls, we would be their next target."

Tasia located the speaker. He was a dark-skinned lord wearing a cream-colored head wrap, with a single long, black braid emerging from the wrap and draping over one shoulder. Oiled and flawless, the shiny braid hung almost to his lap.

Lord M'Tongliss of Terinto. Tasia had met him once at a state dinner. He was a man who seemed perpetually on the brink of amusement, just as he did now, even while addressing the Emperor. As if the war, the council meeting, and everything else was a festival play he watched for the sake of entertainment.

"Due to the proximity of Terinto to the front, we receive a fair number of the army's deserters," Lord M'Tongliss said.

This statement sent a wave of low mutters of surprise through the council room.

"Deserters!" someone exclaimed.

"Most of those running from their duties are found dead in the dunes, of course," the Lord said, continuing as if he had not heard the whispered conversations around him. "Tribesmen bring me the few who survive. They tell stories of an Imperial Army half-starved, half-frozen, and of troops so disheartened that they can hardly be cajoled into picking up their swords."

"I'm sure that is not true," Norix said quickly. "The soldiers of the Imperial Army are highly trained and well-supplied. They are brave defenders of the Empire."

Lord M'Tongliss stroked his short, pointed black beard with one hand. "Perhaps," he said. "But the flame-ringed demons who fight alongside the barbarians would certainly be enough to frighten any man."

There was a moment of stunned confusion around him, but then the low laughter began.

The Terintan carried on as if nothing he said had been particularly remarkable. "Even I, who wear this turban of leadership — " he tapped the cream-colored head wrap " — and am known as the fiercest warrior of my tribe. I would never desert my people, but I know I would quake with fear if confronted with a demon."

Words mingled with chuckles, spreading out from Lord M'Tongliss the way rings in a lake spread once a pebble is dropped. One of the lords sitting at the side of the room laughed so hard that the tea he had been sipping spewed out from his mouth and onto the ambassador sitting across from him.

Tasia had an urge to glance behind her at Joslyn, to see how the guard had reacted to the words of this Lord of Terinto, but it would be inappropriate to appear distracted. And besides that, she knew that the stoic Joslyn would not so much as blink while focused on her guard duties.

"Did you really say demons?" asked an ambassador

once he finished laughing. He wiped tears from the corners of his eyes. "Flame-ringed?" He seemed about to say something else, but another fit of giggles overtook him, and he doubled over, slapping his palm hard against his thigh as he laughed.

"Enough," the Emperor boomed, and the laughter and conversations tapered off. "I care nothing for the nonsense of these so-called demons," he said, "but General Remington has informed me of recent reports suggesting high numbers of desertions and low troop morale. General Remington has been in communication with General Telek at the front and I assure you that the matter will be resolved." He paused a moment, his eyes roaming the council room. "You lords and ambassadors are concerned that this war has carried on for far too long. I am concerned as well. That's why we intend to make this year's spring offensive the largest offensive to date. We will crush the barbarians once and for all, and generations will go by before anyone dares to challenge our border again."

The remainder of the council meeting went by swiftly, with General Remington reading off his parchment how many men and what kinds of supplies the Empire required each Great and Minor House to give. This induced many unhappy grumbles, but all the lords and ambassadors accepted the Empire's requests in the end. What choice did they have but to accept, really?

Unless they wanted to oust the Emperor and seize the crown for themselves. Tasia found her eyes roaming from face to face, wondering once more which of these lords was unhappy enough with her father that they would try to kill her, wondering if they might be conspiring even now to overthrow the House of Dorsa, the only royal family the Empire had ever known.

11

Tasia grunted, her bare feet sliding in the sand as she struggled to lift the rock to the top of the heap. When she at last managed to get it there, she bent forward, panting, hands on her hips as she struggled to catch her breath.

Her hands ached, red and tender from the task of carrying one rock after another to the pile. At least last week's blisters had healed.

"Don't stop yet, Princess," said Joslyn from somewhere behind her. "There are still three more stones to go."

Mylla must've heard the guard from her spot on the blanket a few paces away. Shading her eyes from the sun, she called out to Tasia, "Only three left? You're getting faster, thank the gods. Hurry up, I'm hungry."

Tasia straightened, brushing her sandy hands on the back of the baggy men's trousers she'd rolled up to her knees. She looked longingly at Mylla, clean and dry in a new spring dress and sunhat, buttering fresh bread.

"Princess — " Joslyn started.

"Yes, yes, I know. Three more."

Tasia turned away from Mylla, towards the pile of stones that seemed impossibly far away at the other end of the beach. She took off for them at a jog, angling towards the wet sand closer to the surf so that the dry sand would stop scorching her feet.

Gods was the sun hot today.

Joslyn seemed completely unaffected by the heat; she stood in the black leathers of the palace guard as always, arms crossed against her chest as the breeze from the ocean blew her shoulder-length hair sideways behind her. How could she possibly be comfortable in this heat? Then again, she *was* from the desert.

Tasia wanted to shout at the woman as she passed, ask the guard how moving boulders up and down the beach could be considered self-defense training, but Tasia didn't have enough breath to waste it on words. It was work enough to run to the stones without collapsing.

Self-defense, she thought bitterly as she half-ran, half-stumbled through the sand.

But the maddeningly practical guard had already explained her reasoning to Tasia. She'd calmly explained that Tasia needed to build a basic level of strength and endurance first if anything else she taught the Princess was to have any value.

Three days after that, when the blisters were at their worst, Tasia had marched into her father's chambers to complain, the guard trailing behind at her heels.

She showed the Emperor her blisters.

"Her idea of teaching me to defend myself is to have me run up and down the beach, carrying stones so heavy I can barely lift them!" Tasia had said, jabbing an accusatory finger at Joslyn.

Tasia's father was silent for a moment, stroking his

beard as he sat behind his heavy desk. Then he chuckled — smiling not at Tasia, but at the guard.

"Well done," he said, addressing Joslyn.

Tasia hadn't tried to get her father to intercede again after that. It was clear that she was on her own when it came to the spiteful guard's agenda.

She reached the three stones still left in the pile and bent to pick up the one on top. It wouldn't budge. She tried again.

"It's too heavy," she said when she saw Joslyn approaching out of the corner of her eye. "I can't do it."

"You *can* do it. Bend your knees. Push up through your legs and hips instead of trying to lift it with your arms. That's where real strength comes from — " she touched a finger to Tasia's side " — your center."

"I said I *can't!* It's too much."

Joslyn said nothing, crossed her arms against her chest.

"I'm tired and I'm hungry. I'm joining Mylla for my midday meal," Tasia said, letting go of the boulder and turning her back on the rock pile.

"You can eat when you've moved the final three stones," said Joslyn.

Tasia whipped around, gave Joslyn an incredulous look. "You forget your station. You are *my* servant, not the other way around. I give the orders."

"I am the servant of the Empire," Joslyn said. "Are *you?* Or do you serve only yourself?"

Tasia's head jerked back as if the guard had hit her. No one spoke to her that way. No one except her father.

"How *dare* you," the Princess hissed through clenched teeth at the insolent guard. "What do *you* know about serving the Empire? You're nothing but a nomad from Terinto who happened to get lucky enough in a battle to find yourself with the cushy job of being my sword-wielding wet nurse." She took a step closer to Joslyn. Tasia was shorter than the guard by half a head but stood on her tiptoes to be at eye-level. *"I've* known what it means to serve the Empire since before *you* knew what an Empire even was. I've known it since before I knew my alphabet. Since before I could *dress* myself."

Joslyn's eyes darted up the beach to where Mylla sat. The handmaid squinted at the Princess and her guard with a slight frown, obviously trying but failing to listen in on their conversation.

"You still don't dress yourself, Princess," said the guard.

Tasia slapped Joslyn hard across the face, leaving a red imprint of her hand against the tawny skin.

But the guard only blinked.

"I'm reporting you to my father."

"And what do you think he will say when I tell him you gave up your training to indulge your stomach?"

Tasia narrowed her eyes. "My father wanted me to study rudimentary self-defense in case someone attacked me again. But this…" She waved her arm at the pile of stones. *"This* isn't self-defense."

"What your father wants is for you to become the true ruler of the realms after his time is over," Joslyn said.

"Which means you will order soldiers into battle one day, soldiers who will bleed and starve and die in your name. You will negotiate treaties and political alliances, upon which the lives of hundreds of thousands will depend. And yet you are already prepared to surrender to an enemy no greater than a pile of stones and sore hands. How will you be master of others when you cannot even master yourself?"

Pure shock overrode the Princess's anger, rendering her mute. Joslyn had never spoken that many words in her presence at once. And all of them were disrespectful — practically treasonous. As if the unprecedented disrespect wasn't enough, there was also the small, insistent voice in the back of Tasia's mind that whispered,

She's right. You know she is.

"Finish moving the stones before your midday meal, Princess," Joslyn concluded.

Tasia shook a finger in front of the guard's face. "I will tell my father what you just said. How you spoke to me. I will make sure you pay for this."

"I spoke harshly to a member of the House of Dorsa, you're right," Joslyn said, though there was no hint of apology in her voice. "And it is quite possible I will be held to account for it later. But no one will know I said what I did until these stones have been moved, because you are not leaving this beach until they are."

The Princess glared at her guard. Joslyn did not look away. Finally, Tasia ended the standoff with a sigh. She bent her knees, pushed through her legs and hips, and lifted the rock before her from its pile.

#

Some twenty minutes later, Tasia collapsed on the blanket next to Mylla.

The handmaid glanced at Joslyn, who stood a few yards off, her back to the young women.

"I thought you were never going to finish," Mylla said quietly.

"I thought I wasn't, either. Tell me you were a good girl and saved some food for me?"

Mylla lifted the lid of the basket. Inside was a fine porcelain plate with a cut of roast upon it; cold, congealed gravy formed a grayish sponge around it. A bowl held a few grapes, but they were wrinkled and wilted from the heat of the beach.

Tasia, too hungry to care, reached for the grapes anyway, managing to knock sand all over the cold roast.

"Oh, *pig* shite," she grumbled. She stuffed three grapes into her mouth at once, and they tasted as bad as they had looked.

"Three grapes at a time?" said Mylla. "A rare display of coarseness from our well-mannered Princess. What would the Empress have said?"

Tasia stopped chewing long enough to give the handmaid a withering glare.

Mylla tittered. *"Someone* is in a foul mood."

"You know I don't like it when you bring up my

mother. Especially not like that."

Tasia swallowed her mouthful of desiccated grapes, coughing when they caught in her throat. She gestured for the canteen, and closed her eyes in relief when the cool water crossed into her parched mouth.

"I was only trying to make you smile," Mylla said while Tasia drank. "I didn't realize you were going to insist upon acting the grouch."

Tasia wiped her mouth with the back of one hand. *"You* would be in a foul mood, too, if you'd been made to carry stones all morning. *After* an unexpected, two hour, early morning session with Remington catching me up on the politics of the Kingdom of Persopos." She blew a strand of hair from her face. "Persopos. Who even cares about those hermits? Norix says the Kingdom's involvement is Remington's fantasy, designed as an excuse for the fact that the war lingers on." She shook her head, annoyed to be caught between the rivalries of her father's two favorite advisors. "All *I* know is that being heir so far means I always miss breakfast and end up covered in sand by midday."

Mylla grinned and recapped the canteen. She sighed dramatically. "Oh, the difficulties of being a princess."

Tasia flicked some of the sand that had dried on her palm onto the handmaid.

Mylla squealed. "This is a brand new dress!"

Tasia leaned over her, brushed even more sand onto the light blue silk.

Mylla swatted at Tasia's arm. "Stop, you brat! You'll

stain it!"

Her handmaid's irritation finally broke the spell of gloom that had settled over Tasia. She laughed merrily, hunger forgotten for a moment as she rolled towards Mylla, pinning the girl on her back. Tasia's rough, boy-style tunic and trousers were still covered with sand, and she wriggled on top of Mylla, delighting in the girl's high-pitched protests as she tried to get away.

Something snagged beneath Tasia's knee, and both girls stilled when they heard the sound of ripping fabric.

"See that, Tasia?" Mylla said, genuinely upset. "You've torn it. Now it truly *is* ruined."

Tasia rolled halfway off the handmaid, propping herself up on one elbow, her other arm draped across Mylla's torso. "I'll have it mended. Or buy you a better one."

"That's not the point. You shouldn't have torn it in the first place," Mylla grumped.

"Oh, Myll," Tasia said. "Don't be cross with me." She glanced over her shoulder, saw that Joslyn was still a few yards away, her back facing them. Tasia leaned forward, kissed the handmaid gently. Mylla's posture softened beneath her. The girl reached up, curled a hand around Tasia's bare neck, arched up towards the princess. Tasia allowed herself to get lost in the feeling of Mylla's lips for a moment, eyes drifting closed.

But the kiss couldn't last. Tasia was mindful that Joslyn was within hearing distance and was apt to turn around to check on her charges at any moment. Reluctantly, Tasia broke the kiss, lowered Mylla back down to the blanket.

"I want you," she whispered to the handmaid.

Mylla dabbed at her lips. "You got sand on my face," she whispered back, but her tone was no longer petulant. "And even if you weren't such an insufferable brat, you couldn't have me." Her gaze shifted past Tasia. "Not with *her* around."

"I know," Tasia said. She flopped onto her back, shielded her eyes from the sun's glare with a sandy forearm. She heard Mylla brush the dress clean, then rustle through the picnic basket behind her.

A light touch ran down her forearm. "You're so burnt, Princess. You look like a ripe tomato."

"I *feel* like a ripe tomato."

"My sweet Tazy. Are you still hungry?"

"Starved."

"Do you want some of the roast?"

Tasia sighed. "I suppose. Though it might be disgusting, served cold. But I suppose it's better than nothing."

"Says the girl who's never had anything but the first cut of each meat, when subjects in her own capital go without," Mylla chided.

"Don't. Not today. You sound like Joslyn." Tasia took her arm off her face and sat up, leaning back on the blanket on sore hands. "You'll never believe what she said to me." In a low tone, Tasia briefly recounted the charged conversation she'd had with the guard thirty minutes earlier.

Mylla gasped. "I can't believe her. Anyone else would face the lash for saying something like that. I mean, *I* would speak to you that way," she said, giving Tasia a sly grin. "But only in jest. Never seriously." She took a forkful of roast, swirled it around in the cold gravy. "Here. Eat," she said, bringing the meat to Tasia's burnt lips.

Tasia took the bite gratefully, and despite the fact that it was cold, her stomach rumbled and demanded more.

Mylla clucked at the sound of Tasia's stomach. "My poor Princess." She prepared another forkful. "Sunburnt like a common field hand. Dressed in boys' trousers. Covered head-to-foot with sand. And put in her place by a guard." She lowered her voice. "That nomad is a problem, Tazy."

Tasia nodded and accepted another bite of roast.

"You're too easy on your servants sometimes. And I suppose you have to be, what with the name 'Dorsa' attached to you. But I'm no royal. I can speak how I want without damaging the dignity of the Empire's First Noble House." Mylla gazed past the Princess thoughtfully. "You there — guard!" she called a moment later.

Joslyn looked over her shoulder, walked towards the two young women.

"What are you doing?" Tasia whispered to Mylla.

"You'll see." She winked. "And I know something you don't about your guard."

"Yes, Lady Mylla?" Joslyn said.

"How did you come to be in the Imperial Army?" Mylla asked.

Joslyn glanced from Mylla to Tasia. "I joined when the recruiter visited my village. Like most soldiers."

Mylla made a disappointed noise. "Oh, come now, Joslyn. There must be more to it than that! Give us the *details*. Tell us *exactly* how you joined."

Joslyn hesitated. "That's a rather long story, my Lady."

Mylla shrugged. "We have time. The Princess has a lesson with Wise Man Evrart, but that isn't for another hour or so. And neither you nor I need to be anywhere if the Princess isn't there. So go ahead. Tell us your story."

Joslyn turned her head, gazing out at the sea. The wind caught her black hair, and it blew across her face, temporarily obscuring her eyes. She reached up, tucking it behind one ear with a practiced, easy gesture.

And for some reason, *that* was the moment when Tasia saw it for the first time: Joslyn possessed a kind of wild beauty Tasia had never seen before. She was part imperial soldier, part desert nomad. She was tamed and untamed. She was domestic and foreign, familiar and unfamiliar, safe and dangerous, contained and uncontainable, all at the same time.

"When I was a teenager," Joslyn began, "I lived in the foothills of the Zaris Mountains. At seventeen, I decided I wished to leave. Not long after that, a recruiter from the Imperial Army came to our village, seeking new conscripts. I joined because… it was the easiest way to get away from Terinto."

"And the fact that you're a woman?" Mylla asked. "A slash between your legs instead of branch and berries? The recruiter had no problem with that?"

Joslyn didn't answer for a moment. "Yes. He did have a problem with that. He told me I could join as a cook, but I said I wanted to be a soldier."

"And what happened?" said Mylla.

Something about Mylla's tone was playful. Playful, but not innocent. A cat can be playful when it toys with a mouse it has cornered, but there was nothing innocent about it. That was what Mylla reminded Tasia of now — a cat that had cornered a mouse. The Princess couldn't guess what her handmaid was up to.

"Is there a reason you need to know this information? Lady Mylla?" Joslyn said.

"I'm just curious," Mylla said breezily. She turned to Tasia. "Aren't you curious, Princess?"

Tasia nodded, her eyes on the guard.

Joslyn looked uncomfortable. But she deserved to be uncomfortable, after the way she'd spoken earlier.

"Keep going," Mylla told Joslyn brightly.

The guard sighed. "When I told the recruiter I would only join as a soldier, he insisted upon testing my fighting skills. When I passed his test, he accepted me."

"And what kind of test did he give you?" Mylla asked.

"Combat," Joslyn said simply.

"Elaborate," Mylla said, then quickly added, "Sorry, that's probably too big of a word for you. 'To elaborate' means to give more details, to flesh out an explanation."

Joslyn's stare grew cold. "I know what 'elaborate' means, Lady Mylla."

"Then *elaborate* for us."

Tasia looked from her guard to her handmaid. Mylla was beginning to make her feel uncomfortable. She wanted the guard to be punished for the way she had spoken earlier, but that wasn't Mylla's task to complete. As a princess, *Tasia* could berate her staff, but it wasn't proper for anyone else to do it, not even Mylla.

Joslyn looked seaward again, quiet for a few seconds before saying, "He had all the boys attack me with the new short swords he had provided them with, assuming I would yield after a few seconds."

"But you didn't yield," Mylla said. "Tell the Princess what happened."

Joslyn's gaze dropped and she said something too quietly to be heard.

"Speak up, Guard," said the handmaid.

Joslyn looked up, glancing first at Tasia, then at Mylla. "I killed three of them. I wounded two. Three more yielded."

Tasia's mouth fell open into an *O* of surprise.

"See that, Princess?" Mylla said. "Your new guard's as barbaric as the mountain men in the East. So murderous she killed her own comrades just to prove a point. They truly scraped the bottom of the barrel finding this one for you."

A subtle look of pain flashed through Joslyn's black eyes.

Mylla turned to Tasia, speaking as if Joslyn wasn't still standing there. "I don't know why we allow nomads into the Imperial Army. They're all brutes," Mylla said.

"He didn't just have the boys fight me, Lady Mylla," Joslyn protested. "He ordered them to kill me. All of them at once."

Mylla ignored the guard. "Your father must be desperate to fill his ranks. I mean, in the name of the gods, the *nomads*. They're hardly different from their herds of apa-apa. Next thing you know, we'll be inviting the mountain barbarians into the army."

"Mylla," Tasia said, a warning in her voice.

Mylla arched an eyebrow, asking Tasia a silent *What?* Then she turned her attention back to Joslyn. "I've never met a nomad in person until you." She stood up, looked the guard up and down. "I must say, your crude tendencies and lack of intelligence aside, all your swordplay has given you quite the physique. I think that, if we had met under different circumstances, I might even find you attractive." She paused. "Except for the slanted eyes and the broad face." Mylla turned to Tasia. "Why *do* nomads have such over-large faces, anyway?"

"Mylla, that's enough," Tasia said.

"I wouldn't mind seeing more of that physique of yours." She reached for the guard's leather tunic, but Joslyn took a swift step out of reach. "Oh, and modest, too," Mylla said, grinning. "But I'm sure you weren't always. You were a slave girl, were you not? Which means that you've shared your physique before... Well, 'share' might be a generous word for it, but nomads are little better than animals, especially the women, so maybe you enjoyed it, sharing your body with the various men who owned you. I hear that's what slave girls do. Am I right?"

"Mylla!" Tasia barked. "That is quite enough!"

Mylla heaved a frustrated sigh. She spoke to Tasia but stared at Joslyn when she said, "Your new guard believes she can speak to you as if she is your equal — no, as if she is your superior. Being barely civilized, it's understandable that she doesn't know how to speak to her betters. All I am doing, Princess, is educating her."

Joslyn held Mylla's glare without looking away, her lips pressed into a tight line.

A tense moment passed. Finally, Mylla sat back down on the picnic blanket and leaned back on one hand. "Are you going to finish the roast, sweet Princess?"

Tasia met Joslyn's eyes, trying to convey an apology. The guard's face remained hard, and the Princess looked away.

"No," she mumbled. "I think I've rather lost my appetite."

Mylla flipped the lid to the basket of food closed. "Then let's go," she said. "We both have sand all over us — you especially. So we should head back. I want time to give you a nice long, hot bath before you go see Evrart."

She gave Tasia a devious smile, and the Princess suspected her handmaid had more than bathing in mind.

"Very well," Tasia said, still somewhat disturbed by what Mylla had done to the guard. There was a way to go about correcting servants, and what Mylla had done went too far. But Tasia stood without commenting on it, brushed the sand from her trousers. "Let's go."

12

"And how was your training today?" the Emperor asked. He leaned over his dinner plate to peer sideways at Tasia, looking past the young nobleman placed between them. "Your skin is tanning from your hours on the beach. You'll look like you're from Terinto yourself before much longer."

Tasia dabbed at her mouth politely, gazing across the dining hall at the table of advisors and servants at the other end. Joslyn sat beside Cole. The guard must have felt Tasia's gaze; her eyes flitted briefly to the Princess's before returning to her commander.

"So I will," the Princess said to her father, forcing a smile.

"What training is this?" asked the nobleman.

His name was Mace of House Gifford, and he was the latest suitor of the Princess to be invited to dinner. Just because Tasia had now been named as her father's official heir didn't mean the Emperor had given up his quest to see her married before her next birthday.

Mace was, Tasia had to admit, somewhat less obnoxious than the last five suitors. Tall and dark-haired, like most men of the West, he had so far proven himself to be confident without being boastful, respectful without being sniveling, all while seated between the most powerful man in the realm on one side of him and his heir apparent on the other.

"The Emperor has come to believe that I need to be trained in basic self-defense," Tasia said evenly.

Her younger sister Adela, seated on the Emperor's other side, leaned forward. She giggled and grinned at Mace. "But so far, all her training has been horribly *boring*. The only thing she's done is carry rocks up and down a beach. Joslyn won't let her even *touch* a a sword yet."

Tasia smiled at her little sister. She liked that everything amused the girl, no matter what the discussion was.

Mace took a sip of wine, looking thoughtful. A cupbearer appeared to refill his goblet the moment he set it down.

"Moving rocks?" Mace said, glancing from daughters to father. "Is that so? And who is this Joslyn?"

"Her new personal guard," Adela supplied. The girl pointed across the room and Mace followed her finger to the only female in the black leather of the palace guard. "She's a nomad from Terinto. *And* a war hero. They say she slew ten men single-handedly in the Battle of Hasper."

Mace cocked his head to the side. "A woman war hero. That's rather uncommon." He looked at Tasia. "But you still haven't explained why you're moving rocks."

"My new guard seems to think I need to improve my strength and my endurance before my true self-defense lessons begin," Tasia said.

"Forgive me if I'm being dense," Mace said, "but why would a *princess* need to learn basic self-defense, when surrounded by such competent palace guards?" He nodded across the room at Cole. "If we are going to speak of war heroes, my father tells me that Commander Cole of Easthook is one of the most distinguished military veterans in the Empire, and that he handpicks each member of the palace guard himself. And oft-as-not he oversees their training."

"So he does," the Emperor agreed. "But the Empire has its enemies, Mace. The House of Dorsa has always seen fit to train its sons in the art of self-protection and combat. Many second and third sons of the House of Dorsa have gone on to be great generals. But since I have no sons, I have seen fit to train my eldest daughter in the combative arts. Since she is my heir, it seems only fitting."

The Emperor gave Mace a stare halfway between challenging and inspecting. By now, word had spread that Tasia would be her father's true heir, which meant that any husband of hers would carry the title of "Emperor" but not the attendant power that went with it.

All of which implied that Mace, even if his quest for Tasia's hand in marriage succeeded, would not be the true power in the realm.

Mace nodded slowly, thoughtfully, and Tasia had the feeling the Emperor's implication had not been lost on him.

"Of course," he said. "Very understandable. The Princess will be the Empress one day, and will have need of a variety of different skills that other young women do not need. Including self-defense." He raised his goblet, glancing from side to side. "To the House of Dorsa. Long may its wisdom protect the Empire."

The Emperor gave a pleased nod and lifted his own cup. "Long may its wisdom protect the Empire," he repeated, and his two daughters followed suit.

But Tasia's stomach twisted uncomfortably.

Which fate was worse? she pondered. To be the girl-child of an Emperor and have her role in life pre-determined by the mere possession of a womb? Or to be a girl-child of an Emperor who had decided that, out of a group of poor options, she was the best choice to safeguard the Empire's future?

Both fates seemed a noose around her neck.

She looked across the room, hoping to catch Mylla's eye. But the girl was giggling about something with Adela's two handmaids, their attention far removed from the royal family.

But a pair of dark eyes did catch Tasia's. Joslyn. For the second time, Tasia caught her guard watching her from across the room. For one eerie moment, Tasia had the uncomfortable feeling that the guard had heard her thoughts, that she knew Tasia had been imagining a noose tightening around her throat.

Joslyn nodded at the Princess, shifted her gaze back down to her plate, and the strange feeling passed.

#

Mace and Tasia took a walk through one of the palace's many gardens once the evening meal had finished. Tasia had tried to beg off, stating that she had a headache, but her father insisted that if a headache was what plagued her, the fresh night air would be the perfect cure. And so it was that she found herself strolling beside the young lordling from House Gifford half an hour later, Joslyn trailing a few respectful steps behind them.

"So," Mace said conversationally once they were out of earshot of the palace, "your father tells me you've rejected every suitor he's presented you with thus far."

"He speaks truly," Tasia said.

"And why have you rejected them? If I may ask?"

"Well, let's see," Tasia said with mock thoughtfulness. "Frederick of House Serrell was too fat. Barret of House Kelter was too shy. Preston of House Aventia was too... snobbish."

Mace let out a short, surprised laugh. "Snobbish?"

"He was rather impressed with himself."

"How so?"

"Oh, I don't know," Tasia said, stopping to finger a small, tight rosebud. The garden would be a tapestry of color in just a few more weeks. "The night Preston came to dinner, he was dressed in finery greater than my own, with a ring on each finger, a pendant, and hair so well-oiled that he might have slaughtered a whale on his way to the palace."

Mace laughed again, an easy, fluid sound with no hint of self-consciousness or pretension. "Note to self," he said with an air of ponderousness, turning his gaze skyward, "do not dress too finely or oil my hair when visiting the Princess Natasia."

"When visiting?" Tasia said. "You presume a second visit already? Bold."

"No, no, your Majesty," he said. "In the short span of hours we have known one another, I have already learned to presume nothing when it comes to you. It is rather rare to meet a princess training in self-defense and preparing to inherit her father's crown."

Tasia quirked an eyebrow. "I take it you've met many princesses, then."

"Only three so far," he said nonchalantly.

"Three?" The Princess scoffed. "Did your Wise Men fail to teach you the basics of arithmetic? There are only two princesses in the Empire — myself and my sister."

Mace nodded. "This is true. I have met you, I have met your sister, and I also met a princess of one of the Adessian Islands."

"The Adessian Islands are rather far from the West," Tasia said skeptically.

"So they are," Mace agreed. "My father sent me there to negotiate a trade agreement."

"And you met a princess along the way?"

Tasia stopped at a marble bench beside a willow tree, sitting down and gesturing for Mace to sit beside her, which he did.

"I did." He hesitated. When he spoke again, it was in a different tone. "Princess, may I ask you a frank question?"

Tasia studied him, her face openly curious. "You may."

"Is my fate to be the same as all the other suitors? Am I wasting my time this evening?" He held up a hand. "And before you answer, let me just be clear — your acceptance of my bid, your rejection of it, it's all the same to me. My father is the one who hungers for apartments within the royal wing of the palace, not me. I know I'm not to be shaped into an Emperor or wear your father's crown." Mace took a breath. "And if you're going to reject me, which is fine, then I will cut my visit here short and head home. It's plowing season in our land, and my father has little patience for settling disputes between farmers. I'd rather not have a backlog of cases to work through when I get back."

Tasia let out a small giggle, which grew into a larger one, which evolved into full, long laughter.

Mace blinked in surprise. "I'm sorry; did I say something funny?"

She nodded, wiping tears from her eyes. "What's funny is that I think you care as little about this potential marriage as I do. And you're honest enough to say it."

Mace shrugged. "I take it most of your suitors are not honest?"

"None of them are." She put a hand on his shoulder. "Mace, there's nothing good about marrying into the House of Dorsa for you. You'll be as ceremonial as an Emperor sewn into a tapestry, as powerless as a toothless hound. You'll enjoy very little reward from the crown on your head and yet inherit all of its danger." She took her hand from his shoulder, gestured at Joslyn. "Want to know the real reason she's here? And why I'm learning supposed self-defense? And why Father's chosen me as his heir instead of someone like you?"

Mace glanced at the stoic guard, then back to Tasia. "Why?"

"Because, Mace. Someone tried to kill me recently." She waited for the statement to sink in. "You're about the most bearable suitor I've had so far. But I wouldn't wish this fate on you; I actually *like* you."

The young nobleman stared at Joslyn a moment, then turned his attention back to Tasia. "You are heir because your father trusts no one else," he said. "That seems like a rather reasonable decision to me."

Tasia nodded. "He believes someone is trying to destabilize the Empire, and he's making an effort to determine the would-be killer by process of elimination. I've been eliminated as a suspect, as I am the only highborn he knows who is without a doubt innocent of the attempt on my life."

"But I doubt that's his only reason for naming you heir," Mace said. "It's — well, forgive me for saying so, Princess, but it's almost unheard of for an Emperor to name a girl-child his heir. So it must be about more than trust. He must truly hold you in high esteem."

Tasia gave a non-committal shrug. "Perhaps. Yes, Father says I have a shrewd mind, like my grandmother. But I don't think I'm all that shrewd, given that I nearly got myself killed through my recklessness."

Mace looked into the distance, thoughtful. After a moment, he leaned forward, and this time when he spoke, it was with great earnestness. "Princess, my grandfather was one of the Western lords who rebelled against your father. He died dangling at the end of a rope the year I was born, the same year my father became Lord of House Gifford. Under any other Emperor, my family would have been stripped of our lands and our titles. But my father pledged his loyalty to yours, and your father chose to trust that pledge." He smiled grimly. "I am probably alive today because your father showed mine mercy. And if my way of repaying that kindness is to become a toothless, ceremonial Emperor beside you... well, there are certainly worse fates than being bound to a beautiful woman."

His sincerity — and apparent honesty — softened Tasia, and the smile she returned to him this time was genuine. "You would make a good Emperor, actually. Better than I will make as an Empress."

"You shouldn't say that."

Tasia leaned back, gazing at the rising moon. "It's ironic, don't you think? My sister is the one named for Empress Adela, yet I am the one being asked to fill Adela's enormous shoes."

Mace cocked his head, a glimmer of humor in his eyes. "The Empress Adela had big feet? My Wise Man never taught me that."

Tasia slapped him playfully, and their conversation moved away from heavy things and back to their earlier banter.

Much to her surprise, her father was waiting for them when they returned from the gardens. The Emperor asked Wise Man Evrart to escort Mace to his rooms, then turned to Tasia once they were out of earshot.

"Well?"

"Alright," Tasia said with a resigned sigh. "I suppose he'll do."

#

An hour or two later, having changed out of her evening gown and into her night robe, Tasia brushed her hair by herself at her vanity. Mylla had already prepared Tasia's bed for the night; Joslyn had performed her evening inspection of the Princess's three adjoining chambers — the spacious antechamber, where Tasia entertained visitors and where Joslyn had recently taken up residence; the servant's chamber, which was currently Mylla's room; and Tasia's own bedchamber.

Joslyn approached Tasia, standing behind her and meeting her eyes in the mirror.

"So my rooms are safe for the night?" Tasia asked. "No assassins hiding beneath mattresses? No goblins behind the tapestries?"

Joslyn permitted herself a half-smile. "Goblins can be quite nasty, when provoked."

Tasia set her brush down and turned on her stool. "Was that actually a *joke*, Guard Joslyn of Terinto?"

Joslyn's half-smile grew into a smirk. "I would never

joke about goblins."

"Yes, well. I should've known better than to ascribe a sense of humor to you," Tasia said.

Mylla finished turning down the blankets on Tasia's bed, disappeared into her own bedchamber and shut the door behind her.

"Joslyn," Tasia said quietly. "About what Mylla said on the beach earlier today…"

Joslyn shook her head. "I have been surrounded by the coarseness of common soldiers for the past seven years, Princess. The Lady Mylla said nothing worse than what I have heard before. And she was right that I need to remember to speak with more deference to my… betters."

"No, Joslyn. Mylla was wrong. About all of it." She hesitated, contemplating how much to say. "No one has ever spoken to me the way you spoke to me today. Other than the Emperor."

"I apologize, Princess. I shouldn't have — "

"But you told me exactly what I needed to hear." Tasia let out a long breath. "The events of the last few weeks… the assassination attempt… being named my father's heir… I know I need to change. And I'm trying to change. My father needs me to change. The *Empire* needs me to change. You were only trying to help me do that."

Joslyn gave the Princess a single nod. Tasia hadn't exactly apologized, but she'd come as close as a princess could when speaking to a servant. Somehow Joslyn understood and accepted.

"And over these past few weeks…" Tasia said. She

searched for words, thinking of the late nights she and the guard had spent together when Mylla was out at various functions with her father. They alternated between playing Castles and Knights, which Joslyn had gotten remarkably good at, and teaching the guard to read. "I've come to trust you," Tasia concluded. "When you're a Princess, it's not easy to find people you can truly trust."

The guard's expression was both surprised and appreciative. "Thank you, Princess."

"Just call me Tasia when we're alone." The Princess glanced at Mylla's bedroom door. It was still closed, but she lowered her voice anyway. "And Joslyn, I don't think your face is over-large. And there's nothing wrong with your eyes, either. I happen to think they're... beautiful."

It was a sentiment the Princess hadn't planned to voice, but as soon as she said it, she realized it was true. Joslyn's nearly black eyes were indeed beautiful. And it had nothing to do with the folds around her eyes, or their bottomless depths, or the way the guard's pupils seemed to disappear within the irises. Joslyn's eyes were beautiful because she revealed herself through them. Even when her face and posture remained stoic and formal, her eyes would give her away — sometimes glinting with humor when she surprised Tasia at Castles and Knights, sometimes with earnest sincerity as she copied the letters Tasia wrote for her, and on rare occasions, Tasia thought she saw a genuine affection in the guard's eyes.

And those emotions — the sincerity and earnestness, the flashes of humor or hurt, the attentiveness she directed towards the Princess — they were why Tasia had come to trust the guard.

"Thank you, Prin... Tasia."

Their eyes met. Tasia opened her mouth to speak, but she wasn't quite sure how to end the uncharacteristically personal conversation.

"I should... bid you goodnight," Joslyn said, gesturing at the door behind her to the antechamber.

"Yes," said the Princess, turning back to the vanity. "It's been a long day. And from what I hear, I'm waking up early to move rocks up and down the beach again tomorrow."

Joslyn smiled at Tasia in the vanity's mirror, and her black eyes held a hint of impish mischief. She took a half-step towards the door, then stopped and turned back.

"Princess?"

"Just Tasia, Joslyn."

"Tasia, then." The guard paused, and Tasia had another one of those rare moments of seeing the woman's emotions in her eyes. The mischievousness had given way to something... else.

"Yes?" Tasia prompted.

"I just wanted you to know... I know I said it before, but... no one will ever get close enough to harm you again," Joslyn said. "I mean it. Not while I still have breath to fight."

"Thank you," Tasia said. And while the last time the guard said it, she'd been suspicious, this time, she found the guard's sincerity touching.

"Sleep well, Tasia."

"And you, Joslyn."

The guard disappeared into the antechamber, and the door closed with a click behind her.

Mylla launched herself onto Tasia's bed, sliding across the quilt until her face was just a foot from Tasia's, who still sat at her vanity.

"Oh, Princess," she said in a mocking voice. "You'll always be safe with me. I'll never let those big, bad Cult of Culo priests get close to you ever again. And tomorrow, I'll make you carry even *more* boulders down the beach and speak to you insubordinately again, all to ensure your safety."

"I take it you were eavesdropping?"

"'Just call me Tasia when we're alone,'" Mylla said, imitating the Princess. "Have you already forgotten how she spoke to you today?"

Tasia set her brush down on the vanity with enough force that the jewelry resting there jumped. "Don't," the Princess said, a warning in her voice.

"Don't what?" Mylla asked. "Remind you that she's a brutish, ex-slave *nomad?*"

"Lower your voice. She's only just there." Tasia gestured at the door to the antechamber.

"You're attracted to her," Mylla accused.

Tasia let out a sound that was almost a laugh. "So *that's* what this is? You're jealous? While you go meet with men you might marry every night, *you're* the one getting jealous? Of my *guard?*"

"That's different," Mylla said. "I have no choice about marriage."

"And I have no choice but to have a guard from Terinto follow me everywhere I go!"

"You didn't deny it," said the handmaid, climbing off the Princess's bed.

"Deny what?" Tasia barked.

"That you're attracted to her."

"I'm not — I'm — why on Earth would you think I'm attracted to her?" Tasia sputtered.

"Because I know you," said Mylla. "I know what you sound like when you're interested in someone."

"Even if I was — which I'm not — why would you even care?" Tasia asked, rising from her seat at the vanity. "You and I have both had... plenty of encounters. Was I jealous about Willem? Or Lars? Have you ever been jealous of Markas or Lord Simon?"

"That's different," Mylla said.

"Why? Because they're men?"

"No, because you don't care about them any more than they care about you," the handmaid said.

"Mother Moon, Mylla! I do *not* care about Joslyn!"

Tasia realized that she'd shouted the declaration loud enough for her voice to carry into the antechamber. She glanced over her shoulder at the door as if the guard might burst through to contradict her. She drew in a breath.

"It's late," Tasia said, lowering her voice. She stepped closer to the handmaid and placed a hand on her forearm. "We're probably only arguing because we're both tired. So let's just go to sleep, alright?"

"Yes," said Mylla, pulling her arm away. "Let's." She walked towards her own bedchamber.

"I meant in my bed," Tasia said. "Won't you sleep beside me?"

"I think I prefer my own bed tonight."

The handmaid disappeared into her room and slammed the door hard behind her.

Tasia sighed and climbed into bed alone.

13

"Will Lady Mylla be joining us this morning?" Joslyn inquired.

"No," Tasia said.   She glanced at the closed bedchamber door behind her. "I think the Lady Mylla has had her fill of watching me move rocks up and down the beach."

The corner of Joslyn's mouth twitched up into a slight smile. "She will be disappointed. We are done with the first phase of your training, and move on to the second part today."

Tasia touched a finger to the callouses growing on her palms. "So all my rock-carrying finally made me strong enough to move on to actual self-defense?"

The two of them walked down the empty corridor, away from the palace's royal wing. At this time of the morning, they would be unlikely to meet anyone except the palace's night guard. Which might explain why Joslyn was more talkative than usual.

"No," Joslyn said, the smile growing on her face. "All your rock-carrying has made you humble enough to learn actual self-defense."

Tasia opened her mouth to argue, but then thought better of it. Instead, she matched Joslyn's smile. "You're crafty, you know that? For an ex-slave who barely knows her alphabet."

"Perhaps you have it backwards," said the guard. "Perhaps I'm crafty *because* I'm an ex-slave who barely knows her alphabet."

Tasia chuckled. "True enough. But the next time Mylla is gone for the evening to meet another one of her suitors, we're focusing on your writing. I think I had better handwriting when I was three."

Joslyn glanced at the Princess. "I am happy to apply myself to my studies," she said, "but are you sure you aren't bringing up my letters because I beat you at Castles and Knights last time we played?"

"Quite sure," Tasia said, but she grinned.

They arrived at the beach just as the sun peaked above the horizon in the east, pouring its pink-red light onto the gently lapping waves. Joslyn stood to the side, shedding her black palace guard's leather tunic, revealing a loose, sleeveless linen shirt beneath. Tasia gazed out at the ocean, relaxed. She'd always found the water to be restorative.

"It's beautiful, don't you — " she started, but before she could complete the statement, Joslyn pounced on her. She wrapped one arm tightly around Tasia's throat, cutting off both Tasia's air supply and her squeal of surprised protest.

"The first rule of self-defense," the guard said into her ear, "is to remember that an attack may come at any time, from any person." Joslyn loosened her grip around the Princess's throat, just enough so that Tasia could breathe. "Now that I have you in this position, what are you going to do to free yourself?"

Tasia clawed at Joslyn's arm, but no matter how deep she dug her nails or how hard she tugged at the guard's wrist, the arm didn't move. Finally, the Princess sagged. "I can't fight you. You're too strong."

"Fighting is not about who is stronger or who is bigger," Joslyn said. "It's about who has the advantage in any given moment, and who can keep or steal that advantage. Right now, I have the advantage because I surprised you and grabbed you before you were ready. What can you do to take the advantage back?"

Tasia pulled again on Joslyn's arm, to no avail. "I don't know," she said, frustrated. "There's nothing for me to do to gain the advantage."

Tasia felt the guard nod against her head. "Your attacker also doesn't think you have any advantages to leverage. But that is exactly your advantage. I used the advantage of surprise by grabbing you when you did not expect it. How could you surprise me?"

"By... pulling your arm away from my throat?"

"If that was something you were capable of, it *would* be surprising, but you've already tried and failed that," Joslyn said. "Besides, as your attacker, that is exactly what I expect you to do — pull at my arm. So I was already prepared for that. Think, Tasia: What am I *not* prepared for?"

Tasia tried to think of what Joslyn was not prepared for... and came up with exactly nothing. "I don't know," she said at last, frustrated.

"Right now, you and your attacker are both thinking of the same thing," Joslyn said. "Your throat. The first thing you need to do is get him thinking about something else. Kick me in the shin — "

"Joslyn, I don't want to — "

" — or stomp on my foot."

"I can't stomp your — "

"Stomp on my foot, Tas — "

Tasia lifted her riding boot high and drove the heel down onto Joslyn's foot. The guard gave a soft grunt into Tasia's ear, and the arm around the Princess's neck loosened by a fraction of an inch.

It was enough. Tasia pushed her fingers into the space between her throat and Joslyn's forearm, then pulled her head down and away through the gap she created. The friction against Joslyn's chest yanked the bun from her hair, but she escaped the guard's grip.

The guard grinned. "Good. That's good."

"Did I hurt you?" Tasia asked.

Joslyn let out a rare laugh. "No, not really. Though the stomp was harder than I expected it to be."

"Oh, Mother Moon! I'm so sorry."

Joslyn shook her head. "No apologies, Princess."

"No one else is here. Just call me Tasia, honestly."

"Alright, Tasia," Joslyn said, though the informal nickname sounded awkward when she said it. "No apologies. Your assassin isn't likely to be gentle on you, so you shouldn't be gentle on me." Joslyn wrapped her arm around Tasia's throat again. "Let's do it again. But this time, don't stomp my foot. Do something else — anything else. Be creative. Steal the advantage by surprising me."

The women practiced until the morning sun was high and burned away the haze that hung above the ocean. Joslyn grabbed Tasia from behind, or from the side, or around her waist; for her part, Tasia elbowed, bit, pinched, kicked — anything to take the advantage away from the guard. The Princess suspected that nothing truly surprised Joslyn and that she was going easy on Tasia, but the guard encouraged her anyway, pausing now and again to give her tips on technique or to suggest another avenue of attack.

Eventually, Joslyn's attacks progressed to pushing or pulling Tasia down to the sand.

"If you find yourself on the ground," said the guard as she straddled Tasia's waist, "remember two things: First, you never want to be the person on the bottom. Second, if you do find yourself on the bottom, escape is all about freeing your hips first."

They practiced another thirty minutes that way, rolling together through the sand. Joslyn taught Tasia how to rock side-to-side to free her hips from beneath an attacker, how to maintain control of her arms by keeping her elbows close to her chest, how to use her legs to sweep an attacker off of her.

Tasia succeeded in scoring one unexpected success, in which she somehow managed to roll Joslyn onto her back and pin the guard's arms with her knees. Tasia held the collar of the guard's loose linen shirt with both fists, ending up with her face only inches from Joslyn's. They met eyes, and Tasia could smell the guard's skin. The scent was a mixture of soap, leather, and something that was Joslyn's own — a smell of desert sand and wildflowers, hard sun and steel.

Tasia let go and sat up hastily, unsure why the scent of the guard's skin had so unnerved her.

"It's probably time for the morning meal," she said. "And I'm supposed to meet with my father's advisors after that."

"Yes," Joslyn said, pushing herself up from the wet sand. She wouldn't meet the Princess's eyes as she got to her feet and brushed the sand from her clothes. "That's enough for one morning anyway."

#

They were late for the morning meal, which made Tasia late for the bath Mylla had drawn for her, which made for a cold and unpleasant experience as the Princess washed the sand from her skin. The chambermaid had likewise drawn a bath for Joslyn in the antechamber, and as they both bathed in separate rooms, Tasia couldn't help but think about the smell of soap on the guard's skin, couldn't help but wonder if Joslyn's naked skin puckered with goosebumps from the cold water the same way Tasia's did.

She pushed the thought from her mind with a fierce shake of her head. She couldn't think of Joslyn like that. Joslyn certainly didn't think of *her* like that. And Mylla was wrong. Tasia wasn't interested in the guard.

Was she?

Tasia stepped out of the cold bath as quickly as she could, toweling herself dry and shrugging into the dress Mylla had left out for her.

"Out for the rest of the day with Father," read a note in Mylla's handwriting beside the dress. She'd drawn a small heart at the bottom of the page, and the sight of it made Tasia's chest clench with guilt. She hadn't started the fight last night, but she still regretted it. Everything with Mylla had felt strange and uncomfortable lately, and Tasia wanted to do something to change that.

Joslyn stood waiting in a flawless black guard's uniform when Tasia opened the door to the antechamber.

"Shall we head to my father's office, then?" Tasia said.

Joslyn nodded without meeting her eyes.

Guard and Princess walked side-by-side down the royal family's wing once more, this time in silence. They passed guards and the occasional Wise Man, each of whom hurried along with business of their own.

The corridor that led to the royal family's apartments ended in an interior courtyard with a sunken atrium in its center. High skylights let in the bright light of the mid-morning sun; a fountain in the center of the atrium gurgled at them cheerily as they passed. The lush indoor garden was one of the nexuses of the palace, with hallways branching in every direction like spokes from the hub of a wheel. Down one hall was a series of adjoining ballrooms, where royal functions and balls were held; down another were the offices of the Wise Men; down a third were guest quarters; down a fourth were her father's offices and the council rooms.

A few bruises and sore muscles twinged as Tasia walked, and she rubbed the pad of her thumb against the callouses that had formed on her palm from carrying rocks. A nobleman walking in the opposite direction stopped when he saw Tasia and Joslyn, dropping to one knee and removing his hat with a dramatic flourish. Tasia pretended not to see him.

For all she knew, he was one of the conspirators who'd tried to kill her.

For all she knew, the conspirators would be at the council meeting in just another hour or two, smirking at her while she sat at her father's side, pretending respect for the new female heir but all the while plotting her demise.

"What good will self-defense lessons do, in the end?" Tasia asked Joslyn suddenly. "We know that whoever tried to kill me was a noble or being assisted by one. If they want to find a way to get to me, they will. They've probably been at all the council meetings these past two weeks, laughing at me while they wait to make their next move."

Joslyn said nothing at first. She gave Tasia a quick, sideways glance. "Self-defense on the beach is not that different from self-defense in the council room, Princess," said the guard. "It's still a matter of identifying your advantage, doing what they don't expect, and maintaining your balance."

"Maybe," Tasia said glumly.

"You out-witted the man who tried to kill you," Joslyn said.

"No, I didn't. I got lucky with the two guards being nearby."

They skirted the atrium and turned left down the corridor that would lead to her father's office and the council chambers.

"Why try to kill *me*, anyway?" Tasia said. It was a question that still troubled her, that she still came back to. On the one hand, she knew the answer — she was the eldest child of the House of Dorsa, the child the Emperor had always favored most. But on the other hand, the assassination attempt just didn't make sense.

"To pressure your father," Joslyn answered. "To threaten him, to intimidate him, to take away his blood heir."

"But I'm not his only blood. There's still Adela."

"From what I've seen of your younger sister — "

"Don't," Tasia warned. "If you're going to belittle her, say that she's too frivolous or only cares for ponies, I swear to Mother Moon I will send you back to Terinto."

"That wasn't what I was going to say."

"No? What were you going to say, then?"

"That from what little I have seen of your sister, she is a gentle spirit — a spirit of water and air," said Joslyn. "Yielding. The still waters of a mountain lake or slow-flowing river that rarely build to a tidal wave. Your own spirit is made of fire and rock. Which, once tamed, is better suited for leadership. Whoever tried to kill you must have known that. Must have known you'd be a threat to whatever it is they want."

"Water and air, fire and rock? Spirits?" Tasia gave a half-laugh. "What is this — Terintan astrology?"

"If that's how you prefer to think of it," said the guard with a shrug.

They walked a few more paces in silence, Tasia going over the faces of the lords and ambassadors in her mind. The long-faced Lorent from the Steppes. The carefree Lord M'Tongliss who spoke of demons attacking the Imperial Army even while the others laughed at him. The handsome young Lord Simon, the fat Lord Wendell, the tired Lord Albert. She played through dozens of other faces, wondering which one — or ones — might want her dead. Did Norix have his suspicions? Did her father?

A thought occurred to her, and Tasia stopped short. What if Norix or her father *did* know who had tried to kill her, and naming her his heir was just a way of drawing the killer into the open? What if her father had used her as bait?

"Princess?" Joslyn said. "What's wrong?"

"Why did my father make me heir, Joslyn?" Tasia asked. "I've never done *anything* for him. Or for the House of Dorsa. I mean, yes, I show up to royal functions and bat my eyes at the lords and laugh at their jokes like a good princess is supposed to do, but that's not enough to rule an Empire. What if... do you think my father might just be trying to draw out my assassin by making me his heir?"

"No," Joslyn said firmly. "Your father is not that kind of leader."

"But what if he is?" Tasia argued. "He can't *possibly* see anything in me that would suggest I could be an empress."

The guard studied Tasia for a moment. "May I see your hand, Princess?"

"My... why?"

The guard reached out, took Tasia's hand and turned it palm-up. She ran her thumb across the top of it lightly and nodded her approval. "Callouses. In my experience, not many highborn — outside Terinto, that is — have them."

Tasia snatched her hand away. "I know. They're terribly unsightly. And they are entirely *your* fault. You with your *ridiculous* beach drills."

Joslyn shook her head. "No. Callouses mean you are learning. And you haven't complained about your lessons since the day you slapped me."

Tasia blanched. "I regret having done that."

"I know," said Joslyn. "Never say that you were nothing before you were your father's heir, Tasia. Your hands have undergone a transformation; your mind is undergoing the same transformation. Someone wished you dead because they see the potential in you. We will discover who that someone is in time. Until then, your best protection is to know who you are."

"Who I am? What, the Princess?"

"No. The woman of fire and rock, the woman who carries boulders and knows how to break free from a choke hold." She gazed at Tasia intently. "Your mistake has been to believe you are who they say you are — the Princess. But 'Princess' is not who you are; 'Princess' is a title. *This* — " she tapped the bare skin of Tasia's breastbone with one finger " — and *this* — " she lifted one of Tasia's hands and ran her own rough thumb over the callouses there " — is who you are. No twist of fate, not even death or the threat of death, can part you from that."

"More Terintan astrology." Tasia stared at her guard a long moment. "How did you get to be so wise?"

"I was a slave once," Joslyn said, a tentative smile growing on her face. "And no slave becomes truly free until they realize that 'slave' is just a word and not who they are."

Just then, the time-caller's voice echoed down the corridor from his place in the atrium. "The time is now one of the clock! One of the clock!" he shouted.

"Oh, pig shite," Tasia said. "We're late."

14

Conversation came to an abrupt halt inside the Emperor's office when Tasia and Joslyn walked in.

"You're late," the Emperor said.

"I know, Father. I'm sorry."

His office contained all the usual faces — Commander Cole at his place against the wall, Wise Man Norix seated at the desk next to him, General Remington and Wise Man Evrart on the divan. Wise Man Crestin, another one of Norix's top assistants, was also in the room. Tasia wondered what he might be doing here; Crestin typically handled the writing and dissemination of public announcements. Was her father preparing an announcement? Of what?

"We were discussing the war," said the Emperor as Tasia took the room's only open chair.

She suppressed a sigh. The war. That was all anyone talked about these days. The Emperor and his advisors talked about the war in his private office, the lords debated it daily in the council room, Wise Man Norix and General Remington talked about it to Tasia in their lessons. She was tired of the topic, tired also of the war itself, which after twelve years never seemed to progress beyond stalemate.

"As I was saying before the Princess entered," Wise Man Norix said, giving Tasia a look that might have been annoyed, "the council still seems rather divided on the subject of the war. And with Lord Hermant withdrawing his extra financial support... I'm sure he will continue to pay his taxes, of course. He doesn't want to be in open rebellion against the crown. But without his surpluses from the silver mines..." Norix trailed off with a troubled sigh. "Emperor, I know it's not an easy prospect to face, but we are headed towards a very serious funding problem. And if desertion rates on the front are high now, imagine what they will be like come next winter, when we cut the soldiers' rations even further."

"The council does not yet know that Lord Hermant has withdrawn his financial support," the Emperor said. "That gives us time."

Wise Man Evrart put up a tentative hand. "Your Majesty... I don't think we should assume that the rest of the council does not already know that House Farrimont has withdrawn its support for the war."

Tasia had always liked Evrart. He had a way of speaking his mind while still being respectful — a skill which his mentor Norix sometimes lacked. Norix always condescended to Tasia, and occasionally he came dangerously close to condescending to the Emperor himself. Evrart never did.

"I am well aware of the council's divisions," said the Emperor. "And I am not fool enough to think that Hermant will keep his dissent to himself."

"What if Lord Hermant is right, your Majesty?" Norix said. "Maybe it is time for the Empire to let the East handle its own problem."

General Remington scoffed from his place on the divan. "Are you going deaf in your old age, Wise Man? Or are you choosing to ignore what the Emperor said in the council meeting the other day? The Empire is one body; a barbarian problem in the East is a barbarian problem for us all."

"My hearing is perfect, General," Norix said testily. "But your Majesty, I may risk my head for saying so, but I myself am not sure why this war is so important to you. We have been beating back the barbarians for almost fifteen years, yet what do we have to show for it? For the amount of coin and blood we have shed there, we could have bought half the Adessian Islands!"

"You will never lose your head for speaking your mind to me," said the Emperor. "I value your head and the wisdom it contains. But as Remington said, the East is a part of this Empire, and I have a sacred duty to protect my people there."

"Your Majesty," Norix said, "if you will allow me to be contrarian just a little longer... Frankly speaking, Emperor, the East is weak. And it's poor. If it weren't for the fact that the mineral-rich mountains in the Northeast are a part of it, the East would hardly even be able to justify its existence."

"The East is weak in part because it has been brutalized by war for twelve years," General Remington said. His face reddened as he spoke, a sure sign that Norix's words had angered him. "And its strategic importance is enormous. It is the buffer zone between the Empire and all the other scattered powers on this continent. You're more court fool than Wise Man if you fail to see that."

"What other powers on this continent?" Norix argued, raising his voice. "None of them have even a fraction of our population, our wealth, our military might."

"The Kingdom of Persopos — " General Remington began.

"Yes, yes, we all know your theory that the Kingdom of Persopos is secretly supporting the barbarians," Norix said impatiently, cutting the General off. "Yet you've never managed to produce a prisoner, a document, a merchant captain, or any other artifact that could corroborate your theory. I don't mean to question your experience as a commander of men, General, but wisdom does beg a difficult question: Given that your business is war, is it not possible that you see a threat where there is none, because you prefer to justify a war that seems to have no end?"

Now General Remington's face had gone nearly purple. "If you had let me finish, *Wise* Man," he said, "you would have heard me explain that there is reason to believe that the Kingdom of Persopos has infiltrated our camp in the East at its highest levels." He seemed about to say more, but snapped his mouth closed and glanced at the Emperor.

"It's alright, General," said the Emperor. "It is time they know." He looked from face to face. "What I am about to say does not leave this room. General Remington brought me information some weeks ago that suggests General Telek, who is leading our troops in the East, has come under the influence of the Kingdom of Persopos. He may no longer be trustworthy."

"Bah!" Norix spat. "Forgive me, your Majesty, but that is nonsense. We have not yet seen solid evidence that places the Kingdom of Persopos together with the barbarians. And General Telek's family has been leading the Imperial Army for four generations. His House is above reproach — they are more loyal to the Empire than almost any."

"A House is only as loyal as the individuals within it," said Cole quietly.

Everyone looked at the commander of the palace guard for a moment, having nearly forgotten he was in the room.

"Precisely," General Remington said with a firm nod.

Norix shook his head. "No. I don't believe it."

The Emperor smiled. "I knew you wouldn't. That's why I'm including you on the delegation to the East."

"Delegation to the East?" Norix said. He glanced from the General to the Emperor. "What delegation East?"

"I'm sending the three of you — Norix, Remington, Natasia — to the front," said the Emperor. "I would go myself, but we are in the middle of the spring council meetings, and my presence is needed here to placate the lords. But sending the three of you ahead of the spring offensive is part of placating them. We will show that we are taking their concerns seriously, while at the same time settling the question once and for all concerning the

Kingdom of Persopos."

Tasia grew momentarily dizzy. A journey to the war front in the East. This would be the first real test of her ascendancy, her first real task as her father's heir and representative. She'd never even been outside the Capital Lands, let alone to the East.

"There is no question of their involvement — they are *not* involved!" Norix said, frustrated. "There are only barbarians and soldiers who have both toiled there for a dozen years. The war is indeed infecting the entire Empire. And an infected limb is amputated." He banged his fist on the table for emphasis.

"You know not of what you speak," said General Remington. His voice had gone icy. "You know nothing of wars and even less of Persopos."

"Oh, I don't?" said Norix sarcastically. "I suppose I have been the palace's top Wise Man and the senior advisor to two different Emperors for no reason at all."

"Stop," the Emperor commanded. "Both of you. The first rule of wisdom is the admission that no man knows all," he said, quoting one of the House of Wisdom's most basic tenets. "You will *both* travel East. You will *both* speak to General Telek and test his loyalty. You will *both* return here and give me your conclusion. Most importantly, you will both remain open to the possibility that you are wrong. Am I clear?"

"Yes, your Majesty," mumbled Remington and Norix together.

"I need to know if we can trust General Telek, but it's

more than that," the Emperor continued. "I need to know what's really been going on at the front — why ill-equipped mountain men are defeating our imperial soldiers. I don't believe nomadic superstitions of demons any more than I would believe the Cult of Culo attempted to kill Natasia, but I still need to know precisely why desertion rates have climbed so high. And I want to know what General Telek is going to do to fix it."

He turned to Tasia.

"As for you, Natasia, the expedition has several functions. It is a part of your education, because I want you to see what war looks like with your own eyes. But I also want the Empire's lords and generals and even common soldiers to begin to recognize you as the future of the House of Dorsa, as the voice of the Empire itself. Be strong. Learn. Show them that you are every bit as capable of succeeding me as Nik would have been."

Tasia nodded, the heavy weight of his words settling upon her shoulders.

"Between the three of you," the Emperor said, "I want you to come back with the truth about what's happening in the East. The truth, along with a cohesive strategy for finishing this war once and for all."

"If what you want is an end to the war," Norix said, "I don't see that a delegation East is necessary. I'm sure we can strategize that right now, in this room."

The Emperor turned to face him. "Wise Man Norix. I have listened to your input and I have made my decision. The time for discussion is over. In just a few minutes, we will walk into the council room, and we will present a united front on this matter before the lords and ambassadors. You will journey East and you will do what I have asked you to do. Do you understand?"

Norix would not meet his eye. "I do, your Majesty."

"Good." He glanced at the candle on the wall that marked the time. "Let us prepare for today's council meeting."

#

The council meeting was less contentious than the previous week's. The lords and ambassadors responded well to the Emperor's announcement of the delegation East. Of course, the Emperor said nothing about the Kingdom of Persopos, the potential of a disloyal general, or the disagreement amongst his own advisors over the war's future. Instead, he said that he was sending his heir, his top general, and his top Wise Man to strategize with commanders on the front about ending the war once and for all. This seemed to satisfy almost everyone in the room, and after his announcement, the atmosphere inside the council room tangibly relaxed.

After the meeting, the Emperor invited all the attendees to the ballroom for evening hors d'oeuvres and wine. Tasia nursed a single glass of wine over the course of an hour, smiling generously through multiple rounds and multiple variations of

"Congratulations on your ascendancy, Princess."

"The Emperor couldn't have made a better choice."

"I was surprised to hear the Emperor name you heir. But then again, I wasn't."

"Should we skip the formalities and simply begin to refer to you as 'Empress'?"

"It's about time a daughter of Dorsa ruled her House!"

Tasia smiled until her cheeks ached from the effort. She offered her hand to be kissed so many times that her knuckles became perpetually moist from the kisses of lords, ambassadors, Wise Men, and their sons.

But there were also many council attendees, she noticed, who did not look her way at all during the reception. Many who acted as if she was not in the room. Many who walked away when she walked towards them.

This is how it will be, she thought through another fake smile.

This is how it will be, she thought as she tittered out another fake laugh and said, "Oh, you're too kind, my Lord."

Some of them will pretend to love me. Some of them will not bother hiding their distaste.

Yet there were a few lords who seemed genuinely pleased to hear her named heir, a few who offered Tasia something more than fatuous flattery and hollow compliments.

Lord Simon of House Brundt was one of them. She greeted him warmly when he approached, giving him a smile that was closer to genuine than what she offered to the other lords. They hadn't seen each other, Tasia realized, since their champagne-saturated evening of fun at a palace ball the year before. His father had still been alive then, and Lord Simon had been simply Simon, just another young lordling.

"Your Majesty," Lord Simon said as he approached Tasia. He dropped to a knee, and she offered her hand for a kiss. "It is good to see you again."

"And you, my Lord."

Once on his feet again, he wasted no time on pleasantries. "You are to be my ruler some day soon," he said.

"Soon? Let's not be hasty with my father's demise," Tasia said with a practiced giggle. "I daresay he has a good many years in him yet."

Lord Simon shrugged. "I would've said the same of my own father." He looked away for a moment. "At any rate, it is brave of you — to volunteer for this expedition to the war front."

"Have you met my father?" Tasia asked. "I would not use the word 'volunteer' to describe my involvement."

Lord Simon chuckled. "Ah, yes. The things we do for our fathers, correct?"

"Indeed," Tasia said.

"I hope you will take precautions on your journey and be safe," said Simon. "I would never want any harm to come to the heir to the crown."

"We will travel with a full guard," Tasia said. She gestured at Joslyn, who stood respectfully a few feet behind her. "And in case you haven't noticed, I've acquired a shadow of late. My guard goes where I go."

Simon nodded at Joslyn, then lowered his voice. "I mean it, Tasia. Be safe. There is talk in the council room of another rebellion, but not over Western independence this time. I'm not sure if your father realizes how deeply unpopular his war has become."

Tasia's pulse quickened. There was no mistaking that Lord Simon was delivering a warning — a warning that would certainly put him at risk if the wrong men overheard him saying it to Tasia.

"Do you know something I need to know, Lord Simon?" she asked quietly.

"I've already said it," he answered. "News of your close call with the assassin has not been kept as quiet as I'm sure the palace would have liked." His eyes flitted to Joslyn. "Keep yourself safe, Tasia. And keep your father safe, too."

Lord Simon smiled charmingly then, gave a quick bow, and said at a normal volume, "Alas, fair Princess. If only I had the time to stay longer. But my carriage leaves tonight back to House Brundt. My Wise Man is staying behind for the remainder of the council meetings. I do hope you will find the time to pay a visit one day. My House isn't as grand as some, but we would make you feel most welcome."

Tasia renewed her smile. "Of course you would, my Lord. I will visit as soon as Empire affairs allow it."

He nodded and strode away, leaving Tasia to wonder at his cryptic message.

Tasia turned, facing her guard. "Did you hear what he said, Joslyn?"

"I did, your Majesty."

"And what did you make of it?"

But Joslyn didn't answer. Her eyes looked past the Princess, and she nodded curtly.

Tasia pivoted to see another lord walking her way. She found her smile once more. "Ah, Lord Galen of House Harthing," she said to Mylla's father. "It is always such a pleasure to see you."

Lord Galen, who in his fifty-fifth spring seemed as fit and spry as a man half his age, kneeled before the Princess and kissed the ring bearing the emblem of House Dorsa. She could feel the callouses on his fingers, callouses that Mylla said came from two daily hours of swordplay each morning. It was unlikely Lord Galen would ever see a battle again, but he was the kind of man who kept his fighting skills honed for the sheer exhilaration of it.

He rose. "And you are more beautiful than ever, Princess Natasia. Quite the surprise for all the lords and ambassadors last week to hear that you will be succeeding your father, wasn't it?"

"Believe me, my Lord, no one was more surprised than me."

"Oh, come now, Princess," said Lord Galen with mock chastisement. "I was not surprised. In my daughter's letters, she always praises how clever you are."

"I doubt she meant the kind of clever that can guide an empire," Tasia said, and they both laughed.

"And speaking of my daughter," said Lord Galen, "is she caring for you well?"

"Of course she is," Tasia said. "I don't know what I would do without the Lady Mylla."

"You'll have to learn to live without her soon," said the Lord. "She accepted a marriage proposal a fortnight ago."

Tasia's smile faltered. "Is that so? I thought Lady Mylla was still meeting with potential suitors." Unable to stop herself, she asked, "Who is it?"

Lord Galen chuckled. "No, she only met one suitor. They were quite taken with one another from the start, I must say. She dines with him almost every chance she has, as his grandfather has been staying in the Ambassador Quarter for the council meetings."

"Who?" Tasia repeated, trying her best to feign polite and curious inquiry.

"Umfrey of House Farrimont," said Lord Galen. "So I said 'his grandfather,' but I suppose I might as well have said 'yours.'"

"Umfrey?" Tasia repeated, and now the smile faded from her face completely. "But Umfrey of House Farrimont is my…"

"Your first cousin," Lord Galen confirmed with a nod. "And I must say, a proposal from a House tied so intimately to your own is quite a victory for House Harthing. Between me and you, however," he said, dropping his voice conspiratorially, "I think my daughter worries that she's grown too accustomed to the capital's warm climate. I believe she's thinking of delaying the wedding simply to avoid moving to the Zaris Mountains during winter."

Tasia tried to match Lord Galen's smile, but her mind was spinning.

Umfrey of House Farrimont. Her first cousin. Her uncle's oldest son. Umfrey who would become the Lord of House Farrimont once his — *their* — grandfather died. Why didn't Mylla tell her? Was she afraid of how the Princess would react? And why would Lord Hermant permit such a marriage? House Farrimont was strong, with long-standing ties to House Dorsa. House Harthing, though... there were few noble Houses smaller in the entire Empire.

"Quite a victory for House Harthing, indeed," she said woodenly.

Lord Galen winked. "You know first-hand how charming my daughter can be. I think she simply won the young man over before he knew what was happening to him."

Tasia regained control of the muscles around her mouth and forced her lips to smile again. "I am sure Lady Mylla will want a marriage as soon as she comes of age. A union between House Harthing and House Farrimont will doubtless be beneficial for both families."

"Yes, I believe so." Lord Galen took Tasia's hand again, raising it to his lips and kissing the seal of the House of Dorsa on her ring. "Perhaps you can convince her of that for me."

"I will certainly try, my Lord," Tasia said.

"Good day, Princess."

She watched his receding back as he threaded through the crowd.

A light touch on her elbow brought her mind back into the room.

"Princess?" Joslyn said softly in her ear. "Are you alright?"

"I will be."

"Would you like to stay longer? Or shall we return to your chambers now?"

Tasia felt her head nodding. "Yes. Returning sounds like an excellent idea."

She allowed Joslyn to lead her from the ballroom.

15

"She's getting *married*, Joslyn," Tasia said as they walked back through the long palace corridors.

"Yes, that's what young women tend to do," Joslyn said wryly.

"But she didn't tell me. The proposal came two weeks ago — two weeks! She's known for weeks and she hasn't told me. She's let me believe she's met multiple suitors, and doesn't like any of them."

"Given all the changes you've gone through over the past several weeks, perhaps she didn't want to add to your burden," suggested the guard.

Tasia shook her head. "You don't understand. You don't understand what Mylla and I... you don't understand what we are to each other."

Joslyn was quiet for a moment. "Tasia," she said gently, "I sleep in the anteroom next to your bedchamber. I know quite well what the Lady Mylla is to you."

Tasia felt her cheeks burn. She'd suspected that Joslyn understood that the relationship between Princess and handmaid extended beyond mere friendship, but she supposed she'd preferred just suspecting and not knowing for certain.

"I feel like... I feel like I might shatter," she confessed

to the guard. Tears threatened, but she held them at bay. "My ascendency, the trip to the Eastern war front — why did I agree to that so easily? And now Mylla... and she isn't marrying just any ordinary lord, Joslyn. She's marrying my *cousin*. My mother's nephew. The heir to my grandfather's House." She watched her feet move forward down the smooth marble of the hallway, wondering how they kept moving even when it felt like she wanted to collapse. "It's too much. It's all too much."

"It's not," Joslyn said. "You just need to rest. That is what my *ku-sai* used to say to me: 'When you face a problem with no solutions, rest and look again.'"

Tasia shook her head. "Unless I sleep a hundred years, my problems will still be here when I wake." She paused. "And what is a *ku-sai*?"

"It means teacher."

"Forgive me, but... since when do slaves have teachers?"

"They don't," Joslyn said. "But runaways do. Some of them."

"Oh?" Tasia said, intrigued. The more she learned about her guard, the more she wanted to learn. "I could use a distraction right now, Joslyn. Tell me how it came to pass that you were raised a slave but then ended up with a wise *ku-sai*."

Joslyn's expression turned uncomfortable. "It's not a time in my life that I speak much about, Princess."

Princess. A minute ago, the guard had called her Tasia. But now she was back to Princess.

When Tasia was nine and Nik was seven, they'd tried to tame the rabbits they'd discovered living around one of the ponds on the palace grounds. They'd spend hours sitting perfectly still, a bit of tempting food in front of them, urging the rabbits to come closer. Once they accepted the proffered food, the Prince and Princess had inched closer to the rabbits, then closer, then closer. They'd almost achieved their final goal of feeding the rabbits directly from their hands when their father found out. He was, much to their surprise, livid.

"Wild creatures need their fear of mankind," he'd said. *"If you take that away from them, they are defenseless. You think you have created friends of those rabbits, but all you've done is create victims."*

That was the memory that surfaced when Joslyn called her "Princess" instead of "Tasia." The guard was like a cautious rabbit, advancing and then retreating from Tasia's open hand. Maybe Tasia had been wrong to tell the guard to call her by her name in the first place. Maybe friendship with her servants was one more thing she had to let go of as her father's heir.

The thought made her lonely. She touched her throat lightly as if she could feel an actual noose there.

"My father sold my sister and me when she was seven and I was four," Joslyn said after a long silence had passed between them.

Tasia searched Joslyn's face for a residue of pain, but the woman's face maintained its normal stoicism.

"Who bought you?" Tasia asked cautiously, hoping the

rabbit wouldn't skitter away again.

"A traveling tinker," said Joslyn. "Here in Port Lorsin, people normally think of tinker families as wandering fortune tellers. But it's only the women who tell fortunes. The men earn their coin by fixing things, selling things, trading things — a little of everything."

"I've seen traveling fortune tellers before, when I was very young and used to visit commoners with my mother and father. The women who read cards and palms on street corners always seemed a rather grimy lot to me." Tasia cocked her head to the side, trying to imagine a version of Joslyn that didn't have a sword at her hip. A version where the woman's black eyes gazed into crystals and made vague pronouncements. "Did they treat you well, the tinker family? You and your sister?"

Joslyn shrugged. "We were slaves. The tinkers were not cruel, but we were slaves and we were treated as such."

"But you ran away from the tinkers anyway and found yourself a... a *ku-sai.*"

"No, that came much later." Joslyn hesitated. "The tinker sold me to a man when I was eleven."

Tasia thought she saw Joslyn's face change subtly when she said *"a man."* She was about to press for more details, but they had arrived at the entrance to her apartments.

"Wait for a moment," Joslyn said when Tasia reached for the door handle. "Allow me first." She disappeared inside and returned a minute later. "Everything is clear."

"And Mylla?" Tasia asked. "Is she inside?"

Joslyn shook her head.

Tasia sighed. "Very well," she said, taking the pin of blue feathers from her hair as she walked through the antechamber and into her bedchamber. She'd expected Mylla to be here. She'd planned on confronting the girl, finding out why the handmaid hadn't said anything about the marriage proposal. The proposal she had already accepted.

Tasia sat heavily at her vanity, removing the rest of the pins from her hair and letting it down, massaging her sore scalp with her fingertips. Through the mirror, she could see a fragment of Joslyn, posted by the bedchamber door.

Normally the guard remained in the antechamber. Maybe Tasia hadn't frightened the rabbit away quite yet.

"Do you remember anything about your mother?" Tasia asked the reflection in the mirror, picking up her hairbrush. "Given that you were taken from her at such a young age?"

The reflection stirred. "I remember very little of my mother."

"What do you remember?"

"I remember that she had black hair that hung to her waist once she unfurled it," Joslyn said. Then she added, "Her hair smelled like incense and saffron. But I can't remember her face."

Tasia ran the brush through her hair, watching Joslyn in the mirror thoughtfully. "I lost my own mother. Did you know that?"

The reflection nodded.

"I was seven when she died. My brother Nik was five. Adela was barely walking and talking. It hurts, doesn't it?

Losing a mother when you still need her."

"My *ku-sai* used to say that losing a mother is to slice a wound that never heals."

Tasia gave a faint smile. "I believe I like this *ku-sai* of yours."

For a moment, Tasia lost herself in the memories of grief that had surrounded the weeks and months following her mother's death. Seven year-old Tasia knew from Wise Man Norix that the God of Time was made up, a myth that commoners prayed to because they were too ignorant to know any better. But in secret, after Nik had crawled into her bed each night and cried himself to sleep, Tasia prayed to the God of Time. She prayed to have one last moment with her mother. She prayed to see her mother smiling at her a final time, because the image of her face was already fading from Tasia's mind.

"You are the only mother they will have now," her father had told her, referring to Nik and Adela. *"You must be strong for them. They will need you."*

It hadn't occurred to Tasia at the time to ask her father why *he* couldn't be the strong one for his three children. She had simply nodded like an obedient daughter, and did her best to console her five year-old brother and infant sister. At least Adela would never remember losing her mama, Tasia had thought at the time. That, at least, was the God of Time's one blessing.

"I miss her, Tazy," Nik would say each night.

"So do I," Tasia answered. *"But you are the future Emperor, and I am the Princess. We can only cry when we*

are alone, never in front of Father or the Wise Men or the lords and ambassadors. Understand?"

He nodded. *"Father said we must all be brave,"* he said miserably.

"Father's right," Tasia agreed. *"Father is always right."*

#

Tasia didn't go to dinner, even though Mace of House Gifford had been invited again. She sent a messenger to her father to say she wasn't feeling well and would be taking her evening meal in her room. It was partially true; she was tired from the day's events and had a mild headache. More than that, though, when the time came to bathe and dress for the evening meal, Mylla still hadn't reappeared. The longer she was gone, the hotter Tasia's emotions became — a potent mix of anxiety, anger, and despondency.

She paced the room, going from the window that overlooked the courtyard to scour the space below for her handmaid, then to her bed, to her vanity, to the table in the center of the room.

By the gods, where was that girl?

She opened the door to the antechamber. "Joslyn?" she called. "I need a distraction. Come play Castles and Knights with me."

The guard entered obediently, sat at the table by the window while Tasia set up the board.

"Do you want white or red?" Tasia asked.

"You choose."

"Alright. I'll be red tonight." Tasia lined up her pieces along the Sunrise Mountains, thinking of the barbarians and the routed battalion. The guard watched her, leaning forward over the table and propping her chin in the palm of one hand. The gesture made her look almost girlish. A moment later, the guard began setting up her white pieces in the Terintan desert. In real life, her pieces occupied Lord M'Tongliss's lands.

"Joslyn?"

"Yes?"

"Why do you think Lord M'Tongliss said what he did at the first council meeting — about army deserters raving about demons?"

Joslyn straightened in her chair. "I suspect he said it because he believes it's true."

Tasia let out a half-laugh. "Are all desert nomads so gullible and superstitious? *I* suspect that the deserters just wanted sympathy and didn't want to be turned in to local magistrates for their disloyalty. After all, the penalty for desertion is death."

Joslyn looked down at the board, adding a ship to one of Terinto's two port cities. "I do not find nomads to be very gullible. When you make your home in the desert, there is only life, or death. Those taken in by fables and fantasies quickly find themselves on the side of death."

"So are you saying that you really believe the barbarians have recruited demons to fight for them?" Tasia handed the dice to Joslyn and placed the cards of fortune face down in the center of the board.

Joslyn took the dice and rolled, then picked up a card of fortune.

"I'm saying that the things I have seen and heard on cold nights in the desert and while I lived with my *ku-sai* in the Zaris Mountains might surprise you," the guard said.

The words sent a chill down Tasia's spine.

"Can you read the card for me?" Joslyn asked, showing Tasia the card she'd drawn.

"You read it."

Joslyn sounded out the card with a little help from Tasia, then made her opening move.

"My mother was from the Zaris Mountains. Though probably far to the north of you and your *ku-sai*," Tasia said, taking the dice back. "She used to tell us all sorts of stories about the mountains when we were little, and it wasn't always easy to tell when she was telling the truth and when she was having us on. I was almost nine before I realized there was no such thing as a talking cat."

Tasia and Joslyn shared a laugh.

"In Terinto, it is said that sorcerers sometimes take the bodies of cats so that they can spy upon their enemies," Joslyn said matter-of-factly.

"My mother used to speak of sorcerers," said Tasia. "And witches, too. She believed in them."

"They are both more common than you might think," said the guard without a trace of sarcasm. She moved a cavalry unit to the west, and Tasia cocked her head, trying to understand if the guard was now just moving pieces at random.

"She talked of the race of small men, too," Tasia said. "The ones who build entire cities below the Zaris Mountains. Have you ever met a small man? When I was a girl I used to dream of visiting one of their underground cities. They sounded so fabulous — filled with emeralds and rubies and lit by phosphorescent lakes."

"I've met a few small men."

Tasia gasped. "Really? How? You must tell me everything."

Joslyn chuckled and rolled the dice again. "They used to come to the village where I lived with my *ku-sai* to trade for furs and food. They are notoriously difficult to bargain with. If they don't like the terms of the deal, they will simply walk away, and you might not see them again for months."

"What do they look like? Do they really have eyes that take up almost their entire face, like the stories say?"

Joslyn nodded. "But you rarely see their eyes, because they cover them with gemstone lenses designed to block the sun. They've lived beneath the mountains for so many generations that they can no longer tolerate much sun. Which is why it's much more common to come across them at night."

"Do they — " Tasia started, but the bedchamber door burst open.

Joslyn stood so quickly from her seat that her chair toppled to the stone floor with a clatter. In an untrackable blur of motion, she drew her sword and positioned herself in front of the Princess before Tasia even had time to draw a breath.

16

"Do you intend to run me through, nomad?" asked a familiar voice.

Joslyn relaxed, re-sheathing her sword.

Tasia leaned around the guard. "Mylla? Where have you been?"

The handmaid heaved a great sigh. "Where have I been? Where *haven't* I been? I've been traipsing all over the city, trying to retrieve my gown from the washer woman, and my shoes — and *your* shoes — from the cobbler, and my new hat from the furrier. And after all that, I'm *still* going to be late to meet Father." She moved to the center of the room, dropping an armload of parcels before placing her hands on her hips. "Why can't common people fulfill their obligations to their betters in a timely fashion? 'Oh, Lady Mylla, we thought you were coming tomorrow,'" she said, pitching her voice high in imitation of some unknown commoner. "Do they not understand how important the proper dress can be for an evening? No," she said, answering her own question. "Of course they don't understand. Why would they? They've never owned anything finer than cotton in their lives. They can't even point to where silk comes from on a map, let alone understand the way the right gown can shape the outcome of an evening."

Normally, Tasia found this kind of flustered behavior from her handmaid endearing, but now, given the knowledge about the pending marriage she'd learned about from Mylla's father earlier, she was simply irritated.

"I saw your father today. After the council meeting."

"Oh?" said Mylla as she stooped to retrieve one of her packages. "And did he say anything about your ascendancy?"

"He was surprised," Tasia said evenly. "Though probably not nearly as surprised as I was to hear of your upcoming marriage to my cousin."

Mylla froze. She placed the parcel she was picking up back on the floor and straightened slowly. Her eyes were wide.

Tasia stood from her place at the table and took a step towards the handmaid. "Nothing to say?" she asked. "Do you know how it felt to hear that news from *him* instead of you?"

Mylla's face collapsed, gaze falling to the floor. "Tazy… I'm sorry. I was going to tell you, but…"

"You were going to tell me *when?*" Tasia asked, her voice warbling with tears of frustration. "The night before your wedding? You've known for a *fortnight,* Mylla."

"I've been trying to think of how to tell you," the handmaid said. "But then you've had so much stress with your ascendancy, and the lessons on the beach, and then we quarreled the other night and I — "

"Stop, Mylla," Tasia said, and the tears were flowing in

earnest now. She covered her face with her hands. "Just stop trying to explain."

"Tasia... My Princess..."

Footsteps, then Tasia felt the tug of familiar fingers on her hands, pulling them away from her face. "Why are you so upset with me?" Mylla asked. Her tone was gentle. "You always knew this would happen one day."

Tasia let her eyes be uncovered and tried to stop the flow of her tears with one mighty sniff. Joslyn, she noted, had discretely slipped from the room. Into the antechamber, no doubt. Probably still able to hear every word of the conversation. But no matter. What her guard overheard was truly the least of her concerns at the moment.

"I knew it would happen, Mylla, but you're not even of age yet. I thought we would have another half a year together. Maybe even longer."

Mylla scoffed. "Longer? You know my father better than that, my sweet Princess. He will see to it that I am married and with child within the first week of my eighteenth birthday. I wouldn't be surprised if he plans the wedding for my birthday itself."

"I know," Tasia said, swallowing. "But I thought that we... as long as you were still at the palace, you could still... *we* could still..." Tasia dropped her chin to her chest and covered her face again as a fresh stream of tears issued forth.

"Princess... my sweet Princess... don't cry." Fingers found Tasia's wrists, gently pulled her hands from her face.

"Tazy, come now…"

"I thought you might marry someone near Port Lorsin," Tasia said between hot tears. "I thought that maybe you would stay close, not more than an hour or two's journey from…"

Mylla's lips found Tasia's, as if she could kiss the words away. But the Princess stayed stiff, her mouth contorting with a barely controlled sob. Mylla didn't give up; she continued with her kiss. Slowly Tasia melted into the girl, letting the magic of Mylla's soft lips infuse her whole body.

"Lie with me. Just for a minute," Mylla whispered into Tasia's ear. The handmaid nipped at the earlobe she had just spoken into, and a wave of gooseflesh rolled down Tasia's body.

"I thought you were going to be late to meet your father."

"He can wait. He knows I'm always late, anyway." Mylla guided Tasia to the bed; Tasia allowed herself to be guided. The girl nipped at Tasia's neck and throat, both of which were bare inside the scoop-necked dress she wore. "May I take your necklace off for you, Princess?"

"Yes," Tasia said, barely audible.

She felt Mylla's fingers fumble with the clasp at the back of her neck, while the girl's lips and teeth continued to travel up and down Tasia's throat. Finally the necklace came off, and Mylla stepped away long enough to place it on Tasia's vanity.

"May I help you out of your dress, Princess?"

Tasia nodded, and Mylla stepped behind her, pressing her breasts into Tasia as she slowly unbuttoned the back of the dress. Tasia could feel the warmth of Mylla's breath between her shoulder blades.

"Do you remember the first time you kissed me, Myll?"

The unbuttoning down Tasia's back stopped for a moment. "Yes. How could I forget?"

"It was the first anniversary of Nik's death. Father didn't even remember it. But you did, didn't you?"

Mylla kissed Tasia's bare shoulders. "Of course I did." She unbuttoned the dress the rest of the way. "I missed Nikhost, too. He was my friend. We used to play together when my father brought my sisters and I to the palace when we were all little — do you remember? I chased Nik around the courtyard and tried to kiss him, because my nurse used to tell us that if we kissed the son of the Emperor, we would become an Empress."

Tasia laughed wetly. "I don't think I've ever heard that story."

"It's true." Mylla used Tasia's shoulders to pull herself up onto her tiptoes, and kissed the Princess again, letting her lips linger on Tasia's for a long, sweet moment. "Do you think," Mylla whispered, "that if I kiss the Emperor's daughter instead, I could still become an Empress?"

Tasia turned around, running her hands down Mylla's sides, lacing her fingers together in the small of the girl's back while Mylla tugged the dress open wider.

"I would like nothing more than for you to be the Empress by my side," Tasia said. "If only Nik hadn't died.

He could be the heir instead of me. I would find a way to keep you close to me and love you always."

Mylla kissed her again, pushed her gently onto the bed.

"I still miss him, Myll," Tasia said. "I miss him every day."

"I know, sweet Princess."

"He was the only one who really understood what it's like to… be my father's child."

Mylla's mouth puckered into a slight frown. "I like to think that *I* understand, Tazy."

"You are wonderful, and I love you more than anything," Tasia said. "But you don't understand." She sighed, remembering her sweet younger brother. "That first time you kissed me, after Nik died, I was fifteen."

Mylla nodded. "And I was fourteen. And couldn't stand to see something so beautiful be so sad."

"You were undressing me, just like you are now. And you unlaced my brazier…"

"Like this?" Mylla asked, looping a finger beneath the laces on the side and tugging them loose.

"Yes," Tasia breathed. "And then you…"

Mylla took the brazier off, bent slightly, and caught one of Tasia's nipples between her teeth. Tasia gasped.

The girl released the nipple, cupped Tasia's face in her hands. "Then I did that. And this." Mylla slid forward, kissing the Princess hard. "I have to marry him, Tasia. I can't marry you. We both know it."

"You could delay. As I have for you."

Mylla shook her head. "You can't delay forever.

Sooner or later, you will have to marry, my sweet Princess. We all have to."

Tasia pushed herself into a sitting position. "But you could still refuse him, Mylla. You don't have to marry yet. You don't have to — he lives all the way in the Northeast."

Mylla cocked her head to the side. "Would you refuse him, if you were me? I'm from a minor House, Tasia. A marriage to the heir of House Farrimont — that's more than I ever could have hoped for."

"Is that really all you think about?" Tasia asked bitterly. "Marrying to better your station?"

"Not all of us were born into the House of Dorsa," Mylla said. "Not all of us are lucky enough to be named heirs when we have no brothers. You should be glad that Nik's gone. You get to stay at the palace. You get to succeed your father on the throne."

Tasia stared at her handmaid disbelievingly. "Glad that Nik's gone? How can you be so callous?"

"It's the truth. If Nik were still alive, you probably would already be married, lounging in the bed of a rich lord of your father's choosing." She giggled, pinching one of Tasia's breasts. "Or already *fat,* with infants pulling down on your lovely, perky nipples."

Tasia pulled away from the girl, pressing her fingertips against her temples. All she had wanted was to reminisce about the time her handmaid had soothed her grief with a kiss. Somehow the conversation had taken a twist that felt like a knife blade in her gut. Much like Mylla keeping her upcoming marriage a secret had felt like a knife in the gut.

Tasia opened her eyes. "You're going to be late to meet your father — or Umfrey. Or both of them, I don't know."

"Tasia — " The girl reached for her but Tasia pushed her hand away.

"Don't, Mylla. Just go."

"All I said was — "

"You know what my brother meant to me. You speak as if..." The unfinished game she'd been playing with Joslyn caught her eye. "As if it's all some game of Castles and Knights."

"It *is* a game of Castles and Knights," said Mylla. "You, your brother, your sister — even me. We're all pieces on the board. Don't you know that? Pardon me for pointing out the obvious."

"Pardon *me* for thinking you saw me as something more than just a princess!"

Mylla gave a bitter, sour laugh. "'Just' a princess. It must be nice to think of yourself that way, to be so accustomed to your privilege that you can forget for a while that there's a board, a game, and pieces in play. Do you realize how hard my father had to work to get Umfrey to propose to me?" When Tasia didn't answer right away, Mylla said, "No. Of course you don't. Because everyone clamors to marry you, and you turn them down at your leisure."

"I turned them down because of — "

"Don't say 'me.' Don't you dare say you turned them down because of me. You should know better than that."

Tasia said nothing.

Mylla snorted. "While all Four Realms are ready to bow and kiss your hand, all *you* can do is mope around up here in your tower and feel sorry for yourself. A princess in love with her handmaid. This — " she said, pointing back and forth between herself and Tasia " — could never go on indefinitely. If it did... We'd be nothing but a bawdy comedy waiting to happen, Tasia, don't you know that?"

Tasia could feel her heart shattering at the same time she felt the anger rise like a tidal wave inside her.

The one person she had trusted completely.

The one person she'd allowed herself to love since her brother had died.

The one person she'd thought had loved her, too — not because she was Princess Natasia. Just because she was Tasia.

But it had been a game to Mylla all along.

"Go," Tasia said. "Meet your father. See if you can manipulate him into spoiling you more than he already does."

Mylla snorted. "Oh, that's *rich,* coming from the *Princess.*" She scooped Tasia's dress from the floor and tossed it onto the bed. Then she crossed her arms against her chest. "Do you know the real reason why I didn't tell you about the marriage proposal from Umfrey?"

She waited, but Tasia said nothing.

"Because I knew you wouldn't be able to find a way to be happy for me," Mylla said. "Because I knew the *only* way you'd be able to see it was as me leaving you. Well, you know what, Tasia? Not all of us are princesses. Some of us actually have to *think* about where our game piece is on the board. Some of us have to *think* about improving our family's situation."

"All I think about is improving my family's situation!" Mylla laughed. "Really? Since when?"

She shook her head in disgust when Tasia could find no reply.

"You're selfish, Tasia. You always will be. But I don't blame you; it's the luxury of being *just* another princess."

She spun on her heel and marched to her own bedchamber, slamming the door hard behind her.

Tasia crossed the room, flinging open the wardrobe and pawing through it until she found the baker's girl shift, hidden at the back. She yanked the simple brown dress from its hanger and pulled it on, not bothering to put her brazier back on or change out of her silk undergarments first. She didn't plan on anyone seeing her undergarments anyway, and if they did, she wouldn't be in an explaining type of mood, anyway.

Never having to explain herself was the luxury of her station, wasn't it?

She stuffed her feet into knee-high riding boots — another bit of clothing a baker's girl would never have, but oh well — and stormed out of her bedchamber and into the anteroom.

Joslyn stood just on the other side of the door, as if expecting her.

"I'm leaving the palace," she announced. "And I suppose I have no choice but to bring you with me."

Tasia gave the guard a petulant glare, daring her to raise a challenge.

But when Joslyn finally did speak, she simply observed: "You're dressed as a commoner."

"Yes. This is what I wear when I don't want the attention of being the Princess of the House of Dorsa."

Joslyn nodded but still looked uncomfortable.

"Is there a problem?" Tasia asked sharply.

"No, only…"

"Only what?"

"Only if we're trying to go unnoticed, then I probably shouldn't be wearing the palace guard blacks," Joslyn said. "I will give us away immediately."

Tasia had been prepared for a confrontation. She hadn't expected Joslyn to acquiesce so easily, and now she didn't know how to respond.

"May I have a moment to change clothes, Princess?" Joslyn asked. "I believe I have something that will suffice."

17

Sneaking out of the palace had become second-nature to Tasia, and she led Joslyn through the Sunfall Gate with ease, joking with the night guards and flipping them a silver penny each by way of thanks. As the guards only earned five coppers in a week, a single silver coin was nearly a month's salary. A nice bonus in exchange for turning a blind eye to the Princess's nighttime "meanderings," as Norix had called them.

But Joslyn's expression was pensive as they left the circumference of the palace's lanterns and slipped down a side street.

Tasia watched her out of the corner of her eye. "What?" she finally asked.

Joslyn glanced sideways at the Princess. "Nothing."

"It's not nothing. What are you so sour about?"

"The night guards on the Sunfall Gate," said the guard at last.

"And what about them?"

"They are derelict in their duty if a single coin sways them to conspire with you," Joslyn said. "It presents a breach in security that endangers the entire palace."

Tasia laughed. "Why, because they have enough sympathy that they'll let an imprisoned teenage girl out to play now and again?"

"No."

"Then why?"

"Because if they let you in and out without reporting it up the chain of command," Joslyn said, "who else do they let in and out? What if your assassin was able to work with someone inside the palace due to the negligence of the exact same guards? What if you're not the only one who has bribed them?"

Tasia fell silent. "They are good men," she said after a moment. "They wouldn't do that."

Joslyn did not reply.

The palace was situated on a hill that sloped gently upward from the bay, and north of the palace, which was the direction in which Tasia and Joslyn now walked, the hill declined sharply.

Tasia glanced over her shoulder. Already, the palace behind them loomed large, towering authoritatively above the surrounding city streets. The further down the hill from the palace they traveled, the smaller and more cramped the buildings became. They'd already walked out of the northern edge of the tony Ambassador Quarter and were headed into the slightly seedier Merchant Quarter, a large, diverse district that housed traders and shopkeepers of every stripe, along with a number of taverns, inns, and brothels that served the sailors and other travelers who entered Port Lorsin by ship. From the docks southeast of the palace to the Merchant Quarter was only a short walk — even shorter for those who could afford a rickshaw or hired carriage.

The western side of Merchant Quarter was almost upscale, as it bordered the palace to the south and the Ambassador Quarter to the southwest. The eastern side was rougher, and it was towards the east that Tasia angled as they walked down the long hill.

"Do you have a destination in mind?" Joslyn asked beside her.

Tasia turned right down an alleyway, hopping over a pile of horse manure that she saw just in time. "Not particularly. A tavern where I can get good and drunk." She barked out a half-laugh.

"Is that… wise, Princess?"

"Stop pretending to be Norix," Tasia said. "I don't care if it's wise or not. It's all I can really handle right now."

Joslyn nodded.

The truth was that Tasia didn't even really care if they found a tavern. She was happy just to be outside the constricting walls of the palace, especially after the ups-and-downs of her strange day. The announcement of her trip to the east early in the afternoon; the argument with Mylla over her impending marriage early in the evening.

Mylla. The companion she thought she'd have for a lifetime. The one she'd first started sneaking out of the palace with two years ago. Tasia swallowed past a lump in her throat.

For the Princess, escaping into the city streets while the rest of the palace slept provided the kind of solace that some people received from walking along the shoreline, or meditatively watching a sunset. There was an intoxicating freedom — and peace — in her anonymity here, an anonymity she would lose soon, now that she was her father's heir.

"The first time I snuck out was with Mylla, two years ago," she said to Joslyn as they walked. "I was months away from my eighteenth birthday, and feared my father would force some marriage on me right away. I was so upset after he introduced me to the first suitor — a wealthy lord's son from the Central Steppes — that I locked myself in my chambers for a week and stopped eating. Mylla was the one who first made friends with the night guard. She brought me outside the palace walls in a blindfold, telling me she had a special surprise for me." Tasia smiled at the memory. But the smile, and now the memory, had turned bittersweet. She supposed that every memory she had of Mylla would be tinged with the tang of bitterness soon enough. "I cried when I saw she'd led me outside the palace walls — not unhappy tears, either, mind you. It was the first time I'd ever been out of the palace without a royal escort. I think I fell in love with Mylla in that very moment."

Tasia looked at Joslyn out of the corner of her eye, but the guard's eyes remained focused ahead of them, twitching back and forth as if trying to track each detail, each movement of the street ahead.

"Are you even listening to me?" Tasia asked.

"Of course I am."

"Then what did I just say?"

Joslyn stopped, ushering Tasia behind her as a cart pulled by an old, tired-looking donkey ambled by. "You said..." Joslyn began, and she proceeded to repeat everything Tasia had told her. Verbatim.

"So you do listen," Tasia said.

"Yes. Always."

Tasia groaned. "I should stop talking about Mylla. We need a place to drink." She grabbed Joslyn's wrist and tugged her across the street, heading for a street cast in shadow. "Come on. There's a place down this way — the Speckled Dog. The Sunfall Gate guards talk about it all the time, it's supposed to be a real dive. Filled with off-duty guardsmen and soldiers on leave from the war in the East. I've always wanted to go — to see where the ordinary soldiers drink, that is, not to the East." She shook her head and rolled her eyes. *"Gods.* I still can't believe my father is sending me."

"Going to the front is good," Joslyn said. "It will show the lords that you are more than a figurehead, a symbolic gesture by your father to maintain the locus of power within his own house. It shows you will rule."

"I never asked to rule," Tasia muttered.

"You never would've been happy being only the wife of the Emperor, either," Joslyn countered.

But Tasia was only halfway listening. "Look!" She pointed and grabbed Joslyn's arm, making the guard immediately tense beneath her grip. The sign above them depicted a crudely painted dog, with Xs for eyes and a tankard of ale next to it. There were no words on the sign.

But then again, many soldiers were like Joslyn — illiterate.

An arrow on the sign pointed downwards. Tasia found the top of a set of narrow, steep stairs and followed them down to a plain and windowless wooden door.

"I hope you like bad ale and watered-down whiskey," she said to Joslyn with a grin, and pushed the door open.

#

The Speckled Dog turned out to be every bit as seedy as Tasia had hoped. Every table, barstool, and lantern inside the dim basement tavern was coated with a layer of grime; every surface she touched left her fingertips with an unpleasantly sticky residue. But for Tasia, the unpleasantness itself was pleasant. Dirty and dark meant that for a few hours, she could pretend to be someone other than the Princess of the Four Realms, heir to Emperor Andreth.

And who should she be this evening? She was in her baker's girl costume, but maybe she could be someone else — a washerwoman or a chambermaid. Or perhaps a courier traveling to the capital city from abroad, bearing the letters of rich men writing their cousins in the capital. Maybe a courier who sometimes doubled as a trader, carting apricots from the Capital Lands to exchange for the coveted apa-apa wool that the desert tribes cultivated.

Yes. She would go with that. It would explain Joslyn's presence at her side — her traveling companion, a nomad hired for translation, guidance, and protection through the desert.

The sun was still in its last throes before giving in to night as Tasia and Joslyn walked through the tavern doors, but inside the underground room, it might as well have been midnight.

Tasia stopped just inside the doorway, surveying the space. Her imagination had painted the single-room tavern much larger when the guards had told her about it. The site of epic brawls as drunken sailors tried to prove their superiority to drunken soldiers, and of epic duels as two men fought over the same woman, the Speckled Dog had been huge in her mind. But now Tasia saw it was barely the size of Mylla's bedchamber, nothing more than a series of rough plank tables and stools arranged haphazardly on a dirt floor, with a door in the back of the room that presumably led into the kitchen. The whole place stank of fish and stale ale.

"Are ye going to move, or'm I needin' to push ye out of my way?" said a voice behind them, and Tasia turned to see a short, irritated fat man, with far more hair lining his cheeks and upper lip than his bald head.

"Apologies, sir," Tasia said, stepping quickly out of the way.

He gave her an odd look as he moved past, and Tasia realized her words had been far too formal for a place like this. A muttered "sorry" would've been more than sufficient.

"Let's sit," she said to Joslyn.

They wound through the maze of tables and stools until

they came to a spot near the back, close to the kitchen. It was early yet, with only the two of them, the fat man, and three other patrons in the tavern, but Joslyn's dark eyes darted from side to side before she sat down anyway. She chose a spot with her back to the wall, and as soon as she sat, her hand slipped under her over-large tunic. Tasia guessed that the guard was fingering the hilt of her sword, which made the Princess realize that in her haste to leave the palace, she'd forgotten to strap the dagger Joslyn had given her beneath the baker's girl dress. Although she'd only started to wear it recently, its absence made her feel oddly naked.

Tasia waved the serving girl over to them. "Two ales and… what do you have to eat?"

"Salted pork and wild onion soup tonight," the girl said, managing to sound both sleepy and mildly annoyed by the appearance of the new customers.

Tasia wrinkled her nose. It sounded awful.

"We'll both take a serving," she said.

"It's three coppers a piece," the girl said. "One for each ale, two for each dinner."

Tasia nodded, but the girl didn't head for the kitchen.

"What?" Tasia asked.

"You pay in advance," the girl said.

Tasia reached into her riding boot and fished out a silver penny from the pouch she'd tucked inside. She could feel the royal ring in there, too, the one she always carried, just in case, when she left the palace for her adventures.

She set the silver coin on the table. "I don't have any

coppers. Will this do?"

The serving girl's eyes widened, and she looked from the coin to the Princess as if perhaps someone was playing a joke on her. "We — I don't know if we have enough coppers to give you the difference."

Tasia shrugged. "Open a tab for us. I'm sure we'll drink more before the night is through. You carry whiskey, don't you?"

The girl nodded, her eyes still bug-sized.

"Then bring us some whiskeys after our meal. That should use up a few more coppers, shouldn't it?"

The girl picked up the silver coin from the table and held it to her lips, giving Tasia one more glance before she bit down hard on it. She pulled it from her mouth and inspected the bite mark.

Sounding considerably cheerier, she said, "I'll be right back with your meals and your ale."

"Good," Tasia said. The girl turned to leave, and on impulse, Tasia reached out and smacked her bottom. The Princess cackled with delight when the girl scurried away, shooting the stranger with the silver coin a surprised backward glance.

When the girl disappeared into the kitchen, Joslyn leaned forward and lowered her voice. "We're attracting too much attention as it is. Don't make it worse."

"Too much attention? No one's even in here."

"Not quite no one," said the guard. Her gaze shifted, looking beyond Tasia as she scanned the room. "The sailor behind you saw you slap the girl on her rear. The fruit merchant to his left made note of the silver penny in your boot. And the Imperial soldiers playing darts heard you ask for the whiskey."

Tasia turned around. She saw the men playing darts, another talking to the companion beside him, a spoon poised above his bowl, and the fat man who'd told them to get out of his way. The latter glanced away as soon as he saw Tasia looking at him, picking up his tankard of ale.

"How do you know what they are — sailor or fruit merchant or soldier?"

"Because," Joslyn said patiently, "the bald man has blackberry stains on his fingertips — I noticed them when he walked past us at the entryway. And since it's too early in the season for blackberries here, he must have bought them rather than picked them. The soldier in the corner is wearing the standard issue boots of the Imperial Army. And I could smell the sea coming off the sailor as we passed him."

The serving girl reappeared then, setting down a tray of food and ale between the Princess and the guard.

"So what brings ye to Port Lorsin?" she asked as she distributed the food.

"Just passing through on our way to the Central Steppes," Tasia said with a practiced ease.

The girl made a face. "It'll be cold up there. They say spring doesn't arrive on the steppe until Mother Moon is halfway through her fourth cycle."

Tasia grinned. "That's what we're hoping for. We're bringing apa-apa wool from Terinto to sell. It's the best wool in the world for blocking out the wind." She turned towards Joslyn. "Isn't that right, Jos?"

Joslyn nodded wordlessly.

The girl put her hands on her hips and studied the guard a moment before turning back to Tasia. "Your friend isn't very talkative, then? Does she speak the common tongue?"

"Some," Tasia said with a shrug. "When she wants to. She understands more than she lets on."

The girl glanced at Joslyn again. "Lucky you. Traveling all this way with a fine specimen of a nomad woman to keep you warm when that desert sun goes down."

"The apa-apa wool keeps me warm, not the nomad," Tasia said.

"If you say so," said the girl, and she winked at the Princess before turning back towards the kitchen.

Tasia giggled, pleased with her on-the-spot storytelling. "Did you see that? My slap on the bottom worked. She's flirting with me to see if she can earn a little more of that silver coin! And checking along the way to see if you and I..." she pointed back and forth across the table between herself and the guard. "To see if we were... more than just traveling companions."

Joslyn cocked an eyebrow. "That's what you're hoping for? A serving girl to take your mind off Mylla?"

"What's wrong with that?"

"Nothing," Joslyn said. "But in the army we used to have a nickname for girls who spread their legs quickly for any soldier with a bit of coin to spend."

"What? Whores?"

"No. Saddle burners."

"Saddle burners?"

"For the inevitable rash that would develop after a night with her. Would make riding on his horse rather uncomfortable." She lifted a shoulder. "Or her horse, as the case may be."

Tasia leaned forward across the table. "What, you have personal experience?"

Joslyn said nothing, just raised both eyebrows with a small smirk and sniffed her ale before taking a sip.

"You're so infuriatingly... mysterious." Tasia sighed. "But I suppose you're right. About the serving girl, at least." She picked up her ale and gulped down a mouthful. "Gods be good!" she exclaimed. "This tastes like donkey piss!"

Joslyn chuckled. "Can't say I've ever tasted donkey piss."

"Well, it sure isn't palace wine."

"What palace might that be, my dears?" asked the dart player Joslyn had identified as an Imperial soldier. He had sauntered over and now rested his palms on the edge of the table. "They building palaces in Terinto these days? What do they build it from? Apa-apa dung?"

Joslyn stiffened, one hand automatically dropping beneath the table.

But Tasia turned to the soldier with a broad grin. "Oh, no, of course not. Still not any palaces in the desert. To the south, though — have you ever crossed the Gulf of Adessia and visited the Adessian Islands? Most magnificent palaces in the known world."

"Is that right?" asked the soldier. "And how would you know — did they invite the two of *you* in for a drink?"

"Something like that," Tasia said. "We're friendly with a silk merchant there, and *he* is close to a tailor, and the tailor works for one of the island kings. So we got an invitation to the palace to show the tailor our apa-apa wool."

"And what use does a king of an Adessian island have for apa-apa wool?" the soldier asked. "It never gets cold enough for frost in the Adessian Islands."

Tasia glanced at her guard, hoping the woman could think of something quickly.

"For when he travels to the port cities of Terinto to negotiate trade routes with the tribal elders," Joslyn said easily. "Desert nights are remarkably cold."

"Sounds like a tale I'd like to hear more of," said the soldier. "Are you two lovelies here by yourselves? I hope you'll let a poor old Emperor's soldier buy you a drink."

"An Emperor's soldier!" Tasia said. "How about that. We're the ones who should buy *you* a drink. Have you spent time in the East?"

"Spent time in the East?" The soldier laughed and held up his left hand, wiggling his thumb and first two fingers. The last two fingers were missing. "I didn't just 'spend time' there, lass. I left two of my fingers there to watch over the place until I got back."

Tasia reached around behind her and grabbed the stool

on her other side, dragging it around so the soldier could sit at the end of the table. "Now *that's* a tale I want to hear."

Joslyn watched her do it with a disapproving frown on her face.

18

"...and so then I said to the king, 'But that's what makes it *apa-apa* wool!'" Tasia lifted her overfull tumbler of whiskey at the same time to emphasize the punchline of her joke, and some of it sloshed over the rim, dripping down her fingers and onto the wooden table below.

The crowd of men gathered around her all laughed, and one of them — the fruit merchant, if Joslyn's assessment could be trusted — raised his own tumbler high.

"To the Silk King of Adessia!" he declared.

All the rest of them raised their own glasses and tankards. "To the Silk King!" they shouted in a broken chorus.

Everyone drank, and the ones with a stool to sit on around Tasia slammed their drinks down hard against the table when they finished. It was the fourth or fifth such round they'd shared together — Tasia had lost count — with more men joining them each time.

Tasia looked around at the faces of her new friends, her face flushed with alcohol and the stuffiness of too many bodies in too small a space underground.

"Another round?" she asked, lifting her empty tumbler.

"Another round!" the men agreed.

The serving girl, having heard the boisterous group

finish their latest toast, reappeared on the periphery. She looked both anxious and eager at the same time, Tasia thought. Anxious because everyone was getting so thoroughly sloshed, eager because she probably hoped there might be another silver in it for her and the Speckled Dog. And so, regardless of if she worried over how much the patrons had to drink, the girl reappeared with the clay whiskey jug a few seconds later, refilling all the empty tumblers.

Tasia pressed a third silver penny into her palm. "This should be enough for this round and another one, don't you think?" Tasia asked in a low voice.

The girl smiled, nodded, and scurried away, the silver disappearing between the folds of her skirt.

The only person who didn't look like she was having a good time was, of course, Joslyn. Tasia supposed she could understand why the guard refused any alcohol after her first few sips of ale with her meal, but she didn't understand why the woman had to be so *morose* about it.

Tasia reached across the table and squeezed the guard's forearm. "Don't look so glum, dear," she said. "I'm sure the Silk King will save you some mutton the next time we go."

"Save her some mutton?" asked a flabby man with a bulbous nose and stringy hair to Tasia's left.

She turned to look at him — and immediately wished she hadn't. He spun dizzily in her vision for a few seconds before she managed to blink him into solidity. When she did, she saw that he was grinning.

Hoping for another story from the great apa-apa merchant, Tasia realized.

"Ah, yes," said the Princess, swirling her whiskey in her tumbler. "There was mutton for dinner the last night we dined with him, but my traveling companion Joz here —"

"Which king of Adessia?" a deep, accented voice asked behind her.

Tasia gripped the table's edge, using it to stabilize herself before she turned to face the questioner.

Faces two rows deep flickered with shadows cast by the nearest lamp. All of them peered curiously at Tasia, waiting for her to answer the question.

"Who's asking?" she said.

"I am," said the same voice, except now the voice belonged to a mouth that was moving. A mouth with full lips proportioned just right, sitting above a square, chiseled jaw that had just the lightest coating of yesterday's beard on it.

What a beautiful specimen of a man, Tasia thought through her fog of whiskey.

"And just who are you?" she asked, mainly because she wanted to see the mouth move again.

"I am Yurick, son of Yuros," the mouth said. The owner of the mouth took a step closer to Tasia, and now the lamplight revealed straw-colored hair above sea-blue eyes. A beautiful specimen, indeed. "And I am a sailor for King Terin the Great, King of Bird Isle, King of Sandtree Isle, Protector of the Calsin Channel. So I ask again, who was this King of Adessia who you see fit to make the butt of your crude jokes?"

The men around him shrank back into the shadows a few paces, sensing trouble.

Even drunk, Tasia sensed it, too.

She tried to laugh it off. "Oh, not *your* king, good Yurick. We were nowhere near the Calsin Channel."

"Then where were you?" he asked.

Tasia waved her hand dismissively even as she searched her sluggish mind for some facts about the Adessian Islands that would help her escape the trap she'd laid for herself. "We were somewhere far more remote. The easternmost islands. Very small."

"The Calsin Channel *is* between the easternmost islands," Yurick said. "Are you insulting my king, or just lying to all of us?"

Whether through dumb luck or carefully planned luck, the serving girl graciously chose that moment to return with the whiskey jug.

"Another round, miss?" she asked.

"Who wants another round?" Tasia called.

A chorus of happy cheers answered her.

"Fill everyone up again!" Tasia said. When every glass was filled, she lifted her tumbler towards the newcomer from Adessia. "To Yurick, son of Yuros," she said loudly. "And to his king, Terin the Great. Long may he reign!"

"Long may he reign!" the crowd chanted, and they drank.

But Yurick, son of Yuros, did not drink. Instead, he

took another step closer to Tasia and turned his tumbler upside down, pouring the amber liquid onto the dirt floor at Tasia's feet. A murmur of discontent rolled like a wave through the crowd of drunken men.

"That's no way to respond to generosity," Tasia said.

"And calling a king of Adessia a buffoon is no way to speak about your betters," Yurick said icily. "I don't even think you're an apa-apa merchant. I don't think you know the first thing about Adessia — I doubt you've ever even been to sea."

The murmurs grew louder.

"Who are you?" Yurick asked. "Who are you really?"

Tasia's heart picked up speed, and despite all she'd had to drink, her throat felt unusually dry when she swallowed.

"It's as I said before, my new friend," she said, doing her best to maintain her composure. "My friend and I are simple traders who've had a run of good luck with apa-apa wool. Nothing more."

Yurick reached for something at his waist, and much to Tasia's dismay, she heard the distinct sound of a metal blade coming free from a leather sheath. The sailor of Adessia held the dagger before him.

"Know what I think, girl?" he said. "I think you're nothing more than common scum, a highwaywoman who robs the honest, hardworking traders who travel to the capital to sell their wares. I think you and your friend here robbed some poor merchant and took his coin." His sea-blue eyes grew wide and furious. "We drink from blood money!" he shouted. *"Blood money!"*

Tasia flinched when Yurick threw his empty tumbler to the ground. The cheap glass shattered immediately, spraying shards in all directions.

In a flash, Joslyn was on her feet. She'd sat across from Tasia in quiet, judgmental silence the entire evening, but now she moved with a speed and grace Tasia hadn't even realized she was capable of. In what seemed impossibly fast to Tasia, Joslyn came around the end of the table and placed herself between Yurick and the Princess.

"You will return your blade to its sheath," the guard said, her back to Tasia.

"Why?" Yurick said with a sneer. "So you can rob me, too?"

A mixture of emotions buzzed through the crowd. Some voices sounded alarmed. Others were hostile, but Tasia couldn't tell for certain to whom that hostility was directed. At her, the one who'd been buying them drinks all night and entertaining them with wild stories? Or at Yurick, for disturbing the peace?

Maybe at both of them.

She glanced around at the faces surrounding her — and wasn't encouraged by what she saw. Some of the men she'd been drinking with over the past hour glared at Yurick. But more of them were glaring at her. She supposed she understood why; most of these men were hard-working shopkeepers, merchants, sailors, and soldiers. If indeed she was nothing more than a highway robber woman, then these same men would be her most likely victims.

Which would make it a cruel, twisted bit of humor if she were to use what she'd allegedly stolen in order to buy the same men drinks.

"I'm no thief!" Tasia shouted above the rumble of voices.

"What was the Silk King's name?" a man called out from somewhere in the crowd.

"He was — his name was — I don't remember," Tasia said, desperately trying to break through her alcohol-induced fog to come up with the name of any island king other than King Terin. She knew them. She *knew* she knew them; Norix had made her memorize them all once, two or three years ago.

"You met a *king* and don't remember his name?" said another voice. "If I ever met a king, you can believe I wouldn't forget him anytime soon."

"Put the dagger back into its sheath," Joslyn said again to Yurick. "Do it now, while you still have the chance."

"Men of Adessia defend what is ours," Yurick recited, widening his stance and shifting the dagger from one hand to the other. "We sail the Southern Seas, we dance beneath the stars, we make our riches near, we make our riches far."

"Put the blade away!" someone yelled.

"Stop him!" someone else shouted.

"Stop *him?*" said an answering voice. "What about her? Name the Silk King!"

"Name the Silk King!" several voices said together.

Out of the corner of her eye, Tasia saw the serving girl. She peered around the corner from the open doorway of the kitchen. Then the door closed, and Tasia heard a lock slam home.

"Stand up, thief, and pay for your crimes," Yurick said to Tasia.

"I'm not a..." but the word *thief* was drowned out by several cries of "Stand up!"

Yurick lunged for Tasia, making a grab for her long hair with the hand that didn't hold the knife.

In a swirling blur of sand-colored apa-apa wool, Joslyn's blade flashed. Yurick cried in pain.

His dagger clattered to the floor and he clutched the hand that had been headed towards Tasia a moment before. Blood seeped out between his fingers. His hand dangled in an unnatural, stomach-churning way.

"You bitch!" he spat at Joslyn. He glanced down at the blood pooling at his feet, face filled with shocked fear and agony. "I can't move my hand," he said to the restless crowd. *"I can't move my hand!"*

"Kill the thieves!" someone bellowed.

"Kill them!"

Joslyn's voice rang clear above the growing din. "I severed the tendon that connects this man's wrist to his hand. I will do the same to the next man who moves against us."

For a few seconds, the crowd shuffled uncomfortably. A couple of men near its outer edge melted away into the far shadows of the tavern. Apparently at least some of them seemed to take Joslyn's threat seriously.

But then, like an ocean wave breaking against the

shore, their collective discomfort broke.

"Get her!" yelled a man beside Yurick.

Three men at three different points in the crowd lunged for Joslyn simultaneously, but the desert nomad danced out of the way with ease, her palace guard's short sword in one hand, her dagger in the other. They both glinted in the lamplight, silver tongues flashing like lightning in a dark sky as Joslyn parried and dodged and sliced.

Tasia hunched lower on her stool, wondering if she should try to run for the door even as she found herself too paralyzed to move. Men surged forward from all sides now, but Joslyn or one of her blades always managed to stay between Tasia and the next attacker.

Then the Speckled Dog broke into sheer chaos.

Barstools flew through the air, tables were overturned, ale and whiskey flooded the dirt floor. Everywhere, men shouted — at each other, at Yurick, at Tasia, at Joslyn. The initial reason behind the fighting seemed to have lost its relevance; no one called out *"Thief!"* or *"Get them!"* any longer. They all seemed to fight simply for the sake of fighting.

Tasia shrieked when someone grabbed her wrist, then realized it was Joslyn. The guard hauled Tasia to her feet and shoved her forward through a gap in the crowd. Joslyn cleared a path for the two of them, her short sword hacking left and right like a machete cutting through jungle overgrowth. The fat fruit merchant crashed into Tasia a moment later, but thanks to Joslyn's swift twist on Tasia's dress, the Princess disentangled herself from the merchant before he fell to the ground, knocking over two more men like bowling pins as he went.

Joslyn pushed Tasia ahead of her, the hilt of her dagger pressing into the small of Tasia's back while the short sword continued to leap from side to side. The blade bobbed up and down so quickly that it almost looked to Tasia as if it moved of its own accord.

The Princess focused her attention on reaching the door, the Speckled Dog's only entrance and exit. If she could open that door and escape up the narrow stairs to the street above them, this nightmare could still prove a short-lived mishap. She reached out, stretching towards the door's rope handle.

A man's face suddenly appeared an inch from hers. The mouth split into an angry gash, revealing a row of broken, yellow-and-brown teeth.

"Thief!" he shouted, and flecks of whiskey-tainted spittle sprinkled onto Tasia's cheeks like light raindrops.

He grabbed the neck of Tasia's dress, and without thinking, she lifted one riding boot and stomped down hard on his foot. The man cried out in pain and surprise, stumbling backwards and tripping on the two men behind him.

It looked as if all those hours training on the beach with Joslyn had paid off, after all.

Tasia grasped the door handle and flung it open.

She turned to tell Joslyn that she'd succeeded in opening the door, but the guard already seemed to know it had been opened. Joslyn wrapped an arm around Tasia's waist and, with one final kick into the chest of a man brandishing a grease-coated steak knife, scooped the Princess off her feet and charged up the stairway.

Joslyn didn't stop or set the Princess down when they reached the street. Still holding the Princess against her like an overlarge child, she sprinted up the street a full block, ducking into an unlit alleyway a minute later.

Only then did she set Tasia onto her feet.

"Are you hurt?" Joslyn asked, panting.

Tasia, who was still drunk but sobering quickly, hadn't actually had the time to consider if she was hurt or not. She looked down at her body with surprise, as if only just remembering she had one. She didn't seem to be in pain, but she patted herself down in a rapid inspection anyway, yanking her hand back from her midsection when it encountered the wet, sticky warmth of blood.

Had she been cut after all?

She rubbed her finger and thumb together, looking up at Joslyn with startled eyes. "There's blood on me," she said. Then the Princess saw the gash in the apa-apa tunic Joslyn wore, and realized the blood was not her own. "Joslyn! You're bleeding."

The guard looked down. "Yes. It's not deep."

"We must dress your wound," Tasia said, lifting Joslyn's apa-apa tunic and the linen shirt below.

The guard was right; the cut was long but not deep — a shallow, dark red swath contrasting against Joslyn's bronze skin. It clearly wasn't the first such injury she'd had; her entire flank was crisscrossed with white scars, along with a particularly thick scar that ran almost vertically down her side, like a seam.

Joslyn hastily pushed her tunic back down. "I'm fine," she said, voice gruff. "We need to get back to the palace."

"Yes," Tasia said, still thinking about the map of scars she'd seen on her guard's skin. "Alright."

She let Joslyn lead the way. Guard tugged Princess forward by the wrist at a rapid clip as they traversed from alley to alley, staying off the main streets as much as possible. Gullies of sewage, dilapidated homes, and shuttered shops passed in a blur. The narrow alleys they traveled had no lamps, and the sun had fallen hours ago, giving them only the dimmest of light to navigate by. Had Tasia been leading the way, especially given her drunken state, she surely would've gotten lost within the first five minutes. That, or tripped over some unseen obstacle and fallen face-first into the sewage water. But Joslyn, who as far as Tasia knew hadn't even lived in Port Lorsin until she was assigned to be the bodyguard of the Princess, hurried through the dark city with the same easy assuredness as a mountain goat would navigate a cliff face.

Or the assuredness an apa-apa would navigate a sand dune.

"I'm sorry your tunic got ripped," Tasia slurred from behind the guard. Her feet moved on their own accord, as if Joslyn had somehow automated them. Nevertheless, she stumbled every few yards, sometimes because the guard was pulling her along too quickly, sometimes because she'd tripped on some piece of refuse. But the guard quickly righted Tasia each time before she could fall.

"It's not a tunic," Joslyn said without turning around. "It's called a *brizat*, which makes it more cloak than tunic."

"Briz... *at,*" Tasia repeated, trying to imitate Joslyn's accent. "Wouldn't it be hot to wear so much apa-apa wool in the des — "

"Your Highness, with all due respect, I would prefer that we keep our talking to a minimum until we are safely within the palace walls."

"Tasia," the Princess mumbled. "I'm just Tasia."

She'd really made a mess of things this time, hadn't she? All she'd wanted was to be someone else for a while, to forget about her father and the council and the Empire and the War in the East and the assassination attempt and Mylla's imminent abandonment. It wasn't so wrong to want to escape all that, was it? Anyone else in her situation...

She could almost hear Mylla laughing in her ear. *"You're the Princess of the Four Realms,"* she'd say. *"Soon to be the most powerful woman in the Empire. Why are you complaining?"*

"Because I don't want to be anyone special," Tasia muttered under her breath. "I want to be Tazy, the apa-apa merchant, who travels to the Adessian Islands and meets with the Silk King and has adventures."

Joslyn glanced over her shoulder. "Did you say something?"

"No," Tasia said.

The toe of Tasia's boot slipped on something wet, and

she toppled forward, crashing into Joslyn's back. The guard twisted quickly, catching her and setting her upright again.

"Are you alright?" Joslyn asked. She winced just a little as she spoke. Just a small wince. But Tasia noticed these things in her guard now.

"I am," Tasia said. "But what about you? How is your wound?" She reached for the hem of the *brizat*, but Joslyn pulled away. Tasia saw that the blood stain seemed to be spreading.

"There's nothing I can do about it until we get back to the palace, Princess."

"Tasia. *Please* just call me Tasia."

Joslyn nodded and, with a gentle pull on Tasia's wrist, she resumed her trek towards the palace.

19

"Please don't report what happened tonight to Cole or to my father," Tasia said when they at last made it back to her chambers.

Joslyn hesitated, one hand on the door to the antechamber. "Reporting an incident in which your life was in danger is my duty. It is why your father pays me."

"So that's all I am to you?" Tears threatened, but Tasia had cried enough for one day, and she swallowed them back. "After all the time we've spent together, I'm still just a spoiled princess you have to watch. Just a duty. I suppose that's fair. All I've done is make your life difficult. Even when you've been trying to help me."

Joslyn looked at her for a long moment, like she was trying to come to a decision. "I said it's my duty to report what happened," she said at last. "I didn't say I would."

Tasia sighed with relief. And not just relief that her father wouldn't find out about the night's mishap. Relief that Joslyn cared enough about her that she wouldn't say anything. She *wanted* Joslyn to care about her, wanted the guard to think of her as more than just an assignment.

"How is your cut?" Tasia asked. "I can send for Wise Man Evrart to tend to it for you. He has a gentle hand — and steadier than Norix's."

"I don't require the Wise Man's help. I can mend it myself."

"Alright." She paused, trying to form an acceptable apology in her head. "I'm so sorry you got hurt. Truly. I shouldn't have... I should've listened to you, Joslyn. I shouldn't have attracted such a crowd."

Joslyn opened the door to the antechamber. Tasia moved to go inside, but was stopped by a hand on her shoulder.

"Wait, Tasia."

She turned, observing some sort of emotion playing across Joslyn's face. The Princess felt hope rise in her chest, although hope for what, she couldn't say. "What?"

The emotion disappeared. "I need to inspect your chambers first."

"Oh."

Tasia waited by the antechamber door while Joslyn went through her regular inspection.

"Is Mylla back yet?" Tasia said when Joslyn returned.

Joslyn shook her head.

"I see." She bent to unbuckle her boots, hoping to hide the disappointment on her face.

"Tasia...?" Joslyn said haltingly.

"Yes?"

"I am sorry that the handmaid will be... leaving you so soon."

Tasia's eyes welled with tears, but she still refused to let them fall. "Thank you, but of course it will be fine. I always knew she would leave sooner or later."

Joslyn nodded. "Sleep well."

"I will try," Tasia said. "You, too."

But her bed felt cold and empty without Mylla there to warm it. Why had she fought with the girl earlier?

Maybe Mylla was right. Maybe Tasia was inexcusably selfish, only ever thinking of her own feelings, her own wishes, her own laments. Hadn't she proven so tonight? First fighting with Mylla, then nearly getting herself and Joslyn killed at the Speckled Dog just because she'd wanted booze and entertainment.

She always had to be the center of attention, didn't she? No matter what it cost others.

She sighed, rolling over in the too-large bed. She ran her hand down the spot that Mylla usually occupied. But no. No more feeling sorry for herself over the Lady Mylla of House Harthing. She was to be the Empress soon. How silly for an Empress to cry over a girl who had always been destined to leave her anyway.

What would Nik say, if he were here to see her now?

"You never wanted the crown," she whispered into the dark, to a Nik who was not there. "But what made you think *I* wanted it?"

Tasia rolled to her other side. She missed them so much, her brother and mother. Losing one of them would have been hard, but bearable. But to lose both of them? Nik had been her anchor in the world, her counterpoint. He'd balanced her. Now that he was gone… and Mylla was leaving…

Lamplight flickered in an uneven pattern beneath the

closed door to the antechamber. It had to be Joslyn still moving about, as the light was too strong to be coming from the lamp near the outer door.

Tasia watched the light for a minute, eyelids growing heavy. But a soft, muffled moan coming from the other side of the door startled her back into alertness again.

Cautiously, gently, worried that she was intruding despite the fact that the room technically belonged to her and not the guard, Tasia climbed out of bed and pushed open the door that led into the antechamber.

A dim lamp burned low at the far end of the room in its normal place beside the door. A brighter lamp burned to Tasia's left, illuminating from within the rice paper screens that cordoned off Joslyn's corner from the rest of the antechamber.

Another quiet sound came from the other side of the rice paper screens, this one more a grunt than a moan. Tasia could see the guard's misshapen shadow against the screen.

"Joslyn?" Tasia said.

"Yes?" The guard's voice sounded strained.

"Are you alright?"

"I will be."

Tasia hesitated, taking a step closer to the screen. It hardly constituted a wall; if she wanted to, she could use the tip of her finger to puncture any of the squares of paper before her.

"May I come around the screen?" Tasia asked.

There was no answer for a moment. Then: "If you

wish."

Tasia slipped through the gap between the screen and the wall and into Joslyn's private space.

The guard sat sideways on her cot, bare from waist up except for rough-looking cloth bindings wrapped tightly over her breasts. The gash Tasia had seen earlier looked red and angry in the lamplight. It was much longer than Tasia had realized, running horizontally across Joslyn's ribcage, then taking a sharp upward turn and terminating just below the breast bindings.

And this vertical part of the cut beneath her right arm seemed to be the source of the moaning, as it still seeped blood from the top. A candle burned in the center of a small table before Joslyn; the rest of its surface was littered with blood-soaked rags. The guard held a needle over the candle flame.

"Mother Moon," Tasia said. "You sewed it up yourself?"

No wonder the guard had been moaning. Tasia took a half-step forward, bending closer to examine the wound. Messy stitches had already closed the horizontal part. The vertical segment, though... how was Joslyn going to reach it?

Black eyes flickered over to the Princess before returning to the candle flame. Joslyn pushed hair behind her ear, the movement making her wince.

"Usually only Wise Men are permitted to treat a wound like this one," Tasia said.

"Most of the soldiers in the Imperial Army eventually

learn how to sew closed their own wounds. Wise Men are… not always available on a battlefield."

The Princess sat down on a stool beside the cot. "You're not going to be able to reach the last part."

Joslyn didn't reply.

"I will go fetch one of the Wise Men," Tasia said, rising to leave.

"No," Joslyn said quickly. "I would prefer you didn't."

Tasia frowned. "Why?"

"I would rather handle it myself," the guard said, her eyes still on the needle above the flame.

"But you can't," Tasia said, flustered. "You won't be able to reach it."

Joslyn held up a dull pewter mirror, angling it to see the part of the wound she still hadn't stitched. "I've healed from much worse. Without needle and thread to help. If we fetch a Wise Man, I will have no choice but to explain how I received the injury."

The two met eyes, and Tasia wrestled with the decision. Was protecting her secret from her father really worth Joslyn's suffering?

"It doesn't matter," Tasia said, her decision made. She rose from the stool. "I'm going to get Wise Man Evrart."

"No," Joslyn said again. This time, her voice was as commanding as the Emperor's ever had been. And as if ordered by her father, Tasia sank back into the stool.

Under the orange glow of the lamp hanging above the cot, with her muscled torso bare, Tasia realized the guard had even more scars crisscrossing her body than she'd originally realized. Her back, in particular, was a mess of long, thick scars. Tasia recognized those kinds of scars. They were the kind that could only come from the lash of a whip, flaying open the skin.

She watched as Joslyn threaded the needle. Once threaded, the guard twisted to get to the wound — and immediately a barely audible whimper of pain escaped her throat.

Tasia couldn't stand it any longer. "You have to let me help."

"I can reach if I just — "

"That is a *command,* Joslyn. Now give me the needle and thread."

The guard studied the Princess for a moment, then handed her the instruments. "Hold it at the bottom," she said of the needle. "The rest is too hot to touch."

Tasia took the needle and twisted it right and left to get a better look. "I'm better with a needle than you might guess. I sewed tapestries when I was younger — it was a part of my art tutoring. Many of the tapestries around the palace were sewn by royal women. Art is one of the only acceptable pastimes for princesses and empresses, you know."

But Joslyn didn't seem to be listening. She rooted through a small wooden box beside her, searching for something. She produced what appeared to be a handful of scraggly dried weeds. "Press pinches of this into each part of the wound before you stitch it closed."

Tasia reached for the weed, and it broke off easily in

her fingers. "What is it?"

"Moss. A special type that grows in the foothills of the Zaris Mountains, at the northern border of Terinto. It helps wounds heal quickly and prevents infection."

Tasia looked skeptically from the dried moss in her fingers to the ugly, half-bleeding wound. "I don't want to hurt — "

Joslyn put her fingers around Tasia's own, wincing once more as she guided Tasia's hand towards the wound. Then she pressed Tasia's fingers into the open cut. "Like that," she said, almost breathless. "Then sew that part closed, then add more moss and sew the next part."

Tasia took a breath, bringing the needle close to the cut. Sewing a festive tapestry of hunters and huntresses on a fox chase and sewing closed another person's skin were not the same thing at all. Her stomach twisted, and she wished she hadn't had so much to drink.

"Please, Tasia. The needle is easier to bear when it goes quickly."

"Alright," she said, and Tasia clenched her teeth as she punctured Joslyn's skin with the hot needle.

A few stitches later, she reached for more moss.

"You started to tell me earlier about the man the tinkers sold you to when you were eleven," Tasia said, hoping to distract both the guard and herself from the gruesome task at hand.

"I did not start to tell you anything about the man who bought me," Joslyn said brusquely.

Tasia hadn't expected the sharp retort. "You don't wish

to speak about him — the man who bought you?"

"No."

Tasia held the needle over the candle, turning it several times in the flame. "He was the one you ran away from, then?"

"Yes."

The guard clenched her jaw and looked into the distance. Tasia added two more stitches.

"How old were you? When you ran away?"

"Fourteen."

"Where did you go? Is that when you joined the Imperial Army?" But as soon she asked, Tasia realized it wouldn't have been possible. The Imperial Army's minimum age was sixteen. Besides, the guard had told Tasia and Mylla that the recruiter came to her village not long after she turned seventeen.

"No," the guard said. "I went north."

"Ah — and that's when you ended up in the Zaris Mountains."

"Yes. It's where I met my *ku-sai.*"

Tasia added another stitch. The guard's tone made it clear that she didn't want to talk about her past. And now was as good a time as any for Tasia to practice not being the selfish, privileged princess Mylla had accused her of being.

Tasia sewed the last three stitches in silence, artfully tying off the last one before leaning back and inspecting her work with satisfaction.

"There," she said. She took the cleanest rag she could

find from the table and pointed at a jug on the floor. "Is that clean water? I thought I would wipe off the dried blood from your side."

"You don't need to — "

"I do need to, Joslyn. This is my fault. Hand me the jug."

Joslyn reached down, her face tightening with the effort. "It's not water. It's Terintan whiskey."

Tasia laughed. "All this time you had whiskey in your room? You are full of surprises, Guard. We could've just gotten drunk in your room tonight instead of going to the trouble of causing a fight at the Speckled Dog."

Joslyn didn't smile. "I don't keep it for drinking. Terintan whiskey is much stronger than what they have here. It's used for cleaning wounds as often as it's drunk."

Tasia nodded and wet the rag, then touched it gingerly to the top of Joslyn's wound. She worked her way down carefully, noting the spot where her neat, even stitches gave way to Joslyn's jagged, messier ones.

The sight of the stitches sent a wave of guilt through Tasia.

"I'm a disappointment to the House of Dorsa," she said. "A disappointment to the entire Empire. I'm sorry this happened to you. It's all my fault."

"You don't need to apologize," Joslyn said, her tone softening. "You were upset. All of us are capable of rash decisions when we are upset."

"Including you?"

Joslyn took a moment to answer. "My *ku-sai* taught me

how to stop being rash."

Tasia let out a half-laugh. "Perhaps you should introduce me to him. I could use someone who could teach me not to be rash."

She added more Terintan whiskey to the rag and dabbed the bottom half of Joslyn's wound. Both women were silent for a few seconds, each apparently lost in their own thoughts.

"Thank you," Joslyn said. "For helping me. You were right — I wouldn't have been able to stitch the rest of it on my own."

"'It is a commoner's duty to serve the highborn,'" Tasia recited, quoting from a tome written by an early Wise Man on ethics and government. "'And it is the highborn's duty to protect and provide for the commoner.'"

Joslyn gave Tasia a weak grin. "The Empire has odd notions of service and protection."

"Then what do they say about service in Terinto?"

"Slaves serve masters; free people serve those they deem to be worthy."

"Do you deem me worthy, Joslyn of Terinto?" She'd meant the question lightly, playfully, but somehow it didn't come out that way. She found herself hoping that the guard would say *yes* despite everything.

Joslyn turned her head, dark eyes meeting the Princess's. Tasia's heart seemed to leap of its own accord, as if the guard's gaze had transferred an unexpected energy.

The guard searched Tasia's face for a moment, then she smiled. "I believe you have greater potential than anyone yet realizes. Including yourself."

"And what potential is that?"

"That is for you to discover." Joslyn held out her hand, and Tasia placed the whiskey-soaked rag and the needle in it. "It's late," the guard said. "We should both sleep."

"We should." Tasia rose from the stool and moved to leave. But then she stopped, turning back to face the guard. "Joslyn?"

"Yes?"

But once the guard met her eyes, Tasia was no longer sure what she wanted to say.

"Tomorrow, instead of sneaking out, let's play Castles and Knights again," she said at last. "I'm irritated that you keep beating me."

Joslyn smiled. "That sounds like an excellent idea."

20

Non-stop training.

The week leading up to Tasia's fact-finding mission to the eastern front was filled with non-stop training.

Mornings began before dawn with Joslyn, with Tasia creeping out of bed while Mylla still slumbered. After the night at the Speckled Dog, the Princess had apologized to her handmaid through tears for being such a spoiled brat; through her own tears, Mylla apologized to Tasia for not telling the Princess of her engagement to Umfrey sooner. With each of them set to leave the capital in a matter of days, Tasia forgave all. She cherished Mylla more than she ever had before, loved her more than she ever had before, and it seemed that Mylla did the same. And though they both promised that they would write long letters to one another every single week, Tasia suspected something was ending between them. Ending forever.

Tasia might've felt more sorrow over it if not for the fact that she was so busy. On the beach, as soon as the first orange-and-pink rays of sun bounced across the waves, she ran barefoot from one pile of stones to the next, transporting the rocks one by one until each pile disappeared from one side and reappeared on the other three times. Next came grappling, followed by parrying, thrusting, parrying, dodging with a dagger in each hand as Joslyn tried to find an opening with the heavy wooden practice sword.

Tasia had wanted to learn the sword, too, wanted to mimic the way that the guard could weave the long steel blade through the air like a snake, but it was still too heavy for her to wield easily, despite all the carrying of rocks.

"Besides," Joslyn said, hands on her hips while she caught her breath, "a dagger is easier to hide than a sword."

After the training session on the beach, Tasia broke her fast in the kitchens, sandy and sweaty, with the guard at her side. She slurped down her hot oats and milk with more appetite than she could ever remember having, but no matter how much she ate, the ropey muscles growing down her arms, around her middle, through her legs never seemed to soften. Some days, Tasia felt embarrassed for the new muscles; it seemed that every morning she looked less like a princess and more like the washer woman.

Or like a guard.

Joslyn didn't eat breakfast. She never ate until the noontide meal, though she didn't explain why. She took tea in the morning as Tasia ate, but not the tea Tasia was used to. Joslyn's tea was particularly strong, with a smoky scent to it that lingered around the guard for hours afterward.

"You're still breaking the line of your wrist on the forward thrust," the guard said one morning while Tasia helped herself to a second helping of hot oats.

Ever since the night Tasia sewed her wound closed, Joslyn was slightly more open and relaxed with the

Princess, but her primary topic of conversation remained self-defense.

"It's a good way to have the knife taken from you," Joslyn continued, "or to shatter your arm upon the blow." She tapped Tasia's forearm with one long finger.

The Princess looked down at the finger upon her arm. She swallowed her oats too quickly, scalding the back of her throat. "Can't you stop teaching long enough for me to eat my meal?"

It looked for a moment as if the guard might smile. But she didn't.

Tasia shook her head. "It's bad enough that Norix and old One-Leg drill me through two bottles of lamp oil on military operations every evening. 'How many men in a battalion?' 'How many in a division?' 'Describe how to execute a flanking maneuver.'" Tasia took another bite of oats.

"You really shouldn't call General Remington 'old One-Leg,' Tasia," was all Joslyn said in response.

Tasia waved her hand impatiently. "I know, I know. He was the greatest war hero of his generation. The difference between the Empire losing the Western Rebellion and winning it. Someone I should deeply respect, blah blah blah."

Joslyn chuckled, but she seemed pensive.

"What?"

The guard shook her head.

"I didn't think it was possible for you to grow more serious than you usually are anyway, but every day that we get closer to leaving for the front, your face becomes more stone-like than the day before," Tasia said. "What troubles you?"

Joslyn sipped her tea, let out a rare sigh. "We are headed to the Sunrise Mountains in less than a week, Princess," she said. "The tribes east of the mountains have been pouring over in such quantities that they overran an Imperial outpost and destroyed an entire battalion, razing villages along the way."

"So I've heard."

"I've fought in the East. The barbarians have never had enough men to route a battalion," Joslyn said. She took another sip of tea. "Perhaps I am troubled because we ride into a danger that makes little sense."

Tasia grinned. "Scared of a few mountain men? Or is it Lord M'Tongliss's talk of demons that has you upset?"

Joslyn shrugged, eyes taking on a far-away glaze.

Tasia glanced around the kitchen. She and Joslyn sat on tall stools at a rough-hewn table in the center of the hot, steam-filled room. A fire crackled in a large hearth to their right a few yards away, and one of the cooks, plump from sampling her own work for too many years, waddled over to it. She pulled a long-handled wooden spoon from a peg next to the fire and stirred one of the large cooking pots. The smell of the noontide meal — lamb in a citrus sauce — wafted towards them.

Besides the cook, who was occupied enough and far away enough that she wouldn't overhear them, Tasia and Joslyn were alone. Nevertheless, Tasia lowered her voice as she said to Joslyn, "I haven't felt safe since the night I was attacked. I think a part of me... I'm sure it sounds strange to you, seeing as how you've seen the horrors of battlefields first-hand, but... I think a part of me wants to go East to get away from whoever is trying to get me killed here."

"It's not strange. But there's nothing to say that whoever tried to kill you won't follow us East," she added cryptically.

Tasia took another bite of her hot oats while Joslyn sipped her smoky tea.

"Do you look forward to the journey?" Tasia said. "After all, we will be traveling through Terinto where the province touches the Zaris Mountains. That must be near your old village."

"It wasn't ever really 'my' village," Joslyn said. "It was the village nearest to where my *ku-sai* lived, so he sent me there for supplies once or twice per moon cycle. But I never thought of it as home."

Tasia hesitated. "How did you come to join the Imperial Army, Joslyn? I don't mean the story Mylla made you tell on the beach," she added quickly. "I only mean... It seems that you liked living with your teacher. And I know most nomads have little love for the Empire. So why leave your village? Why leave your teacher?"

"At the time, I believed I had learned all I could learn from him," Joslyn said. "I was young and hard-headed and wanted a chance to prove myself."

Tasia waited for the guard to say more, but when Joslyn

went back to sipping her tea, Tasia realized she would have to prod if she wanted more details. "Have you gone back to see him? Since joining the Imperial Army?"

"Once. But he wasn't there."

"Where did he go?"

Joslyn shook her head. "It's a long story, Tasia. One I do not believe you have time for."

She pointed at the candle mounted to the wall across from them. The pewter backing was marked with twelve even hashes, and the candle flame flickered beside the hash three-quarters of the way down.

"Nearly eight and a half of the clock!" Tasia exclaimed. "You should've hurried me along sooner." She stood from the stool and scooped the last bit of hot oats and milk into her mouth with little decorum. She'd already been late to her lessons with Norix once this week, and she didn't want another lecture on the importance of consistent punctuality from him.

#

On the day of Mylla's departure to the Northeast, where she would spend the last few months of her betrothment at House Farrimont before her eighteenth birthday, Tasia feigned the stomach cramps of her monthly blood in order to skip her lessons with the Wise Men and spend a little more time with her departing handmaid.

Her departing love.

Mylla was aflutter with nervous energy, packing and repacking gowns and trinkets into her three wooden chests. The day before, she'd cleaned out her bedchamber, emptying it of all the things Tasia had come to think of as marking it as distinctly Mylla's. The Western-style tapestries had come down from the walls, rolled up and stowed away in one of the three chests. The small cedar jewelry box, appropriately humble for a handmaid, and yet appropriately rich for a noblewoman, was also gone from its normal place atop Mylla's dresser, along with the small oval mirror which normally sat beside it.

Tasia lingered at the dresser, skimming one finger across its top, staring at the place where the missing box and mirror should've been.

Four years. For nearly four years they'd been... well, if not always lovers, then something significantly more complicated than princess and servant. From the time Mylla was fourteen and the time Tasia was fifteen. Before Mylla, Tasia had hardly had the confidence to touch her own body, let alone that of another.

She watched the handmaid — no, the Lady engaged to be married to a lord's heir — silently for a moment as Mylla pressed down on the dresses piled high in a chest. The handmaid looked up, blowing out a puff of air from cheeks red with strain and hurry.

"Tazy? Help me with this, will you?"

Tasia walked over to where Mylla still wrestled with the dresses inside the chest. At last they managed to force the lid closed, the two of them sat on top of it while Mylla snapped the brass latches down into place.

"There," she said, nearly breathless. She glanced at Tasia and smiled.

"I'm going to miss you," the Princess said.

Mylla grinned. "So you keep telling me. But I have no doubt that as soon as you get to the front, you'll find a handsome soldier or two to warm your tent at night. Then you'll forget all about Lady Mylla of House Farrimont."

House Farrimont. Lady Mylla, wife of Umfrey, of House Farrimont.

"We will be cousins soon," Tasia said.

Mylla leaned over, pecked Tasia on the cheek. "We shall. I will be the cousin of the Empress. I suppose it's as close to royalty as I will ever manage to come."

Tasia tried to return her lover's smile, but found she couldn't. She supposed she understood Mylla's obsession with furthering her House's position within the Empire; after all, advancement was the primary focus of most of the nobles she knew.

She sighed. In her mind's eye, as if from a bird's view, Tasia saw a sea of humanity covering a hill, with each man, woman, and child clamoring desperately to make it to the top. They crawled over one another like lice, with no regard for whom they crushed underfoot as they pushed their way closer to the crest.

And at the crest of the hill? What was there? What prize awaited them? Nothing. It was just the top of a hill, nothing more.

It was crush or be crushed, because there was no getting off the hill. Mylla understood that. But Tasia, because she had been born at the top of the hill, had never had to climb.

"What are you thinking about?" Mylla asked her.

Rather than answer the question, Tasia brushed the hair that had come loose from Mylla's bun off her cheek. The Princess leaned in, pressed her lips against Mylla's forehead. "Do something for me, Myll."

"What, sweet Princess?"

"When you have your first daughter, name her for me."

Mylla's eyes grew misty, and she laced her fingers with Tasia's. "Oh, Tazy. Of course I will."

They kissed goodbye a few minutes later.

Tasia couldn't have realized that when they met again it would be on opposite sides of a new battlefield.

Part II:

The East

"To the contemporary reader, as he considers the sequence of events that unfolded from the safe vantage point of thirty years after the end of the War in the East, the tragedy that unfolded within the Empire appears to be so undeniably obvious and inevitable that it seems the key players of the time — the Emperor Andreth, his chief Wise Man Norix, his war generals, and even the Princess Natasia herself — were as if willingly blind.

"'How could they not see what was right in front of their eyes?' cries today's reader. 'How could they not have acted sooner to avert what happened?'

"But what such a reader fails to realize is that, at that time, the facts as they presented themselves seemed entirely too preposterous to be facts at all. And so, rather than seeing the truth, those players mentioned previously could only see the warning signs in front of them as the most elaborate of fictions."

— Wise Man Tellorin, *The Updated Histories of House Dorsa*

21

Boredom, anxiety.

Anxiety, boredom.

It was the fifth day into their journey east, and when Tasia didn't feel one, she felt the other. Bored because, day after day, she spent every daylight hour jostled along a bumpy road in a stuffy carriage. Her arse was sore from all the bouncing; she sweated beneath her traveling clothes; and the constant movement made her seasick. On the first two days of their journey, she tried reading, but found the ever-rocking carriage nauseated her whenever she looked down at the page.

Norix and Joslyn shared her carriage, and the three of them talked sometimes.

Or more accurately, Joslyn and Tasia talked when Tasia could get the guard to string together more than a sentence at a time, while Norix often lectured for hours on end. Which meant that being inside the carriage with him was like being trapped inside an interminable lesson.

Occasionally, he would change carriages to ride with General Remington, where the two of them no doubt either argued nonstop about the Kingdom of Persopos or else conspired together on how to script exactly what Tasia would say when she visited the generals in the field.

"She's obstinate and childish," she could imagine Norix complaining. *"I don't know what the Emperor was thinking, naming her his heir."*

"And she still cannot accurately describe the difference between heavy cavalry and light," General Remington would answer.

They could both lecture her all they wanted to. She listened to Norix and Remington, but she didn't intend to follow their script. She had her own instincts, her own mind. Ultimately she was the one who'd be commanding these generals one day, not her two advisors. That was one of the pieces of advice her father had given her before she'd left:

"Always recognize the value of your advisors, and respect the wisdom they bring to the table. But also recognize their limitations," he said. *"Norix is the wisest of the Wise Men, that is certain, but I didn't choose you as my heir simply because I could be assured of your loyalty. I chose you because I believe your instincts are in line with my own."*

It was the kindest thing he had ever said to her in almost nineteen years of life, and similar to something Joslyn had told her almost a month before. Tasia was determined to prove them both right.

But there was also the anxiety.

At least her lifelong tutor's lectures provided her with some distraction. When he left her alone with Joslyn, sometimes they would attempt a game of Castles and Knights, but most of the time, they just stared out the carriage window at the passing landscape. It gave Tasia far too much time to dwell upon the task ahead of her.

Almost anything could happen once they arrived at the front in another ten days. She might be successful in her mission: She would talk to common soldiers, to officers and generals, bringing them words of encouragement, boosting their morale, and restoring their will to fight, all while Norix and Remington worked behind the scenes to find out the truth about General Telek and what was going wrong in the war.

But then again, she could just as easily fail. She could fail to inspire anyone. And Norix and Remington could fail to learn anything that would help them end the war once and for all.

She comforted herself by thinking that even if the mission failed to bring back anything new and valuable to her father, at least she was doing something useful for once. At least her father and the council knew she cared about the future of the Empire.

That counted for something… didn't it?

Anxiety. Boredom.

Boredom. Anxiety.

#

On a sunny mid-afternoon on the sixth day of the voyage, after a water and hay break for the horses and a short meal for the travelers, Norix excused himself to one of the other carriages and Tasia found herself riding alone with Joslyn once again.

She watched the guard across from her discretely, trying to think of a way to open a conversation. It wasn't really that she had a burning desire to converse with her guard as much as that she was terribly bored and conversation with Joslyn seemed as if it might be at least marginally better than conversation with Norix.

"Are we practicing with the daggers again tonight, before bed?" she asked after a minute or two, her mind finally seizing upon a topic she might be able to get the guard to discuss.

Joslyn pulled her attention away from the carriage window. "That was my intention."

"Ugh. I'm so *sick* of daggers," Tasia said, although it was a lie.

Joslyn lifted an eyebrow and looked away, turning her gaze back out the window.

Why couldn't Tasia simply admit the truth to Joslyn? Why couldn't she tell her that she actually liked dancing around the evening campfire every night with the twin blades in her hand? She felt strong when she carried the daggers Joslyn had given her. She felt powerful. She felt like the generals she would soon meet would be wrong to underestimate her.

So why not tell the guard that?

Tasia hesitated. "I'm sorry," she said. "The truth is that… I have been grateful for your service. And I'm probably the only Princess of Dorsa in all of history who's ever learned how to wield daggers in both hands. That makes me unique. Doesn't it?"

"Why did you agree to this mission?" Joslyn said instead of answering her question.

It was rather pert to ask, and it took Tasia a moment to decide if she would answer the question at all. But she'd learned to expect such occasional audacity from the guard, so she answered anyway.

"Because someone needs to boost the morale of the troops in the East, and who better to boost them than the Princess of the Four Realms," she said. Then she added, "And while I'm there, Norix and Remington will make a detailed analysis of the Empire's war efforts, get a better sense for the generals and their field commanders, and understand clearly what's been going wrong. Then we can report back to my father so that he can decide what best to do next."

Joslyn stared at her impassively, said nothing.

"What?"

The guard tilted her head to the side, studied Tasia for a long moment, and shook her head.

"What?" Tasia said again, irritated. "If you have something to say, Joslyn, just say it."

"Your father named you his heir," Joslyn said at last. "Not the Wise Man. Not the General. Yet you seem content to play the part of princess rather than ruler."

"What do you mean? I *am* the Princess. And I'm doing exactly what Father asked me to do," Tasia huffed.

"Are you sure about that?" said the guard. "He made you heir because he trusts your loyalty and your instincts.

He does not trust Norix, and his patience with General Remington has worn thin."

Tasia was taken aback. "I don't know what you're talking about. Norix and Remington are the two advisors he trusts the most."

The Princess waited for Joslyn to elaborate, but the guard only shrugged.

"He trusts Norix," Tasia said again.

"Why do you think so?"

"Because he's served my father since Father was younger than I am now," Tasia said, thinking the answer was obvious. "Since Father was Adela's age. And Norix served my father's father, too, when he was the Emperor. He's always served our family." She paused. "Why do you say my father doesn't trust him?"

"The Wise Man assumes too much familiarity with the Emperor sometimes," Joslyn said. "Your father encourages his advisors to speak their minds, but sometimes Norix speaks out of arrogance, and your father knows it. Arrogance is dangerous; it blinds us. That's why your father sent the Wise Man on this journey. To humble him."

"You seem to know a lot about Norix, for someone who's only been living at the palace for a month," Tasia said.

The guard didn't answer.

Tasia contemplated Joslyn's words, and at the same time recalled some of the meetings she'd attended in her father's office. Joslyn had a point, she realized. Norix was always angling for position, always trying to prove that his own viewpoint was the right one. And lately, what had his viewpoint been about? Always about proving the War in the East to be a bad investment for the Empire — a bad use of men, a bad use of funds, a bad use of time. Norix held to that view no matter what anyone else, such as General Remington, pointed out.

"Let me ask you something," Tasia said suddenly. "You've fought the barbarians. You've served on the front lines. What is your opinion of the war? Is it something the Empire should still be fighting?"

"I'm not your advisor, Tasia. Just your bodyguard."

"I know. But I still want to hear your opinion."

Joslyn drew a long breath, let it out slowly. "My opinion is… My opinion is that the war has changed in the past two or three years. The barbarians have changed."

"How so?"

"They used to fight us from shadows, in small bands of ten, fifteen raiders," Joslyn said. "They would find a way to attack our supply chain, or overrun a group of scouts, or steal horses while we slept. But a few years ago, that changed. The barbarians started to attack in bigger groups, using better weapons, with something that actually resembled strategy."

"Why did they change?" Tasia asked.

"I don't know," said the guard. "I am intrigued by General Remington's theory about the Kingdom of Persopos. Some of the weapons we found on dead barbarians certainly seemed to be of higher quality. But as the Wise Man Norix argues, it's also possible they acquired those weapons raiding merchant caravans or through trade."

Both women lapsed into silence. Joslyn shifted her position, leaning her head against the carriage window and closing her eyes. Tasia watched her sleep — or pretend to sleep — for several minutes before speaking again.

"You should be more than my bodyguard," she said. "You're much too smart to be just a guard or a foot soldier. You should be my advisor."

The guard's eyes opened. She regarded Tasia with dark eyes before finally saying, "No one would accept that. I'm just the illiterate ex-slave nomad who's good with a sword." Bitterness tinged her words.

"They'll accept it if I make them accept it," Tasia said.

"If it were a move in Castles and Knights, I would have recommended against it." The guard closed her eyes again. "I'm going to rest a while before we stop for the day. It will enable me to be more alert once night falls."

"Alright," said Tasia, trying to mask her disappointment.

But neither knew just how important the guard's alertness would be in a scant few hours.

22

"It's no use," Tasia told the guard. "It's too hard."

Joslyn shook her head. "You have mastered other techniques, Princess," she said patiently. "Remember the first time you attempted the double-parry?"

"Yes. My wrist was sore for a week."

"But you learned it," Joslyn said. Without warning, she thrust the blade of her short sword towards Tasia's abdomen. Acting on an instinct built from weeks of repeated practice, Tasia sidestepped and caught the oncoming blade inside the X of her crossed daggers.

Tasia blinked when she saw how easily and without thought she'd parried the blade and avoided the kill stroke.

"You could've stabbed me!" she shrilled.

Joslyn smiled. "No, I wouldn't have. I knew that you would block the blade."

"And if I hadn't?" Tasia said. "You would've impaled the Princess of the Four Realms just because you were trying to prove what a good teacher you are."

"I wasn't proving what a good teacher I am," said Joslyn. "I was proving what a good student you are."

"So you keep telling me," Tasia grumbled.

"And I wouldn't have impaled you, Princess."

Tasia sighed, rolling the dagger in her right hand across

her palm. She glanced behind them. A handful of the soldiers accompanying their journey East still sat in clusters of two or three around the cook fire, and occasionally they cast furtive glances at Tasia and Joslyn. One of them, a younger soldier whose beard was little more than a few black wisps at the end of his chin, looked away quickly when he saw the Princess gazing in his direction.

"They are my future subjects," Tasia said to Joslyn in a low voice, "and right now they're all watching me fail."

"Fail? They just watched you execute a perfect double-parry against a master swordsman."

Tasia lifted an unimpressed eyebrow.

"The sooner you hit the target, the sooner we can be done for the night," Joslyn said.

"You're much too bossy for a commoner, Guard."

Joslyn crossed her arms against her chest and said nothing.

"Fine, fine, fine," Tasia said. She took a deep breath and concentrated on the bail of hay once more.

"It's mainly about wrist control," said a voice behind her. Tasia jumped, turning to see General Remington standing a few yards behind her. Next to him was Captain Mannick, the young army captain whose unit had been assigned to accompany her and her entourage east.

"And breath control," said Captain Mannick with a grin.

Tasia had liked him until that moment. Now it seemed he was looking for a way to make fun of her. He must be highborn, she decided. A commoner would be too bashful to speak like that to a princess.

Acutely aware that she now had the attention of more than half the camp, Tasia took another breath, steadied her aim, and whipped the knife towards the bail of hay. Its tip stuck — but only for a moment. Then it drooped and fell to the ground.

Joslyn walked to retrieve it while Captain Mannick applauded.

"That's really quite impressive," he said. "I don't think I've ever seen a princess throw a dagger before."

"I take it you've seen a princess do a great many things?" Tasia retorted, annoyed.

Captain Mannick was handsome, in a way. He had wavy brown hair that hung to his shoulders and a neatly trimmed mustache and beard that was much in fashion in Port Lorsin at the moment. Tasia supposed that if they had met under different circumstances, she might have been intrigued by his rough good looks and cocky attitude.

But not under these circumstances.

Joslyn extended the dagger back to her, hilt first. "Fluid," she said to Tasia. "Your throw is too stiff at the moment."

"Let me show the Princess," said the captain, advancing towards the spot where Joslyn and Tasia stood.

"That's alright," said Tasia. "My guard is a very good teacher."

Mannick stopped, looking Joslyn up and down. "Really? I didn't know that nomads taught much of anything. Unless you count horse-thieving."

Joslyn stiffened beside Tasia.

"Here," Mannick said, reaching out a hand for the dagger. "I'll show you how it's done."

Tasia could feel every eye in the camp turn her way.

"Thank you for your offer, Captain," Tasia said with a polite smile, "but I'm really quite happy with my current teacher."

Mannick reached for the dagger anyway. In a flash, the blade of Joslyn's short sword rested upon his bare wrist.

"Princess Natasia has twice informed you that she is not interested in your assistance," Joslyn said in a low voice. "It would be better if she did not have to tell you a third time."

Captain Mannick took a half-step backwards, glancing between Joslyn and Tasia. He, too, seemed to realize that he had attracted the attention of the entire camp. His face soured, but he gave the Princess a quick bow.

"My apologies, your Highness," he said. "I did not mean to offend you."

"No," said the Princess with the same stiff smile. "I'm sure you did not."

"Come, Mannick," said General Remington. "Let us finish our conversation."

Mannick backed away, eyes flashing anger at Joslyn before he turned around.

Tasia waited for the two of them to walk away before she spoke. "You made an enemy unnecessarily tonight."

Joslyn did not answer, but the muscles of her jaw worked back and forth.

"I thought your *ku-sai* taught you not to make rash decisions?" Tasia prodded. She knew the guard had only meant to protect her, but with everyone in the camp watching, drawing a sword on the commanding military officer had not been the most diplomatic means of doing it.

Joslyn muttered something unintelligible.

"What?"

"I said, 'I don't like the way he watches you,'" Joslyn said quietly.

"Watches me?"

"Yes. He's been doing it since we left Port Lorsin."

"I haven't noticed that at all," said the Princess, surprised.

When the guard said nothing more, Tasia turned back towards the bail of hay. She squared her hips and bent her knees the way Joslyn had showed her, then drew in another breath.

A light touch on her arm broke her concentration.

"Elbow closer to the ear, Princess," Joslyn said quietly behind her, gently guiding her arm to the right place. Tasia could feel the guard's warm breath on the back of her neck, and she shivered involuntarily.

She let out the breath and closed her eyes for a moment, clearing away the sensation of Joslyn's touch, the unnerving new knowledge about Captain Mannick, the desire to finish this task swiftly and retire to her tent. Once the thoughts quieted, she visualized the blade striking the center of the bail the way Joslyn had taught her to do.

Tasia opened her eyes and took a breath through her

nostrils, feeling the chill of the night air fill her lungs. She flicked her elbow and wrist forward, releasing the dagger just as her hand traveled past her cheek. The dagger spun end over end, and stuck in the bail with a satisfying *thunk*.

"I did it!" Tasia exclaimed, hopping up and down like a child before she realized what she was doing. She smoothed her traveling gown and lowered her voice. "Did you see that, Joslyn? I'm not as hopeless as you thought I was, after all."

"I never said you were hopeless, Tasia," she said, using the Princess's nickname softly enough that she couldn't be overheard.

"Thank you," Tasia said. "For everything," she added, knowing Joslyn would understand she meant far more than self-defense lessons.

"You're welcome. And I'm sorry if I acted rashly earlier."

Tasia glanced over her shoulder. Most of the men had retired for the evening; only one or two clusters remained.

"It's alright," said Tasia.

Joslyn retrieved the dagger from the center of the bail and handed it to the Princess. "Don't forget to — "

"Sharpen and oil the blade? Yes, I will. You remind me every night, you know."

Joslyn gave the Princess a lopsided grin.

She's smiling more lately, Tasia thought, taking the dagger back. *Maybe it's the journey — maybe she prefers being here, at the edge of her homeland, than in the city. Her childhood must've been like this, sleeping in tents on forgotten roads in the middle of nowhere.*

Tasia watched as the guard cleaned up their practice area.

She liked the guard's smiles. It was too bad that they were coming more frequently lately simply out of nostalgia; it would have been nice if they were coming because Joslyn was developing some kind of affection for the Princess.

But that was probably too much to hope for. She turned towards the tent she shared with the guard and pulled back the flap.

#

The problem with using a chamber pot in the middle of the night was being stuck with the smell until dawn.

Most palace residents used chamber pots at night; only the private chambers of the royal wing had individual garder rooms. Tasia had always been pampered, she supposed. She had grown up without the need to use a chamber pot. And on the rare occasion when she did use one, someone else always emptied it for her.

But now, with the cold night of northern Terinto blanketing them with inky darkness, the only sounds the calls of foreign owls and other unknown night creatures, Tasia lay in bed wide awake, debating whether or not to use the chamber pot or venture outside to use the latrine ditch the soldiers had dug.

She might not debate the question if all she needed to

do was urinate. But unfortunately, the night's heavy, greasy supper meant she had to… do rather more than just urinate. Which brought her mind back to the smell. And being trapped with it in the tent until morning.

She glanced down at Joslyn, who slept on a nomad's woven straw mat on the floor near the tent's entrance. Joslyn wouldn't want the Princess leaving the tent in the middle of the night on her own like this.

But Tasia could take the daggers. That would at least be a precaution — not that precaution was really needed. This northern tooth of Terinto was virtually uninhabited. It was surprising even the owls could find enough to eat here. Or trees enough to sleep in.

She would take the daggers anyway. Joslyn had taught her that they should never be further than arm's reach away, and even now they sat on the simple table next to Tasia's cot.

Should she wake Joslyn?

No. That was too embarrassing.

The guard would not be pleased, though, if she discovered that the Princess had stolen out of the tent in the middle of the night on her own.

Next time, use the chamber pot, she would say. *I have been in the Imperial Army; I have fought in wars. I have smelled much worse.*

Her stomach gurgled; she felt a painful cramping somewhat south of her abdomen. Tasia winced.

She had to make a decision — now. Chamber pot or latrine ditch.

As quietly as she could, she pulled the rough woolen blankets back and sat up. The cot creaked beneath her. She stood slowly beside the bed on bare feet, her white sleeping robe falling shapelessly to her ankles.

Tasia lifted one of the daggers from the table. It was one of Joslyn's own; the long and weighty handle was wrapped in well-worn calfskin, the pommel was a simple ball of steel.

(*"It can be used to bludgeon, if need be,"* the guard had told her during one of the lessons, and the statement was followed by an additional fifteen minutes of practicing different ways to use the handle and the pommel as weapons unto themselves.)

Holding it in her right hand, the dagger seemed to whisper reassurance, seemed to nod along with Tasia and agree that her decision to seek out the latrine ditch was the right choice.

Cautiously, with dagger in hand, Tasia made her way to the tent entrance, giving the sleeping Joslyn a wide berth. She looked back once over her shoulder to make sure that the guard hadn't stirred, then crept out, taking care to disturb the tent flap as little as possible.

She hadn't bothered with a second robe or shoes. It was certainly not royal behavior — wandering around a camp comprised almost entirely of men in the dark in bare feet and only her sleeping gown — but she assured herself she would make it to the latrine ditch and back before anyone was the wiser.

It only occurred to her after she slipped out through the

half-opened tent flap that she might have to sneak around the night watch. But that shouldn't be hard. Each guard shift consisted of three men, and they patrolled the circumference of the camp with a steady, unchanging pace and route. She knew this because their voices had woken her up on several previous nights as they walked behind her tent. Tasia had been avoiding palace guards all her life; getting past these three soldiers without notice wouldn't be any different.

She stood still outside her tent, listening for the voices of the guards, but all she heard was a distant *coo-WAH, coo-WAH* of some night animal. For a brief moment, the eerie sound made her think about Joslyn's tall tale a few days earlier of desert hyenas controlled by sorcerers, and she shivered.

That woman and her desert wisdom. Tasia shook her head with a smile.

She heard the voices of the guards approaching and crouched down, obscured by the shadows cast by her tent. Despite being on the edge of the high desert, where the skies were almost always clear, tonight was overcast, and the moon was only a dull silver hangnail in the sky. Of all the nights to sneak around the guards to the latrine ditch, tonight was a good choice.

The men spoke and laughed in low voices as they walked their circuit, only one dim, red-orange torch between the three of them. Once their backs faced Tasia again, she stood and picked her way across the dusty ground towards the outer edge where she'd watched the men dig the latrine ditch. Her stomach clenched again, as if reminding her to hurry, and she placed the hand that didn't hold the dagger on her gut lightly.

She picked up her pace.

It was the smell that warned her to slow down and scan the ground. Despite its pungency, she was glad for the smell's alert; without it, she might have tripped in the dark and fallen into the latrine face-first.

Tasia held her breath when she got closer, placing the dagger on the ground beside her right foot before straddling the ditch and lifting her night robe. She closed her eyes and willed herself to concentrate on making quick business of her task.

But before she could finish, a strangled cry — a cry that sounded like someone trying to call for help had been silenced before the call could be voiced — echoed across the quiet camp. Tasia stood up and listened, but there was nothing else.

The torch light was gone.

She stepped to the far side of the latrine, picking up her dagger and peering into the darkness. The landscape was flat in this northern sliver of Terinto; the earth wasn't exactly desert sand, but it was dry and dusty and supported nothing except for a few twisted, stunted trees. There was no bush or boulder or high grass around her where anyone could hide behind to ambush Tasia, yet the light from the dying campfire was weak here, and the world disappeared into utter blackness only a few feet behind her.

She strained to hear the jocular voices of the three

guards; she squinted towards the main body of the camp, looking for the procession of their torchlight, but she heard nothing. Saw nothing.

Maybe the sound was unimportant. Maybe it had been another animal's noise in the night.

Yes. It was probably nothing. She was jumpy from being out here by herself, when she really should've at least woken Joslyn to go with her. Tasia nodded to herself. That was it — she was just jumpy. And she was close enough to finished with her business that she should head back to her tent.

She took a step in the direction from whence she had come — and heard another sound coming from the same direction as the first had. This sound was wet and hoarse — a man's muffled scream, Tasia was sure of it this time — and it was followed by a heavy thud. The sound of something (or someone?) toppling to the ground.

Heart like a jackrabbit in her chest, and without first pausing to consider which of her options would be the most rational choice, Tasia gripped the leather-wrapped dagger hilt tightly and called into the night, "Hello? Who's there?"

A low-throated chuckle came from behind her, and Tasia whirled.

A man stood there, nearly featureless in the dark. But there was enough light that Tasia could see he had stringy, shoulder-length black hair and a mouth framed by a thick black mustache.

"Well, well," the man said as he gave another menacing laugh. "It's the Princess herself, am I right? Out to take a shite in the middle of the night." He stepped over the latrine ditch and towards Tasia in two long strides. "Never thought I'd be lucky enough to be the one to kill the big quarry, but I guess old Jack's luck might finally be taking a turn for the best," he said, and it seemed he spoke more to himself than to Tasia.

In that moment, with the man merely an arm's length away, Tasia regained her senses. She turned to flee, but her sprint towards her tent only lasted a single step before Jack was on her, tackling her to the ground.

He used his weight to pin her to her stomach, clapping a leather-gloved hand to her mouth before she could scream.

"Don't make it hard on yourself, Princess," Jack whispered into her ear, and Tasia's mind went reeling backwards in time, back to the night when a stranger dressed as a Wise Man had also pinned her to the ground and told her that fighting him would be a useless thing to do.

You're only making it harder on yourself, Princess, he'd said.

Like a seedling pushing itself free from the earth for the first time, something blossomed in that moment inside Tasia's heart. She wouldn't be the helpless game piece of men anymore — not her father's, not her would-be assassin's, not the lords and ambassadors, not the Wise Men. She wouldn't be the one who always needed saving from someone like Joslyn. She was done with that. Thanks to hours upon hours moving rocks up and down a beach, grappling, parrying and thrusting, she was stronger now; she had a power in her body she'd never had before.

And she had a dagger.

A calmness arose from somewhere deep inside her, enveloping her in its smoothness. She would survive this, she knew. And she knew it not as a hope or as a desperate wish but as a simple fact. As elementary as the truth that the sun rose in the east, set in the west, and the sea lay to the south.

"The first rule of grappling is to never be the one on the bottom," Joslyn's voice whispered in her mind. *"And if somehow you do find yourself on the bottom, then the second rule of grappling is to free your hips first."*

Improbably, the man on top of her smelled like fish, and his hair smelled of the sea. It seemed a strange thing to notice at a moment like this, but the observation did nothing to dull Tasia's sharp new focus. In the next instant, she also observed that he had become distracted; he was no longer holding her mouth so tightly, and he put no effort into holding her down with his weight. What was he distracted with? Tasia felt his hips flex and wiggle above her; he reached down with the hand not on Tasia's mouth towards his belt. At first she thought he was preparing to rape her, but his hand was reaching for something else.

A knife, she thought.

All of it — the smell of fish, the man's distraction, Tasia's realization that he was reaching for his knife — occurred in a fraction of a second, in the same amount of time it takes to draw a breath.

And one breath and one distraction was all Tasia

needed.

She braced her bare heels in the dusty earth and thrust her hips up. It wouldn't be enough to throw his weight off of her, but that wasn't what she needed. She simply needed to make him more distracted than he already was — and to do it before he had a chance to pull the knife from its sheath.

By the time he grunted his surprise, Tasia had already lifted her dagger and plunged it into his side, driving it into the gap between his padded leather shirt and his belt. He screamed like an injured animal, loud and panicked and shocked. Tasia pulled the dagger from his side and bucked her hips again, and this time he rolled off her. She clamored to her feet, keeping the dagger in her hand the whole time.

"Joslyn!" she screamed into the night. "Captain Mannick! Imperial Guards! General Remington! Norix! *Joslyn!"*

A blood-slicked hand wrapped around her bare ankle and pulled, and Tasia tumbled to the ground. Something hard and pointy struck her in the back of the head, and the spinning world dissolved into the night.

23

Sounds:

The clang of metal on metal. The grunting of men. Shouts, screams, fire, footsteps.

Tasia woke to find herself lying on the ground, a dull throbbing emanating from the back of her skull. How long had she been unconscious? Long enough that the previously quiet camp was now engulfed in chaos. She reached towards the pain at the back of her head automatically, and her fingers encountered something warm and sticky — blood.

Something about the feeling of her own blood on her fingers roused her into full alertness, and her eyes flew open.

She screamed.

The man who had attacked her — Jack, the greasy-haired one who smelled of fish and seaweed — was an inch from her face.

Tasia scrambled to her feet, Joslyn's dagger still firmly in her hand. She prepared to defend herself against Jack's next attack, but he did not rise from the ground.

And when she saw that it was only Jack's head lying on the ground, and that the rest of his body lay nearly a yard away, Tasia screamed a second time.

Joslyn. She needed to find Joslyn. Or one of the soldiers. Or… someone.

Tasia turned towards the main camp, away from the latrine ditch, and realized immediately she could not run in that direction. Two of the larger tents, including Norix's, were ablaze. A dozen half-dressed soldiers, weapons in their hands, ran in a dozen different directions. Even as Tasia watched, an arrow struck one of them squarely in his bare back. For a moment, his arms opened wide, as if he was a bird about to take flight. Then the short sword dropped from his fingers and he fell face-first to the ground.

The enemies all looked like the beheaded Jack — mismatched armor with mismatched weapons, all of which looked like they had seen better days. But the problem was not their weapons; it was their number. There had to be at least sixty or seventy of them. Tasia's own entourage included only fifty soldiers and assorted personnel. And from the looks of it, probably half of them were either dead or wounded.

The camp was minutes away from being completely overrun.

Clutching the dagger in front of her, Tasia crossed the latrine ditch once more and ran, angling for the shadows behind the nearest tent. The most she could hope for was to hide until the fighting was over, and hope that somehow, miraculously, the Imperial soldiers would re-organize and beat back the larger force. Perhaps discipline and training would make up for what they lacked in numbers.

Perhaps.

She reached the long black shadows cast by the tent, crouched beside the canvas wall, dagger still in front of her.

Nothing to do now but wait. Wait and pray.

Tasia's mind spun with a hundred questions. Where had these men come from? What did they want? Were they just simple-minded bandits, lying in wait on this road for a quarry — any quarry — worth robbing? It seemed unlikely; Norix had chosen this route through the empty northern edge of Terinto specifically because it was generally free from trade traffic, which meant their journey would attract less attention.

Norix.

Tasia had never been overly fond of the palace's head Wise Man, her father's chief advisor and her tutor since childhood. The old man's condescending attitude towards Tasia was something she'd always chafed beneath. But that didn't mean she wanted anything bad to happen to him. His tent was a raging bonfire in the night; had he already been killed?

Mother Moon, Tasia mouthed silently, *and any other gods who are listening: Spare Norix. Please.* The irony of Tasia's prayer was that Wise Men didn't believe in the gods; that was what made them wise. The gods, they said, were naught but metaphors, and prayers and sacrifices and incense burned in their name were all just superstitious, ignorant drivel that belonged to the distant past.

Norix wouldn't approve of her appeal to Mother Moon. Tasia kept praying anyway.

He's just an old man. He doesn't deserve a death like this. Not after so many years of serving the Empire faithfully. He —

But Tasia cut off her prayers when a voice rang out above the din of the fighting. She couldn't quite make out the words, but it was commanding. And feminine.

It was as if Mother Moon herself had decided to answer.

"...to me!" said the voice, and Tasia knew she was hearing the conclusion of whatever the command had been.

It wasn't a goddess. It was a guard.

"Joslyn," the Princess whispered to herself, and the name itself was almost a continuation of her previous prayer. Either she was praying *to* the guard or *for* the guard. "Please remain unharmed. Please."

The "to me" Tasia had heard was most likely directed at whatever Imperial soldiers were still alive. Joslyn was not one of the soldiers; technically she was no longer part of the Imperial Army. Nevertheless, the "to me" Tasia had heard meant the guard must be taking control of the soldiers. Joslyn had made herself the rallying point, was calling the survivors to circle around her.

Tasia was a survivor. She should rally to the guard, too.

"No," she whispered into the shadows. She was the Princess of the Four Realms, the eldest child of the Emperor, the future Empress. She couldn't endanger herself by running into a battle bare-footed in a sleeping gown, with only a dagger to defend herself.

Yes, the shadows seemed to whisper back.

She was the Princess of the Four Realms, the eldest child of the Emperor, the future Empress. The soldiers were pledged to protect her, but wasn't she as responsible for their lives as they were for hers? Precisely because she *was* the Princess?

She should at least see what was happening. When all of this was over, she didn't want to be found cowering in the shadows — no matter who won. She wouldn't allow her enemies to find her this way, and she didn't want the men to know that she had run and hid at the very moment they needed a symbol of hope the most.

Tasia stood, glancing left and right to make sure none of the enemy had wandered far enough from the melee to see her. Once she was sure the route was clear, she sprinted from her hiding spot towards the tent to her right.

And promptly tripped on the rope staking it down, which the darkness had rendered invisible.

Tasia flew forward, arms outstretched before her, dagger bouncing from her grip when she hit the ground chest-first. The impact knocked the air from her lungs, and for a terrifying moment, she thought her lungs had collapsed in such a way that she would never take a breath again. Her face skidded across the dusty earth, and something sharp scraped down her chin.

A moment after her landing, she gasped in a breath, relieved that she hadn't killed herself.

But the dagger. Where was the dagger?

She crawled forward in the dark, cursing her ineptitude as she groped for the dropped blade. Her men were being slaughtered, and she wasn't even competent enough to run from one point to the next without nearly killing herself.

Tasia's fingers met warm leather. She wrapped a skinned palm around the dagger's handle, letting out a breath she hadn't realized she'd been holding.

It wasn't over. She could still go to them, and if Mother Moon and the other gods would have her die this night, then she would die alongside the Imperial soldiers, dagger in hand, fighting for them just as they fought for her.

More cautiously this time, she edged around the corner of the tent she was behind, trying to see what was happening. On the other side of her hiding spot, the fighting still raged.

She still needed to get closer.

She took off at a jog for the back of the next tent, taking care this time to skirt the ropes and stakes that bound them to the earth. Three tents later, the sound of fighting intensified. She was behind Captain Mannick's tent, she realized, only one tent off from her own.

Her back pressed against the canvas of the Captain's tent, Tasia inched forward, stealing a quick glance around the back edge of the tent towards the thick of the battle.

Joslyn's rallying cry had done some good, it seemed. The Imperial soldiers were still outnumbered, with one man in the House of Dorsa black and silver for every two or three scruffy ruffians. But the remaining soldiers had managed to create a kind of oval formation, standing shoulder-to-shoulder as they worked to beat back the onslaught against them.

Joslyn stood in the center of the oval's front line, a sword in each hand. Painted an angry orange-red by the blazing tents, the tongues of steel flicked forward, backward, sideways at speeds almost too fast to track with the naked eye.

An enemy lunged forward; Joslyn's right sword plunged through his throat. Another enemy swung a hatchet at the man beside her; the left sword severed his weapon arm at the elbow. The fighter screamed and fell to his knees, clutching his arm. The soldier he'd been about to attack finished him, driving a short sword through his chest.

It was gruesome and bloody and chaotic and Tasia didn't want to see it. She wanted to cover her eyes and drop back into a crouch behind the tent, but she wouldn't. She would help.

As she debated what to do, she heard a cry of pain. There had been many of those tonight, but this one sounded too familiar. She ventured another glimpse around the edge of the tent and saw Joslyn crumple forward at the waist, dropping to one knee as she clutched her side and struggled to keep her feet. One of the swords lay on the ground beside her, no longer dancing in the firelight. A bearded man twice her size lifted his sword with an animalistic growl, preparing to deliver the final blow.

Tasia didn't think. She stepped around the corner of the tent and lifted her dagger —

Elbow in. Left foot forward. Hand straight back. Flick

the wrist.

— letting the blade fly with a perfect form she didn't even think about. The dagger turned end-over-end as it whistled through the night air. Much to Tasia's own surprise, it struck the man holding the sword above Joslyn in the throat, burying itself up to the hilt in his jugular.

The battle lust that had filled his eyes a moment earlier was replaced with shock. The sword tumbled uselessly from his hands as he reached for the dagger in his throat, clawing ineffectively as blood spurted like a fountain from the wound. He made a gurgling noise, and more blood poured from his mouth. With a grunt of effort, Joslyn pushed herself to her feet, roared in defiance as she drove her sword through the man's belly. He fell backward, bouncing against the ground once, then moving no more.

Tasia stood frozen. She'd done it. She hadn't just thrown her dagger into a hay bail target; she'd thrown it at a man. During a battle. And she killed him. She'd taken life.

"Charge and flank!" Joslyn shouted. Her voice was reedy, lacking the command it had possessed before. She held one sword; her other hand still clutched at her midsection.

But reedy or not, the other soldiers heard her and obeyed. As one body, they broke the back half of their oval in its center, half of them moving to the left and half to the right. They closed on the remaining enemy fighters like a crab's closing pincer, trapping the ones still alive between them.

It was all over a few minutes later, with the last of the enemies impaled from behind by a soldier's short sword. When that last man fell, the surviving Imperial soldiers all seemed to sag at once. Swords, axes, pikes, and halberds drooped from hands like wilted flowers. Exhausted men fell to their knees, while the injured tore off strips of their tunics or the tunics of the dead to bind their wounds.

Joslyn fell, too, collapsing in the center of all of them, dropping to both knees and then pitching forward as if she'd been pushed from behind. She braced one hand against the earth, barely supporting herself. The other hand stayed across her belly, and in the firelight, Tasia watched in horror as blood seeped from between her fingers.

Tasia rushed from her spot between the tents to the guard. The Princess kneeled before the guard, putting both hands on Joslyn's shoulders, trying to push her upright again. "Joslyn? Are you alright?"

Joslyn lifted her head, face a pale mask of pain. Her normally ruddy bronze skin was ghost-white, despite the warm light cast by the blazing tents. "I need the... my box... in the tent..." She pointed weakly in the direction of the tent she'd been sharing with Tasia.

"Alright. Okay. I'll get the box," Tasia said, and she ran into the tent. No one seemed to notice her — a princess in a dirty sleeping gown, running bare-footed into the largest tent in the campsite. Those who were still alive were all too busy doing other things: Men chased down horses and pack animals, some of whose hobbles had been cut by the raiders and, in their fright, had scattered across the barren plain. Other men ran with buckets of water from the nearby pond to douse the burning tents, while still more tended to their fallen comrades, seeking out the ones who might still survive.

Tasia returned with Joslyn's box and set it on the ground before the guard, who had shifted into an awkward sitting position, legs splayed wide before her.

"What can I do?" Tasia asked.

"The armor…" Joslyn reached down to lift the padded leather armor off her torso, but when she tried to pull it off, she let go with an anguished cry. "Help me get it off… so I can treat the wound," she panted.

Joslyn raised her arms with a grimace of pain, and Tasia pulled off the armor as gingerly as she could, cursing when a metal rivet tangled itself in Joslyn's raven-black hair. The linen shirt below the armor was soaked in dark red blood, and Tasia took this off, as well. When she did, she saw that the shallow wound in Joslyn's side, the one she'd gotten defending Tasia at the Speckled Dog, was still a tender pink with fresh scabs.

A wave of guilt washed over Tasia. She was nothing but trouble for Joslyn.

Beneath the shirt, there was so much blood covering Joslyn's torso that at first Tasia worried that the woman had been completely gutted. But the guard used the ruined shirt to swipe away the blood, and Tasia was relieved to see that there was only one long, horizontal slash across the middle.

"It wasn't a puncture," Joslyn said with a strained

voice, as if reading Tasia's thoughts. "If it was… it would be much more dangerous. But it didn't go deep enough to… deep enough to…" She grimaced as she trailed off.

Tasia forced herself to look at the wound again, despite the fact that the blood and cries of pain from the dying men around her were making her stomach queasy. But she was the Princess. She would not allow herself to look away from pain.

She took the shirt from Joslyn and dabbed gingerly at the slash. The cut was deep enough that layers of Joslyn's muscle and fat were exposed, but not so deep that any organs had been penetrated. Joslyn was right: The wound wasn't as bad as it could have been. Had it gone even a half-inch deeper, it might have cut through her entrails, and then, even if she survived being sewn up, she might've died from what the soldiers referred to as "battle poisoning."

With a shaking hand, Joslyn reached for her box.

"Here," Tasia said, quickly opening the lid and bringing it closer to Joslyn. "What do you need? Let me help you."

Joslyn supported her weight with one hand; with the other she reached inside the box, fumbling through its contents until she produced a small glass bottle with a clear liquid inside. She pulled the small cork out with her teeth and groaned as she dropped back on her elbow, tipping the bottle towards the gash with a trembling hand.

"Let me," Tasia said. "Please." She took the bottle from Joslyn. "How much?"

"Half the… half the bottle," Joslyn managed.

Tasia dabbed more of the blood away and then carefully

poured the clear liquid onto the wound. It foamed and sizzled when it struck the guard's skin, yellowing as it dried. Joslyn sucked in a breath between clenched teeth and let her head fall backwards.

"Are you okay?" Tasia asked.

With effort, Joslyn sat up a bit straighter and nodded. "Yes," she breathed. "That part is always the hardest. Now the moss."

She dipped her chin in the direction of the box, and Tasia pulled out a bundle of the scraggly dried weeds she'd seen before, the last time she'd sewn closed one of Joslyn's wounds.

"Do you remember how to…?" Joslyn said.

"I do," Tasia answered, pulling out the needle and the thick black thread. "But I need to heat the needle first." She glanced behind her, wondering if she could find a live ember to light Joslyn's small candle and heat the needle.

"There's… no time for that," Joslyn said. "Use the solution from the… from the bottle. Put the needle in it."

Tasia did as she was told, sticking the long, curved needle into the bottle as far as she could. Then she broke off some of the dried moss, packed it into the first few inches of Joslyn's wound as gently as she could. She lifted the needle. "Are you ready?"

Joslyn nodded and closed her eyes.

24

By the time Tasia finished sewing closed Joslyn's abdomen and binding it with clean white gauze from her box, the survivors of the attack had put out the fires, recovered the horses and pack animals, and bandaged the wounded.

It was darker and colder now with the two tents extinguished, and the night's foreign sounds seemed stranger than they had before. A kind of muted disquiet took over the camp, with men whispering and speaking in low voices to one another rather than speaking at a normal volume. A woman sobbed somewhere, probably the washer woman or her daughter. A solemnity hung like a shroud over those who had survived. Despite the fact that they had emerged from the battle victorious, all those who remained nevertheless recognized that, somehow, they had also lost.

Tasia could almost taste the mood. It had a sour, bitter taste — sharp and unpleasant like a piece of fruit that had just begun to turn. The mood was a poison, she knew, and if it didn't dissipate it would sicken the camp's survivors.

She left Joslyn sitting on the ground, still in the same place where she had fallen, while she retrieved a fresh tunic from the guard's canvas bag of belongings. As she rifled through the bag, she marveled at the woman's simplicity. The canvas bag was all the guard had brought with her — it was filled with a few tunics, a few trousers, spare undergarments, and a few tools to mend weapons, armor, and her own body. That was all.

Tasia, by comparison, had brought no fewer than three large trunks with her, filled with gowns and traveling clothes for every occasion, enough to keep the washer woman busy each day. A separate, smaller box was nestled inside one of the larger boxes with nothing but Tasia's jewelry and face powders. Another small box held her bath salts, soaps, and perfumes — all of which she'd barely had occasion to use.

Joslyn was sitting straighter by the time Tasia returned to her, cleaning the blood off one of her swords with the ruined linen shirt.

"Here," Tasia said, showing Joslyn a clean tunic. The guard reached for it. "No, I don't want you pulling out your stitches. I'll help you."

It took the two of them a few minutes, but they managed to get Joslyn's tunic on without too much pain.

Tasia looked for a place to sit down without getting dirty, found none, and squatted next to the guard.

"So," she said. "Who were they — the men who attacked us?"

Joslyn shook her head with a frown. "I think they — "

"Princess!" someone called.

Tasia turned to see an ash-smudged Norix waddling towards her as quickly as he could. Like the Princess, the old Wise Man was in his sleeping gown and bare-footed. Also like the Princess, he was covered in dirt, but also smudged with ash. Two bedraggled soldiers walked on either side of him.

"Thank the Mother Moon you're alive!" he exclaimed when he reached her.

That was how Tasia knew just how upset Norix was — he had let slip a *Mother Moon*.

He dropped down to both knees in front of Tasia, patting her arms and sides as if to reassure himself — or her — that she was truly unharmed. "How did you escape?"

"I was actually... using the latrine ditch when the attack began," Tasia said, hoping that the fire's light was too dim to reveal her blush. "A man found me. We fought and I stabbed him, but — "

Norix blinked in surprise. "Stabbed him?"

"I took one of the daggers Joslyn has been training me to use with me to the latrine. So yes, I stabbed him in the side, just below his armor, but he pulled me down, and I must've hit my head..." She trailed off, trying to penetrate the gap in her memory from the time she fell and the time she woke again.

"I beheaded him," Joslyn supplied. "The man who attacked you. I heard you scream, and by the time I got there, he had a knife to your throat. I would've stayed with you after I took off his head, but by then they were attacking the camp from every side, and when I saw the Wise Man's tent catch fire, I left to help the soldiers putting out the blaze."

"You should never have left the Princess's side," said Norix stonily.

"The Princess was in the dark, hidden from view," Joslyn said. "You were trapped in an inferno."

"It does not matter what happens to me," said the Wise Man. "I am just an old man. I'm destined for the crematorium's inferno soon enough anyway. *She* is the Empire's future." He jabbed a finger in Tasia's direction, as if his statement was part accusation.

"I was satisfied that the Princess was temporarily safe," Joslyn said stiffly. "And I am glad that you remain uncremated. Sir."

Norix grumbled inaudibly.

"Where did you go?" Tasia asked her tutor, hoping the change of topic would dissipate the tension between guard and Wise Man.

"I ran," he said. "Found a copse of fruit trees on the other side of the pond, covered myself in leaves and hoped I would remain undiscovered." He looked her over, gestured at her dirty robe. "And you? Wisdom must have dictated that you do the same, I see."

She shook her head. "No. Wisdom dictated that I could not leave the soldiers to fight in my name while I hid behind a tent. So I — "

"Princess!" Norix gasped, his eyes widening. "Tell me you were not fool enough to join the battle!"

"I could not leave soldiers to fight for me while I hid," Tasia repeated firmly. "So I kept myself hidden, but…"

She glanced at Joslyn for a brief moment. "But I kept looking for a way that I could help."

"And she found it," said the guard. She spoke to Norix, but kept her eyes fixed on Tasia when she said, "Were it not for the Princess's true aim, I would be amongst the dead right now."

Norix's brow creased and he looked at Tasia for an explanation.

"A man was about to drive his sword into Joslyn," Tasia said. "I threw my dagger at him, and it struck him in the throat." She shuddered at the memory of the blood squirting from his throat in all directions.

I took a person's life tonight, she reminded herself.

Norix nodded slowly. "Well. It seems as if your father's plan for teaching you to defend yourself has paid its dividends at last." But he didn't sound happy about it. Norix glanced briefly at Joslyn. "Although I find it intriguing that the guard set to protect you was defended by *you,* and not the other way around."

Tasia bristled, the sympathy she'd felt for her old tutor earlier evaporating now that she was face-to-face with his typical condescension. "Perhaps you didn't hear the part where Joslyn beheaded the man who had been about to kill me?"

"I also heard the part where she left you there," Norix said. "Perhaps you didn't hear the part in which she might not have needed your defense if she had stayed by your side as she was commissioned to do. But I suppose even nomads sometimes feel the need to play the hero."

Tasia swallowed at least five angry comments, which stuck like shards of glass in her throat. As she had seen her father do sometimes, she decided to redirect the conversation. "Does anyone know what happened to General Remington?"

Norix's face fell and he dropped his eyes. "Amongst the dead," he said sadly. "The General came out of his tent just as I came out of mine. I saw a raider plant a dagger in his back. That was when I ran."

General Remington, dead. Just like that. The old war hero who'd saved the Empire from breaking apart during the Western Rebellion, who'd orchestrated the War in the East for twelve years, who'd survived the loss of a leg and a host of other battle wounds, was dead from a coward's dagger in his back. He'd never been someone Tasia had felt much affection for — a boring and condescending lecturer, like Norix, but he'd been a faithful servant of the Empire for decades, and the Emperor had trusted his advice almost unconditionally when it came to matters of war. Who would advise the Emperor on military matters now? And how would Tasia tell her father that her most trusted military advisor had died from something as ignoble as a dagger in the back?

What would Father do? Tasia wondered.

Joslyn's dark eyes caught hers, held them for a moment. When chaos had overwhelmed the camp and threatened to destroy them all, Joslyn had seized control and restored order. With the single cry of *"...to me!"*, the guard had turned the tide of battle.

The camp was in shambles. Two tents and likely untold supplies had burned or been otherwise ruined. Too many of their already small fighting force was dead. The entire mission was in jeopardy.

The guard had turned the tide of battle; could Tasia turn the tide of its aftermath?

"We must find General Remington's body and send it to Port Lorsin for a proper funeral," Tasia said. Somehow she'd managed to find her royal voice, the one that sounded authoritative and confident. She turned to the two soldiers who'd escorted Norix. "Where is Captain Mannick?"

The younger of the soldiers, brown eyes weary and face smudged with ash, nodded. "Killed, Princess. Saw it m'self."

Tasia thought a moment. "Who is the ranking officer now?"

The soldiers exchanged a glance. "There were two lieutenants assisting the captain," said the older one. This one had bright blue eyes and a shock of blond hair — probably a native of the Steppes or the mountains of the Northeast. "We're not sure if..." He cleared his throat. "We don't know if either of them survived."

Tasia placed a hand on the blond one's forearm and squeezed. "You fought bravely tonight," she told him. "Search the camp. Bring me the ranking officer who still survives." To the younger one, she said, "As for you, count how many able-bodied men we have left, how many are injured, and how many survive. Bring me numbers. I will be in my tent with my advisors."

"Yes, your Majesty," both boys mumbled, and they shuffled away.

"That was well-handled," Norix said after the boys were out of earshot.

Tasia nodded. "Join me in my tent," she said to Norix. She stood, looked down at Joslyn. "And you, too, Guard. The three of us have decisions to make."

Norix glanced from Tasia to Joslyn. "Since when is the bodyguard an advisor?"

"Since she kept all of us from getting slaughtered tonight," Tasia said. "And with Mannick and Remington both dead, she might be the ranking officer still alive."

"I was never an officer, your Majesty," Joslyn said, still sitting on the ground. "I was an enlisted foot soldier. And now I am not even that, given that I am no longer a part of the Imperial Army."

"I must agree with the guard, Princess," said Norix. "She is not qualified to advise you."

Tasia pressed her lips tightly together. If she had seen a mirror, she would have recognized the expression as an echo of her father. "I am of age, am I not, Norix? If my father were dead today, I would hold the crown and be qualified to make my own decisions, correct?"

The old Wise Man looked momentarily befuddled by her question. "Yes, Princess, but I do not see how — "

"Then I believe I am perfectly capable of deciding who can and cannot advise me." She turned to Joslyn. "Do you need help getting up, Guard, or can you stand on your own?"

The warrior from Terinto rocked forward, managed to come to her feet without accepting the Princess's outstretched hand. But she winced and hunched once on her feet. Through the light linen of her tunic, Tasia could see a dark red line forming already, blood seeping through the stitches and through the bandage.

Tasia stopped herself from rushing to the guard's side, offering Joslyn help as they walked towards the tent. Joslyn wouldn't appreciate it. And somehow Tasia knew better than to touch her so intimately in front of Norix. But silently, Tasia decided she would keep a close eye on the guard. Someone would need to change the bandages regularly and ensure that the guard rested enough to heal, because Joslyn would push herself too hard if left to her own devices.

25

"Continuing our journey would be unnecessarily dangerous," Norix repeated for a third time. "We need to turn back."

There were no tables and only one chair inside Tasia's tent, so she sat while Norix and Joslyn stood. Norix was red-faced with frustration, which, when combined with his dirty sleeping gown, made for a nearly comical combination. Joslyn was the opposite of red-faced; she remained pale and slightly hunched forward, one hand bracing herself against the table. Tasia herself had pulled a traveling cloak over her sleeping gown, washed her face with clean water from her basin, and put her hair into a simple, tidy braid. She intended to address the rest of the entourage soon, and she needed to look presentable when she did it.

"If the raiders somehow knew our route, which it seems that they did, then returning from whence we came will be just as dangerous as moving forward," Tasia said. "And given that there is as much danger behind us as ahead of us, I would prefer that we complete our purpose before returning to Port Lorsin. General Remington had reason to suspect General Telek of being a traitor to the Empire. We cannot begin the spring offensive while our commander's loyalty is in question."

"General Telek's loyalty has *never* been in question," Norix grumbled, almost to himself.

"More than half of our fighting force was killed tonight, Princess," Joslyn said. "We should take that into account. If we continue East, we will not be as well-protected as we have been up to this point."

Tasia contemplated this. The soldier she'd sent to inventory her troops reported that twenty-seven of the fifty soldiers they'd been traveling with had been killed, including General Remington, Captain Mannick, and one of the captain's lieutenants. The other lieutenant was alive but badly wounded; it was unlikely he could sit a horse, let alone command men in battle should another raid occur. Tasia fully intended to make Joslyn their temporary commander, but had so far kept the decision to herself.

The soldiers weren't the only ones who perished during the battle. Several servants, including the washer woman and the cook's assistant, had died in one of the tent fires. The washer woman's daughter was still alive; she was the one Tasia must have heard sobbing in the battle's aftermath.

"The purpose of the raid also remains unclear, Princess," said Norix. "They seem to have been simple bandits, but if they — "

"They were not simple bandits," Joslyn said. Norix looked displeased to be cut off. "The one who almost killed me wore the vulture emblem of the Golden Soldiers on a ring."

Norix's brow crinkled and he glanced from Joslyn to

Tasia. "Mercenaries? Are you completely certain?"

Rather than answer, Joslyn shuffled from the tent. A few seconds later, she returned holding a thick golden ring up to the lamplight. She wiped the blood off the top of the ring to reveal its flat face. "Yes. I'm sure."

Sure enough, the golden ring was inlaid with emeralds in the shape of a vulture, the rather portentous crest of the underground and illegal mercenary army, the Golden Soldiers.

"So someone hired Golden Soldiers to attack us," Norix said grimly, pacing away from the table. "Now the twofold question is: Who and why?"

Tasia thought back to her encounter with the man who called himself Jack at the latrine, the one Joslyn had beheaded. "I think I can answer the 'why,'" she said. "They came to kill me. The man who almost took my life called me 'the big quarry.' He recognized me right off."

"Then the raid was another assassination attempt, made to look like bandits besetting our party in the middle of the night," Joslyn said.

Tasia looked at Norix. "You're the Wise Man. Who did this? Who keeps trying to kill me?"

"I wish I knew, Princess," he said with a sigh. "All we can say for certain is that whoever it is — individual or group — it is someone with means. Means enough to hire an assassin with the skills to resist the truth serum, then with means enough to hire a band of mercenaries. Unfortunately, though, we already knew that."

"Whoever it was also had knowledge," Joslyn said.

"They ambushed us on a road that should have been deserted at this time of the year. It was chosen specifically for that reason. They must have known our path."

"Then there is a snake in the hen house," Norix said. His tone was dark, foreboding. Tasia had never heard him sound so heavy and old, and it gave her a chill. "We must return to Port Lorsin immediately and tell the Emperor what has happened."

The three of them fell into thoughtful silence.

"No," Tasia said after a moment. "Our mission was to travel to the war front in the East, encourage the soldiers, gather first-hand intelligence for the Emperor, plan an end for the war. We shall not return to Port Lorsin until the mission is complete."

"Continuing at this point is a fool's errand, Princess," Norix said. "We will turn back immediately."

Tasia shot him a sharp look. "Wise Man Norix, you are my father's most trusted advisor. And you have been my tutor since I was a child. But I will not tolerate you calling me a fool. Or assuming you can dictate my actions."

"I was not dictating your — "

"You did not say 'we *should* turn back,' you said 'we *will* turn back,'" Tasia said.

"Your father sent me on this journey in part to guide you, Princess," Norix said, "and I don't think you — "

"Exactly," Tasia said. "To *guide* my actions. Not to direct them. I am capable of making my own decisions, and I have decided that we will not turn back."

Norix did not look pleased, but he averted his gaze.

"As you wish, your Majesty."

"We will send a messenger back to Port Lorsin," Tasia said. "Without the burden of our entire entourage, they will make swift time — they will reach the Emperor much faster than we could. Meanwhile, we will change our route to the East and press on. Once we reach the front, we will be surrounded by Imperial troops and be well-protected. By the time our mission is complete, we will have our reinforcements and fresh supplies."

Norix shook his head slowly as the Princess spoke. "This is unwise, Princess. We must assume that whoever hired the Golden Soldiers will soon find out that the raid on our camp was thwarted, and they will send a second band to attack us, stronger than the first."

Tasia was about to argue, but Joslyn spoke first.

"It will make no difference how many men the Golden Soldiers send," the guard said, "if they cannot find us." Joslyn limped towards her canvas sack of belongings, kneeled with obvious effort, and produced a folded piece of parchment. She hugged her side with one hand, unfolded the parchment with the other, laying it across the rug at Tasia's feet. It was a map, marked in Terintan characters.

The guard placed an index finger on the northern edge of Terinto. "We traveled north to avoid the Great Sand, which places us here." She tapped a finger on the parchment. "If we travel a little further to the north, we can follow the West Snake River into the Zaris Mountains, then cross the river just south of its headwaters, here. It would put us onto the Yellow Plateau, and from there we could angle south and east to the front through lands that are very sparsely populated."

"That would add *weeks* to our journey," Norix said.

"If we were traveling with fifty soldiers, extra servants, and carriages, yes, it would add weeks. Actually — with the carriages, a journey through the mountains might not even be feasible. But if we leave the carriages, traveled by horseback only... it would add five days. A single week at the most."

Joslyn looked up from her place on the ground, meeting Tasia's eyes and waiting for an answer.

Norix scoffed. "Abandon the carriages? Ask the Princess to travel through the mountains on horseback? That's ridiculous."

Joslyn shrugged, untroubled. "We travel light. We change our path. Not many know the Zaris Mountains, and so they avoid them. We stay safe this way." She turned to Tasia. "If you want to complete the journey, it's the best choice."

"What about our injured?" Tasia said. "I doubt many of them can even mount a horse at this point."

Norix's expression was incredulous. "Princess, you can't seriously be considering — "

Tasia lifted a finger, silencing the Wise Man, who gurgled as if he had choked on the remainder of his sentence.

"I have an idea about the injured, Princess," Joslyn said. "An idea which might also provide us with even more time to slip unnoticed into the mountains. But it may not be to your liking. And it would put some of your people at risk."

Tasia met the guard's eyes. "Go on."

#

Forty dead.

Twenty-seven soldiers killed in battle, ten servants killed or burned alive. Three more soldiers who died in the quiet hours before dawn of their wounds, including Captain Mannick's surviving lieutenant.

They lit a funeral pyre that burned the rest of the night and into the noontide meal the next day. Tasia's hair still smelled like smoke and burnt flesh even after washing it twice. The two messengers, including the soldier from the Steppes with the blond hair she'd met the night before, had been sent at full speed back to Port Lorsin with their best horses.

Another assassination attempt, read the message to the Emperor. *Multiple dead. Returning to Port Lorsin; please send support troops.*

At the bottom of the message were two marks that, to the untrained eye, would appear to be stray quill blots — accidental and meaningless hashes. But her father would know what they meant. The first mark indicated that a piece of Tasia's message was deceptive. The second mark indicated that more information would be forthcoming.

The Princess wrote the message, including the two code

markings at the bottom, by her own hand. She pressed the emblem of the House of Dorsa into the wax seal and prayed the messengers would not be intercepted by the traitors.

She prayed no more death would occur on her behalf.

But that is the burden of royalty, she reminded herself. *The burden of leadership. They die for us again and again.*

"General Remington is a tremendous loss," said Norix beside her as they watched the pyre burn. "Your father had intended for him to return to Port Lorsin from this journey with a clear strategy for ending this war."

Tasia nodded. Regardless of what she had said when she stood up to Norix earlier, Tasia knew she wasn't the one who was supposed to be in charge of this mission. She had been sent along partially to be a figurehead, a proxy for her father, but more because he had wanted to test her, to give her something that actually required her to act responsibly for a period.

Tasia wasn't the one who had been meant to gather intelligence. General Remington was. But now he was gone, making the task truly Tasia's, as Norix had already made it clear that he would not even entertain the idea that there might be a problem with General Telek.

After the noontide meal, Tasia went to the washer woman's daughter, looked her up and down.

The Princess smiled, taking both the girl's hands in her own and squeezing them. "You look radiant," she said.

The girl, no older than fifteen, blushed a fierce apple-red. Her eyes looked almost bruised from all the tears she had shed. "Thank you, Princess," she said, sniffling. "I've never worn finery such as this before."

She had on one of Tasia's blue silk gowns, and it was far too big on her. Where Tasia had height and curves, the young woman was petite, with the thin, straight lines of a child who'd been underfed for a lifetime. The dress's hem had already dragged along the earth, turning the bottom a drab brown.

"For your sake, I hope you never have to again," Tasia said. The girl's smile faltered in confusion. Tasia waggled a finger at her playfully to dissipate the tension. "You take care of my wardrobe."

"Yes, your Majesty, I will."

"And make sure they treat you like a real princess."

The girl giggled and dropped her gaze, her cheeks blazing brighter.

"You are very brave to do this for me, Sanda, especially after what happened to your mother," Tasia said, feeling the pressure of tears in her eyes as she took the girl's hands again.

Sanda shook her head but wouldn't look up. "No, Princess. It is my honor. And it is what mother would have wanted me to do. How often does a washer woman's daughter get to be a princess? Not ever, really."

Tasia's smile didn't quite reach her eyes. "I hope you enjoy being a princess more than I have, dear heart." She took a breath and stepped back, meeting the eyes of the healthy soldiers she was sending with Sanda and the injured. "Now. We really must get all of you on your way while there's still daylight to be had."

Tasia made one more round amongst them, squeezing the fingers of injured soldiers, encouraging the able-bodied ones who would accompany them. With the luck of Mother Moon, they would all survive the journey back to Port Lorsin. They would survive their journey west, she would survive her journey east, and Sanda would have tales of the time she was Princess of the Four Realms for a week to share with her children and her grandchildren.

With luck, they would all live. And Tasia's second message to her father, the truthful one hidden at the bottom of one of the trunks of gowns she was sending with Sanda, would make it to him.

Another assassination attempt, this time by the Golden Soldiers, it read. *We suspect a traitor within the palace, someone close enough to have known the route. Continuing to the front to complete our duty; please send reinforcements to accompany us on the homeward journey.*

She waved goodbye to the carriages as they rolled away with Sanda, the surviving servants, the injured, and the handful of able-bodied soldiers sent to protect them.

When they were gone, she turned to Joslyn, Norix, and the ten soldiers who still remained. "We strike camp and travel north until we lose daylight," she said to them. The light-hearted tone she'd used with Sanda had vanished. "I thank each of you for your courage and your service. I don't know what lies ahead of us, but I know this: Your bravery and fighting spirit in the face of peril will bring even more hope to the Imperial Army fighting the barbarians in the East. We will not let your brothers and sisters in arms on the front down; we will deliver the hope and support of the Emperor as promised, and we will be the Emperor's own eyes and ears there. Our journey is invaluable to the Empire, and nothing will have been in vain."

Her eyes caught on Joslyn's, and the guard gave a subtle nod. It was a nod of approval, a nod that said, *You have spoken well.*

Norix stood next to the guard. His expression contained none of the same encouragement. Here was a man who doubted Tasia's course of action, who fretted for his own safety and the safety of the Empire, who wished he had joined the injured and the servants and was already on his way back to the comfort of the palace.

"Rulership," her father had told her once, *"primarily consists of a series of impossible choices. The ruler's duty is not to make the right choice, because there is rarely a 'right' choice. The ruler's duty is to force whatever course of action he chooses to serve the Empire, through the brute power of his own will."*

Tasia might not have Norix's learning or wisdom, but she was still her father's daughter. Force of will was something she had in abundance.

She looked down at the tunic and riding trousers she had borrowed from Joslyn. They pulled and pinched in some places, felt too loose in others. For a flash of a moment, Tasia felt the clothes as a metaphor: She wore her leadership uncomfortably, but she wore it nonetheless.

"We leave," she said to the dozen faces around her, both the approving ones and the doubtful ones. And with nods and mumbled assents, they scattered towards their respective duties.

26

It was late spring, and while the scrubby savannah in northern Terinto had bordered upon hot, the mountains further north were still cool. Cold, even: The first two nights had been so frigid that Tasia had barely slept but had lain on her mat shivering until dawn. She finally slept on the third night, but only thanks to exhaustion.

Living so close to the ocean, Tasia was accustomed to morning fog rolling in, but that fog was warm and tropical. The fog she rode through on the fourth morning of their northbound trek into the Zaris Mountains was chilling and damp. It soaked through her cloak, her skin, her muscles, until it settled with a thick heaviness into her bones.

She tugged on the drawstrings of her hood with one hand, gripped the reins of her horse tightly in her other. Tasia had been riding horses since she was a girl — almost all noblewomen were trained to ride — but usually when she traveled any distance, she went by carriage. As a member of the House of Dorsa, riding horseback was typically reserved for an occasional parade or royal hunt or country jaunt; Tasia had never ridden for longer than an hour or two at a time. And the saddles she'd ridden in those instances had been decorative and padded, heavy on the horse but comfortable for the rider. The saddle she rode in now had been designed more pragmatically, with agility and the animal's endurance in mind... which maximized the impact on the rider's bottom.

In other words, Tasia's backside was already badly chapped, from her tailbone all the way down to the insides of her knees. Her legs and feet were numb and raw, and even when she had the chance to get off the horse, she couldn't shake the sensation of still being on its back.

The mountain air's damp hadn't been making things any better, either. South of the mountains, it was water that had come at a premium, water that they'd had to ration and manage carefully. Now that they were north, water seemed to cling to every surface. Nothing stayed dry; nothing got dry once it was wet. When they'd struck camp earlier that morning, the riding clothes she put on were already clammy and sticking to her skin.

Tasia peered down the trail ahead of her, trying to squint through the fog. But she could barely see beyond her own horse's nervously twitching ears.

The ghost forms of trees and boulders appeared in phases; first they were nothing more than grey outlines in the gloom, then the outlines darkened, filling in with the silver-white of birch bark or the flecked black of a rock face. More than once, Tasia had to duck as a previously invisible low-hanging branch suddenly materialized through the heavy soup around her.

It was like riding inside a dream, where the landscape was an indistinct shapeshifter that could not be relied upon.

Tasia knew she wasn't the only one who felt the

eeriness in the pre-dawn murk. The men around her barely spoke to one another, and when they did, it was in quiet voices and short sentences. Even sounds seemed to lose their shapes and melt away into the mist.

Movement on the trail ahead of her. Tasia's heart quickened; she leaned forward on the neck of her horse, close enough that its mane tickled her face.

A rider approached, emerging like a silent mirage.

Joslyn.

Tasia let go of the breath she'd been holding, kicked her horse into a brisk walk only to realize there wasn't enough room on the trail to move around the three riders between her and the guard.

Joslyn dismounted, waiting for the winding train of soldiers to reach her. When the riders in front of her stopped, Tasia hopped off and threaded through the birch trees, wet brown leaves clinging to her riding boots.

"The way ahead is clear, Princess," the guard said wearily as Tasia approached.

"But the markings?" Tasia asked, referring to the odd white runes they kept seeing on rocks and trees.

Joslyn's gaze shifted away for a moment, thoughtful. "I suspect… There are pockets of small men who still live in this part of the Zaris Mountains, isolated from their larger tribes further north."

"Small men," Tasia breathed, the words sending a thrill through her chest. She'd always wanted to see the small men her mother used to speak of. "Did you see any?"

"We won't see them," Joslyn said. "Not unless they

want to be seen."

"That's what the runes we keep seeing are? Small men?" asked the soldier, Alric, who'd been riding point. He was one of the oldest soldiers of the ones who still rode eastward, and unofficially he had become the commander in the absence of any officers. Joslyn and Norix had worked together to talk Tasia out of making her bodyguard the commanding officer; Joslyn didn't want to do it because she felt her primary duty was still to guard the Princess, Norix didn't say why he didn't like the idea, other than that it would be "improper." Tasia suspected he didn't like the idea of a nomad leading the expedition. Especially a female nomad.

Joslyn's brow creased, troubled. "I'm not certain that the runes are from the small men. But it seems likely — given the height, the style. If there were ordinary men near here, I would have found them."

Tasia nodded.

Joslyn had left them the day before, when the sun had begun its western descent. Tasia had sent her to scout the trail ahead and figure out where the mysterious white runes had come from. The guard had been gone the rest of that afternoon, the whole of the night, the better part of this morning.

Even though Tasia had been the one to send her to scout ahead, Joslyn's absence had left the Princess feeling unsettled. She trusted Joslyn. And with time to contemplate it further in the silence of their morning's ride, Tasia realized she trusted her guard more than she trusted anyone else in the entire entourage, even more than Norix.

"What makes you so sure you would find men, if indeed there were men to be found?" asked Alric.

Joslyn gave a half-hearted shrug. "Because I would have."

Alric grunted, unconvinced.

"Joslyn lived in the Zaris Mountains for several years," Tasia said. "Before she joined the Imperial Army."

Alric looked askance at Joslyn. "I thought you were a desert nomad?"

"I am," Joslyn answered, and offered nothing more.

"Since when do desert nomads live in the Zaris Mountains?"

Joslyn shrugged again and said nothing.

Alric continued to stare at Joslyn, openly taking his measure of her. Tasia thought to intervene, to say something on her guard's behalf, but it would be inappropriate to allow her favoritism to show.

"Well," said Alric, turning to the soldiers on his left and his right, "if small men do appear, I'm sure we could impale two per sword, eh, boys?"

One man chuckled uncomfortably, the other man managed a smile, but it looked more like a grimace.

"Small men are peaceful," Joslyn said. "They do not pick quarrels unnecessarily."

"Small men?" asked a gruff voice behind Tasia. She turned. Norix. She hadn't realized the Wise Man had come up behind her.

Alric nodded. "That's what the nomad woman says.

That the runes we've been seeing are the work of small men."

"Hmmpf," said Norix. Ever since Joslyn had convinced Tasia to journey north into the mountains, the old man had been particularly cranky.

"What can you tell us of the small folk, Wise Man?" asked one of the soldiers.

"That they are small," Norix said. "Child-sized cave dwellers with childlike minds, who care only for shiny baubles and hiding beneath their mountains."

He turned without waiting for anyone to reply, heading back towards the bow-legged pony that served as his mount.

"The sun is coming up. We should ride," Joslyn said.

"Aye," said Alric. "We should."

Tasia was glad that the two had found something they could agree upon, but tension still hung between them, suspended in the mist.

"We should be able to make it to Goat's Beard Pass by sundown," Joslyn said. "If we hurry."

"Then let's hurry," Alric said. He swept an arm forward, and there was a touch of condescending sarcasm in his voice when he said, "Lead the way, desert nomad of the mountains."

Some of the other soldiers chuckled.

But Joslyn did not react to his words. She simply nodded and mounted her horse, taking over the responsibility of riding point.

Tasia sighed and returned to her own horse,

disappointed that she would be riding with only her own thoughts for company yet another day.

27

They did indeed make it to Goat's Beard Pass in time for the evening meal, setting up camp on a flat outcropping of rock at a cliff's edge. As usual, Tasia took her meal inside her tent, away from the soldiers.

She wanted company — she'd barely spoken a word all day — but ever since the night of the raid, she'd discovered a fresh determination to prove herself the princess who would inherit her father's crown one day. She'd killed a man. She reminded herself of it each night. She hadn't run. She hadn't hidden. She'd followed the sounds of chaos and killed a man who meant her people harm. And then she'd overruled the counsel of Norix and ordered the injured home as she herself continued east.

She was the Princess of the Four Realms, heir to the crown, future Empress of House Dorsa, and she had killed a man. It was no longer for her to sit around the campfire and banter with the soldiers. She would eat apart and sleep apart and speak apart.

But she was relieved when Joslyn finished her inspection of the camp's perimeter and pushed open the tent flap, stooping low to make it through the entrance.

They'd sent the grand tent of the Princess back to Port Lorsin with Sanda. In fact, they'd sent all their large, comfortable tents back to Port Lorsin — which, now that Tasia thought about it, might have been another reason why Norix was so grumpy. The tents that remained were small affairs, soldiers' tents. And even though Tasia had the largest of them, it was tall enough at its peak only to kneel in, and barely wide enough for herself, Joslyn, and their two packs.

"Is the campsite secure?" Tasia asked the guard, thinking of no other way to open a conversation. Speaking felt odd after being silent most of the day; the words felt foreign in her mouth, and for the briefest of moments she wondered if she had spoken in the common tongue or something else.

"Yes," Joslyn replied, and her own voice was heavy with exhaustion. She settled cross-legged on her sleeping mat, pulling an oilcloth from her pack and unsheathing her sword.

The guard seemed ready for more silence, but Tasia wasn't. "Tomorrow we descend onto the plateau?"

"Yes. And hopefully we will descend off the Yellow Plateau and into the valley as well, depending on the freshness of the horses after the descent."

She ran the oilcloth down the length of the blade, her hand moving in slow, rhythmic strokes. The kind of strokes that told Tasia the guard had repeated this ritual hundreds of times — no, thousands of times. Perhaps a hundred-thousand times.

"And how long until we reach the front?"

Joslyn paused without looking up. "Another week,"

she said. She moved the cloth down the sword again. She twisted, reaching behind her for the scabbard, and Tasia did not miss the way her face suddenly curdled into pain.

"Your wound," Tasia said. "Did you change the dressing on it while you scouted?"

Joslyn shook her head, bringing the scabbard back to her lap. "There was no time. I did not leave my horse's back once." Although she did not wince again, Tasia noticed how gingerly she moved this time, how slow she was when she put the sword back into its sheath.

Tasia clucked her tongue against the roof of her mouth. "You didn't sleep?"

Joslyn shook her head again.

"You must be so weary."

The guard hesitated, gave a subtle nod.

"Take off your tunic," Tasia said, scooting closer to Joslyn. "I'll help you change your bandages."

Joslyn made no move to lift her tunic at first, hand still resting on the sword lying across her lap. Then she sighed and put her weapon beside her, lifting the tunic with stiff movements.

Blood showed through the white bandage. It was dark underneath, bright red closer to the surface.

"Joslyn! How long have you been bleeding like this?"

"I don't know. My mind has been elsewhere."

Tasia crawled forward, splaying her own legs on either side of Joslyn's crossed ones so that she could reach the bandage across the guard's middle.

She unwound the cloth as gently as she could, but

Joslyn's breath still hitched and fell in a shallow, rapid pattern. Tasia tossed the bloody cloth aside and pulled the lantern over. She leaned closer to the wound.

"Mother Moon and Father Sun," Tasia muttered. She looked up, meeting the guard's eyes. "You managed to pull out about half of your stitches, did you know that? What do you have to say for yourself?"

Joslyn said nothing. Her face was pale. Not as pale as it had been the night of the battle, but still too drawn, too worn, with circles too dark beneath her eyes.

Tasia grinned to show that she wasn't actually cross with the guard. "You must enjoy needles in your flesh."

The smallest of smiles appeared around the edges of Joslyn's mouth. "It depends on who's doing the sewing."

"Well, you must like it when I'm the one doing the sewing, because this is the third time I've had to sew you closed."

"I do like it," Joslyn said. "You have a gentle touch. If you hadn't been born a princess, perhaps you could have been a surgeon or an apothecary."

"No. Only Wise Men are apothecaries and surgeons. And Wise Men are all... well, *men.*"

Tasia saw the small black box that contained Joslyn's medical supplies peeking out from her sack, and she reached for it so that Joslyn wouldn't have to.

"Emperors are usually men," Joslyn said.

"Emperors are *always* men. Empresses are *always* women," Tasia said, glad to banter with the guard.

"You know what I meant."

Tasia pulled out Joslyn's box of medical supplies. A scrap of parchment stuck to a corner of the box and came out with it.

The Princess picked up the scrap of paper. "What's this?"

"It's…"

But Tasia unfolded the parchment scrap before Joslyn could answer. A dried purple flower with a yellow center tumbled out of it.

"…a flower," the guard finished.

Tasia glanced up, a question in her eyes. Something about the guard's own expression gave her pause. Joslyn looked as if she might speak, but then she simply shook her head.

"A flower?" Tasia said.

In the months that she'd known the guard, she'd never seen her say or do or possess anything that hinted at frivolity. Everything about Joslyn served a purpose, and her pack was a good example of that. Until now, Tasia had thought it contained only her medical kit, a map, her tools for sharpening and polishing her weapons, and a few spare changes of clothes.

But… a flower? Tucked away at the bottom of the canvas pack? What could it mean?

"We should mend my stitches, Princess," Joslyn said. "Tomorrow will be another long day."

Tasia nodded and opened the box, pulling forth the needle, thread, the small bottle of clear liquid, and dried moss. She knew the routine at this point, and needed no instruction.

"Why do you have a flower?" Tasia asked as she threaded the needle. She wouldn't meet Joslyn's eyes, probably because she knew that she was intruding. But nevertheless she felt compelled to ask.

"Someone gave it to me. A very long time ago."

"Who?"

"A girl," Joslyn said simply.

Tasia took up the business of sewing closed the guard's flesh where the stitches had come out. Except for a slight quickening of breath, Joslyn gave no indication that she even felt the needle. Tasia wondered idly if so many years of pain — at the hands of slave masters, at the hands of enemies on various battlefields — had somehow inured Joslyn to normal levels of pain. Perhaps she truly barely felt the needle. But perhaps she only pretended, refusing to reveal her pain to Tasia.

"You know that you can talk to me, don't you?" Tasia said. "Whatever you tell me about yourself, I'm not going to share it with anyone else." Tasia spoke without looking up from her work, dabbing at the blood that still seeped from the wound. "Gods, you know more about my own life than I ever wanted you to or expected you to."

The guard let out a strained breath as the needle slipped into Joslyn's skin again.

"What do you mean?" the guard asked.

Tasia's eyes darted up, then back to her work. "I assume you're joking, Joslyn, because I know you're not dense." She wiped the needle off, turned her attention back to her work as she spoke again. "For one… You figured everything out about Mylla without my ever telling you. I don't think anyone else knew — well, a chambermaid or two, probably, but no one who really mattered."

"So chambermaids don't matter." Joslyn's carried the edge of an accusation.

"Chambermaids don't generally overthrow empires. And the chambermaids at the palace have served my family for generations. Our families are… what do you call it? Symbiotic." Tasia tied off the last stitch, reached for a fresh bandage. She'd boiled the ones from two days ago, which made them clean, but they were still stained with the faint dark brown of dried blood. "And while the chambermaids may have known about Mylla, they don't know about what it's like to go to council meetings. Or to be berated by my father in front of his advisors. Or to sneak off to the Speckled Dog only to nearly lose my life over my own foolishness. But you've been there. For all of it."

Joslyn said nothing.

"So don't you think it's only fair? You know so much about me. But you won't tell me anything about yourself."

"I'm your bodyguard, Tasia. Not your friend."

"Not my…"

Tears rose in Tasia's chest without any warning, unwelcome and unanticipated. *It's because I'm so tired,* she told herself. She swallowed them before they could show.

"Then Mother Moon must have decided that I am to

have no friends," Tasia said. "Not you. Not Mylla." She snorted. "Mace of House Gifford. Maybe I will make a friend of him once he serves his purpose of impregnating me with the Empire's precious heir." Tasia shook her head, and for some reason, she thought of her brother, her mother. "Did you ever think, Joslyn, that maybe you and I are both slaves, just in different ways?"

She didn't expect the guard to reply. Talking to Joslyn was often like talking to herself, for all the guard ever said. She reached around behind the guard's back with the bandage, fingertips brushing the place where the guard's muscles sloped inward to meet her backbone.

"Anaís," Joslyn said.

Tasia stopped, her hands still on the guard's back.

"Her name was Anaís. The girl who gave me the flower," Joslyn said.

Afraid that Joslyn would stop talking if she asked one of the thousand questions that had suddenly flooded her mind, Tasia said nothing. She focused on wrapping the clean bandages around the guard's abdomen. And listened.

"I loved her," said Joslyn. "Or thought I did. And I assumed that she loved me, too." She sighed and shook her head. "We were so young. Old for our age, maybe, and world-weary, but still young. Looking back now, that's all I can see — how young we were."

Tasia continued to wrap the wound, her hands unfurling the bandage as slowly as she could, as if by slowing the process of treating the guard she could also make the story last. Joslyn's eyes took on a far-away cast, and somehow

Tasia knew she wasn't really in the tent anymore. She had traveled down a tunnel into her past.

"There was a huge fountain in the center of the city; it was where the slaves and the servants congregated as we drew water for the men and women who owned us," Joslyn said. "That was how I met Anaís. She was a slave, too." She paused. "No one had ever loved me before; that's probably why I allowed myself to become so... intoxicated by her. We helped each other escape, and I assumed that escaping together meant we would run away together. But there was a boy. A stablehand for the family that owned her," Joslyn said, and the statement was dark, like gathering thunderheads. "He was the one she ran away with. On the night we all ran away, she left me with the flower as... as a way of saying goodbye. As a 'thank you,' I suppose." Bitterly, she added: "The stablehand got Anaís. I got the flower."

Tasia tied off the bandage at Joslyn's side as the guard had taught her to do, tucking the ends of the knot beneath the cloth. She waited for Joslyn to say more, but nearly a minute passed in silence.

"I'm sorry, Joslyn. That she did that to you."

Tasia kept her eyes on the bandage instead of the guard's face as she spoke, measuring her words carefully, sensing that how she responded to this slight opening Joslyn had given her would decide whether or not the opening would widen or close forever.

"I know it's not the same thing as what I went through with Mylla," the Princess said. "We weren't slaves, of course, and I always knew she would leave me for a boy eventually, but... But it didn't break my heart any less. So I'm sorry."

Joslyn shrugged. "It was a very long time ago. And I was hardly more than a child."

Tasia hesitated. "Yes, but... sometimes I wonder if a broken heart ever truly heals. Or maybe it does heal, but it heals the way a broken bone does. Forever crooked and misshapen."

"My *ku-sai* used to say that when the body repairs a broken bone, it rebuilds it stronger than it ever was before." Joslyn let out a long breath, winced. "I like to think the heart is the same way. That once it heals, it is stronger than ever."

"And yet you still carry her flower in your pack." Tasia reached over and plucked the dried purple flower from the mat where it had fallen, carefully placing it back into the parchment. She handed it to Joslyn.

The guard accepted the parchment, studied it for a moment without opening it. "Yes. I still carry the flower."

"Why?"

Joslyn looked up. "Perhaps I keep it to remind myself never to allow someone to exploit such a vulnerability again. A part of my heart's new strength."

"Perhaps," Tasia said. "Or perhaps there's a part of you that still loves her, despite what she did to you."

Joslyn reached out, and for an instant Tasia thought she was reaching for her. But the guard reached around Tasia, picking up the lantern and setting it down between them.

Joslyn unlatched the lantern and swung open its hatch, dipping the piece of parchment with the dried flower into the flame. It caught immediately, fire eating the old paper with a soft *whoosh*. Joslyn dropped it to the bare earth before it could burn her fingers, then licked a thumb and ground out what was left of the flame before anything else could catch.

"I can't believe you just did that," Tasia said, breathless. The flower was nothing more than a smudge of ash.

"I should've done it long ago." Joslyn picked her tunic up off the sleeping mat and shrugged into it, taking care not to stretch too much to disturb the fresh stitches and bandage. She laid down on her mat, her back towards Tasia, her face a foot from the tent's entrance. "I should catch up on sleep," she said, voice muffled in the small space.

Tasia made no move to lie down. She didn't want to accept the abrupt end to what had practically passed as an intimate conversation between them. But she knew Joslyn well enough by now to know she wasn't going to get anything else out of the guard tonight, and so she gave a nod that Joslyn couldn't see and settled down onto her own sleeping mat, wrapping the wool blankets around her as closely as she could.

She came up on one elbow. "Joslyn?"

"Hmm?"

"Thank you. For telling me all that."

There was no answer, so Tasia turned down the lantern's light and closed her eyes.

And then, in the darkness: "You're welcome, Tasia."

28

Tasia's sleep was fitful and troubled. At first she couldn't sleep at all, and when she finally did nod off, her dreams were restless, disturbing. She dreamed of Mylla, stabbing her in the side with a black iron knife, then handing her a purple flower with a yellow center as she bled to death on the floor of her bedchamber.

"I will always love you," Mylla said to a dying Tasia.

"Why did you do this?" Tasia asked her.

"I had to," said the handmaid simply, and she walked away.

That dream morphed into another, and this time Tasia was on horseback, riding through a birch forest in which spring had never arrived. Snow made everything unnaturally silent, and her breath fogged in small puffs of moisture before her. A horse came galloping towards them, and there was something odd about the burden it carried on its back. As it came closer, Tasia recognized first the horse, then its load.

"Joslyn!" she cried, heeling her own horse in the flanks.

Joslyn's horse slowed to a trot before Tasia reached it. The Princess leaped from her saddle and sprinted the rest of the way, but as so often happens in dreams, the distance warped and her feet were as if submerged in river mud —

she couldn't make it to the guard no matter how hard she ran.

The body of the guard rolled off the horse's back and landed at an unnatural angle. Her face was white and ashen, her black eyes were open but glazed and dull.

The horse had carried a corpse back to the Princess.

"No!" Tasia screamed. "No, you cannot die! I *command* you not to die!"

The words came through frustrated tears as she continued to try — and failed — to run towards the guard.

"She was a slave," Norix said grimly beside her. "She ran away. And the punishment for a slave running away is death. You know this, Princess."

Tasia woke with a start, breathing hard and still panicked.

Which was why she thought she was just imagining it when something seemed to move in the darkness.

But then something moved again, a shuffling motion beside her. She screamed.

Joslyn sat straight up, pulling a dagger from beneath her sleeping mat at the same time.

"Tasia?" she said, completely awake.

"Something's in the tent," the Princess whispered.

Joslyn fumbled with the lantern. Dim light filled the small space.

Tasia blinked... and opened her mouth to scream again when a face with huge eyes emerged from the darkness two feet away from her.

But Joslyn was faster than Tasia's scream. She clapped

a hand over the Princess's mouth and pulled her backwards.

"Shh," she said in Tasia's ear. "It's a small man. He won't hurt you."

The eyes blinked, pupils set in ghost-pale blue shrinking to the size of pinpricks.

Tasia had never seen a creature with eyes so big relative to its face. She'd seen an owl once in the daytime — the tiny, shrieking kind that was common in the Capital Lands. The owl had overlarge eyes compared to the rest of its head, but those eyes were like peas compared to the eyes that stared back at her now. Each was the size of her palm, with a small, button nose set between them and a smallish mouth beneath.

Norix had been right: Small men looked childlike.

But the skin on the face disrupted the illusion. The small man's skin was wrinkled and cracked like old leather. The small man wasn't just old; he was ancient.

Her heart quickened. A small man — an actual, living, breathing small man. Except for his wrinkled skin, he looked exactly like the small men illustrated in Mother's old children's books, the ones she used to read to Tasia and Nik when they were little.

The small man pointed a crooked finger at the tent entrance. "Come," he said. "Follow."

He stepped over Tasia's ankles and pushed open the tent flap. He turned back, glancing over his shoulder. "Come. Follow."

Tasia looked at Joslyn, but the guard had already pulled on her boots and was busy strapping her sword to her waist.

"We're following him?" Tasia whispered. "Is it safe?"

"Yes," Joslyn said. "If he meant to harm us, we would already be dead. Small men do not usually make themselves known unless they have a very good reason. And when they ask you to follow, you follow." She picked up the lantern and stepped outside the tent.

Tasia steadied her nerves, pulled on her trousers and boots, and followed.

#

Soundlessly, the small man picked his way through the small encampment on bare feet. Like his saucer-like eyes, his hands and feet were also disproportionately large compared to the rest of his body. Despite the fact that he barely reached Tasia's waist, his hands were at least as large as the guard's, though his stubby fingers lacked the elegance of Joslyn's long, graceful fingers. His feet were nearly twice Joslyn's size. But even though the hands and feet made him look impossibly out-of-proportion, his movements were graceful, fluid.

He led them away from the ridge and into the forest, parting bushes to reveal a game trail. He glanced over his shoulder once to make sure that Tasia and Joslyn still followed, then disappeared into the undergrowth.

The small man proceeded down the game trail the same way he had walked through the camp — gracefully and silently. Joslyn managed to move quietly as well, like a practiced huntress. Tasia, on the other hand, stumbled through like a drunken sailor. Between the dark, the protruding roots, and the interfering brambles and branches, her progress was slow. She knew she was being too loud, too conspicuous, but she couldn't help it. She wasn't a small man and she wasn't the ever-talented Joslyn. She was a princess, in the woods, at night, following a fairy tale down a nearly pitch-black trail on the side of a mountain.

Tasia couldn't say how long they followed the game trail; it might have been fifteen minutes, it might have been an hour — she was too busy concentrating on trying not to fall to mark the passage of time.

She wondered where the small man was leading them, wondered if he actually had a destination in mind or was simply leading them into some remote part of the woods to ambush them. He was tiny, she reminded herself; so tiny that she could probably overpower him without Joslyn's help. But would that matter if he took them someplace where his cohorts were already waiting? Could she overpower five of them at once? Ten of them? Twenty? And how many small men would it take to defeat Joslyn?

Eventually, the trail grew broader, smoother. Tasia was able to catch up with Joslyn and whispered to the guard, "How far have we gone from the camp? What if he leads us into a trap?"

Joslyn only shook her head and put a finger to her lips.

Despite Tasia keeping her voice low, the small man must have overheard her. He glanced up at her, meeting her eyes.

"Close," he said. He pointed into the forest.

They moved uphill, birch trees spreading further apart, undergrowth thinning. It became harder to distinguish the trail from the rest of the land around them. As they crested the hill, the trees disappeared altogether, and the undergrowth was replaced by low, scrubby grass, glistening a moist yellow-green in the moonlight.

The grass wasn't the only thing that gleamed in the moonlight. White runes, similar to the ones Joslyn had investigated a few days ago, were painted on boulders scattered along the top of the hill. On first glance, Tasia thought the boulders with the runes were randomly placed, but upon second glance, she realized they marked a rough circle.

Something other than moonlight emanated upwards from the other side of the hill, giving the horizon a soft orange glow. That was puzzling. It was much too early for dawn, and although Tasia's sense of direction wasn't as accurate as either of her two companions, she was relatively certain they weren't facing east.

"Here," said the small man. He waited until Joslyn and Tasia stood next to him, then crouched low in the grass and indicated the bottom of the opposite side of the hill.

Tasia followed his gaze and saw a bonfire glowing below them, a bonfire surrounded by another, much tighter ring of rune-marked boulders. Beyond the boulders, staring at the fire, were small men, dozens of them. One held a steel-tipped spear at least twice its height.

She knew it. He'd led them into a trap. She and Joslyn

were about to be impaled by a midget with a seven-foot spear.

But just as Tasia moved to seize Joslyn's arm and run with the guard back down the hill, she realized that the bonfire wasn't a bonfire at all. The fire was rapidly moving — *bouncing,* even — from edge to edge of the ring of boulders.

She squinted. How could a fire move like that?

There was something inside the fire. A figure. She made out a face, then hands, then...

Tasia gasped. The figure wasn't *in* the fire. The figure *was* the fire.

What had seemed like ordinary flames at first were not flames but ever-morphing features. Now it was a white and yellow and orange fire, now it was a long face, with fangs the length of a man's hand and huge, curled horns like a ram. Now it was a burning branch, now it was an arm, thin and spindly, finishing in talon-tipped fingers. Then the thing morphed again, and there were only ordinary flames, licking the night sky, sending off sparks that floated lazily higher on the updraft of hot air.

The fire — the creature — the *fire-creature* — shrieked with what could only be interpreted as an all-too human frustration.

Tasia seized Joslyn's arm, but this time it wasn't because she wanted to run from the small man. She grabbed her guard on instinct, the way one might grab onto a chair or table when feeling faint.

"Did you see...?" she managed to say.

"Yes," Joslyn said, and the word was barely more than a breath.

"Have you ever seen something like...?" Tasia whispered.

"No."

The small man observed Tasia and Joslyn's reactions. He nodded, possibly in approval.

"Safe," he said. Then the wrinkled skin of his face folded into a deep frown. "But circle weak. Not hold much longer."

Joslyn drew her sword.

The small man reached up, tapped the flat side of the blade. "Not work," he said. He pointed at the fire-creature. "Ancient. Only work power."

"Power?" repeated Joslyn.

The small man nodded. "Only work power. Come."

He beckoned them forward, walking down the hill towards the spear-wielding small man.

One of the small men broke away from the group as Tasia, Joslyn, and their guide approached. The new small man must have been younger; his skin lacked the cracked leather appearance of the one who'd brought the Princess and guard. He glanced at the newcomers, then said something to their guide in a tongue Tasia had never heard before. The language was gravelly, deep, like the shifting of boulders deep under the earth. The elder small man responded, and when he spoke in his native tongue his voice carried more weight, more bass.

The younger one nodded and returned to his spot,

planting the butt of his spear in the ground next to his companions.

Tasia counted the small men surrounding the rune-marked stones that were apparently containing the fire-creature. She counted in part because she was curious, because her mother said it was rare to see more than five or six small men at one time, but she also counted because she couldn't bear to look at the fire-creature. She couldn't bear to listen to it shriek, to watch it bounce from one side of the circle to the other as it morphed from shapeless flame into terrifying almost-human features.

Twenty-seven. There were twenty-seven of the small men, staring gravely at the fire-creature. Their lips moved back and forth, but the fire-creature's shrieks made it impossible to know if they were making any sound.

"Why did you bring us?" Joslyn asked the small man.

The elder pointed at her. "Warrior," he said. "Small men have power. Tall men forgot. But small men — no warrior."

"Joslyn," Tasia said, a warning in her tone. "He's not suggesting you fight it, is he?" She shook her head. "I forbid it."

Now the small man looked directly at Tasia, his huge eyes solemn and rimmed red by the light of the creature behind him. "Circle weak. Fail soon. Circle fail, then *undatai* kill small men, kill tall men. Kill all things." He held out a hand, and the small man with the long spear trotted forward, handing the spear to the elder. The old small man extended the spear towards the guard. "Warrior kill. Small men keep *undatai* in circle."

Joslyn said nothing. She did not accept the spear.

"Oon-duh… tie?" Tasia said.

The small man turned his head, regarded the fire-creature gravely for a moment. *"Undatai.* Monster from mountain of fire." He offered the spear again to Joslyn. "Warrior kill *undatai* or *undatai* kill all."

Monster from mountain of fire. It was exactly what the thing looked like. Tasia stared at it a long moment, terrified and mesmerized at once, watching as horns, talons, fangs, tail appeared and disappeared from the flames.

"It's too dangerous," she said out-loud, though she wasn't sure if she was talking to the small man or to Joslyn.

Joslyn ignored the Princess and nodded at the spear. "I thought you said weapons would have no effect? Only… power?"

The small man rotated the spear, pointed to a spot halfway up the shaft. A white rune was painted there, carved into the wood.

"Power," said the small man.

It didn't look like power to Tasia. It looked like an odd squiggle with two horizontal lines and a dot above it. Children's gibberish.

Power. What did the small men know about power? They were cave dwellers frightened of the world of men, superstitious big-eyed children who cared only for their gems and their gold.

And yet…

And yet there was a fire-creature only a dozen yards

away from her, apparently contained by a circle of rocks painted with more children's gibberish.

Joslyn unbuckled her sword belt and dropped it to the ground. She took the spear she had been offered earlier.

"No, you can't," Tasia said, growing frantic.

"*Undatai* break circle soon," the small man said to Tasia. "Warrior kill. Or all die — small man people, tall man people."

"Joslyn..."

It seemed as if the *undatai* knew its fate was being discussed. The flames grew taller, licking the night sky. The creature roared, and the sound seemed to rattle the entire mountainside.

The small man's voice took on an urgent tone. *"All* die when *undatai* break circle. *All.* Warrior must kill soon!"

Joslyn tested the spear's weight, spinning it before her. She looked at the Princess. "I don't think there's much choice in this, Tasia. We can't let this thing break free."

Tasia grabbed the guard's wrist. "How do we know he's telling the truth?"

"Small men are not liars."

"But why you?" Tasia asked. "We should go back to the camp, get Alric and the others. *They* can fight this thing. I don't want you getting close to it."

She glanced again at the *undatai* inside its invisible prison. Tasia wasn't sure if it could be described as having eyes, but somehow it saw her. And it looked at her — into her, through her, and even though the creature was a multitude of flames, Tasia felt suddenly cold inside, as if her heart had been doused with ice water. The *undatai* charged towards her. She flinched backward on instinct, but although she could feel the heat of it warming her face, the flames never reached her — they bounced back from the circle of rune-marked boulders.

The creature's form solidified into something that vaguely resembled a human made of flames, lava, embers. Its eyes were huge, bug-like, lacking irises or pupils; the top of its head split into two thick, curled horns; long arms hung from a broad torso; each spiderish finger ended in a wicked talon. Where the bottom half of its body should have been, though, there was only a tornado-like whirl of flames.

"Time running out," warned the small man.

Tasia seized the guard's arm. "What if it kills you?" she asked the guard.

"If it kills me... return to camp as quickly as you can and get the men far away from here."

"Not without you. I can't lead them without you."

"You can. You have been the whole time," Joslyn said. She took a breath. "Small men understand things that we don't, and they chose me for a reason. I have to do this, Tasia."

But Tasia didn't want to look at the *undatai* anymore. She'd already seen enough. It was a nightmare come to life, the kind of monster that only existed in the imagination of frightened children. It shouldn't even be here. *She* shouldn't be here.

"Tasia?" Joslyn said.

The Princess shook her head. "No," she said, although she wasn't sure what she was saying *no* to.

The guard hesitated, then rested a hand on Tasia's shoulder. "If this fight is one I don't survive, I want you to know that I... that it has been a privilege to serve you."

"No," Tasia said again. "I can't lose you."

"Warrior," the small man said. He sounded anxious. "Power hold only little time left."

Joslyn grasped the spear in both hands, holding it across her body. She moved closer towards the *undatai's* prison, hesitated. She turned back towards Tasia. "I believe you will make an excellent Empress one day."

And without waiting for the Princess to respond, Joslyn stepped inside the circle of rocks.

29

Tasia couldn't watch Joslyn fight the living nightmare. But she had to watch. She looked — then looked away. It was too hard to see the guard she had come to care for facing the monster made of fire.

Joslyn was graceful and nimble, always one step ahead of the wild swipe of the creature's flame-engulfed talons. It shrieked and swung; Joslyn danced away. It shrieked again, this time with a jet of fire streaming forth from its mouth; Joslyn danced away again.

The Princess couldn't watch. She had to watch.

Tasia's breaths came in ragged pants, as if she'd sprinted all this way to watch the battle between guard and monster. And then her breath wouldn't come at all, as if her chest was being crushed under a huge stone.

Joslyn was nimble, but the creature obeyed none of reality's ordinary rules.

The spear thrust outward, but the creature flickered like a sputtering candle, and the spear passed through nothingness. Joslyn spun, ducked, kneeled, thrust: The spear passed through nothingness.

After a long stalemate in which neither fighter managed to gain the upper hand, they both slowed. Joslyn and the creature circled one another with careful deliberateness, each one of them a hunter stalking prey, a cat toying with a mouse. But which was the cat and which was the mouse?

Joslyn darted forward, feigning a thrust that turned into a sideways jab. The spear tip finally struck home, burying itself in a knot of flames as the *undatai* screamed in agony. Joslyn yanked the spear back, and something molten and orange dripped from the long tip.

Blood?

But retaliation came faster than Tasia could have imagined: One moment the *undatai* was in front of Joslyn, writhing in what could only be interpreted as pain; the next moment it was behind her, its talons digging deep into the guard's back.

Joslyn's torso arched backwards and she let out a high-pitched wail of pain. In slow motion, the guard collapsed to her knees, then face first into the dirt. A wet smear of blood between her shoulder blades shone in the light of the *undatai's* flames.

The spear rolled from her fingers.

A woman screamed, the sound carrying in the clear night sky. It wasn't until the scream ended that Tasia realized it had come from her.

"Joslyn!" she shouted when she recovered her wits. Tasia didn't think; she charged into the circle, landing hard on her knees beside the guard.

When Tasia was a child, her mother had given her a glass bauble. Inside was a miniature world that depicted her mother's home in the Northeastern mountains. There was a small hut made of logs with a couple holding hands outside it, alpine trees, mountains jutting up in the distance. And when Tasia shook the bauble, snowflakes swirled — a blizzard around the hand-holding couple that gradually slowed to a light dusting.

On hard days, especially after her mother died, Tasia used to stare inside that perfect glass world, dreaming that she was one half of the couple that stood outside the humble cabin. She would be a commoner, living a simple life in the mountains, surrounded by snow and the scent of pine trees.

Stepping through the invisible barrier marked by the rune-painted boulders was like stepping into the glass bauble. The world beyond the barrier shimmered and distorted, like something seen through a thick window pane. And inside the circle was a silence so complete that Tasia couldn't even hear the sound of air in her ears.

She screamed Joslyn's name, trying to shake the guard awake, but the sound that came from her mouth was muffled, like screaming underwater. Tasia had the eerie sense that she was both *here* and also *not here*, and that Joslyn was somehow even more *not here*.

Tasia tried again, even as she sensed the *not here* fire-creature had discovered her presence and would be upon her any moment.

"You cannot leave me," Tasia said in the guard's ear. On impulse, the Princess turned Joslyn's face and kissed her full on the mouth.

Joslyn coughed, blood speckling her lips. Roughly, she shoved Tasia away, grabbed the spear, and rolled onto her back. She brought the spear's gleaming tip up just as the *undatai* pounced onto the space the Princess had occupied a moment earlier.

The sound of the monster's howl was deafening, and if she'd truly been inside her mother's glass bauble, the glass would have exploded outwards in a million tiny bits.

Tasia scrambled backwards, shielding her eyes from the blinding flash of light that came from the space above Joslyn. The air around her rippled, glistening like sunlight striking water.

Then all was still. And dark.

Joslyn dropped the spear, and it clattered to the ground with exactly the sound a spear *should* make when it fell. There was nothing muffled about it. Nothing *here* but *not here*. Joslyn fell back to the ground. Her eyes fluttered closed.

Tasia scrambled on hands and knees to the guard's side. "Joslyn?" She shook the woman's shoulders. "Wake up. Please? Wake up."

The guard inhaled — a long, rasping breath that sounded like wind sucked through a narrow pipe. Her dark eyes opened, but they were dull and distant, unseeing.

Tasia shook her again. "Come back to me. Please come back."

The guard's eyes did not blink. She breathed, but she did not answer.

Tasia patted one of Joslyn's cheeks, softly at first, then with more force. Joslyn did not respond. She shook the guard, first saying her name, then screaming it. Joslyn did not respond.

Tasia felt the presence of someone beside her, and looked up to see the small man standing over her, his expression grave.

"What's wrong with her?" Tasia asked, frantic. "She's... she's awake but not awake. Is she..." She didn't know how to finish the question. *Is she still alive?* didn't seem to be the right question, since she could see that the guard was definitely breathing, and her eyes were open. "Help me roll her over," Tasia commanded the small man. "I need to see the wound."

The small man made no move to help her, but Tasia didn't care. She rolled Joslyn onto her side, leaning closer to see the place where moonlight shone on something dark and sticky. Three deep puncture marks in Joslyn's black leather guard's uniform marked the place where the *undatai* had dug its talons into her back. The dark, sticky patch was almost dry; no fresh blood flowed from the wound.

That was strange. Tasia ran her fingers over the three punctures, pressing gingerly, expecting more blood to seep out, but nothing happened.

She looked up at the small man beside her. "What's happening to her?"

"Warrior kill *undatai*," the small man said. "But *undatai* take warrior back to own world. Warrior still fights."

"What do you mean, 'back to own world'? What world?"

"*Undatai* world. Other world."

"There is only one world," Tasia said, but she heard the doubt in her own voice. "Everything else is superstition — the Wise Men proved that centuries ago."

The small man said nothing.

"I don't care where she went. She needs to come back," Tasia said. "Do something."

The small man shook his head. "Do nothing. Warrior must find own way back."

"And if she doesn't find her way back?"

"Body stay *here*." He tapped his chest. "But mind stay *there*." The small man paused, studying Tasia. "Then warrior become *undatai*."

Cold gripped her heart.

She clasped Joslyn's hands in her own, pressing them to her chest, squeezing them as if the pressure alone might rouse the guard from her catatonic state. "You can't leave me, Joslyn. I need you here, with me."

Silently, she added, *I think I love you.*

#

Hours passed, and the night sky shifted from inky black to deep navy. Stars began to fade from view; the moon's brilliance dulled. Tasia still kneeled next to Joslyn in the same position, still rocked back and forth with both her hands wrapped around one of the guard's, pressing it to her chest. Her knees were wet and sore from kneeling so long on the damp earth; her head was stuffy and ached from too many tears.

She was vaguely aware that, early on in her vigil, the small men had conferred together, speaking in their own language, and then dispersed. The elderly small man, the one who had guided her and Joslyn to the *undatai* in the first place, was the only one who remained behind.

He stayed a respectful distance away from Tasia, and the two of them did not speak as the minutes passed into hours. But finally, as the sky began to lighten, Tasia turned on him.

"Why did you bring us here?" she asked, but the question carried the weight of accusation.

He nodded as if he had been expecting the question. "Small men watching you. Watching warrior. Small men knew warrior could kill *undatai*. We trapped inside power circle for warrior."

"Where did it come from?" Tasia asked.

"Under mountain." His large eyes grew sad. "Killed many small men. Entire city."

An entire city of small men, slaughtered by the *undatai* before they managed to trap it on the mountainside. Tasia could believe it. The creature seemed capable of unfathomable destruction.

"How did you trap it?"

The small man picked up a rock from the circle that had marked the undatai's prison, brought it to Tasia. Despite the fact that the rock was nearly the same size as his chest, the elderly small man carried it with ease. Tasia supposed that his surprising strength wasn't so surprising; the small men were miners at heart, and probably carried such stones each day of their lives as a matter of course.

He dropped the small boulder next to Tasia. With a wrinkled finger, he traced the white lines of the rune. "Old language contains power," he said.

"Old language?" Tasia looked at the white lines. They didn't resemble any letters she'd ever seen. They looked like nothing but random scribbling. "What old language?"

"Language of tall men. The old tall men. Small men learned power from tall men, but tall men have forgotten. Small men still remember."

Cautiously, Tasia let go of Joslyn's hand and reached out towards the white rune. Half-afraid something strange would happen to her when she touched it, she allowed one finger tip to brush the white line. But she felt nothing special — no thrum of the so-called power, no change in texture or in temperature. It was just a white marking on a black stone, not any different from the many markings her party had seen since they began their journey through the Zaris Mountains.

Beside her, Joslyn shuddered. The guard let out a long and ragged breath, the sound of an exhausted sigh.

Tasia spun. "Joslyn? Can you hear me?"

Joslyn's eyes fell closed, slowly opened again. She blinked a few times, like one just waking after a long and deep sleep. Dark eyes found Tasia's, and at last there was a spark of consciousness in them. The guard pushed herself halfway up, supporting her weight on one elbow.

"Princess?" she said. She glanced around, troubled expression passing over her face like a shadow.

"Yes, Joslyn, I'm here," Tasia said, relief washing through her chest.

"What place is this?" the guard asked.

Tasia frowned. "The mountainside. Where the small man led us."

Joslyn glanced from Tasia to the small man. "Where I fought the *undatai*?"

"Yes, of course. You never left."

Joslyn yanked away the hand that the Princess still held, then scrabbled backwards on hands and heels. She snatched the spear that had killed the *undatai*, and before Tasia understood what was happening, the spear's tip hovered an inch from her chest.

"Joslyn! What are you doing?" Instinctively, Tasia leaned backward, away from the spear tip.

In a flash, and without letting go of the spear, Joslyn leapt to her feet.

"Who are you? Who are you *really?*" she demanded, holding the spear within thrusting distance of Tasia. She cast a sideways glance at the small man, who remained crouched in the same spot he'd occupied before, seemingly untroubled. "Who are you both?"

"Joslyn. You know me," Tasia said, voice wavering. "It's me. Tasia."

The guard jabbed the spear in Tasia's direction, stopping it a few inches short of her chest. "Prove it!"

Tasia held up both hands. "Calm down," she said, trying to put authority back into her voice. "You killed the *undatai* a few hours ago, but it injured you and..." She hesitated and glanced at the small man, who nodded. "And you went to the *undatai's* world. But you found your way back now."

"You have proven nothing." Joslyn's voice was ice-cold.

Tasia got to her feet. "I am the Princess Natasia of House Dorsa," she said sternly, placing her hands on her hips. "Daughter of the Emperor Andreth the Just and Empress Crestienne the Fair."

"What did you call your brother?" Joslyn demanded.

Tasia glanced down at the spear's tip, still only a foot away from her. "His name was Nikhost. I called him Nik."

"The name of your handmaid?"

"Lady Mylla of House Harthing." Tasia hesitated. "I loved her, once."

"False!" Joslyn roared. "The *real* Princess still loves her handmaid."

"You're wrong. I speak the truth," Tasia said calmly. She stepped forward, let the cold tip of the spear bite against the light fabric of the sleeping gown covering her chest. "I *did* love Mylla once, but it was a child's love for another child. She cares for nothing but the advancement of her House. I care for… more than that."

This seemed to give Joslyn pause. "The real Princess never told me that," she said, but some of the fury had drained from her voice.

Something occurred to Tasia. "My love for Mylla was like your love for Anaís."

The tip of the spear wavered, then dropped a few

inches. Tense seconds passed in silence.

"What did I burn in the lantern, the night I fought the *undatai*?" Joslyn asked.

"A dried flower. The flower she gave you on the night she ran off with the stable boy."

The spear's tip fell to the earth. "Tasia?" the guard whispered.

Tears pricked the Princess's eyes. "Yes, Joslyn. It's me."

"Warrior is home now," the small man said without rising from his crouch. He pointed at the pile of ash that had been the *undatai*. "Ash of *undatai*." He pointed at the ring of boulders. "Circle of *undatai* trap." He pointed at the spear that the guard held. "Spear marked in old language."

Joslyn's eyes flitted to the spear, to the spot where the white rune had been carved into its shaft.

"Am I back?" she said softly. The question was filled with wonderment, and seemed posed mainly to herself. "Am I truly back?"

"Warrior is home now," the small man repeated with a nod.

The guard let go of the spear and it fell to the earth. Tasia closed the distance between them in two long steps, throwing her arms around the guard and pulling her into a tight embrace.

The guard stiffened, then relaxed and returned the embrace.

"You scared me," Tasia whispered. "I thought I'd lost

you. I don't know where you went, but you're home now."
She stood back from the embrace. "I promise you are."

"Home," Joslyn repeated. Her tone was odd somehow. Strained. In the dying moonlight, her eyes shone with more emotion than Tasia had ever seen there before. "Yes, I suppose I am home, aren't I?"

30

The decision not to speak of the small men and the *undatai* to Norix, Alric, and the rest of their traveling companions was not one Tasia and Joslyn needed to discuss aloud. At some point, Tasia supposed, it might become relevant for them to know. But she wasn't ready to talk about it and hadn't yet thought of a way to explain it to them. Besides the fact that she personally wouldn't have believed the story of the *undatai* except that she had seen it before her very eyes, she didn't know that the *undatai* was particularly relevant to their journey. There had been a fire monster that emerged from deep underground, terrorized and slaughtered small men, and somehow escaped to the surface, only to be recaptured by magical runes by the surviving small men. Then her guard had killed it but then spent an indefinite period of time in what was apparently a world apart from the one they both knew.

Staying silent about the incident was easy. Speaking of it would only make her seem as if she had lost her mind.

What *was* difficult, however, was not being able to talk to Joslyn about it. For days after the battle with the fire-creature from deep beneath the mountain, the guard was even more distant than usual. At every opportunity, she left the group to scout ahead. At every opportunity, she avoided Tasia's attempts at conversation, finding excuses to sleep or eat or tend to her horse or sharpen her blades by herself. Even the nightly lessons in self-defense came to an end.

Which was how it came to pass that the Princess found herself sparring each evening with Alric, instead.

"I yield," he said breathlessly for the third time one evening as Tasia pressed the flat side of one of her daggers against his neck.

She released his wrist from the lock she held it in at the small of his back, sheathed the dagger.

Alric turned, wiping sweat from his brow and regarding the Princess with a bemused expression.

"Well, your Majesty," he said. "I must admit that I had planned on taking it easy on you tonight, given how long we've ridden today. But I s'pose the joke's on me, ain't it?" He shook his head. "That guard of yours might be a nomad, but she knows her way around a blade. She's taught you well."

Tasia felt eyes upon her and she turned her head, glancing past the campfire. Joslyn looked away quickly, returning her attention to the sword laying across her lap.

Tasia sighed. "Yes, she certainly has. Thank you for practicing with me, Alric."

The old soldier bowed his head respectfully. "Honor's all mine, Princess." He hesitated. "Will you be needing anything else this evening?"

In her peripheral vision, Tasia saw a knot of soldiers sitting on rocks and stumps with playing cards in their hands. She smiled.

"What's the wager for tonight?" she asked Alric.

He grinned. "Ahh, that'll be latrine digger duty for tomorrow night's camp for the loser, a portion of everyone else's rations for the winner."

"I see." One of the card players saw Tasia watching them and blushed a ferocious crimson, visible even from where she stood some fifteen feet off. She turned back to Alric. "Just don't eat too much of their rations, Alric. Joslyn says we'll spend the day ascending out of the valley tomorrow."

He chuckled. "I live to please you, Majesty. I'll make sure the boys got enough to keep their bellies full."

"Very good. You're dismissed, Alric."

Alric gave a short bow and joined the card players.

Tasia headed Joslyn's way, hoping to catch the guard while she still focused on polishing her sword, but she was intercepted halfway there by Wise Man Norix.

"A private word with you, Princess?" he said.

A few feet away from them, Joslyn packed up her sword and disappeared into the tent she shared with Tasia.

"Of course, Norix," Tasia said, even though all she actually wanted was to follow Joslyn into the tent and gauge how the guard was feeling.

The Wise Man nodded and led Tasia in the opposite direction from the tent.

"With all the single-file riding through the mountains, we have spoken very little since the night of the raid," Norix said. "Between that and the time you spend with your guard, I feel like my wisdom is hardly needed anymore." His tone was light, conversational, but Tasia sensed something else in it. Sensed that he was probing for something.

"You and I have spoken some," Tasia said carefully. "And I am sure that when we arrive on the front, I will require your wisdom as I parlay with our generals, given that the task falls to me instead of General Remington now."

"Ahh, indeed. The generals," said Norix, nodding. They walked in a slow circle around the outer perimeter of the camp, strolling as if they were back in one of the palace gardens instead of the remote wilderness of the eastern edge of the Zaris Mountains. "And about our generals... what do you plan on saying of the raid?"

The question was not what Tasia expected. She assumed Norix had pulled her aside to complain or to attempt to steer her decision-making, both of which he had been doing frequently since she had taken charge of the expedition.

"I haven't given it much thought," Tasia said honestly. "I suppose I will simply convey the basic information we have, that we were set upon by mercenaries and we — "

"It might not be wise to reveal that much, Princess," Norix interjected.

Tasia frowned. "It is too much to say that we were unexpectedly set upon?"

"By *mercenaries*," Norix said. "We still do not know who hired them. Though I do not believe we have anything to fear from General Telek — I always disagreed with Remington on that point — I promised your father I would keep an open mind. An open one, and now, more than ever, a cautious one."

"You're right, Wise Man," Tasia conceded. "Now I remember why Father holds you as his most trusted advisor. Even small details like the word 'mercenaries' make a difference."

"So they do, Princess."

"There's so much to remember all the time. About everything."

Norix patted her back and gave her a grandfatherly smile. "No Emperor — or Empress — has ever ruled alone. You would do well to remember that. You will need allies around you whom you can trust — not only in their loyalty, but also trusting in their wisdom." He paused. "And on the topic of allies, is there something... amiss... between yourself and the nomad of late?"

Tasia hesitated, wishing for the first time to tell Norix the truth about what happened the week before with the *undatai*. But a small voice inside her whispered, *"Wait."*

Wait for what, Tasia couldn't say. All she knew was that she wasn't ready to speak of it to Norix.

Not yet.

"No," Tasia said. "I think Joslyn has just been tired lately — all the scouting ahead means that she rides longer than anyone else every day, with half as much sleep."

"Mmmm, yes," said the Wise Man, nodding. Tasia could tell that he was not satisfied with the answer, but he chose not to press the point.

"Speaking of sleep..." Tasia said. She glanced pointedly towards her tent.

"Yes, of course, Princess. We should all protect our sleep, given how little we get these days." He gave her a smile that didn't reach his eyes. "At least for old men like me, who are more accustomed to beds than to the cold ground."

"I will see if we can find another sleeping mat for you, Norix. To make your nights more comfortable."

"Oh, no, no. No need for the trouble," he said, false smile growing. "Such are the inconveniences of serving the future ruler of the Four Realms. Sleep is but a small price to pay."

He reached for her hand, and she extended it automatically, watching as he pressed cracked lips to the ring that bore the emblem of the House of Dorsa.

He turned to go, but paused and looked her over. "I must say, your Majesty, I will be glad to see you in your gowns again. I suppose I understand the need for your lessons in self-defense, especially given the raid, but I cannot seem to grow accustomed to your new... wardrobe."

Tasia looked down at herself. She'd been wearing men's riding breeches and tunics for so many days now that she'd practically forgotten to think of missing her gowns. She'd saved some finery for her meetings on the front lines, of course, but she'd gotten used to dressing like this — more like a soldier than a princess. And although she, too, would be glad to get back to her normal clothes, there was something about this outfit that she appreciated. Something that made her feel... well, "strong" might be the right word.

"I feel the same way," she lied. "Goodnight."

"Goodnight."

When Tasia entered her tent, she found Joslyn laying on her mat, eyes closed but not asleep. The Princess stepped over to her own sleeping mat. Tasia didn't bother changing into her sleeping gown. Since the night she'd awoken to find the small man in their tent, she preferred to sleep like Joslyn did — fully dressed, ready for anything at any moment. The only thing she took off before she slept were her riding boots.

"I know you're awake," she said to he guard's back. "You don't have to pretend to sleep."

Joslyn rolled over, opened her eyes. She regarded the Princess silently for a moment. "I wasn't pretending. I never sleep until you do. And even then... sometimes I do not sleep at all."

The statement concerned Tasia, and she let her face show it. "Aren't you exhausted? Riding all day, every day makes me feel as if I could sleep for a fortnight and still be tired."

"I am exhausted," the guard admitted. "But when I sleep long enough, I dream." There was a long pause, long enough that Tasia was surprised when the guard spoke again. "They are dreams that make me want to stay awake."

"What do you dream of?" Tasia asked. And then, because she'd asked the guard many questions in these last few days but had never gotten a real answer, she put her hand on Joslyn's shoulder. "Tell me. Please."

Maybe this question about unsettling dreams would be easier to answer than all the other questions Tasia had asked — *What happened in those hours on the mountainside? Those hours when I feared you dead and you stared at nothing? Where did you go? What did you see there?*

The guard's answer to those questions had always been the same: A silent shake of her head, followed by, *"Nothing I want to speak of."*

Joslyn looked away. "Sometimes I dream of my *ku-sai*. He tries to tell me something, but I never understand the words. The wind takes his voice, or a storm comes and I cannot hear him, or..."

Tasia waited for the guard to finish, but several long seconds passed with nothing. "Or what?" the Princess finally prompted.

"Or an *undatai* slaughters him before my eyes. Not the fire demon that you saw, but a different one. One made of sand and glass and rotting things. One that looks like a... like a living representation of all the worst parts of Terinto."

"Do you think there are more of them?" Tasia said.

It was a question she'd fretted over each day on their long rides through the wilderness. With the guard far ahead of the column, scouting, and no one else who knew what had happened that night, Tasia had nothing to do but worry over the same fears over and over again. And now that Joslyn had finally given her an opening, the questions bubbled out of her.

"Do you remember what Lord M'Tongliss said — at the council meeting before we journeyed east?" the Princess asked. "He said that the deserters the tribesmen found in Terinto spoke of flame-ringed demons. What if this was what those deserters meant? What if they ran because they saw *undatai?* What if that's what we're facing in the East?"

Joslyn shook her head, said quietly, "Then mankind will not hold dominion over this world much longer."

They held one another's gaze for a long moment.

"Joslyn. What happened while you were... gone that night? If this is truly what the Empire faces, I need to know. If you won't tell me as your friend, tell me because you are a soldier of the House of Dorsa, and I am your future Empress."

The guard dropped her gaze. For a moment Tasia thought she would be reduced to begging, or to commanding, but finally, Joslyn spoke.

"It's not that I haven't wanted to tell you what happened. It's that... It changed me. And I've been trying to come back to myself. But I fear that... I fear that if I talk about what happened — who I saw and who I almost became — what if I never find my way home to myself again?"

She looked up, and Tasia saw something in those dark

desert eyes she'd never seen before: fear. Whatever had happened in those hours she'd been *"away"* on the mountainside, it had shaken her to her core.

And the idea of Joslyn, the fiercest woman Tasia had ever met, being afraid of something... that made Tasia afraid.

"What are you afraid of?" Tasia whispered.

Joslyn shook her head.

"Tell me."

"I can't," the guard said.

"You can. How can you conquer your fear if you cannot name it?"

"I fear that I... I fear the..." Joslyn let out a frustrated sigh.

"Just say it. No matter what frightens you, I will never think you a coward. Never."

The guard closed her eyes. Barely audible, she said, "I fear the blackness inside my own heart. I fear that it will grow, and consume me, and that I will become an *undatai* in a human body."

It was not what Tasia had expected. "There is nothing black about your heart, Joslyn."

"You don't know that. You don't know the things that I have done. Or the things that I did while I was in that other world. You don't know the things that I might yet — "

The impulse had come a few times before this moment, but now when it came, Tasia acted on it. She leaned forward, cupped the back of the guard's head with one hand, and silenced the guard with a kiss.

"There is nothing black about your heart," Tasia said again, this time in a whisper that matched the guard's. She stroked Joslyn's cheek. "You have one of the purest hearts I have ever known."

Roughly, Joslyn pushed Tasia's hand away. "I killed you. In that other world, I killed you again and again. I drove daggers through your heart, I slit your throat, I cut open your stomach and laughed while your entrails spilled onto the ground. When I woke up... when I pointed that spear at you again... I almost killed you in this world, too. By the time I realized that I was really back, that the nightmare was over, that you were truly *you*..." She shook her head. "I almost killed you, and it would have been too late, and I would have had to live out the rest of my life knowing that I had killed the woman I..."

She pushed herself up from the mat. Before Tasia had a chance to recover from her shock, Joslyn had ripped open the tent flap and stormed out into the night.

31

Tasia caught up with the guard a hundred yards from the camp. Joslyn leaned against the rough trunk of a pine tree, breathing hard as if she had been running.

She opened her eyes when she heard Tasia approaching.

"If you wish to dismiss me from your service, I will understand," the guard said. "I can go back to the Capital Lands on my own. Or I will go back to Terinto. It will be easy enough to find work there, and — "

"Guard. You are *not* dismissed. Nor do I ever intend to dismiss you."

Joslyn's head fell to her chest. "I am supposed to protect you," she said in a small voice. "But what if I have become a danger to you? Every time I fall asleep, I go back to that world of nightmares, and it seems so real. I spend my nights fighting for my life, killing whatever comes my way. And you're there sometimes, but you..."

"But I what?"

Joslyn looked up. "Tasia, don't you understand? Something has changed inside me. I brought back... something dark from the place I went. I can't explain it, but I can feel it." She touched her chest. "Here. Like a living thing that is not me, but is me. Like a parasite."

Tasia stepped closer, rested a hand gently on the guard's

shoulder. "Then we will face it together. Overcome it together."

"I don't know if it's possible to overcome it. Whatever it is... it's making the line between this world and the other one... *thinner*, somehow." Joslyn paused, and for the briefest moment her eyes looked catatonic again, sending a thrill of fear down Tasia's spine.

Joslyn lowered her voice. "What if... what if one day I cannot tell the nightmare from the reality, this world from that world, and I hurt you?"

"You would never hurt me," Tasia said. "I know you."

Joslyn shook her head. "But you don't. You know nothing about me."

Tasia reached out, took the guard's hands in her own. "I *do* know you, Joslyn of Terinto. I know that you saved my life that night at the Speckled Dog, and I know you could have told Cole or my father what happened, but you didn't. And I know you saved me again the night of the raid, when you beheaded the mercenary who had been about to kill me."

"You saved my life that night, too. You owe me no debt."

"I saved your life only because *you* believed in me enough to teach me how to fight," Tasia said. "You have believed in me from the start, even when I didn't believe in myself — and not just because I have the title 'Princess' before my name. No one has ever believed in me like that, not since my brother Nik." She squeezed Joslyn's hands. "Which is exactly why I believe in *you*. Your heart is *not* black, Joslyn."

She took another step, feeling the texture of the rivets of the guard's leather armor through her tunic. She kissed Joslyn's jaw tentatively.

The guard turned her head away. "Tasia," she said, and the name was a sigh on her lips. "You should not kiss me."

"Maybe it is exactly what I should do. Maybe what you need to make the nightmares go away isn't more steel. Maybe it's..." She started to say *love,* but she stopped herself. They might not have been speaking the Old Language that the small man spoke of, but even this language had words that were endowed with power. And she sensed the moment was too fragile to use a word with so much power. "Maybe you need to know how much you're cared for," she finished.

"Do you care for me?" Joslyn asked. "Truly?"

"I care for you." Again the Princess struggled to find the right words. Struggled to know how to express what she needed to without blundering and sending the guard back into silence, without scaring the rabbit away. "I care for you more than I can say," she said at last. "Truly."

Joslyn reached up, brushing a tentative thumb across Tasia's cheek. "You were the one I returned for."

Tasia wanted to ask, *Return from where?* but she knew better. "I'm glad you came back for me," she said instead.

The Princess could feel the callouses on Joslyn's hand as the guard cupped her face, but there was nothing about the touch that was rough or hard. In fact, of all the hands that had touched her face — her mother's, her nursemaid's,

Mylla's, a host of young lordlings — Joslyn's touch seemed to be the most gentle she'd ever known.

The guard leaned forward slowly, cautiously, as if expecting a rebuke at any moment. But when none came, she pressed her lips softly to Tasia's.

Tasia felt the kiss through every part of her body — every hair seemed to stand on end, every inch of skin seemed to pucker into gooseflesh. She wanted to grab both of Joslyn's arms and *pull* the woman into her, pull until there was no space between them, pull until they had merged into a single being. But she knew better than to do that, too.

Instead of getting closer, Joslyn moved her face away from Tasia's. Not far — only an inch or two.

"I… shouldn't," Joslyn said. Then, more firmly: "I can't."

"Why?" Tasia asked. "Why can't you?"

"I am your servant," the guard answered. "And as you said, you will be my Empress one day."

"That doesn't mean you can't," said Tasia quietly.

Joslyn moved away, and this time it was feet instead of inches. She let out a bitter laugh.

"I can't," she repeated. "I can't because I want far more from you than a servant should ever rightfully want from her mistress. I can't because I want to slap Lady Mylla every time she rolls her eyes at you, because I want to run that snide Mace of House Gifford through with my short sword. I can't, because I want you all to myself. And I know that's one thing I can never, ever have."

She walked a few paces away from Tasia, heading back to the camp. Over her shoulder, she called, "Princess. We should get some sleep. We still have two or three days of hard riding left before we reach the front."

"You can," Tasia said to her back. "You can have me. Because I offer myself to you, Joslyn of Terinto, guard of the Princess of the Four Realms. I am your mistress, and that means I can give any gift to you I like. And the gift I choose to give is myself."

Joslyn stopped walking but didn't turn around. Instead, she put out a hand and leaned heavily on a nearby birch, leaned as if the narrow tree was the only thing in the world holding her up.

"I ask for one thing in return," Tasia said. She waited.

Joslyn turned around. "What?"

"I ask for you. I ask for all of you." The Princess took a small breath, let it out again. "I ask for stories of your childhood in Terinto, of the family you scarcely remember, of the tinker who bought you, of how you escaped your second master, of your *ku-sai,* of your time serving my father in the Imperial Army. I ask for your thoughts and your dreams, and in the quiet of night, I ask that you confess your fears. You can have all of me, but that is the price I demand in return."

Joslyn stared at her without speaking, until silence itself rang loudly in Tasia's ears.

"Say something."

"It is a high price," the guard said.

"Say you'll pay it," said Tasia, a plea trembling in her

voice.

Joslyn closed the distance between them, and for the second time that night, she put her lips on Tasia's. "I will pay," she said when the kiss broke. Joslyn moved her mouth from the Princess's lips, to her jaw, to her throat. The guard's teeth skimmed the side of Tasia's neck. "I will pay," she said into Tasia's ear. A tongue tickled the earlobe. "I will pay all that and more."

"Joslyn," Tasia said, the name sighing out of her in a whisper. She lifted the guard's tunic. Tasia had touched Joslyn's skin many times before in the process of sewing closed her wounds, but now she let herself do what she had always wanted to — she caressed the skin below.

She let her fingers slide across Joslyn's stomach, between the bandage's bottom edge and the top of the guard's trousers. Joslyn sucked in a breath, muscles contracting beneath Tasia's palm.

Tasia's legs turned liquid, no longer able to support her weight. She leaned back against a birch.

Joslyn's mouth continued its slow exploration of Tasia's body, working from ear back down to throat, throat to collarbone, and then, after tugging at the strings holding together Tasia's riding tunic, from collarbone to breast. Tasia's head fell backward, her eyes closing, letting the world dissolve away and all her attention narrow to the sensation of Joslyn's mouth on her bare skin.

Suddenly, the guard dropped to her knees before Tasia, causing the Princess to lift her head in surprise. But before she could ask Joslyn what she was doing, her tunic was being pushed up, and the guard's tongue had found her bare stomach. Joslyn's mouth roamed from one hip bone to the other, tongue and teeth teasing the skin just above Tasia's trousers.

She tugged at the drawstring that held the trousers up, then stopped, looking up at the Princess.

Tasia found the guard's dark eyes, barely visible in the still shadows of the forest. That half-illuminated Terintan face, gazing up at her with an unspoken question on it — Tasia was sure she'd never seen anything so beautiful in all her life.

"Yes," she said, answering the silent question. "Please."

Joslyn pulled the knot from the drawstring, and Tasia felt the trousers loosen, falling around her hips. Joslyn pressed her face into Tasia's plain linen undergarments. The warmth of the guard's breath weakened Tasia's knees even further, and she slid a few more inches down the birch trunk.

The guard's long, deft fingers made quick work of the ties that held the undergarments in place. Tasia felt the rush of cool night air meeting the most tender parts of her body. But the chill was quickly replaced by heat as hands moved up and down around her thighs and a mouth enveloped her slit.

The Princess let out a little cry when she felt the pressure of Joslyn's mouth against her, then realized that a hundred yards into the forest was still much too close to the camp for her to make any noise. She bit down hard on her bottom lip and squeezed her eyes shut as a tongue flicked into the folds between her legs. The pressure the tongue applied was gentle and light at first, the faintest teasing of the parts of Tasia that throbbed and begged for attention. But then Joslyn's fingers tightened their grip on Tasia's backside, and the tongue moved harder, faster, with just the right amount of friction. Tasia bit down on her lip so hard she was sure she would draw blood.

Just when she thought she couldn't take another moment, when she was sure she would burst from the pleasure of it all, from the strain of holding in the moan that she so desperately wanted to let out, two long fingers slipped inside her, moving up and down in harmony with the tongue.

"Joslyn — *gods,* Joslyn — no, don't stop," Tasia said when the guard looked up at the sound of her name. Greedy, the Princess wound her fingers into Joslyn's hair and pushed the woman's face back into her. "Keep going," Tasia breathed. "Please keep — *oh!"*

It had been too loud, Tasia knew, and she clapped a hand onto her own mouth. She bit a finger when the orgasm came a few minutes later, jaw clenching hard around a knuckle while the sensation danced like lightning from the core of her to every part of her body.

When it was over, she wilted, drooping over Joslyn like a flower past its prime. But Joslyn held her up, getting to her feet while supporting Tasia at the same time. She wiped off her mouth with the back of one hand, then wrapped her arms around Tasia, rocking just a little while the Princess clung to her.

"You are... extraordinary," Tasia said. "Everything about you."

The guard kissed Tasia's forehead, squeezed her a moment longer before releasing her. "We should go. We don't know who might have seen us leave."

"I care little for who saw us leave," said Tasia.

"I care," said Joslyn. "The last thing we want to do is invite more trouble to this expedition."

"Alright. I suppose you have a point," Tasia said, conceding. "Will you carry me back?"

"Carry you? Why?"

"It's the only way I can touch you without arousing suspicion," Tasia said with a grin. "And I don't want to stop touching you. Now that I've started, I don't think I ever want to stop again."

Joslyn pulled up Tasia's undergarments, then her trousers, tying each one in place tenderly before lifting the Princess from her feet.

"We'll say you twisted an ankle, if anyone asks," Joslyn said. "It might also explain the... noises."

No one asked. Most of the camp was already asleep by the time the guard carried the Princess back into their tent, with only two men on guard duty giving them a slightly puzzled look when Joslyn walked out of the woods with Tasia in her arms.

They spent the rest of that night with their sleeping mats pushed together and their limbs a tangled mass. Tasia slept more easily than she had on the entire journey and

Joslyn, it seemed, slept without nightmares.

Perhaps, the Princess thought as she drifted off, she should consider what this new aspect to her relationship with the guard would mean. Perhaps she should weigh the consequences. But then Joslyn shifted, Tasia burrowed into her arms, and the thought was forgotten.

32

Joslyn stopped scouting quite so far ahead after that night. She said that the reason was that they were close enough to the front now that it was unlikely they would find enemies bold enough to try another raid — anyone close enough to raid them was also likely to be close enough to be noticed by Imperial troops.

Tasia supposed the guard might be telling the truth... but she also suspected that her previously long scouting missions had mainly been a way to get away from the Princess. And now, getting away from Tasia seemed rather less important to the guard than staying near.

After their weeklong trek north through the mountains and then south and east through the foothills, Tasia's expedition had finally rejoined the Emperor's Road. In this rural part of the East, where the land had been nearly emptied by twelve years of on-and-off war, the road was little more than a winding dirt track. But compared to the roadless land they had come from, even this dirt track was a luxury. Humans, horses, and pack animals alike seemed to breathe a sigh of relief when they reached it.

"It's nice, ain't it, your Majesty?" said Alric on the next-to-last day of their journey. He had dropped back a few places to ride beside her for a while; Joslyn rode point.

"Do you mean the road?"

"I do," said Alric, nodding. "That, and the fact that this ill-fated trip is nearly over." He looked away from Tasia, gazed somewhere ahead of him. "I have to admit. I was wrong about the nomad. She's clever. And she might be better with a blade than anyone I've ever met — and I've met a lot in my time."

Tasia dropped her eyes to her horse's neck, thinking it might hide her smile.

"Alric," she said after a moment. "You fought in the East, didn't you?"

He snorted. "Fought in it? The edge of the Sunrise Mountains is practically me second home. After Shipper's Quarter, that is."

"Shipper's Quarter," Tasia mused. "I thought that was a Port Lorsin accent. Shipper's Quarter explains why it's a bit... mushed."

Alric gave a hearty laugh. "Ah, your Majesty. If only me accent were the only part of me that were 'mushed.' My ma used to say I was soft in the head. She was probably right."

"I have come to know you well enough to say that you are definitely not soft in the head, Sergeant," said Tasia. "But let me ask you. While you fought in the East, did you ever see anything... unusual?" She struggled for words, trying to think of a way to describe the *undatai* without using words like *monster* or *demon*. "Like... like a fire burning where it shouldn't be?"

Alric drew his bushy brows together. "No, Majesty.

Can't say as I ever saw fire except in a campfire or on the tip of a mountain man's arrow."

Tasia nodded. She wasn't sure if she felt disappointed or relieved.

"I will tell you this, though," said Alric after a minute or two of silence. "The mountain men... I served in the East at the very beginning, when the 'war' wasn't more than pushing a few raiding tribes back across the mountains where they belonged. I took a few years off after that, working as a hired guard for caravans and such through Terinto. When I re-enlisted two, three years ago..." He trailed off with a shake of his head. He wasn't looking at Tasia anymore; his eyes had taken on a troubled, far away sheen. "It's a proper war now. These mountain men, who don't hardly know the difference between a sheep's arse and their own wives — pardon the language, Princess — now all the sudden they fight like they have tactics. And they've gone from wooden clubs and rocks to steel. Fine steel, too."

Tasia listened to Alric without speaking, thinking back to similar things Joslyn had said to her, and to General Remington. General Remington had been convinced that the Kingdom of Persopos was arming the mountain tribes. But Norix had been dismissive, arguing that the barbarians had learned tactics from fighting the Imperial Army for so many years, and that their fresh equipment was most likely stolen in raids. Norix painted General Remington as a paranoid old soldier who wanted to see a bigger conflict where there was none. And the Emperor, for his part, didn't seem to know whom to believe. Either man's theory could easily be the correct one.

That had been the point of this expedition. If the General was right, if the Kingdom of Persopos had infiltrated this far west and was fighting the Empire with the barbarians as their proxy, that was dangerous and disconcerting. And if it were true, if men ranking as high as General Telek had been compromised, then abandoning the War in the East was absolutely not an option.

But if Norix was right, if the barbarians had simply gotten more sophisticated with time, then negotiating a treaty and exiting the war might save more lives and more of the Empire's precious, dwindling treasury than continuing to fight. House Druet might need to cede some of the lands that had been in their family for generations, but the Empire as a whole would come out stronger for such a concession. That was certainly what Lord Hermant and some of the other lords thought.

Tasia chewed on the inside of her cheek. Norix was old and stubborn, and there was a high probability that he would see only what he wanted to see once they reached the Imperial Army's winter encampment. It was up to her to discover the truth of things; she was the only one left willing to humor General Remington's theory.

#

"How is your twisted ankle, your Majesty?" Joslyn asked once the Princess caught up with her.

Tasia made a face. "Better, thank you. I still can't believe I twisted it."

"Perhaps it will remind you not to run headlong into the woods at night," Joslyn said. Her face was serious but her eyes twinkled with mischief. "I think if the Wise Man knew, you would be strongly censured for relapsing into impulsivity."

"Says the guard I followed into the woods," Tasia said with mock irritation.

A subtle smile appeared on the guard's face, but she kept her attention on the road ahead.

"We should arrive by mid-morning tomorrow," Joslyn said.

"Good. I don't think my arse can take much more of this horse." Tasia leaned forward and patted her mare on the neck. "Not that you haven't been a kind and gentle mount, my friend."

The horse nickered as if comprehending the Princess's words.

Joslyn chuckled. "She's come to like you. You've treated her well; horses are not always easy beasts to win over."

Tasia smiled. "Neither are men." She turned slightly in her saddle. "Joslyn. Show me the road ahead. I'd like to see what lies in store for us."

Joslyn quirked a quizzical eyebrow. "You wish to ride ahead of the column?"

"I do."

"As you command, Princess." She urged her horse into

a trot, moving around the soldiers ahead of them. Tasia did the same.

"Your Majesty?" Alric called as first Joslyn and then Tasia passed his point position.

"I'm riding ahead a bit with Joslyn," the Princess called over her shoulder. "We will wait for you down the road."

"Your Majesty, I'm not sure you should go unguarded," Alric said.

"I'm not unguarded. I have Joslyn." She laughed and patted the daggers strapped to her side. "And I have these, which I'm rather handy with. As I believe you know."

Alric chuckled. "I suppose you're right, Princess. Still, I would feel more comfortable if you allowed a few more of our men to accompany you."

"I appreciate your concern, Sergeant," said Tasia. "And I am sorry for your discomfort."

With that, she nudged the mare into a canter. Joslyn matched her pace, and the two rode away from the rest of the group.

Only when they were a good half-mile ahead did Tasia slow her horse back to a walk.

"You wished to speak privately?" Joslyn asked.

"I did."

Joslyn glanced over her shoulder. "We have privacy together each night. In your tent."

"Our tent," Tasia corrected, "but this isn't about sex, Joslyn."

"Yours. I am there because I guard you, even at night," Joslyn said.

The guard looked somewhat uncomfortable at the mention of sex. Although they had slept cheek-to-cheek in the two nights since what Tasia had come to think of as *the incident in the woods,* neither had initiated more lovemaking. Tasia knew the absence was not about lack of desire but about practicality; in the small camp, with the tents bunched tightly together for protection, even careful nighttime activities could easily be overheard, and it would not do for the new aspect of their relationship to be discovered by the others. Tasia was still working on earning their respect and loyalty.

Which was what she wanted to discuss with Joslyn.

"I trust you," Tasia said. "And I trust your opinion, especially when it comes to knowing the minds of others. I think you have an uncanny knack for it."

Joslyn's head bobbed with a single nod, showing that she was listening.

"The men we ride with." She hesitated. "Do you think I am overconfident to feel that they have transferred their loyalties from General Remington to me?"

The guard thought a moment. "No, not necessarily. When we left Port Lorsin, our expedition had three leaders — General Remington, Wise Man Norix, and you. The soldiers naturally looked to the General as their leader, because they recognized one of their own. The palace servants we traveled with looked to the Wise Man, because they were accustomed to recognizing him as an authority figure."

"And me? How did they see me?"

Joslyn took a breath. "You are a member of the House of Dorsa and the heir to your father's crown. They honor your House out of reflex."

"They honor my *House*," Tasia repeated. "But not me."

"Tasia..." The guard looked over at her. "Please do not be offended when I say that many of them saw you as the Princess known for sneaking out of the palace. The Princess known for..."

"Bedding too many lords' sons?" Tasia smiled at the guard's slight grimace. "It's alright, Joslyn. I'm not so dense that I don't know what people say behind my back." She thought a moment. "So they saw my participation in this journey as largely symbolic. As a gesture my father was making to show that I was being educated in statecraft."

"I think that's a fair description. Yes."

"But since the night of the raid? With General Remington dead and me demanding that we carry on with our mission...?"

"We sent the palace servants who were loyal to Norix back to Port Lorsin," Joslyn said. "With the General, Captain Mannick, and his two lieutenants dead, the men at arms were naturally looking for someone to lead them."

"And they found... me?"

Joslyn frowned. "Tasia," she started carefully, "I think they — "

"You don't have to soften it for me. Just tell me the truth."

"They put their trust in Alric," Joslyn said. "Men with swords typically listen only to other men with swords."

"I see. But you also said that I wasn't wrong when I said they transferred their loyalty to me," Tasia said. "Explain."

"The men trust Alric. Alric trusts you. You may not be a man with a sword, but you *are* a woman with daggers." She paused. "The night of the raid, Norix fled from the camp and hid. You did not. You stayed behind; you made your first kill defending those who defended your House. And since then, you have sparred with Alric. You have bested him more than once, proving your kill that night was not a fluke. I believe that surprised him."

"So you think he sees me as the leader of this expedition now. Not Norix."

Joslyn nodded. "I think he has little love for Norix."

"Why not?"

Joslyn shrugged and gave a wry grin. "Norix is difficult to love. And soldiers in general have little use for Wise Men. Wise Men study military tactics, military history. They sit beside lords and emperors and tell them where to attack. But you'll never find a Wise Man on a battlefield. Not unless he's there to sew up the wounds of dying soldiers or perform funeral rites."

"Do *you* trust Alric?"

The guard was silent for a long minute. "I do," she said at last. "He is straightforward and honest. He judges those around him based on their abilities and their actions, not on title or sex or... origin."

Tasia nodded, reaching a decision. "Good. I was hoping you would say that. We arrive at the camp mid-morning, and I am going to be immediately surrounded by highborn military men who will all want me to paint a pretty picture of them and their supposed victories to my father when I return to Port Lorsin. But I need a clear idea of what's really happening in this war, and I don't trust the generals to give me an honest answer. Talk to Alric privately for me — I don't want Norix to see me speak to him directly. Tell the Sergeant I want him to move amongst the camp's ordinary foot soldiers. Maybe he knows some of them already and has an excuse to invite himself into their card games. Tell him we need to hear the common man's sense for this war, for why it's going all wrong."

"Alright," Joslyn said. "I will."

The next morning, Tasia put on a traveling gown instead of riding breeches. It felt odd to wear a gown again after more than a week in trousers and tunics. Part of her welcomed the end of the journey; part of her realized that riding through the wilderness had been the easy part. Once she rode into camp, the truly difficult part would begin.

33

Riding regally sidesaddle for the last few miles was far less comfortable than Tasia had remembered. She felt as if she would lose her seating on her horse at any moment, and the daggers she now always kept strapped to her waist felt cumbersome and entirely too visible within the folds of her dress.

The royal party's arrival in the camp was met with little flourish, rather to Norix's disapproval.

"The Princess of the Four Realms has traveled all the way from the Capital Lands, her entourage has been set upon by mercenaries and forced to hide like refugees in the mountains, and the best they can send to greet us is a junior captain?" Norix grumbled behind Tasia as they followed their escort into the heart of the makeshift fort.

"It is standard procedure, designed by the Wise Men themselves," Joslyn said. She rode between Norix and Alric, just behind the Princess. "Whenever a member of the House of Dorsa visits a war front, they are treated with respects no higher than any other dignitary, so as not to attract undo attention from the enemy. One must always assume the enemy is watching."

Tasia recognized Joslyn's last line — it was a direct quote from one of the volumes on military strategy that

Norix had made her read. Tasia smiled to herself. How did an illiterate soldier know to quote a text written by a Wise Man? The guard never ceased to surprise her.

"Hmpf," was all Norix said. He couldn't argue with that, of course. He recognized what she had quoted.

The junior captain led the bedraggled travelers to a cluster of tents on a small hill near the outskirts of the camp. He led Tasia and Joslyn into the grandest of the group, leaving a lieutenant to help settle Tasia's men into the smaller ones. Tasia noted with appreciation that it had been stocked with two cots, rugs to cover the packed earth, a dressing table, and a basin of steaming hot water in a far corner. Once they were inside the tent, the junior captain dropped to one knee and kissed the ring with the House of Dorsa's emblem.

"Princess," he said, voice filled with awe. "Please forgive me for not giving you a formal greeting sooner — I'm sure you understand it is procedure. You have no idea what an honor it is to have you here." Instead of releasing her hand and standing again, the captain carried on in the same tone of wonderment. "My father took me to see a parade on Victory Day in the capital one year when I was just a boy. He held me on his shoulders and we climbed up the base of a statue of Emperor Godfrey — forgive us for that — and I was able to see your father and your mother and you and your brother. I was moved that day, to be so close to the Emperor and his soldiers. It's what inspired me to volunteer for the Imperial Army."

"I thank you for your service," Tasia said with a

gracious smile. The young captain seemed completely earnest in his devotion, and the Princess found it endearing. "The Empire needs men of loyalty now more than ever."

"We do, your Majesty, yes we do," the young junior captain agreed, nodding vigorously.

"It's not every commoner who rises to the status of captain," said Tasia. "You must have distinguished yourself along the way. I'm sure your parents are proud."

Still on one knee, he gave Tasia a broad smile. "My father also served in the Imperial Army, and his father before him. My family is from Everly, on the edge of the Capital Lands. Many of the men Papa's age fought on the side of the West during the Rebellion, but not him. He always believed in being loyal to the Emperor. And he always told me a unified Empire is a strong Empire." He bowed his head. "Truly, Princess Natasia, it is an honor to meet you and to serve you."

Joslyn took a half-step towards the kneeling captain. "You can release the Princess's hand and stand up now, sir."

"Oh — of course," said the captain. He rose awkwardly, dusting off his knees. "I will tell General Telek that you and your men are settling into your tent." He glanced from Joslyn back to Tasia. "Although we were expecting a larger...?" He phrased it as a statement, but spoke it as a question.

"It is a long story, and will come out in due time," said Tasia. "Please ask General Telek to call before the evening meal. I should like to meet him in person before meeting with all the other generals."

"Yes, your Majesty." He turned to go.

"Wait, Captain — what is your name again?"

"Danson of Everly, your Majesty. And actually, I am really just a junior captain."

"I heard your rank earlier, Captain Danson," Tasia said. "Before you go to speak to your General, tell me — what has the atmosphere been like here in the camp, since what happened to Fox Battalion?"

For the first time since they'd entered the tent, Junior Captain Danson's eyes couldn't hold Tasia's. He glanced to one side, away from Princess and guard, as if he suddenly found the tent's canvas walls particularly interesting.

I think he's been instructed not to tell me anything, Tasia thought with a small shock.

He looked back at the Princess and cleared his throat. "Since Fox Battalion… the men were disheartened for a time, but they are the bravest men in the Empire, and they are already looking forward to the spring campaign. They are ready to go on the offensive, to avenge our brothers of Fox Battalion. Word arrived only a week ahead of you that reinforcements are on their way from all over the Four Realms. The common soldiers do not know that yet, but the officers do. When the first reinforcements arrive, they will see for themselves that the Emperor has not forgotten them."

Tasia nodded. "No doubt the first troops for the spring offensive will arrive even while I am still here in your camp."

"Yes, your Majesty. They certainly will."

"Thank you, Captain Danson. I'm sure I will see you again soon."

He gave a boyish smile. "It's Junior Captain, really, your Majesty. I was only promoted from lieutenant recently."

"Junior Captain Danson, then." She mirrored his smile back to him.

"If there's anything you need, your Majesty, anything at all I can provide to make your stay with us more comfortable, all you need to do is send for me. Some of my men are posted around your tent, and all you need to do is send one of them for me and I will be here as soon as I can."

"Thank you," Tasia said again. "I am in your debt." She glanced at the tub of steaming water. "I think I will get to freshening up now."

"Of course, your Majesty," said Junior Captain Danson of Everly, bowing deeply. "I know Senior General Telek will be as pleased to see you as I have been."

"As I will be pleased to see him," Tasia said. "Our Wise Man speaks very highly of him. I believe he knew General Telek as a boy."

"Yes, I'm sure General Telek would love to tell you about the years he spent at the palace when he was younger," said the Junior Captain, but he seemed uneasy. His gaze wandered to the tub. "If there's nothing else, your Majesty…?"

"No, nothing else, Junior Captain. You're dismissed."

The young man gave another low bow and left the tent

still hunched and walking backwards.

"Did you notice?" Tasia said to Joslyn once he had left.

The guard nodded, dark eyes serious. "Someone has told him to keep his lips sealed about Fox Battalion. Perhaps by General Telek himself."

Tasia sighed and rubbed her temples. "One of the hazards of being royal, Joslyn, is that no one is ever completely honest with you. Not even the honest ones like him are honest all of the time. Everyone has an interest to protect, be it their family, their reputation, or simple self-preservation. It makes getting to the truth hard."

"The truth is always hard to get to," Joslyn said. "Royal or not."

"Perhaps, but..." Tasia took a step towards the tub, dipped her fingers into the hot water. She gave Joslyn a sly backward glance. "Would you be so kind as to help me out of my dress, Guard?"

Joslyn returned the smile. "Gladly, Princess."

"You must wish for a hot bath yourself, after so many days hard riding."

"I would not turn down a hot bath, if it were offered, Princess," Joslyn said. She shed her guard's black leather tunic as she approached Tasia and the tub of steaming water, setting it carefully on a chair. When she reached Tasia, she found the buttons at the back of the dress and undid them one by one.

Tasia felt the guard's breath on the back of her neck and let out a long, contented sigh. Now that she'd earned this tender side of Joslyn, she hoped she would never lose it again.

"Do you think we're safe here?" Tasia asked. "For now?"

Behind her, the guard's fingers paused in undoing the buttons. Then they began again as she spoke. "There is something in this camp that makes me keep my hand on my sword. A restlessness in the air that does not bode well."

Tasia unpinned her hair from her head, shook it loose. It had been far too long since she'd washed it, and it smelled of horses and campfires.

"I know," she said. "I feel it, too. Something charged in the air. Something lurking just beneath the surface."

"Yes." Joslyn opened the dress gently from behind, pushing it off Tasia's shoulders. "It might only be leftover emotions from the routing of Fox Battalion."

"The soldiers are probably shaken by the knowledge that five hundred of their own were so easily overrun," Tasia said. "That would explain the dark looks on their faces. Wouldn't it?"

"Probably."

"But only probably?"

"Tasia, I won't feel safe until we know for certain who's trying to kill you." Joslyn hesitated, and her voice was quiet when she spoke again. "Or until my nightmares of the *undatai* end."

"I'm sorry, Joslyn. They still come each night? Even with you wrapped up in my arms?"

The guard nodded. "Even wrapped up in you."

Tasia lifted her hands high, and Joslyn pulled the dress

up and over her head. The Princess shrugged out of her undergarments and turned to face Joslyn, naked. Tasia reached up, laced her fingers behind the guard's neck. "Do we have to keep talking about wars and soldiers and monsters and barbarians? Can we just have a few hours of true rest?"

Joslyn leaned in, kissed Tasia's forehead. "Yes."

Tasia cocked her head. "But there's something still on your mind. What are you thinking?"

"There's one more thing to say. Then I promise — we can rest until we are called for the evening meal."

"What is it?" Tasia asked, worried.

"There's something you should understand about soldiers," Joslyn said. "And about war. Something that the Wise Men probably don't teach the heirs of the House of Dorsa."

"Go on."

"Imperial soldiers may wear the emblem of the House of Dorsa on their chests," said the guard, "but their first loyalty is to the man on either side of them. Their second loyalty is to the officer they trust the most. Their loyalty to the Empire — and to the House of Dorsa by extension — is… somewhat less of a priority."

"And Junior Captain Danson? He seemed practically effusive in his love for my father."

"He is an exception. His appreciation for your House is genuine, I think."

Tasia considered the guard's words. "Which officers do the soldiers here follow? Who owns their loyalty?"

"I don't know yet," Joslyn admitted. "But we should keep our eyes and ears open at the evening meal. I think the truth will be visible enough."

"Gods," Tasia muttered. "Why did I ever agree to be my father's heir? It would have been so much simpler to find some young lord to marry and let him wear the crown."

A ghost of a smile touched Joslyn's lips. "You would not last very long as a dutiful and subservient wife."

Tasia arched an eyebrow. "You're such a cheeky commoner, Joslyn." She looked down at the guard. "How is it that I am here wearing only my skin and you are still fully clothed? I thought you were going to join me in this bath before the water cooled."

Joslyn lifted her arms over her head and Tasia laughed, pulling the linen tunic up and over the guard's head. Beneath the tunic were still Joslyn's breast bindings, long, thin strips of linen wrapped tightly around the guard's chest.

"Do you realize," Tasia said, "that for all the nights we've shared a tent, for all the times I've sewn you closed, I've never seen your breasts?"

She searched for the place where the binding ended, then tugged it loose. Joslyn responded with a smile that didn't quite reach her eyes.

"What's wrong?" Tasia asked. "You take it off to wash, don't you?"

"Yes. But usually I'm alone when I wash."

Tasia gradually unwound the cloth around the guard's

chest, and the looser the bindings became, the more the shape of Joslyn's breasts revealed themselves.

Joslyn closed her eyes, her breath coming quicker.

"Are you alright?" Tasia said.

"They are... not like yours."

"All breasts are more or less the same, from what I know," Tasia said. "Some big, some small, some pink nipples, some brown. Yours can't be much different."

"Mine are... mine are ugly."

Tasia snorted. "Nothing about you is ugly, Joslyn. You're one of the most beautiful creatures I've ever laid eyes on."

"You don't understand — " Joslyn started, but then the last of the bindings fell away, and Tasia *did* understand. She sucked in a small breath.

"Oh, Joslyn," she murmured. She ran her fingers along the scars that covered the guard's breasts. She already knew Joslyn had her share of scars — between being a slave and being a soldier, her back was crisscrossed with scars from the lash; her flanks and limbs carried all manner of scars big and small from swords, knives, spears, and arrows.

But the scars on Joslyn's breasts were different. They were, if Tasia was not mistaken, burn marks. Dozens of them.

"How did this happen?" she asked.

"The man who bought me was fond of fire," Joslyn said softly. Her voice was small, and it startled Tasia. She'd never heard the guard sound small before, so vulnerable like this.

With slow, deliberate affection, Tasia stripped off the rest of the guard's clothes, pulling down her trousers, her man's undergarments, removing both boots and the stockings beneath them. More burn scars covered Joslyn's most tender parts. Where a wiry patch of hair should have been, there was only a mass of scar tissue. The sight made Tasia angry — furious, even — but she was careful not to let it show to the guard. Joslyn would talk about it when she was ready. For now, Tasia only wanted to make sure the woman knew she was beautiful. So beautiful. She took Joslyn's hand and guided her to the tub of water.

"Get in, Joslyn of Terinto. Today I, Princess Natasia of House Dorsa, future Empress of the Four Realms, will bathe you. And you will know by my touch that each inch of you is perfect."

34

The dining tent for the senior officers was every bit as elegant as Tasia's tent, only larger. It was practically the length and breadth of the Great Hall in the palace, lit by a string of lanterns hanging from its wooden support beams, tapestries decorating its canvas walls, fresh reeds strewn across a packed earth floor. The table that took up most of the interior wasn't as nice; it consisted of rough-hewn timbers that looked hastily cobbled together, surrounded by rough-hewn benches. But at least it was set with pewter dishes, ample clay jugs of wine, and bouquets of wildflowers.

The officers all rose when Tasia entered the room with Norix and Joslyn at her side. This was her first actual test as her father's heir. She'd attended council meetings while she'd been at the palace, true, but she'd always done so with her father at her side. She'd also taken charge of the expedition to the East after the mercenaries raided, but that had been with a small group of men, none of whom were highborn. This dinner, in which she would be surrounded by the most important officers in the Imperial Army, all of them the sons of nobles, was the first time her future subjects would truly take her measure.

She flashed back to a moment some twelve years

earlier, at her mother's funeral. *"Hold your heads high,"* her father had whispered to her and Nik, *"and remember that you are members of the House of Dorsa."*

Tasia held her head high and did not rush to her place at the head of the table. She had a bench for a seat, too, but at least it had been covered in rabbit furs. She waited, keeping her face placid while a cupbearer pulled it out for her. Once Joslyn and Norix found their seats on either side of her, she sat and said to the room:

"Gentlemen. By all means, please sit down."

And as they sat with a rustle of benches and creaking leather and jostled sword belts, the Princess stole a glance at Joslyn. The guard was not accustomed to having a seat at the table; she was accustomed to standing somewhere in the shadows behind Tasia, hand on her sword pommel and eyes scanning the room. Her Terintan features held the slightest trace of tension in them. It was enough for Tasia to recognize that the guard was uncomfortable, but not enough for anyone who didn't know her to notice.

On her other side, Norix looked perfectly at ease. Pleased, even. It occurred to Tasia that it didn't seem to matter who sat at the head of the table, Norix always managed to be seated to their right.

Next to Norix was Senior General Telek of House Serrell, one of only three Senior Generals in the entire Imperial Army. He was the head of the First Corps, which was fifty-thousand men strong. He was also the General who had been overseeing the war in the East for the past six years — half the war's lifespan.

But the last three years of the war had been far more devastating for the Imperial Army than any of the previous ten years. It was a fact that surely hadn't escaped General Telek's notice. And he must have realized that part of the purpose of this expedition was to size him up and decide if the Empire would be better served by a different Senior General.

The Senior General of the Second Corps, General Franzen of House Brundt, was also somewhere within the dining tent, but Tasia hadn't spotted him yet. General Franzen's corps had been split, with half of them fighting here in the East, the rest of them "maintaining the peace" in Terinto and along the southern coast, which was a polite way of saying that they were there scouting for pirates, smugglers, and any nomadic tribe that still thought it could test the might of the Empire. Given the need for more troops, however, that half of the Second Corps was en route to the East, where they would take part in the spring offensive.

Senior General Telek leaned around Norix, a broad smile on his face. He opened his mouth to say something to the Princess, but Tasia decided she should be the first one to speak. It was important that she establish who she was from the start and that they see her that way — as the future Empress and not as just another nineteen year-old highborn girl.

Tasia raised the goblet of wine before her and said to the room, "A toast. To Senior General Telek, to all the other officers in this room: May the Empire prevail in the battles to come, and may our efforts provide peace and prosperity for our easternmost border."

General Telek raised his own goblet. "To our success," he said, and glanced up and down the table to the other officers in the room.

It was only at the General's gesture that the rest of the men came alive. They raised their glasses, repeated the phrase unevenly, drank only after the General drank.

Joslyn's comment about how soldiers followed the officer they trust the most first and foremost came back to Tasia. The Princess might be sitting at the head of the table, but the fulcrum of power in the room was located a few seats to her right, in the General's chair.

He caught Tasia's eye again, still smiling. She nodded and lifted the goblet to her lips. The wine was of better quality than she expected, and she wondered idly if the officers always dined so well or if they'd brought out their best barrel because the Princess of the Four Realms and heir to the throne had come for a visit.

"Here, here," Norix said next to her, a little slow with his own response to the toast.

Attendants brought the meal's main course then — roasted duck with potatoes and wilted greens — and again the quality surprised Tasia. She'd been expecting somewhat rougher fare.

She chatted cordially with one of the colonels seated across from her, agreeing that she was happy to have a cot instead of a sleeping mat again.

"But I'm sure even the finest tent in the encampment

cannot compare to your private apartments at the palace," he said.

"What palace?" Tasia joked. "I have apartments in a palace? I scarcely remember them."

The man chuckled. "Now you know how we feel. Sometimes when I visit my manor back in the Steppes, I take a blanket and sleep in the stables, because the ground and the fresh air have become more comfortable to me than my stuffy bedchamber."

"I'm sure your wife must wonder at your choice," Tasia said.

"Oh, but she appreciates his choice very much," General Telek said, entering the conversation with his same broad smile. "She always did say the Colonel smelled like a horse, so I'm sure she appreciates his distance from their bedchamber."

A ripple of laughter moved in a circle out from the General. The Colonel from the Steppes laughed, too, raising his goblet of wine with a nod.

"You speak the truth, General," he said.

General Telek's face grew serious once the laughter died down. "We were so sorry to hear from Wise Man Norix this afternoon of the bandit raid that took the lives of so many within your party. I must say that we were surprised to see you arrive with such a small entourage. And doubly surprised to see the Princess of the Four Realms herself riding on horseback instead of arriving within one of the royal carriages."

It occurred to Tasia that Senior General Telek of House

Serrell was everything one could hope for in a general. Still broad-chested and muscularly lean at the age of fifty-something, he carried himself with a practiced charm and relaxed tact that served him as well in the dining hall as his brawn served him on the battlefield.

"Yes, we traveled light and sent all the carriages back to the Capital Lands after the attack," Tasia said, and noted that several other officers had begun to listen intently to her conversation with the General. "My advisors and I considered turning back, but I felt our visit to the front was too important to abandon." She smiled. "I didn't want to miss the opportunity to meet all of you in person and thank our Imperial soldiers for their courage in the face of danger."

"And the soldiers so appreciate your presence," the General said. "Although most of them do not yet realize that it is the Princess of the Four Realms herself who is staying in our best guest tent." After another sip of wine, the General said. "I understand from the Wise Man that Senior General Remington perished during the bandit raid."

"He did," Tasia said. "Along with more than half of our armed guard."

The General pressed his lips together and shook his head. It was an expression of regret and sadness that Tasia didn't think quite reached his eyes.

"Senior General Remington was one of my mentors," said General Telek. "I served under him during the Western Rebellion. Rarely has the Empire had such a brilliant military mind as his. For him to die so ignobly... in nothing more than a bandit's raid…" He shook his head again.

"General Remington died defending the Emperor's heir," Norix said. "I am sure that there was no other death he would have preferred."

The horse-smelling Colonel across from Tasia lifted his goblet. "To General Remington of House Aventia," he said loudly. "May his memory live on."

"May his memory live on," the table chorused.

The men around her began to eat and talk amongst themselves, and Tasia picked at her duck. She half-listened to the snippets of conversation around her.

" — said that Adessian wine is better than the Capital Lands, but I think — "

" — fat as a summer hog — "

" — so he says to me, 'And that's why I can't hold more than one woman at a — '"

General Telek leaned close again. "I take it you met my personal assistant, Junior Captain Danson?" he said, breaking into Tasia's thoughts.

"I did," Tasia said. "A charming young man," she added, despite the fact that the boyish officer was probably older than her by a few years.

"Indeed," General Telek said. He sipped his wine. "Exceptionally clever. For a commoner. Of course, his birth means he can never be a general, but I believe he will certainly retire as a colonel."

"The Empire needs more men like Captain Danson," Tasia said, nodding in agreement.

"Yes. I asked him to be at your beck and call during your stay with us." He chuckled. "I believe he is the perfect choice; he is rather enamored with the name 'Dorsa.'"

Tasia cocked her head to the side, giving the General an appraising look. "The House of Dorsa has guided the Empire for the entirety of its existence. I would assume there are many people here enamored by its name. I know I certainly am."

"Oh, as am I, Princess," General Telek agreed quickly. "I only meant to indicate that the Junior Captain is particularly zealous in his love for your family."

"More so than you?"

"Now Princess," said the General, a hint of admonishment in his tone. "You know I did not mean to imply that."

"No, I'm sure you didn't mean to imply that," said Tasia, holding the General's eye.

There was an uncomfortable pause. The General shifted in his seat.

"I assume that General Remington's journey here was intended in part to pass along the Emperor's instructions for the spring offensive," General Telek said, changing the topic. "Are those instructions you will be providing me with, instead?"

Tasia opened her mouth to reply, but Norix, who had been listening to their exchange intently, spoke before she could answer.

"We do indeed. I can go over the Emperor's wishes

with you in the morning, General," said the Wise Man.

"We both will," Tasia said.

Norix's brow crinkled for a moment. "I'm sure you'll want to sleep in after your long journey, Princess Natasia."

"I'm sure you will want the same thing, Wise Man Norix," Tasia countered. "But the outcome of our war in the East is rather more important than catching up on our much-needed sleep, don't you agree?"

General Telek glanced between Norix and Tasia, a curious expression on his face. No doubt he wondered which of them held the real power.

Tasia didn't intend to let him wonder long. "Nothing is more important than victory over the barbarians," she continued to Norix. "And with General Remington gone, it is even more important that I am present at our meeting to discuss my father's wishes."

Norix deflated somewhat. "Yes, Princess. Of course you're correct."

"It seems her Wise Men have taught her well," said General Telek, trying to dispel the tension.

Norix gave a hollow smile and spread his hands. "The House of Wisdom does the best it can with its pupils."

#

The rest of the dinner passed without further incident. Tasia and General Telek seemed to reach an unspoken agreement to leave alone the thornier topics and stick with evening meal niceties.

Once the General became engrossed in conversation about supply routes with one of his colonels, Tasia tuned into Joslyn's conversation beside her.

"...through the Zaris Mountains," the guard was saying.

The Captain next to her nodded. "Ah, yes. A good choice." He washed down his duck with a large gulp of wine before lifting his fork again. "But I'm surprised you know the Zaris Mountains. Your features mark you as being from further to the south."

"I am from Terinto's nomadic desert tribes, if that's what you imply," Joslyn said without any hint of animosity. "But I lived in a village on Terinto's northern border for a time. Before I joined the Imperial Army."

"We may have been neighbors without knowing it," the Captain said. "I'm from the Northeast myself, not far from Terinto."

Joslyn nodded politely.

"You didn't, ah, you didn't see any small men on your journey perchance, did you?" the Captain asked.

Tasia straightened. She could feel Joslyn tense beside her, but the guard's tone remained neutral as she answered. "No, we didn't."

Her answer seemed to relieve the Captain somehow. "Shy little boogers, aren't they? They used to come to my father's lands once every spring and once every fall to trade. Used to give me nightmares when I was a boy."

"Nightmares?" Tasia asked, leaning forward so she could see the Captain. "Whatever for? You would have been bigger than them even as a child."

The Captain's cheeks pinked. "Yes, I suppose I was. But have you ever seen a small man, Princess Natasia?"

Tasia hesitated only a moment. "No. My mother was from the Northeast, though. She used to tell us stories about them."

His chest seemed to puff at the mention of Tasia's mother. "Yes, I knew that about the Empress. My own father was good friends with your grandfather, Lord Hermant of House Farrimont." He took another sip of wine before speaking. "The thing about the small men," he said, lowering his voice as if he were about to reveal a secret, "is their eyes. Their eyes take up half their faces, and it's incredibly unnerving to behold. You get the feeling that they're as comfortable in the dead of night as they are at the height of the day. You get the feeling they might be anywhere in the dark."

"We saw no small men on our journey, but we saw their runes," Joslyn said.

The Captain turned from Tasia to the guard. "Beg pardon?" The question sounded strained to Tasia.

"Their runes," Joslyn said again. "We saw markings of the small men everywhere once we entered the mountains — on trees, on boulders. I recognized them from when I lived in the Zaris Mountains before, but I hadn't ever seen so many at once. It struck me as unusual." The guard studied the Captain carefully. "Have you ever seen that? Dozens upon dozens of runes?"

Whether it was the wine or embarrassment, the Captain blushed again. "Ah, runes, yes, well," he said, then broke into a coughing fit. "Excuse me," he said between coughs, holding a fist to his mouth with one hand and slapping his chest with the other. He gulped down the rest of his wine once the fit subsided and attempted a smile. "Pardon me. Too many winter nights spent sleeping in a tent. It's hell on an old man's lungs. What is it you were asking? Something about the small men's runes?"

Joslyn nodded. "There were dozens of them."

The Captain shook his head. "Dozens, eh? That *is* unusual." Then he shrugged. "But small men keep their own council. They are odd creatures, more like cave rats than men, really — don't you think?"

Joslyn didn't respond, simply gazed at the man. The guard's stare seemed to make him uncomfortable, and he looked away, patting his wine-red lips with a napkin.

Rarely had Tasia witnessed a poorer attempt at hiding information. She would remember this man, find a way to pressure him into telling her what he knew once she could get him alone.

But there was more than one way to get a man to talk. Joslyn had her way; Tasia had hers. And the Princess's way included far more charm. Tasia smiled pleasantly and extended a hand to the man. "I don't believe we have been properly introduced."

He took her hand and planted a clumsy kiss on her ring. "Captain Ellis. Of House Hafnell."

"Ah, House Hafnell," Tasia said. "Didn't one of your sisters marry into House Brundt, in the West?"

"Yes, that's right," said Captain Ellis. "My sister Aama

married the lord of House Brundt."

"I know your nephew, then — Lord Simon is my contemporary," Tasia said. "I've known him for many years."

Captain Ellis smiled proudly. "Simon is a bright boy. But I was sorry to see him have to take on so much responsibility, so young when my brother-in-law died. He hadn't even found a bride yet."

"Condolences for your brother-in-law and your sister, to be widowed still so young," Tasia said. "I knew Lord Simon's father, as well. But Simon has certainly risen to the occasion."

"Indeed, Princess. Indeed."

Joslyn caught Tasia's gaze as the Princess and the Captain continued to chat. The guard's eyes seemed to carry the same thought Tasia had earlier: *Be wary of men who know more than they will say.*

35

"What did you make of your first fancy dinner?" Tasia asked Joslyn once they were back in her tent.

"It wasn't exactly my first."

"Your first in which you sat at the head of the table rather than stood behind it. Or at the servants' table."

Joslyn smiled. "I suppose that's true."

"So? What did you think?"

"I thought the duck was dry."

Tasia laughed. "Ah, and once again the guard proves that somewhere underneath all that armor she *does* have a sense of humor." She poked Joslyn in the chest.

"I thought you handled Norix well," Joslyn said. "He seems... rather determined to assert his dominance."

Tasia grunted. "And he will find that I am determined to remind him which of us is the heir to my father's crown. I cannot have him undermining me like that in public."

"He will learn."

"Or he won't," Tasia said. "And I will be forced to somehow remove him one day." She sighed. "But hopefully that won't happen. Hopefully my father still has a decade or two ahead of him before his heir needs to begin the business of orchestrating the Empire. And old Norix will be sleeping in the House of Wisdom's catacombs by then, may Mother Moon watch over him."

She unpinned her hair, used her fingers to loosen it and let it fall to her shoulders. She turned to Joslyn, and found the guard was watching her. Under the guard's gaze she felt somehow already undressed.

She took a step towards the guard, closing the distance until their chests were only inches apart. Joslyn tilted her head, pressed her lips against Tasia's.

"Princess Natasia?" A hesitant voice from outside the tent.

Joslyn stepped away from Tasia swiftly, opened the tent flap a few inches. She peered outside and turned back to Tasia. "It's one of the Junior Captain's men. He's got Alric with him."

"Let him in," Tasia said. She smoothed her hair and sat down in one of the tent's small wooden chairs, leaving the other one open for the old sergeant.

Alric was troubled. Tasia could see it on his face from the moment he walked into the tent. She gestured at the open chair and he fell heavily into it without looking at her, brow furrowed and gaze angled downward.

"Alric?" said Tasia. "Did you make friends amongst the soldiers?"

He shook his head, still not looking at her. "I don't know what I made, Majesty."

Tasia waited.

Finally the old veteran looked up, met her eyes. "I've fought in your father's army since before the Western Rebellion. Since I was a pup." He tipped his head to indicate Joslyn, who stood silently behind him at the tent entrance, one hand on her sword pommel. "I was younger than you are now when we took Terinto. Lost many a friend to the nomads. Lost even more, in a different way, when half of my Western friends deserted our ranks to join the rebellion. I've seen a lot in my time. Men strung up on cross beams in the desert by their — beg pardon, Princess. There are things I shouldn't say to a proper lady."

"You can say anything you want to me, Alric."

He nodded. "What I'm trying to say is that I thought I'd seen everything, heard everything. I thought there was nothing under Mother Moon that could surprise me anymore."

He stopped speaking. His gaze fell again.

"Go on, soldier," Tasia said.

"I played cards with some of the soldiers tonight during your dinner, just like you asked," he said. "The ale was watery — ale at the front always is — but I got the boys talking after a tankard or two anyway. Asked 'em about the desertions. About the mood in the camp after what happened to Fox Battalion. What they told me... what I saw..." He trailed off, hesitating. "I don't know if I have anything valuable to tell you, Princess, because I don't know what I believe myself."

When he fell silent again, Tasia wanted to grab his shoulders and shake it out of him. But she couldn't let her impatience get the better of her.

Give him room to say what he needs to say, she told herself, and she held her tongue.

"Fox Battalion had only twelve survivors," he said after a moment. "Twelve. Out of more than five hundred men. *Imperial* men. Well-trained, well-equipped. Veterans of this war, most of them. When I asked how a group of ragtag mountain barbarians could route five hundred Imperial men inside a fortified position, they didn't want to talk at first. Looked at each other, like..."

#

Like they've been told not to talk, Alric thought to himself. Like some highborn officer or another threatened them with the whip if they did.

The campfire illuminated the soldiers' faces in oranges and reds, and even by firelight, Alric could see that these were weary men. He had been there before; he had been amongst those left behind in the winter encampment while his mates went home, back to farms and villages and cities where they would sleep beside their wives and play with their children for a month or two or three.

It was a lonely business, wintering along the front. A cold, tiring business. And these men were some of the most tired he'd ever seen.

"A dozen men?" Alric said again. "Out of the whole battalion? Even when we were routed in the Battle of Mount Rannard, a third of our fighting force still got out with their heads and most of their limbs in tact."

The men around him said nothing. They arranged the cards in their hands; they drank sullenly from their tankards of ale.

Finally, the stout one they called "Brick," either for his reddish, brick-colored beard or for his squat, rectangular shape, shrugged and stood up.

"May as well show 'im, eh boys?" he said to the men sitting around the fire.

Alric held his tongue and stole a glance at the faces of the others. The one named "Horse," who, along with Brick, seemed to be the leader of this informal band of companions, pressed his already thin lips together and glared at Brick. The four other men avoided looking at Brick. Or at anything at all.

Alric laughed, put his cards down, and stood up across from Brick. Over the years, he'd learned that, when it came to soldiers, when a simple request didn't result in action, a challenge to their courage often did.

To the men still sitting, he said: "What's wrong? You all look like my little daughters when they know they've earned a switch."

Two of them glanced from Brick to Horse, wondering which one of their leader's example they should follow.

One of them, the youngest of the bunch by the looks of it, threw his cards down. "To hell with what the Captain said. Let's show the man."

He stood up. And one by one, reluctantly, the other soldiers put their cards down and stood, too. Horse was the last one to stand.

"Just remember it wasn't my idea," he growled, though to whom the comment was directed was unclear.

Brick gave an assessing glance around. No officers were in sight; those with the highest ranks were likely at the banquet held in honor of the Princess's arrival. The lower-ranking officers likely appreciated the absence of their superiors and were relaxing in their own dining tents.

"If we're going to go, let's go," Horse said, like a man bracing himself to lead a mission across enemy lines.

Brick led the way, weaving through other clusters of talking, laughing, and arguing soldiers until their little group arrived at the outside edge of the camp, where moonlight against the wooden stockade that marked the camp's outer perimeter cast long shadows upon the ground. This far from the ring of campfires, the ground was nearly black and the men became featureless silhouettes. Alric found himself watching his feet and the back of the man in front of him closely, lest he misstep and twist his bad knee.

As they moved deeper into the darkness, Alric began to form a plan in his head. If these men turned on him and attacked, he would take out Horse first, mainly because his size and the knife hidden in his boot made him the most dangerous. Once he took the knife from Horse, he would use it on Brick, either to threaten him or, if it came to it, slay him. With both of the group's leaders neutralized, the rest of the men would give up quickly.

It wasn't that Alric didn't trust this particular group of soldiers, it was simply that he'd been a soldier for so long that forming two or three contingency plans for every situation was second nature to him.

He wasn't the only one, either. The nomad woman who

guarded the Princess was the same way, assessing every situation, identifying her escape routes, positioning herself between the Princess and each potential threat.

He didn't like nomads, as a rule. But he couldn't help but respect Joslyn, even if he would never say so out loud.

The men ahead of him were slowing. Alric slowed as well, chanced a glance away from the ground and past the group in front of him.

He could make out a low building, not much taller than a man stands, taking up about a quarter of the stockade wall that marked the far end of the camp. Three figures stood outside it, and as Alric got closer, he could see that they were armed.

Guards? What would be inside a small building at the far corner of the camp that required guards?

He heard sounds coming from inside the building. The murmur of conversation, maybe. But as he got closer, he realized it was too monotone to be conversation.

It was moaning. The moaning of many voices at once, broken only occasionally by maniacal laughter or animalistic snarling.

"Evening, mates," Brick called out cheerily as they approached the three guards. He held up both palms as he walked, showing he carried no weapon.

"Brick?" one of them said. "Is that you?"

"'Tis."

"Who's that with you?" said another.

"Oh, just the boys. Horse, Bratton, Vic. A couple others." He stopped a couple of yards from the three guards, jerked his thumb over his shoulder. "And a special guest."

"Guest?" one of the guards said, suspicion already lacing his voice. His hand went to his sword pommel, and Alric tensed.

"Yes, indeed," said Brick. "Name of Alric. A sergeant what hails from Port Lorsin — Shipper's Quarter. Part of the royal entourage that arrived this morning."

The way he said *royal* had a mocking edge to it, but Alric wouldn't show himself affected. He understood why the edge was there. He'd been a soldier like Brick before.

"We thought we'd show our new friend Alric Fox Battalion," Brick said, and his tone was entirely too jovial for a soldier standing in the dark, talking to guards who watched over a moaning outbuilding.

"Brick. You know we can't do that," said one of the guards. "Captain Riker would — "

Brick turned his head, spat loudly at the ground. "Captain Riker can go bone his mother, for all I care," he snarled, and for the first time, Alric heard real hate in his words. "Way I see it, if the highborn are going to lie to the Wise Men and lie to the Emperor about what's going on here, maybe we need to find a way to send our *own* message to the Emperor, before we all die out here. And maybe Alric's the one what's going to do it for us." He rounded on Alric. "That's what you came around for, isn't it, mate? She sent you here to snoop on us, didn't she?"

The other men shifted uncomfortably. They weren't as shrewd as Brick was. And apparently Alric wasn't, either.

Nothing the smaller man had previously said or asked indicated that he had any idea Alric had befriended them on orders of Princess Natasia.

Alric only hesitated for a moment. An Imperial soldier was dangerous. A *smart* Imperial soldier was much more dangerous. And a smart Imperial soldier who caught you lying to him was the most dangerous of all.

"Yes," Alric said. "Princess Natasia sent me out to befriend the common men. Get the mood of the troops, see if there was a gap between what the foot soldiers said and what the generals said. And yes: She wants to know what really happened to Fox Battalion."

One man cursed under his breath; a few more whispered to one another.

Alric's hand twitched involuntarily. He had a dagger hidden beneath the back flap of his leather armor; he had two more sheathed against each boot. He didn't have his sword, but the three guards all had theirs.

He was still near the back of the group. He could run, if he had to. There was no shame in a man running sometimes; the only soldiers who'd never learned that lesson were the dead ones.

"See that, Nevin?" Brick said to the guard. "A princess outranks a captain. So we're operating on higher orders. That's how I see it."

The guard named Nevin glanced at his two companions. One of them shook his head; the other shrugged.

"If Captain Riker finds out, tell 'im I was the one who

let them in," said the shrugger.

"Captain Riker ain't going to find out anything," Brick said harshly, his Port Lorsin accent thickening alongside his anger. "Because that would mean one of the men here talked." He looked from face to face, despite the night making it impossible to make anyone's features out. It still had the effect he was hoping for. "And no one here would say nothing, right?"

One by one they all nodded, including the guards. Alric made a note to learn Brick's real name. He had genuine leadership potential. The man reminded Alric of the Princess in that way, a woman he'd be happy to call his sovereign one day. He'd known it from the moment he'd seen her strike a dagger into the enemy's throat from some ten yards away. It wasn't often that a Princess came along who cared about her own people's lives so much that she was willing to sully her own hands by fighting, even more rare that a Princess came along who could throw a dagger with deadly accuracy.

"Alright," Nevin said. "But we shouldn't all go in. Who knows how it will set them off."

"I'll take him," Brick said immediately. "Light the jar for me."

Jar? Alric assumed he'd just misunderstood, but a moment later, Nevin produced a small clay bowl, took off its cork top, and handed it to another guard to hold. Then he pulled out steel and flint and struck it over the open jar. A moment later, the clay bowl glowed with a soft blue flame, smelling faintly astringent.

Now he recognized what it was. It was the gel the Wise Men made from spirits, the kind that would burn for hours before the fuel was used up. It was precious stuff, rare and extremely expensive. Alric was surprised to see it in the hands of common soldiers.

Brick held the blue flame in front of him, illuminating his face in a cool, gentle light. Nevin hesitated a moment, then pulled a ring of keys from his belt and unlocked the heavy iron padlock. The door swung open softly, and the moaning sounds grew louder.

Brick glanced over his shoulder at Alric. "You sure you're ready for this, mate?"

Alric responded with a single, tight nod.

Brick gave him an assessing look. "You tell her Highness what you saw in here tonight. You tell her what really happened to Fox Battalion." There was real urgency in his voice.

"I will," Alric said solemnly.

Brick nodded and stepped through the open door. Alric followed.

#

"They were all there, Princess. All twelve survivors of Fox Battalion," Alric said. He let out a shaky breath. "If you could call it surviving. They've built a makeshift prison for them in that building, a separate cell for each one of them. Hands and feet in shackles, iron collars around their necks with another chain attached to the rear wall of the cell."

"Shackles?" Tasia repeated, astonished. "That's no way to treat Imperial soldiers!"

"I said the same thing at first," Alric said. His gaze fell. "Later... I understood the need for the chains."

"They deserted?" Tasia asked. It was the only reason she could think of for putting the few survivors of the devastating battle in chains.

Alric looked up from his lap. "No, they didn't desert. There was something... *wrong* with them. One moment they were normal men, pleading to be let out, promising they could control themselves. But then... something would happen to them. Hatred filled their eyes, they would begin to shout and snarl and... and their hands transformed into flames."

Tasia's breath caught in her throat. Out of the corner of her eye, she saw Joslyn subtly shift her weight.

"Alric... what do you mean, 'their hands transformed into flames'?" Tasia asked.

The old soldier shook his head. "I mean what I said, your Majesty. Before my very eyes, their hands..." He held up his own hands in front of him, staring at them as if they had suddenly become unfamiliar to him. "One moment their hands were just hands, and they were normal men. The next moment... Their arms were like torches, their hands became flames. And they would scream then — but not as a man in pain. They screamed as if... as if..."

"As if they were not human. As if they wanted to kill everything in sight," Joslyn said.

Alric looked up in surprise. "Yes, exactly. I wouldn't have believed it if I hadn't seen it with my own eyes, but I suppose that's why Brick wanted to show me. He said that at first it was just the tips of their fingers that would turn into flames. Then it was the fingers themselves. Now it's the whole hand. Sometimes they are able to speak, like normal men. Other times, they can only groan and growl, like beasts."

Part man. Part flame. It sounded far too familiar.

Tasia met the guard's eyes, saw through the stoic determination and into the undercurrent of fear beneath. Joslyn looked away.

The Princess turned back to Alric. "Why is this happening to them? What do Brick and the others say about when it started?"

Alric shook his head. "The survivors arrived at this camp in ones and twos and threes, and not all at once. Each of them told slightly different tales about what happened to Fox Battalion. Some said that fire rained down from the sky and burned the men alive. Others said the barbarians transformed into fire demons that slaughtered the soldiers by the scores. But fire must've come from somewhere, because all of the survivors arrived in camp with burns."

"Why is this the first we are hearing of this?" Tasia said. "The attack on the Fox Battalion outpost was nearly two and a half months ago."

"The first survivors didn't appear until several weeks after the battle," Alric said. "And their finger tips didn't begin to blaze until another fortnight after that. Brick and the others told me that the officers wrote them off as having battle delirium at first, but when the flames and the bursts of rage came, they created a prison for them and commanded the soldiers not to speak of them. By that time, word had arrived that a royal entourage would be coming to the front. The officers seemed to fear that loose talk of fire demons and men with burning hands who snarled like beasts would only result in them losing their posts."

Tasia clenched her jaw, trying to control her anger. "Has any effort been made to cure them?"

"I don't know," said Alric. "But my guess would be 'no.' Wise Men are rare on a battle front. Officers tend to rely upon their own wisdom here."

Tasia fell into a thoughtful silence. In her mind's eye, she saw the *undatai* trapped in the circle of runes, morphing from a man-shape into a beast made of flames, then back again. Was that the fate of the men? Were they slowly transforming into *undatai*?

Would that be what happened to Joslyn?

"I want to see these men myself," Tasia told Alric firmly. "And I want Wise Man Norix to examine them, to see if he can learn — "

A commotion came from outside the tent — several voices mingling with the distinctive thumps of weapons thudding against leather armor.

"Step aside, soldier," a man said, and Tasia recognized the voice immediately: General Telek. "Princess Natasia?"

the General called. "Are you dressed?"

Tasia's brow crinkled. What was he doing here at this hour? "I'm dressed, General, but I'm meeting with — "

The tent flap flung open, and the General strode inside. Soldiers followed him, flanking him on both sides, hands on their sword hilts. Behind them stood Norix.

Joslyn took a few steps closer to the Princess, positioning herself between Tasia and the men. "The Princess is in the middle of a meeting, General." Her tone carried a warning in it.

"Then the meeting is over," said the General curtly. "The Princess is under arrest."

"Under arrest?" Tasia exclaimed, incredulous. "I am the Princess of the Four Realms, heir to Emperor Andreth of the House of Dorsa. You can't place me under arrest."

The General smiled wolfishly. Tasia had seen his broad politician's smile at the dinner earlier, but this smile was predatory. "Oh, but I can," he said. "The Emperor is dead, and you stand accused of his murder."

36

"Father is... dead?" Tasia said, too stunned to think of anything else to say. "When? How?"

Two soldiers stepped forward, moving past Joslyn. They each reached for Tasia. Joslyn moved to pull her sword from her sheath, but stopped when the General spoke.

"I wouldn't do that, if I were you, nomad," he said. "There are no charges against you yet, but there's ample space in my stockade for a spare nomad who fancies herself a palace guard. Tempt me and I'll be happy to put you there. And I'm sure the drunkards I keep there would be happy to have a woman to entertain them."

"Stand down, Joslyn," Tasia said, her voice shaking.

Joslyn looked from the General, to the Princess, to Norix. With a pained expression on her face, the guard re-sheathed her sword and stepped aside.

The soldiers pulled Tasia up from her seat.

"Hands *off,*" she said, shrugging out of their grip. "I am perfectly capable of standing without your help."

"As long as the Princess doesn't fight, you can take your hands off her," the General said to his men. "Traitor or no, she remains a member of the House of Dorsa. We will treat her as such unless she gives us a reason not to."

Addressing Tasia, he added, "Which also means I will move you to my quarters without the use of shackles. If you are going to cooperate?"

Tasia's head spun.

Her father, the Empire's sole leader since the time he came of age at eighteen, was dead. He'd extended the Capital Lands to make the untamed nomads of Terinto into the Empire's subjects when he was twenty; he'd put down a rebellion that had nearly toppled the House of Dorsa when he was just twenty-five. For the twenty years after that, despite the War in the East, the Empire had enjoyed peace and prosperity under his rulership. Andreth the Just — firm but fair. But now he was just Andreth the Dead.

Dead.

Dead — and apparently murdered. And they thought *she* had done it. She hadn't always been a model royal, but how could anyone have thought she would murder her own father? What motivation would she have?

"Princess?" said the General.

"I'm sure it's all just a misunderstanding," said Tasia, speaking as much to herself as to General Telek. "Of course I'll cooperate." She attempted a smile, looked past the General to Norix. "Without doubt, Wise Man Norix has already told you that I would never present a threat to my own father."

"Quite the contrary, Princess," said Norix. His tone was surprisingly untroubled. "Everything makes sense now — the faked assassination attempt to throw off suspicion, the convenience of an assassin who died before we could finish questioning him. A raid that eliminated your father's top military advisor and which was likely designed to eliminate me, as well. A veteran war hero died, yet somehow a nineteen year-old *girl* managed to escape unscathed?" He shook his head. "It puzzled me at the time. But now I understand — it was all a part of your scheme to seize the throne. Did you also convince your father to name you heir?"

Tasia stared at him disbelievingly. "You *know* I didn't."

This Wise Man, who'd known her since birth, would disavow her so quickly?

"I was surprised that you took the life of one of your own hired mercenaries," Norix continued. "But I suppose that in retrospect, your parlor trick of landing a dagger in his throat successfully drew suspicion even further away from you and ingratiated you with your men." He tapped his temple. "Clever. Wise."

Tasia shook her head. "No," she said. She fought to keep the desperation out of her voice. "No. That's not what happened at all. Norix — you know me. You've known me since I was a child. You know I loved my father. You know I'd never do anything to — "

"Yes," Norix said. "You are right: I've known you since you were a child, Natasia. I've known you as a bratty, petulant child who has always been impulsive and short-tempered and more prone to following her self-indulgent appetites than following the advice of her father or her tutors."

Understanding dawned on Tasia. A thousand small

facts, facts that had all been insignificant until this moment, suddenly fell into place.

"You," she breathed.

She knew her assassin had been hired by someone with means. Means, and with the knowledge to train him to outwit the Wise Men's truth serum. The assassin had known her movements. The mercenaries had known which route they would take. And Norix had somehow escaped the mercenaries, while his primary rival for the Emperor's ear, General Remington, had died.

"This was *you*," Tasia said. *"You* survived the mercenary raid that night, even though your tent burned to the ground. *You* were the last one to question the man who tried to assassinate me before he turned up dead. *You* made sure I was prepared for my father to make me heir. Why, Norix? Why would you do this to me? To Father?"

The smug expression on his face faltered, but only for a moment. Long enough for Tasia to recognize the shift; short enough that no one else saw it before he recovered.

But it was long enough to tell Tasia that her hypothesis was right.

"Me?" Norix said. He smiled smugly, as if the accusation amused him. "Princess, I have been with you during this whole journey. I only just learned of the assassination myself. I am not the one leveling these charges against you. They come from the palace." He sighed, shaking his head with false regret. "I knew you were reckless, but never did I think your lack of wisdom would descend to the point of murder. My own lack of insight, I'm afraid. I accept the responsibility as your teacher."

"You cannot blame yourself," the General said indulgently.

Tasia glared at him. General Remington had suspected him of being a traitor. Norix had vouched for him. Was Telek a part of this conspiracy against her? Or was it mere coincidence?

"Then if you have not accused me, who says I — did this terrible thing?" Tasia had meant to say *"who says I am responsible for my father's death,"* but she couldn't get the words out. Saying *"my father's death"* would make it real, would mean the he was truly gone.

"According to the letter we received," General Telek said, "your handmaid, the Lady Mylla of House Harthing — actually, of House Farrimont now — confessed when she heard of your father's death."

Mylla?

No. No, it couldn't be Mylla. Mylla loved her. They had parted with hugs, tears, kisses. She wouldn't ever do anything to hurt Tasia.

"Poor thing," Norix said, shaking his head sadly. "She couldn't hold your secrets inside any longer. She broke down into tears when the news came, and admitted to her husband that you had told her your scheme long ago."

"No," Tasia said, verging on hysterical. "Mylla would *never* say such a thing of me."

"Are you so sure, Princess?" Norix said, and now his smugness was almost gleeful. The occupants of the tent seemed to hang on his every syllable. "She also told us you forced her into a shameful silence using the… *unnatural* favors you demanded of her. It seems as though the girl has been quite traumatized by you. I'm sure it is a relief to finally have the chance to tell her story."

"No," Tasia said again. She could think of nothing else to say.

She wasn't sure why, but her father's closest advisor was somehow at the center of a plot to murder him. That was hard enough. But to find out that Mylla had also been involved…? Maybe she had been coerced. That had to be it. They had forced her to make this false confession, perhaps under threat of torture. There was no other explanation.

She looked at Joslyn standing in the corner. The guard's dark eyes were wide, alert, concerned. Joslyn knew better than to believe this — didn't she? She knew Tasia was a foolish and spoiled princess sometimes, maybe, but not a murderer.

"It's time to come with us, Princess Natasia," General Telek said. "Come voluntarily, and we will keep you secure within my own private quarters until the day after tomorrow."

Tasia swallowed. "What happens then?"

"You will be sent back to Port Lorsin for your trial," the General said matter-of-factly.

"To be followed by your execution," Norix added.

She swiveled, locked eyes with her former tutor. "How could you have done this to him? He trusted you, and you *murdered* him."

Norix smiled, glancing at General Telek. "The desperate will say anything to shine the light of inquiry away from them."

"How could you have?" Tasia repeated. "You served him his entire reign. Are you really so cold-hearted as this? And why?"

"Princess — " the General said, a note of warning in his voice.

"Was it your idea?" she asked the old man, taking a step forward. The soldiers moved to block her. "Or are you just a foot soldier in someone else's conspiracy?" Tasia turned to the General. She jabbed a finger at Norix. *"He* is the one you should arrest, not me."

"Princess Natasia. I would really prefer not to parade you through camp in shackles," said General Telek.

"They haven't thought this through," Tasia said to the room of soldiers. If she couldn't appeal to her Wise Man and the General, she would try to get through to the commoners. They outnumbered their superiors, after all. "Why would I have my father murdered? It is only through him that I have any station at all."

"And it is through his death that you ascend to wear the crown," said Norix.

"The crown I never asked for! Do you know who takes the Emperor's place, if there is no heir in place at the time of his death?" Tasia said, glancing from face to face. "If I am executed, then the remaining member of the House of Dorsa is my younger sister, Adela, who is not of age. Do you know who rules then? Do you know who becomes her Regent? The palace's senior Wise Man!"

Norix scoffed, but his eyes flitted nervously towards the soldiers. "Your very question contains your answer. If I truly wanted to rule the Empire as Regent, I could have taken your father's life after Nikhost died."

Tasia knew how to read the expressions of men, and she saw her counter accusation had injected doubts in their minds. Regardless of what happened next, they would always wonder if the Princess might be right about the Wise Man.

"Desperate is the falsely accused," Tasia said, reciting from the work of one of the early Wise Men philosophers. "Even more desperate is the truly accused."

Norix lifted an eyebrow. He was triumphant when he said, "My point exactly, my dear."

The General's expression hardened. "For the last time, Princess Natasia, will you be walking out of this tent with or without shackles?"

The Princess lifted her chin, met each man's eye one by one. She saved Alric and Joslyn for last, hoping they could hear the plea for help contained within her gaze.

"Without," she said.

#

Tasia paced the General's tent like a caged lioness. She should be grateful for her royal status; without it, she would likely be sitting in the cold mud in the stockade, surrounded by the camp's petty thieves, drunkards, and insubordinates. The General's tent was not quite as fine as her own, but at least it was comfortable.

At first she'd wondered why she had to be kept under guard here instead of her own tent, but as the guards escorted her here, she understood. His tent was at the very center of the camp. Her own tent, reserved for high-ranking guests, was set in the quiet, private outer ring. She was being held in what was probably the most secure location in the entire camp. Further, the tents nearest to the General's all belonged to his senior officers, each of whom, Tasia knew from the welcome banquet, were ferociously loyal to him. Beyond the top officers' tents was a sea of barrack tents, each of which held a dozen or two soldiers. General Telek must have reasoned that it would be nearly impossible for Tasia to escape from here.

The thought of him made Tasia clench her fists in frustration.

It was ironic that her tutor had betrayed her, because it was his voice Tasia currently heard in the back of her mind, repeatedly playing one of his most consistent lectures:

"The best weapon you will ever have is your wisdom." He'd said that to her countless times over the years, for as long as she could remember. Sometimes he used it as admonishment, sometimes as praise. *"Even if you find yourself without allies and surrounded by enemies, wisdom will remain your loyal companion."*

But it was hard to keep panic at bay. What good would wisdom do her here, inside the General's tent and surrounded by two dozen armed men? None of Norix's lessons, nor any of Joslyn's self-defense tricks, could protect her against what was to come. She couldn't throw a dagger at this enemy, nor could she use her royal status as a lever.

This is a game of Castles and Knights, Tasia told herself every time one of the waves of anxiety threatened to wash her into an ocean of despair. *In Castles and Knights, one's pieces can be depleted, but with the right strategy, one can still come from behind and win the game. It is merely a matter of protecting some small corner of territory and mounting a comeback from there.*

She told herself this, but she wondered if she held any territory at all.

The tent flap rustled, and Tasia tensed, bracing herself for whatever — or whomever — she was about to confront next.

But it was only Junior Captain Danson of Everly, carrying a tray of food. He pushed backwards through the tent flap, then paused when he turned to see Tasia watching him.

"Your noontide meal, Princess," he said.

"Thank you, Captain," said Tasia as graciously as she could.

"Where should I put it?"

Tasia gave a dismissive half-wave towards the low wooden table in the center of the tent. There was no proper place to eat or drink in the General's quarters, only an uncomfortable divan beside the stained and rough-hewn table. The whole tent smelled faintly of fish and a certain pungent musk that Tasia guessed was the General himself.

Captain Danson set the tray down on the table by the divan. The earthy scent of hot oats wafted towards her from inside the pewter bowl; a hard heel of bread sat beside it. It was plain by any standard, but Tasia suspected her royal status meant that she was being fed better than most of the inhabitants of the camp, even if she was considered to be a traitor now.

"I saw your bodyguard this morning," Captain Danson said. His tone carried a strained lightness. He lifted a steaming clay mug of tea from the tray. Beneath it was a small square of parchment, folded in half. "She asked me to send her regards."

He met Tasia's gaze, tried to impart some kind of message to her. He clearly wanted to say more, but beyond the canvas walls of the tent were the two dozen guards. They could doubtless hear every word.

Tasia glanced from the Captain to the parchment and back. "Thank you."

She sat down on the divan, whose dusty cushions should certainly have been taken out of commission a decade earlier, and reached for the parchment. When she unfolded it, a crumpled purple flower tumbled out of it. Across the parchment, in the guard's unpracticed, child-like handwriting, was written *"Tonite."*

Tasia's heart leapt with hope.

"Please tell the guard... please tell her I received her message and appreciate her well wishes. If you see her again."

"I expect I will see her tonight, Princess," said the Captain. "I will pass along your message." He turned to leave. "I must be returning to my duties."

"Of course. Thank you very much for bringing me my meal."

Captain Danson exited with a quick bow.

Tasia picked at her bread. She had little appetite; her stomach was a twisted knot of anxiety, anger, and grief. Her father was dead. The handmaid who had been her lover had accused her. Her lifelong tutor was either at the center of the plot to take her father's life or at least a significant part of it.

In the past twelve hours, her world had imploded. How much could change in a single night.

Mylla's betrayal hurt almost as much as her father's death. The girl could be shallow, vain, and self-serving, but she wouldn't have done this to Tasia. Not without being forced into it. Yet the handmaid made the perfect tool against Tasia — no one was closer to the Princess. No one spent more time with her. Everyone in the palace, from the lords closest to the Emperor to the lowest chambermaid, knew that. No one's accusation could carry more weight, could be more believable.

What levers had been used against Mylla to convince her to turn on her dearest friend and lover?

Something tugged at the edge of Tasia's memory, something surrounding Lord Galen's appearance at the palace for the council meetings, the marriage proposal from

Tasia's cousin that Mylla had kept a secret, the way Mylla had been ferried away to the Northeast only a day before Tasia's own departure East. The answer was there, right in front of her, if she could only put the pieces together...

And then it came together.

"Pig shite," she muttered to herself.

Mylla's marriage to Umfrey, future Lord of House Farrimont, had never added up. House Farrimont was one of the richest houses in the entire Empire — probably second only to House Dorsa. House Harthing, on the other hand, was small and poor. There was no advantage for the Lord of House Farrimont to marry a Lady of House Harthing. Unless that Lady had something of value to offer.

Something like access to the heir to the crown.

Tasia flashed back to the last time she saw her grandfather, Lord Hermant, storming out of her father's office after declaring he would withdraw his additional financial support for the war.

It was all related — Lord Hermant's anger, the unlikely marriage between Mylla and Umfrey, the "confession" Mylla made to frame Tasia. Maybe Norix wasn't at the center of this conspiracy against her father after all. Maybe it was Lord Hermant.

Tasia unrolled the cloth napkin and picked up the soup spoon that fell out of it. She took her first bite of the watery hot oats. It was terrible, but she would eat the whole thing. She would need all the strength she could get for what would come.

37

At least they'd brought her clothes from her original tent. Tasia put on her sleeping gown, but beneath it, she wore the trousers and tunic she'd worn during their journey through the Zaris Mountains. Her riding boots were here, too, stuffed at the bottom of the trunk. The same boots she'd donned when she took Joslyn to the Speckled Dog months ago.

It seemed like an eternity ago now.

She put the boots on and climbed into the cot, arranging the blanket in a bunch at her feet so that the shape of the boots wouldn't give her away if anyone came into the tent. Now there was nothing to do but wait.

Tasia laid in bed, eyes feigning sleep in case anyone should peek in on her, but ears open and alert for the slightest sign that the time had arrived for her to make her escape.

And escape she must. Nothing awaited her in Port Lorsin but death. Her father's death for certain; her own death if she was unlucky enough to be returned there. She was a royal, so she would have the benefit of a trial — speaking on her own behalf in front of the council before they passed their judgment on her — but with Norix now at the head of that council, she stood little chance of escaping execution.

Tasia imagined what the executioner's rope would feel like around her neck, imagined the crowd of people who would come to see a princess hang. It wasn't every day a royal met their death in such a public manner, and the people of the Empire, mercurial and driven primarily by immediate gratification, would have qualms about cheering her death.

Wait. It wouldn't be a hanging at all. It would be a beheading. It had been so long since a member of the House of Dorsa had been executed that Tasia had forgotten that detail.

She rubbed her neck absently, then realized that she still didn't know how her father had died. A knife in the back? A poisoner's concoction? She remembered how the Wise Man who'd tried to kill her had died of poison; now she assumed it had probably been Norix who'd poisoned him, to keep him from saying whatever he knew.

Which other Wise Men were part of the conspiracy? Evrart? He'd always been kind to her, if a little bumbling, but he was the Wise Man in the palace who was closest to Norix. It was clear to see that Evrart was absolutely obedient to Norix; Tasia was certain that if Norix brought in any other Wise Men from the palace into his conspiracy, Evrart would be his first choice.

"Hey there, mates," said a jovial man just outside Tasia's tent.

She knew the voice. It was Alric. Things were about to change, for better or for worse.

"You aren't supposed to be here," one of the guards said gruffly.

"Oh, but I am," Alric said with a happy chuckle. "I have a message to deliver."

"What message?" asked another guard. "No one's allowed to see or talk to the Princess."

"The message isn't for her," said someone else. It was a male voice with a distinctive Port Lorsin accent, but Tasia didn't recognize it. "It's for you."

"What do you mean, for us?" asked the first guard.

"The message is: Support the rightful heir to Emperor Andreth, or let us kill you," said Alric in the same happy-go-lucky tone.

"Princess Natasia is a traitor who murdered her father," growled another guard.

"Stand down," said the man from Port Lorsin. "Help us get the Princess out of the camp, or die fighting for the wrong side. Those are your choices."

Tasia sat up in the cot, the sleeping gown covering her trousers and most of her boots. Out of habit, she patted her hips to check for the daggers Joslyn had given her, but of course they had not been included in the trunk of belongings that the General had permitted her.

Hoarse laughter. "How d'you figure you're going to get the Princess past us? There's two of you and a dozen of us."

"Does that mean your answer is no?" Alric said. "Last chance, boys."

Laughter again, but this time it was nervous. "You're

the one with one last chance. You two get out of here before we clap shackles on you and let the General hang *you* for treason."

There was a pause. Then the man from Port Lorsin said heavily, "Sounds like they're saying no, Al. I don't like killing fellow soldiers."

"Neither do I," said Alric, and there was nothing light in his tone anymore.

A burst of sounds came from outside the tent — steel rang against steel, men grunted and groaned, bodies struck the earth with heavy thuds.

It was over in a matter of seconds, not even long enough for the guards to shout for help. When everything fell silent, Tasia dared to part the flap to the tent open a few inches.

Alric squatted next to the body of one of the General's fallen men. He wiped a spray blood speckles from his cheek, leaving behind a gruesome streak that ran from jaw to forehead.

"Actually," Alric said to the dead body, "there were four of us. But the nomad probably counts for about eight."

Tasia stepped out from the tent, glancing around frantically for Joslyn. The guard stood above another dead man, gazing down at the corpse with an unreadable expression.

Tasia rushed to her, throwing her arms around the guard and pulling her into a tight embrace. "You came for me," the Princess said, tears of relief spilling onto her cheeks.

Joslyn gave Tasia a quick squeeze before releasing her

and pushing her back a few paces. "I promised your father that I would protect you. That I would give my life for yours, if necessary. His death does not release me from that pledge."

"Begging your pardon for being cheeky, Princess," said a short, stout man with a thick red-brown beard. He was the one with the thick Port Lorsin accent. "But we need to leave. Now."

"The rest of Brick's friends are waiting for us," Alric said, gesturing at the man. He looked the Princess up and down. "I hope you don't mind getting a bit muddy."

#

After the slaughter of the General's guards around her tent, the dead bodies were hastily shoved inside the General's tent, and Tasia was hidden away in a wheelbarrow, under a stack of burlap sacks and broken bits of armor. Her four rescuers — Alric, the Port Lorsiner called Brick, Junior Captain Danson, and Joslyn — scattered in different directions. Brick was the one who stayed with Tasia and the wheelbarrow.

"Ye ready?" he asked, thumping the side of the wheelbarrow. Gruffly, he added, "Don't answer that. A talking wheelbarrow might be suspicious."

Despite the fact that her heart hammered frantically in her chest, Tasia couldn't help but smile.

Brick rolled her through the camp at a steady, plodding pace, greeting the soldiers he knew along the way, occasionally whistling a merry drinking tune as he went. Tasia stayed still beneath the burlap sacks, willing her heart to slow down.

"Where you going with that, Yeoman?" asked a man in a tone and accent that marked him as upper-class.

Tasia held her breath.

"And a good evening to you, too, Lieutenant," Brick said cheerily. "Me and my mates, we're sending our armor to get repaired at the smithy's. Spring's on its way, which means we reckon we'll be fighting again soon."

"It's an awfully late hour to be transporting broken armor to the smith's workshop," said the Lieutenant.

"Eh, well," said Brick. "Better late than not at all. That's what my Papa used to say." There was a pause. "Which explains a lot about him, now that I think on it."

The Lieutenant laughed. "Very well, Yeoman. Carry on."

"Thank you, sir. You sleep well tonight. Never know when a good night's rest will come in handy."

"True enough."

The wheelbarrow began to move again, and Tasia let out a tense breath.

A minute or two later, Brick whispered, "See how easy it is for a commoner to play tricks on the highborn? They think us all stupid and slackards. Court fools. Say anything that confirms it and they're likely to believe whatever you say. Didn't even matter that I'm headed in the opposite direction from the smithy's."

Tasia smiled to herself. Brick went back to whistling.

Gradually, the sounds of the camp faded, and Tasia felt her humble carriage moving downhill.

At last the wheelbarrow stopped, and Tasia felt the armor and sacks lifted off her.

"We're here," Brick said. "So are most of the others." He helped her out of the wheelbarrow and pointed to the faces that surrounded them in a semi-circle, their backs to the log stockade wall that marked the camp's outer perimeter. "This is Bratton, from Port Lorsin like me'self," he said, pointing at a young soldier on the semi-circle's outer edge. Bratton bowed awkwardly. "That's Vic, who's from some mud hole in the West, Jugger from right here in the East, and Fats, also from a mud hole in the West. And the ugly cuss on the end, we call him Horse. You can tell from his long face and horrid smell that he's a Steppes man."

Tasia gave them all a formal curtsy. "Thank you for your service. The Empire will never forget what you've done this night."

Horse grunted. "I place little faith in the Empire's memory. But your father pardoned my uncle for thieving once. For that, I owe him."

"Someone approaches," Bratton said.

The men all drew their swords; Brick pushed Tasia behind him. Over his shoulder, Tasia saw three silhouettes moving rapidly towards them in the darkness. Then they came close enough to see, and the men all relaxed.

"Were you planning on running us through, mate?" Alric asked, slowing to a walk.

"Aye," said Fats grimly, sheathing his sword. "If you were the wrong sort."

Junior Captain Danson and Joslyn came into view behind Alric.

"An *officer*, Brick?" Horse said. "And a woman nomad. I don't know which is worse." He shook his head. "The gods have cursed me. We're all going to die."

"Quit whinging. We ain't got time for it," Brick said. He nodded at the stockade wall. "Do the honors, Vic."

Vic nodded and turned to the wall, dropping down on a knee. He brushed at the earth with his hands, revealing a plank that had been hidden before. With effort, he pried the plank up. There was a dark hole beneath.

"A tunnel?" Tasia asked.

"How else d'you think we men make our way out of the camp in search of better ale and women during this gods-forsaken winter?" Brick said.

Tasia eyed the hole. It was just wide enough and deep enough for a man the size of Fats to wiggle through, and it seemed to go straight down.

"Like I said, Princess," Alric said behind her, "I hope you don't mind getting muddy."

38

The Imperial Army's winter encampment was situated on the central of three hills. There had been trees on each of the hills once; now stumps dotted them like stubble of an old man's beard. Except for the scrawniest of saplings, all the trees had been cut by the troops for fortification or fuel within the past year. The part of Tasia that still felt herself on an information-gathering mission for her father noted the absence of trees and wondered what the camp now used to keep their fires burning each night.

Then she remembered that her father was dead now. That made it a fact-finding mission for herself. The Empress.

The naked hills also meant that Tasia's small party was forced to scurry away from the fortified camp like exposed roaches. That was what Tasia thought of, anyway.

The group of them half-jogged, half-walked down the hill. They encircled Tasia like an oval, with the long-legged, long-faced Horse leading the way, angling them towards a copse of trees that rose like a black uprising of earth in the distance. Joslyn stayed at Tasia's side, never further than arm's distance, while Alric and Brick hung back as rear guard.

No one spoke. When the soldiers needed to

communicate, they did so in a language of fluid hand signals that Tasia couldn't read.

They'd nearly reached the trees when the camp's alarm bells began to ring, the sound reminding Tasia of the frantic fire bells that sometimes broke the silence of night in Port Lorsin. And just like the fire bells, one ringing bell became two; two became four; four became a dozen, and soon the camp behind them was a cacophony of bells, shouting men, and barking dogs.

The camp's gates would open soon. And half of the Imperial Army would charge out, tilting towards a new enemy.

Joslyn exchanged glances with the men, then pressed a hand into the small of Tasia's back. "We run now," she whispered.

The oval broke into a dead run.

Tasia ran as fast as she could, not wanting to slow them down. Joslyn helped by keeping a hand firmly clamped around her arm, pulling her forward every time she stumbled or slowed. But a small voice in the back of Tasia's mind warned her that it didn't matter how fast or how slow they went. They'd never outrun their pursuers. The men who chased them had horses and dogs and archers; her ragtag band had only determination and, she hoped, wits.

They reached the trees just as the first dots of torch lights appeared behind them, floating and bouncing down the hill like ghostly yellow orbs, accompanied by the echoing shouts of commands and instructions.

A few yards inside the trees, the group stopped when Horse raised a fist.

Joslyn pulled Tasia close, wrapping a protective arm around her waist. She and the Princess watched as Brick, Horse, and Alric exchange hand signals at furious speeds. Joslyn nodded at the men when they finished and placed her lips next to Tasia's ear. "We part ways here," she said quietly. "Half of the men will go north, half of them south, to draw off the dogs. You and I continue east, alone."

"But the only things to the east are the mountains and the barbarians," Tasia said.

"Which is why we head that way," Joslyn said, breath still tickling Tasia's ear. "It is the last direction they would think to look."

"Will the others be caught?" Tasia asked. The last thing she wanted for these brave men was for them to die on her behalf.

But the guard wasted no more time with words. As the men peeled off, Alric leading some of them north, Brick and Horse leading the rest south, Joslyn seized Tasia's forearm and pulled her deeper into the forest. They didn't attempt to move quietly anymore; speed mattered more than stealth at this point, and the pursuing soldiers were probably still too far away to hear. They crashed through the underbrush, with Tasia stumbling every few feet on roots and rocks. But Joslyn was as sure-footed as ever, making the Princess wonder if her bodyguard were part cat or part owl, able to see in the dark.

Just when Tasia was about to say that she had no breath

left for running, the guard slowed.

"There is a stream we'll cross ahead. The water will make it harder for the dogs to catch our scent," she said. "Brick says there's a ruined village not far past this point. We will find a place there to hide for the night. Then we continue east at first light."

Tasia nodded in breathless agreement and followed Joslyn down a short embankment and into babbling water. The sound of barking dogs was getting louder.

"Hurry," Joslyn commanded. They scrambled up the opposite bank and continued their mad dash through the woods.

"Joslyn," Tasia said after another hundred yards of half-running, half-tripping through the dark, "I can't keep going."

"It's alright," Joslyn said. "We're here."

Tasia looked up. They stood on a low ridge at the edge of the forest; a cluster of derelict huts formed a ring in the depression below them. A fire must have ruined the village; the stones that formed the huts were smudged with black, and most of the thatch roofs were either gone completely or collapsing in on themselves.

This is what war looks like to commoners, Tasia found herself thinking as she surveyed the burned out village. *Fire and death.*

"That one," Joslyn said, pointing. "It still has a door that's serviceable."

Tasia squinted, following the guard's gaze to a hut at the far end of the village, past a pile of burnt timbers. She wondered how Joslyn had picked it out from its neighbors with such little moonlight to mitigate the darkness. The hut's front door hung askew in the frame from one corner of the doorway, splintered at the bottom. But at least it provided them with something to hide behind.

They hurried into the hut.

"How long will we — "

"Shhh," Joslyn hissed.

They slid inside the broken door. Tasia retreated into the small hut's back corner, while Joslyn stayed near the door, peering outward. Tasia pressed her back against the cold stone wall behind her. Despite the chill in the night air, her palms grew slick with sweat.

What would come of her if the soldiers caught them? Her escape attempt would no doubt be interpreted as an admission of her guilt. And the people who helped her — Joslyn, Alric, Danson, Brick, and the others — would all certainly be deemed guilty of treason and hung. As a member of the House of Dorsa, she would have the opportunity to defend herself at the trial in Port Lorsin; the rest of them were commoners and would receive no such consideration.

A wave of grief struck her, and she struggled to control her tears.

Everything was happening too fast. Her father's death. The accusations against her. Mylla's betrayal. The realization that Wise Man Norix was almost certainly a traitor. And now? Now a group of ordinary soldiers who had nothing to gain and everything to lose from helping her had put their lives at risk in an escape attempt that might not even work.

She covered her face with her hands. Maybe this had been a mistake. Maybe she should have found a way to tell Joslyn to leave her. She could have thought of something on her own that might save her at the trial. And then all these soldiers would have had a better chance at going home to their families alive.

"It seems the ruse worked," Joslyn said, stepping away from the ruined door. "I don't hear any signs of pursuit."

Tasia took her hands away from her face. Her racing heart slowed some. "They aren't coming?"

"At least not now."

"What about the others? If the ruse worked... Are they in danger?"

Joslyn took a deep breath. "It's possible."

"Joslyn, I don't want anyone risking their lives on my behalf."

"You are the Empress now, the living symbol of the Empire," Joslyn said. "People will always risk their lives for you, because you are more than a person. You are the representation of order and safety and stability. They are protecting themselves, but they are also protecting their own way of life."

Tasia slid down the wall, sat heavily on the packed earth of what had been the hut's floor. "It doesn't matter how much they teach you about rulership. No one can prepare you for what it feels like to be responsible for the lives — and deaths — of others." She looked up at the guard. "And my father's dead," she whispered. "I'm an orphan now."

"I know, Tasia," Joslyn said softly. She stepped away from the broken door, crouched in front of the Princess. "But he chose you for a reason. So tell me: What advice would he give you, if he were here now?"

Tasia gazed at Joslyn, thinking. She wondered then about the last moments of the Emperor's life, if he'd known who had betrayed him or if he'd died in an anonymous way, with poison in his wine or a knife in his back. She wondered if he'd known that it was Norix, his closest advisor, who'd pulled the levers that led to his death, or if he'd died in ignorance. Which death would have been kinder for him?

"He would say…" Tasia began. "I don't know what he would have said. The truth is, I don't think he'd planned on having me be his heir until recently. He spent less time teaching me than the Wise Men — Wise Man Evrart, Wise Man…" Norix's name soured on her tongue, and she refused to say it. "And General Remington."

"And what did General Remington teach you about how armies behave when they are pinned down and outnumbered?"

"They find a defensible position, hunker down, and send for reinforcements. Or if they can, they escape through trickery and subterfuge."

Joslyn nodded. "Then you have followed the General's advice, which is indirectly your father's advice. We have found the most defensible position we can, and your companions are working to lead them away from you via trickery and subterfuge."

"My companions are all likely to die because of me," Tasia said morosely.

"Give them more credit than that," Joslyn said gently. She rested a hand on Tasia's arm. "They are all veteran warriors of the Imperial Army. Believe in them to find a way. The way that we believe in you."

Tasia exhaled heavily. "I guess we should try to rest while we can, huh?"

"Yes," said the guard. "We move east as soon as there's enough light to walk by."

39

Tasia woke an hour or two later, heart racing. Just a dream, she realized. They hadn't actually been attacked by soldiers, there was no *undatai* roaming the deserted village, and Joslyn — she glanced around in the darkness until she spotted the nomad — was still alive.

Once her eyes adjusted to the darkness, Tasia studied the guard. Joslyn sat a few feet away, back against the hut's wall, short sword resting across her raised knees. Her head was turned, and she stared out the half-ruined door, whose dilapidated state let in the scantest quantity of moonlight.

Joslyn's profile, like the rest of her, was beautiful.

Without turning her head to face Tasia, the guard said, "Why are you staring at me?"

"How did you know I was awake?"

"I heard your breathing change, and then you were unnaturally still," Joslyn said. "Then the back of my neck prickled with the feeling of eyes on me."

"The back of your neck always prickles when someone looks at you?"

Joslyn looked back at Tasia, face lost to the shadows. "Yes. When your childhood is spent hiding from those who would hurt you, your instincts for sensing a creeping predator become as sharp as a field rabbit's."

"A sword master like you shouldn't compare yourself to a rabbit," Tasia admonished. "You are far more than that. You should say you are something else... like a hawk."

"A sword master who wants to stay alive should never forget that she's as much prey as predator." She let out a small, tired sigh. "Better to think of myself as rabbit than hawk."

"But the rabbit doesn't always know when the hawk stares at it," Tasia countered. "If it did, there would be no hawks. And far too many rabbits."

"There are foolish rabbits born into every generation to feed the hawks," Joslyn said. "Coyote made sure of that."

Tasia was confused for a moment. Then she remembered Wise Man Evrart's folklore lessons, when he taught her the myths some commoners still believed regarding the old gods. Every region throughout the Empire held to slightly different myths, but all of them believed in some version of the trickster god. In the West, people still cursed Gwydion, the prankster god who caused milk to spoil, small items to go missing, donkeys to stumble and break their legs unexpectedly. In the Northeast, it was Raven, the half-man, half-bird god; and in the lowlands of the Central Steppes, it was Tayu, a shapeshifting god whose favorite form was the raccoon.

In Terinto, the trickster god was Coyote. Whereas most trickster gods were minor figures, Coyote was the most important god in the Terintan pantheon. The nomads saw themselves as the tricksters, fooling the barren desert landscape into providing them with what they needed for survival. Coyote was the one who had given them that power.

"You're a true child of Coyote, then," Tasia said, remembering the phrase as being a high compliment in Terinto.

"No," Joslyn said, her voice weary. "I'm just a rabbit with a long streak of good luck."

Tasia shook her head to argue, then realized that Joslyn probably couldn't see the motion in the dark. "You're so much more than that."

Joslyn didn't reply. Tasia opened her mouth to say more, but the guard, as if sensing that the Princess was about to press her argument further, cut her off. "You should sleep. Tomorrow will be a long day."

"*You* should sleep," Tasia said. "I'm awake now. Let me watch. You can get some rest."

"It's alright," said Joslyn. "I'm quite used to — "

"The fools back in that camp may think I'm a traitor who no longer deserves the name of Dorsa," said the Princess in a regal tone. "But you and I both know that I am the rightful Empress of this land, which makes me your superior. If I tell you to sleep, you should sleep."

There was a low chuckle in the darkness, followed by a moment of quiet.

"Your command does no good, Empress," Joslyn said. "My nervous rabbit's mind will not sleep even if Eiren and Eirenna themselves demanded it."

"Eiren and Eirenna... the god of the midday sun and the

goddess of dawn?" Tasia said, remembering more of her Terintan folklore.

"Yes — though Eirenna is also goddess of the sunset. The chieftain and his consort who rule us all." The guard's voice was serious, bearing no trace of irony. Tasia wondered if Joslyn believed what she was saying or was just using the gods for the sake of metaphor.

Tasia pushed herself into a sitting position. "Then let us both stay awake, because I can't sleep, either."

"Alright," Joslyn said, then added, "but we still leave at Eirenna's first appearance over the Eastern Mountains."

They sat together quietly, each pondering their own thoughts. For Tasia's part, she wondered, as she often had before, about her mysterious guard — about how she'd grown up, what she'd lived through to make her so stoic and serious, what she believed and didn't believe, and if there would always be a part of her that would remain a wild desert nomad.

She also wondered what it was Joslyn thought of her.

"Joslyn?"

"Hmm?"

"Why continue to support me?" Tasia asked. "Why risk yourself this way? If they catch you, they'll hang you without a trial."

"I swore an oath to the Emperor to protect you," Joslyn said. "That's what I'm doing."

"Surely the oath is void if the Emperor dies. Especially if the one you swore to protect is accused of his murder."

"You had nothing to do with the death of your father,"

Joslyn said sharply.

"But how do you know that?"

"You forget how much time we have been spending together." Joslyn let out a short laugh. "You are many things, Tasia, but a murderer is not one of them."

Tasia was glad that the night covered her blush. She knew that not all of the *many things* Joslyn referred to were flattering.

"You have seen me at my worst," Tasia said to the guard. "At my most manipulative, my most spiteful. It's shameful."

"Perhaps," Joslyn said thoughtfully. "But I've also seen you admit your mistakes, right wrongs, and make an effort to become the heir your father needed. You are honorable."

"Honorable," Tasia repeated. She gave a disapproving grunt.

The breeze picked up, whistling through the half-broken door and sending it to rocking. Tasia shivered. When they forded the stream, water had flowed inside her riding boots, setting both feet in a miniature lake the rest of their flight. The water was still there, but she hadn't wanted to show any sign of discomfort to Joslyn, who never seemed to complain no matter what the circumstances were.

"You're cold," the guard said.

"I'm fine," Tasia said nonchalantly. But it took all her willpower not to shake uncontrollably.

Without seeking permission, Joslyn pulled off one of Tasia's riding boots and turned it upside down. Water trickled out of it.

"Tasia," the guard chided. "Have your feet been wet since the stream?" She pulled off the other boot and upended it. The second had even more water in it than the first. Joslyn leaned over the Princess, patting her ankles and calves. The wind blew again, and this time Tasia couldn't help herself; she shook hard.

"Mother Moon," Joslyn muttered. "Both your legs are soaked. You should've said something *hours* ago."

"It hasn't been so bad," Tasia said, but the uncertainty in her voice gave her away.

"You're going to catch a chill," Joslyn said sternly. The guard reached under Tasia's sleeping gown, making Tasia start in surprise. Joslyn fumbled until she found the top of each stocking above the knee of the trousers, then rolled them down Tasia's legs inch by inch, because they were too wet to simply tug off. "You're going to need to take the trousers off, too. They're wet to the knees."

Tasia smiled slightly. "If I didn't know any better, Joslyn, I'd say you want to get into my pants."

The guard ignored the comment. "I should've realized how wet you were earlier," she grumbled in response. "I can't believe I let you sit here sopping in stream water."

"'Sopping' might be an exaggeration," Tasia said as she wriggled out of the wet trousers.

Joslyn wrung out one of the stockings, resulting in a pitter-patter of water hitting the earthen floor. Then she wrung out the other. She dropped them both a few feet away and fixed a hard look on Tasia.

Well, Tasia *assumed* it was a hard look. She couldn't actually see the guard's eyes in the dark.

"Sopping," Joslyn said again. She reached for Tasia, fumbling for the hem of the sleeping gown. "How wet is the gown?"

"It's not as bad," Tasia answered honestly. "The stockings got the worst of it."

Sword-calloused hands patted up her bare legs, her thighs. Tasia shivered again, but for entirely different reasons.

"Don't say I have to take it off," Tasia said, voice wavering. "I don't have anything else to wear. And I definitely wouldn't be warmer without it."

Joslyn shook her head. "No, you wouldn't be warmer. And it's not that wet. Still..." She hesitated a moment, then unbuckled her sword and dagger belt. Then reached around to her side, unbuttoning the padded leather armor of her guard's uniform. She stripped it off.

"I don't think your armor will fit me," Tasia said. "And what if you need it?"

"I'm not putting it on you," said the guard, gingerly setting the leather tunic aside. She always handled it with careful reverence, Tasia realized. Even now that the Empire would disavow her for helping the traitor Princess.

The guard scooted closer to Tasia, until her chest was inches from Tasia's shoulder. "The armor... it's hard to transfer any body heat through it." She sounded embarrassed. "May I — if you let me..." She trailed off.

Tasia's brow furrowed in confusion.

Joslyn raised her arms, miming an embrace. "I can warm you," she said. "With my own body heat."

"Oh," Tasia said. "Of course."

She slid a few inches closer to the guard, rotating so that her back leaned against the guard's chest. Her heart pounded. She and the guard had been intimate twice before, and ever since the night in the woods, they'd developed the habit of falling asleep in each other's arms. So why did she feel so nervous to be pressed against Joslyn now? Tasia was a far cry from virginal. The guard's touch shouldn't make her feel like a fumbling new bride.

It was different this time. Tasia couldn't explain it to herself other than that — it was just different somehow.

Joslyn wrapped both arms tightly around the Princess and pulled her close. Tasia could feel the guard's breath against her neck.

"Are you comfortable enough?" Joslyn asked.

"Yes," Tasia breathed, the word hardly more than a whisper.

They sat in silence. Tasia listened to the twin sounds of their heartbeats, the way they seemed to speak in harmony to one another. Her thoughts wandered to Mylla, of the nights the handmaid had spent holding her much like Joslyn held her now. The memory of Mylla holding her led to a memory of her mother holding her, who'd held Tasia only rarely and who'd died much too soon. Her mother's death triggered thoughts of Nik; Nik triggered thoughts of her father. Quietly, Tasia began to cry.

"What's wrong? You're still cold?" Joslyn said, the

words tickling the side of Tasia's neck.

"No," Tasia said. "That's not… I'm not shaking from cold."

Joslyn craned her neck forward, inspecting Tasia's face. She lifted one hand and touched the Princess's cheek, then rubbed the tear she'd captured between her fingers.

"You're crying."

"Only a little," Tasia said.

"Why?"

"It's nothing," said the Princess. She took a breath. "Or it's everything."

Joslyn said nothing, but the arms around Tasia tightened.

"What am I going to do, Joslyn?"

It took the guard a moment to respond. "My *ku-sai* used to say that there is no such thing as a useful worry. He said that when enemies wait in every direction, find a wall to put your back against and focus on one blade at a time."

Tasia considered the words. "I don't see how that applies here."

"For tonight, we focus on rest," said Joslyn. "We deal with tomorrow's problems tomorrow."

Each word was a warm caress of air against the side of Tasia's throat.

"And if there is no tomorrow?" Tasia asked softly. "If tonight is all we have…?"

The guard didn't answer with words, but the harmony of both women's hearts sped up.

"Joslyn…" Tasia murmured, and she turned in the

guard's arms. The dark was no obstacle; Tasia's lips found Joslyn's and fit them there as if that was the place they were always meant to be. "I have to tell you something. I — "

"No," said the guard. "It is I who has something to tell you. Empress Natasia, I, Joslyn of Terinto — "

" — love you," both women finished at once.

40

Tasia kissed the guard again. Joslyn's hand made its way to the small of Tasia's back; the other pressed into the place between her shoulder blades.

Something constricted tightly deep inside Tasia's chest, and, in a way she couldn't yet articulate in words, she knew she never again wanted to kiss a mouth other than this one, she never again wanted her fingers along a jawline other than Joslyn's.

The feeling was unexpected; despite her youth and her station — or perhaps because of it — Tasia had known many men and a handful of women. Never before had it occurred to her that she would abandon all the others in favor of one — not even for Mylla, whom she loved.

A great rumble and crack emanated from the sky, making Tasia jump and Joslyn reach for her sword. A moment later, lightning whipped through the black of the night, illuminating everything in bright white for a moment. Seconds later, rain poured down into the roofless hut. The women paused, looking up. Then both began to laugh. Tasia's laugh was a high giggle, the manic laughter of nervous energy that had just found release. Joslyn's laughter was lower, steadier, the kind of sound a person not prone to frivolity makes when they finally find something worthy of their amusement.

"So much for drying you," the guard said wryly.

"I don't mind being... wet," Tasia said slowly, putting special emphasis on the last word.

Lightning flashed again, thunder boomed. For a brief second, Tasia could see Joslyn's face, could see her already soaked black hair hanging around her face in thick, wet ropes. And in the momentary flash of light, Tasia thought she saw something in the guard's dark eyes she'd never seen there before — a relaxed, simple happiness.

Rainclouds obscured the moon and plunged the world back into darkness the moment the lightning disappeared, but it was as if the lightning had struck the core of Tasia's desire, and she burned hotter for Joslyn than she ever had before. Roughly, Tasia pushed the guard back against the scarred stone wall, and this time her kiss was one that brooked no argument, its earlier hesitancy replaced with a fierce insistence.

Joslyn responded in kind, kissing Tasia back just as hard. She allowed herself to be pushed back against the wall for a moment, but by the time the lightning flashed for a third time, the balance of power had shifted. The warrior had laid the Princess back against the earthen floor, pulled her sleeping gown up, then her undergarments down.

At the next bolt of light that cracked through the sky, Tasia saw that the guard's eyes had changed again. This time they contained raw desire, a hunger that matched her own. She wrapped one hand around the back of Joslyn's neck, fingernails digging into the guard's skin. With her other hand, she reached downward, searching for the top of Joslyn's trousers. She fumbled for the drawstring, but froze when the tip of a finger slipped inside her.

Tasia gasped, eyes fluttering closed involuntarily and toes curling against the floor. But then she remembered her task. They'd done this twice before already — the time in the woods in the foothills of the Zaris Mountains, and the time when they bathed together after first arriving in the Imperial Army's encampment. But both times, Joslyn hadn't allowed herself to be touched. This time, Tasia refused to be denied.

She tugged at the drawstring holding up Joslyn's trousers, feeling the waistband loosen when the knot finally gave way. Then she walked her fingers downward. Smooth, bald skin met her fingers, the burn scars she'd seen before when they'd bathed together. Tasia looked up at the guard's face. But there was no lightning, only rain, and in the darkness, Tasia couldn't read Joslyn's eyes.

Joslyn wrapped a gentle hand around Tasia's wrist. "No one has touched me since…" But she trailed off.

Tasia waited, but when Joslyn didn't finish her statement, she asked, "Since when?"

A chin bobbed in the darkness. "Since… *him.*"

A surge of emotion sent tears welling up in Tasia's eyes. "Oh, Joslyn." She put both hands on the side of the guard's face, and in the darkness traced the contours of the woman's cheeks and nose and lips. Then she kissed her with soft tenderness. "I'll kill him one day," she said fiercely. "I will hunt him down in Terinto, or wherever he's hiding, and I will plunge the dagger into his heart myself."

Joslyn shook her head. "It's too late," she said. Her voice was rough, and Tasia realized she was holding back tears. "I slit his throat the night that I ran away."

"Good," Tasia said, kissing the salty damp spots leaking from the corners of the guard's eyes that mingled with the raindrops. "Good," she said again, and filled Joslyn's mouth with her tongue.

The rain continued to pelt down on them, thunder rumbling and lightning cracking intermittently. The torrential downpour had slowed, but the rain was still coming down hard. Joslyn and Tasia stayed pressed together, their mouths and hands each exploring the other while the storm raged on.

Tasia pushed back after a minute or two. "Does it mean... will it hurt if I touch you there?"

"I don't know," Joslyn said quietly.

"Do you mean to say that a few nights ago, in the woods, and then during our bath, was that the first time you...?"

Joslyn shook her head. Leaning forward until her lips tickled Tasia's ear, she whispered, "I have had many women, but I... but no one's ever... no one has..."

"You've touched them," Tasia said. "But you never let them touch you."

Joslyn nodded.

With the kind of slow, deliberate movements a person might use when trying to avoid frightening off a child or a small animal, Tasia pulled Joslyn's tunic up a few inches and flattened her palm against the woman's bare stomach. Gradually, she slid her palm down, past Joslyn's belly button, beneath the waist of the guard's rain-soaked trousers. When her fingertips encountered the smooth, scarred skin again, she asked softly, "May I try? Will you allow me to touch you?"

Joslyn hesitated, then nodded once, her face brushing against Tasia's.

Tasia's fingers crawled carefully across the guard's most private places. The scars seemed to be mostly on the outside — across Joslyn's pubic bone, crisscrossing on the insides of her thighs. But the center of her, the very center, where heat emanated and which was wet without the help of the rain, that part of the guard seemed to be unscathed.

Tasia put the tip of her index finger on Joslyn's clit, then pressed lightly. The guard sucked in a breath.

"Are you alright?" Tasia asked. "It doesn't hurt, does it?"

Joslyn shook her head. "No. It doesn't hurt. It — "

But Tasia had added a second finger as soon as Joslyn shook her head and began stroking the guard in small, tight circles. Whatever the guard was planning to say transformed into a muffled cry that she let out against Tasia's neck. Encouraged, Tasia lengthened her strokes, then dipped the tips of both fingers inside Joslyn.

The guard stiffened immediately, pulling Tasia's hand away. "No," she said, sitting halfway up. "No, I can't — I'm not — "

"It's alright, shh, it's alright," Tasia soothed. "You're

not ready for that. It's fine."

Joslyn relaxed, easing her body back down over Tasia's. The Princess brushed wet hair from Joslyn's cheeks while continuing to shush her. The rain had slowed to an insistent drizzle above them, but by now they were both soaked to the bone. Tasia wriggled close again, in part for intimacy, in part for warmth. She kissed Joslyn, relieved when the guard kissed her back.

"I want to make you feel good," Tasia said quietly. "The way you've made me feel good. Can I touch you again? Please? I won't go too far. And I won't do anything you don't want me to, I promise."

Instead of answering with words, Joslyn caught Tasia's hand, guided it beneath the line of her trousers once more. Her breathing quickened when Tasia's first two fingers slipped between her folds and found her clit once more.

"I'll just... we can stay with this, alright?" Tasia said, resuming her slow, stroking circles. The guard was still on top of her, supporting most of her weight on her forearms. It was an awkward angle for Tasia; the whole business would have been much easier if Joslyn was the one lying on her back. But she worried that if she tried to roll Joslyn over, the guard would balk and pull away again.

And besides, this seemed to be working. Joslyn's breath had sped up, and she was starting to rock her hips in time to Tasia's circles. Tasia pressed harder, and Joslyn sucked in a ragged breath, her hips jumping forward. Tasia went faster, harder still, and Joslyn hissed out hoarse, guttural syllables that Tasia assumed were something either dirty or prayerful in Terintan. Whatever it was, the sound only turned Tasia on all the more, and she stroked even faster.

The rain picked back up as Joslyn ground against her. The guard said something else in Terintan, but most of it was lost beneath an angry peel of thunder. Then she dipped her head and administered a near-frantic series of kisses and half-gentle bites along Tasia's jawline, throat, collarbone. Tasia moaned with pleasure, keeping up a steady rhythm against Joslyn despite the fact that her wrist and fingers ached from the effort. Panting raggedly, Joslyn lifted her head just as lightning forked through the sky above the hut. The flash of light illuminated above Tasia a mouth that was half-open, eyes that were half-closed. The panting stopped, and Joslyn let out a long, low moan. She shuddered violently, then grew still. A moment later, she rolled off Tasia, lying heavily on her side next to the Princess.

All was quiet except for the sound of the rain and Joslyn's heavy breathing.

"Thank you," she said a few seconds later. She kissed Tasia's cheek. "Thank you."

"You're welcome," Tasia said. "More than welcome."

She didn't intend to fall asleep. But it was already the middle of the night; she was exhausted, wet, and cold, while the guard next to her radiated heat. Tasia burrowed closer to Joslyn, pressing her face to the guard's chest. The mingled scent of rain and Joslyn's skin lulled her, and before she knew it, she was drifting off. She woke up with a start a few minutes later, a fuzzy recollection nagging that someone — at least one of them — was supposed to stay awake. But then Tasia slept, and she slept hard.

Which made the chorus of baying dogs that finally roused her at dawn all the more unpleasant.

Part III:

Accusations

"The violent capture and subsequent trial of the Princess Natasia was a dark hour for the Empire. It was bad enough that the Princess had been accused of arranging for the murder of her father. Worse still was the fact that the trial, its aftermath, and the lack of firm leadership became a distraction that led to disastrous consequences for the real threat to the Empire that was quietly growing in the Eastern Mountains."

— Wise Man Tellorin, *The Updated Histories of House Dorsa*

41

Joslyn scrambled away from the Princess, cursing under her breath in Terintan. She snatched her leather armor from the middle of the hut and jerked it on, fumbling with the buttons that ran up the side.

Tasia sat up too quickly, disoriented and dizzy. Where was she? She'd had the sweetest dream about Joslyn. She dreamed there was a rainstorm, and a hut with no roof, and she'd made love to the guard to the musical accompaniment of thunder and lightning.

Tasia opened her eyes, blinking a few times to clear them. Her body was impossibly stiff. She sat on the floor of a burned out hut, her sleeping gown streaked with mud. Early morning light filled the hut, filtering in through a door that hung askew from only one top hinge. The sky above was less blue than it was violet, the last remnants of the blanket of night still lingering as dawn struggled to wake.

Tasia sucked in a breath. Everything from the night before — both the good and the bad — came back to her in a sudden rush. The barking sounds of dogs grew more distinct, and all at once she understood why Joslyn was strapping her sword belt on with such haste: The soldiers had found them.

The Princess leaned forward, peering through the sizable crevice between the hanging door and its frame. She caught a glimpse of what she expected — a hillside swarming with running men, at least two dozen of them, with three on horseback.

"Gods be cursed," Tasia muttered. She grabbed her two stockings, still saturated with stream and rain water, and wrestled them onto her feet. She had her wet trousers and wet boots on a moment later — the material clung and chafed, but she hardly noticed the discomfort.

Joslyn crouched against the wall beside the broken door, her sword drawn and held at the ready. Her face was blank and hard, a stone statue of a nomad warrior. Tasia noticed that Joslyn had put her leather tunic on crooked; the seam where the buttons ran up was slightly out of place. But other than that one slight mar, the guard showed no sign that she, too, had just woken from a deep slumber.

Joslyn turned her head, catching Tasia's eye. Slowly, she raised a finger and put it to her lips. Tasia nodded. The Princess knew not to make another sound — she didn't move an inch from her place behind Joslyn. She hardly even breathed.

The broken door gave her a partial view of what was happening beyond, in the burned-out village. Through its slit, she caught glimpses of the dogs. They weren't the pampered, well-groomed lap dogs Tasia was used to seeing noblewomen carry with them to garden parties. These were war dogs, at least half the size of ponies. They had square faces with frothing jowls, and jaws that looked like they could snap through a man's arm without too much effort. Tasia counted them as they loped past her narrow field of vision.

Four. Five. Six, seven... and there was eight. And now the handlers, jogging along behind them, shouting commands at the great beasts, thick leather leashes draped over their shoulders.

"All clear here!" a man shouted.

"Clear here, too!" shouted another in response, and this second voice was closer than the first.

Tasia's pulse quickened. She wondered if the dogs had tracked them here by scent, or if the soldiers were searching the village out of routine diligence. It hardly mattered which it was; if the soldiers conducted a hut-by-hut search of the village, then there was no doubt she and Joslyn would be found.

They were trapped.

Heavy footsteps crunched nearby, but Tasia saw no one through the door's crack. She heard a grunt, then a sound that was unmistakably a neighboring hut's door being kicked open.

"Clear!" came a shout, so close this time that the soldier could only be one or two huts away.

More footsteps. A shadow obscured Tasia's view out the door. Then she realized it wasn't a shadow, but a man in the dark brown leather of the Imperial Army. Light as a cat, Joslyn rose to her full height and stepped back from the door. She sheathed her sword with perfect silence and drew the dagger that hung on the other side of her belt.

The irony struck Tasia for a brief instant before the man kicked the door in: This man was an Imperial soldier, the kind of man who would normally be awestruck to see the Princess of Dorsa, who, under any other circumstances, would fall all over himself with bows and obsequious compliments in an attempt to win her favor. And now? Now he was just one more foot soldier hunting the Princess down with dogs.

How fickle was Mother Fortune.

WHAM!

His booted foot connected squarely with the door, and instead of swinging open, its last hinge creaked out a death cry and gave way. Fortunately, the falling door missed Tasia, who still huddled in the corner when it crashed inward and struck the stone wall behind it with a noisy clatter before falling to the ground.

Morning light streamed into the hut, catching the swirling motes of dust and ash and turning them golden. The man standing in the door frame, backlit by the rising sun, was of average height and build but with a slight paunch, bald with a trim brown beard and matching brown eyes. A thick-corded dog's leash was slung over one shoulder. His eyes widened, seeming to take up his whole face when he saw Tasia sitting in the corner. He drew in a breath to yell out his findings, but Joslyn's hand clamped down on his mouth and the point of her dagger drew a single drop of blood from the side of his neck.

"Tell them that you're clear or I'll slit your throat," Joslyn hissed into his ear. "Do we understand each other?"

The man, whose wide eyes now shone with fear instead of surprise, nodded vigorously, then winced when the motion pressed more flesh against Joslyn's razor-sharp dagger.

"I'm going to take my hand away so you can tell them you're clear, but the knife stays where it's at. One wrong syllable from you and you'll be swallowing your own blood."

He nodded, careful to avoid the dagger's tip this time.

Gradually, Joslyn took her hand away from his mouth. He hesitated only a moment, then shouted, "All clear here!"

Joslyn gave a a satisfied nod. Then she seized the man's head and slammed it hard against the door frame. The soldier's knees buckled beneath him. Joslyn caught the weight of his limp, collapsing body, easing him to the hut's floor and quickly dragging him away from the open doorway. She gestured for Tasia to come closer, and the Princess crossed the small room in two long strides.

Tasia stepped over the soldier's motionless form. At first she thought Joslyn had killed him, but the faint rise and fall of his chest showed that he was merely unconscious. The Princess sighed in relief. The men who hunted her were innocent — game pieces on a Castles and Knights board moved by other hands. She didn't want them to die if they didn't have to.

Joslyn put Tasia behind her. Their backs were pressed against the same wall the hut's doorway was on, so that if anyone were to give a quick glance inside, they might very well presume the building to be empty.

Now the only thing to do was wait.

Minutes ticked slowly by. Tasia listened to the voices of the soldiers, sometimes able to hear their accents but not their words. That one who sounded like he was talking around a mouthful of hot oats, he had to be from the Northeast. That was a deep mountain accent, the kind the miners of her mother's homeland had. She heard the lilting sing-song accent of Port Lorsin, the gravelly burr of the West, and the forced, breathless speech of the Central Steppes. All her citizens were here, soldiers who represented every part of the realm.

And if they found her, they would put her in chains and kill Joslyn without hesitation.

Occasionally, she caught a word or two of conversation. Brisk and efficient, they commanded their dogs, asked and answered questions of one another with methodical discipline.

"Left hut, three, four, five?" asked a Western man who must have been an officer.

"Searched and cleared, sir."

"Favin, Seamus!" the officer called.

"M'Lord?" came the distant response.

"Take your dogs, search the woodpile, then the well. See if they can pick up the scent."

"Yes, m'Lord."

Footsteps. Hooves against pea gravel. Dogs yipping, barking. A single snarl, followed by a high-pitched yelp.

At last it sounded like the search was concluding. The shouts of "All clear!" died down, and the conversation became too distant to hear.

But then a problem came. One amongst them had gone missing.

"Ocker!" someone hollered. "Ocker, time to go!"

Two more voices took up the call.

"Oc-kkkker! Where are you?"

Tasia stared at the man on the floor, still out cold.

Ocker. It was a Western sort of name, and she wondered which region he'd been from. Maybe he was Ocker of West End, or Ocker of Kreave. Perhaps he was Ocker of Harthington, and had known the Lady Mylla or Lord Galen.

"Ocky?"

That voice sounded particularly young. And particularly close. Tasia stopped breathing again.

A shadow passed before the hut's missing door. Then the worn toe of a boot appeared. Then a leg. A hand grasped the door frame, pulled the head and shoulders of a skinny teenager with wild blond hair into view.

"Ocky, are you in — " His eyes landed on Ocker, then on Joslyn and Tasia. He froze. "Oh, *shite,"* he cursed softly.

Joslyn sprung at the youth, dagger flashing. But the boy stumbled backwards out of the doorway and bolted before she could reach him.

"Colonel!" he yelled as he sprinted from the hut. "Colonel Pyter! They killed Ocker!"

"Tasia, let's go!" Joslyn barked, no longer trying to stay quiet.

Tasia followed the guard out the open doorway of the hut. They ran at full speed, angling for the woods at the far end of the village. Shouts and barks and hoofbeats rang out behind them, their pursuers gaining ground far faster than the women could add it.

We aren't going to make it, Tasia realized.

"In here!" Joslyn said, snatching Tasia by the wrist and pulling her into a nearby hut. Joslyn positioned Tasia behind her once again. She drew her sword and pressed her shoulder against the wall. "We make our stand here," she said, not turning around. "Prepare yourself."

42

It took less than a minute for the soldiers to find them. Joslyn had chosen a hut with a narrow open doorway. Like the rest of the huts in the village, its thatch roof had burned away, but at least this hut had four complete walls. Likely built to trap as much heat as possible as protection against the harsh Eastern winters, it was also one of a handful of huts in the village that had no windows. Four walls, no windows, a narrow doorway — Tasia understood why Joslyn had picked this one. The doorway was the only way in or out, and it would create a bottleneck the soldiers would have to force their way through to get to them.

"Here they come," Joslyn said. She twirled her sword the way a traveling performer might twirl a baton, spinning it deftly at her side in a full circle, the hilt dancing across her palm before she clenched her fist again. The movement was fluid, graceful, and done without any apparent thought, like a reflex or a twitch. With the other hand, Joslyn pulled a long dagger from her boot, one Tasia hadn't seen before.

But there was much of Joslyn Tasia hadn't seen yet. The Princess closed her eyes, whispered a silent prayer to Mother Moon, Coyote, and any other gods who might be listening that they would both live long enough to see all of each other.

The sound of barking reached them first, then snarling and men yelling. Tasia backed into the corner of the hut. Without her daggers, there was nothing she could do to help Joslyn except to stay out of the way. Joslyn stepped through the doorframe, thrusting her sword at the same time. Tasia heard a high-pitched yelp of pain from one of the dogs, followed by more yelling.

Seconds later, steel rang on steel. Joslyn was pressed back into the hut by a bear-sized man wielding a double-headed battle axe. Fluid as running water, fluid as blood, the nomad melted out of the way every time he swung. She stepped deeper into the shadows of the hut, as if retreating, and he took her bait, lunging after her. It provided the opening that she needed. She side-stepped him and her sword sliced through the air so quickly that Tasia couldn't track its movement with her eyes. Blood spurted from the huge man's throat, then from his mouth. He dropped the axe, whose twin blades were each the size of a serving tray, and clutched at his neck, but it did nothing to slow the bleeding, and he fell like a giant tree, causing the hut's wooden floor to shake from his weight.

He hadn't even finished falling when two more men attacked. Joslyn put them down with the same speed and efficiency as she'd dropped the big one. Those two were followed by a fourth, the fourth by a fifth, and a bittersweet hope formed in Tasia's chest.

Bitter because these men were her subjects, her duty was to keep them safe, yet she had to let Joslyn kill them to save herself. *Sweet* because she allowed herself to entertain the idea that she and the guard might just survive this ordeal without arrest or death.

But then she heard a whizzing noise, followed by a hollow thunk. Joslyn had narrowly missed an arrow, which now protruded from the wooden doorframe like an ill omen. Tasia stared at it, worried at what it might mean, when she heard another whistle, followed by the sound of metal hitting stone. She rushed to the fallen arrow, scooping it up from the hut's floor where it fell. She didn't know what she would do with it, but it was the closest thing she had to a weapon, and so she clung to it, waiting for a signal from Joslyn to do something with it.

But there was no signal forthcoming, and the guard might not have even noticed that Tasia had picked the arrow up — her blades were too busy. Soldiers and dogs cried in pain, falling dead or lame in a semicircle around the hut's narrow doorway. Tasia counted the bodies and came up with seven.

One of the bodies she thought was dead began to move. His face was splattered with blood, making it difficult to tell his age, but as he crawled towards Tasia, she saw he was another young one, not much older than she was. Perhaps even younger.

"Help me," he whispered. One of his arms had been nearly severed by Joslyn's sword, and he dragged it along the ground as dead weight.

Tasia dropped to her knees before the boy, clutching the arrow before her like it was a scepter she might grant a benediction with.

"I'm sorry this happened to you," she whispered back to him. She reached a hand towards his face, possibly to smooth back his blood-stained sandy brown hair.

His face changed, contorting into an animalistic snarl. With his good hand, he grabbed Tasia by the wrist and pulled her toward him with surprising strength.

"Traitor!" he shouted. Spittle mixed with flecks of blood and spattered across her face. "Father killer! King killer!"

"I didn't!" Tasia said.

"Traitor!" he cried again, and Tasia did the only thing she knew to do: She took the arrow still in her free hand and jabbed at the boy's jugular as hard as she could. It pierced the skin, but only barely.

"Gods curse you!" said the boy-soldier, still clinging to Tasia's wrist. "Curse you!" he repeated as Tasia stabbed him again. The fingers around her wrist loosened, and she pulled her hand away. Wrapping both fists around the arrow, she drove it down into his throat again, and again, and again, until dark blood pooled beneath his face and he went still.

"Tasia?" Joslyn said, the commotion between Tasia and the young soldier drawing her attention away from the doorframe for a moment.

But a moment was all it took.

The arrow struck her in her sword arm, piercing the black leather guard's uniform. Joslyn staggered back a few feet, her face slack with surprise.

"Joslyn, *no!*" Tasia cried.

A screaming soldier leaped over the pile of bodies blocking the door, his short sword thrusting towards Joslyn. She dodged the blow, but not with the same fluid grace she'd shown seconds earlier. Joslyn tried to lift her sword arm, but the arrow was deep, and the movement seemed to cause her pain. So she dueled the new soldier with her dagger only, her sword hanging limply by her side.

Another soldier joined the first, and now she dodged and parried with her dagger against both of them.

Tasia saw the realization dawn in the second soldier's eyes when he understood Joslyn's weak point. Knowing she could hardly lift her sword arm, he hacked at that side artlessly while the first soldier kept her dagger impossibly busy. Pale and grimacing, she managed to lift her sword enough to fend off some of his attacks, but then another arrow whizzed past her, narrowly missing her head. She'd dodged the arrow, but that was her fatal mistake: The second soldier thrust his sword into her side, right at the place where her leather armor, put on earlier in haste, was still crooked. The guard let out a long, low cry, then fell to her knees. Blood pulsed from the wound in her side, pouring down like an overturned bottle of port.

But even still she fought, managing from her knees to slash at the legs of the two attackers before her. She even nicked one of them, but at last she didn't get her sword up in time: The second soldier, the one who had been hacking mercilessly at her sword arm side, landed the kill stroke. His blade bit into Joslyn's neck, just above the leather collar of her uniform. The sound the blade made as it bit into her unprotected flesh was a sick, squelching noise, a sound that would haunt Tasia's nightmares for years to come. It bit so deeply that he had trouble dislodging his blade, managing to get it free only by planting a foot on the guard's chest and pushing her away while simultaneously pulling on his sword.

Joslyn crumpled backward at an awkward angle, sword and dagger falling from her hands, hitting her head on the floor with a *thunk*. Her ashen face was only inches from where Tasia still crouched with the arrow in her hands. The guard tried to speak, but no sound came out, only blood. Then she was still.

Screams. Ear-splitting screams filled the hut, ricocheting off the stone walls, escaping up into the open sky.

The first soldier covered his ears with his hands against the sound; the second soldier stepped forward and backhanded Tasia hard across the face.

"Shut. *Up,*" he said coldly, and only then did Tasia realize the screams had been her own. He snatched the arrow out of her hands. "Give it to me, you murderous cunt."

"Nice work, Wendt," the first soldier said.

Wendt gave the other man a grim look, then wiped the blood off his blade against Joslyn's black leather. Then he spat in the guard's lifeless face.

"Nomad bitch. She killed Hammy," Wendt said.

"And Tom," said the other.

"I'm glad we killed her before she could be hanged,"

said Wendt. "Hanging would've been too good for her. Go get the Colonel. Tell him it's done."

The first one nodded, this time stepping gingerly over his fallen comrades. "Colonel Pyter?" Tasia heard him call. "Over here, sir." His voice faded, and the two soldiers who were left looked the Princess over.

"So you're the one, eh?" Wendt said when they were alone. "The traitorous princess we lost almost our whole squad and our lieutenant over?" He glanced over his shoulder at the dead bodies that littered the front of the hut and the doorway. "The lieutenant, he was a spoiled little rich lord's son, we won't miss him. But Hammy... and Tom... They were good men. Now they're dead men, thanks to you, ya dirty whore."

But Tasia hardly heard his words. All her attention was focused on Joslyn, who lay motionless and pale on the floor. She was still breathing, but only barely; each breath came shorter and shallower than the last, and her eyes had gone glassy.

"She's still the Princess, mate," the other soldier said to Wendt. "I don't think you should talk to her like that."

"What's she gonna do?" asked Wendt. "Order me arrested?" He snorted.

"She might not, but I still will," said a low, commanding voice from beyond Tasia's line of sight.

Both men started and went rigid.

"Colonel Pyter, sir," said Wendt. "I'm sorry, I — my lieutenant's in that pile," he said, sounding appropriately mournful. "Dead, his throat slashed by the nomad bit —

woman. And it's all on account of the girl who had her father murdered."

A tall figure stepped into the doorway, blocking the sun. Tasia looked up, recognizing the long-faced, long-haired colonel from the Central Steppes whose wife said he smelled like a horse. She'd met him a few nights before, at the dinner. The last hours she'd served in her royal role, before everything had unraveled.

"As your colleague said, boy, that *girl* is still a Princess of the House of Dorsa," said Colonel Pyter. "And until her trial confirms her guilt, you will treat her as such." As if bent on proving his point, he gave a fluid, graceful bow in Tasia's direction. "Your Highness? It is time to go."

He said it as if he was escorting Tasia down a palace hallway to a ballroom instead of re-arresting her after a long night of being a fugitive.

But the respect, the bow, the tone of voice — it all triggered an automatic response in Tasia. She pushed herself to her feet. Her legs trembled and she was vaguely aware that her sleeping gown was in tatters. But she couldn't bring herself to care about that, anymore than she could bring herself to care about the fact that her hair was a tangled mess and her face and neck were spattered with the blood of the soldier she'd killed.

All she cared about was Joslyn. She'd stopped breathing. And the last breath she'd taken had been long, shallow, gravelly. Tasia finally knew why they called it a "death rattle."

The three men — the first soldier, Wendt, and Colonel

Pyter — watched her cautiously. Despite Colonel Pyter's harsh reprimand to the common soldiers, Tasia knew he wouldn't hesitate to use force to remove her from this hut if he had to. And all the self-defense lessons in the world wouldn't allow her to overcome three men while weaponless and trapped.

Tasia took a deep breath to settle herself and set her face into the best regal bearing she could manage. *"Castles and Knights,"* said her father's voice in her head. *"Don't be fooled into thinking it's mere frivolity. All of life is a strategy game, each person you meet is a piece on the board, and if you don't learn to think three steps ahead of your opponent, you'll find your own piece swept to the side in short order."*

It was time to start thinking ahead again. She forced herself to look at Colonel Pyter, forced herself to forget that the guard laid on the floor, dead.

"Very well," she said after a moment.

Pointedly, his eyes darted to her hands, then back to her face. Tasia followed his downward gaze and realized she was still clutching the arrow. She dropped it, then wiped her hands on the sleeping gown.

She took a step in his direction, then stopped. "What of my bodyguard?"

"What of her?"

"If you are taking me back to Port Lorsin, I wish her to go with me," Tasia said. The composure with which she spoke surprised even herself. Somehow she had managed to put all her emotions into a tightly sealed box inside her chest. She would let them out again later. When it was safe to do so. When she was alone. "I will arrange for a proper funeral for her."

"You are a Princess of the House of Dorsa," said the Colonel, "and until mere days ago the undisputed heir to the Emperor of our great land. I will treat you as such." His gaze traveled down to Joslyn, and his face changed. "But that nomad trash lying on the floor killed nine of my men, including a noble-born officer, before a brave soldier put her down like the animal she was. I will not waste the Empire's resources to transport her back to the capital." Then he glanced around the room, meeting the eyes of his men. "The nomad lies here, alone and forgotten. Let the dogs and wolves and raccoons have her body."

Tasia hated the Colonel in that moment, but hate was an emotion, and though it banged on the box inside her chest, demanding to be let out, the cold, logical part of Tasia knew that she was in no position to argue with him. She nodded graciously and followed him out of the hut without so much as a backward glance towards the fallen guard.

"Go," Tasia imagined Joslyn telling her. *"As your father said, it is all a game of Castles and Knights, and it is time for your next move."*

43

The journey back to Port Lorsin took considerably less time than the journey east. There was no additional trek through the narrow, winding paths of the Zaris Mountains; there was no raid by mercenaries pretending to be bandits. There was only Tasia, alone in a carriage she should've shared with Joslyn.

But the Princess couldn't think of her guard. She couldn't glance at the shelf above the carriage seat where the travel set of Castles and Knights was stored. Every time she did, the image of Joslyn's lifeless eyes lodged itself in her mind.

Occasionally Norix would ride with her, smug in his success but careful to reveal nothing of his involvement in her father's death.

Tasia wanted to mourn. She wanted to shed tears for her dead father, for her dead guard who, for a week or so, had also been her lover. But the tears would not come. Nothing would come, neither the bitter tears of grief nor the burning fire of anger. She wanted to unpack the box of emotions she'd stored near her heart, but somehow she couldn't find the box anymore, leaving her empty, numb, cold. Burned out like the village she and Joslyn had sought refuge in. Tasia supposed there was a certain safety within her numbness; as long as she was passionless and silent, she ran no risk of saying something to Norix that he could later weaponize and turn against her.

The trial would come soon. It hovered at the edge of her awareness like a distant thunderhead on the savannah's horizon, but she felt no more emotion towards it than she did about anything else.

The trial would be a farce, of course. But at least she would learn, based on which nobles said what, who the other conspirators were.

Not that it would do her much good. The trial was a bit of palace pageantry, a minstrel show without the music. It would confirm her guilt and, because she was royal, the judgment would end with an axe instead of a noose.

The axe was meant to be one last show of respect, a swift end in front of the Emperor's council in an obscure, out-of-the-way courtyard inside the palace grounds, rather than the public spectacle of hanging in Port Lorsin's gallows.

But it had been so long since a member of the House of Dorsa had been beheaded that Tasia doubted there existed an executioner in the Empire who could provide her with a swift, one-stroke death.

Joslyn could have.

But Joslyn was dead.

As her locked carriage bumped along the road back to Port Lorsin, her hand kept returning to her neck, her throat. A blade would separate her neck from the rest of her soon enough. But for now, she preferred to remember the three perfect times when a woman — a woman Tasia was sure she cherished above all others — had kissed the spot the executioner's blade would soon bite.

#

Two weeks passed like two days. Before she knew it, a still-numb Tasia found herself being escorted by palace guards back to her apartments. The sight of the black leather armor worn by the guards broke through her shell for a moment, causing her breath to hitch as she remembered Joslyn pulling on her armor too hastily, buttoning it crookedly. A blade had slipped in where the buttons hadn't been quite right.

Tasia pushed the memory away as quickly as it came, retreating further into the hollowness inside her chest.

Nevertheless, something bothered Tasia about the guards, irritating her like an itch in a hard-to-reach place. They were almost to her apartments when she realized what it was.

"Where is Commander Cole?" she asked. "Why is he not here to escort me?"

One of the guards walking with her merely scowled sourly, looking at her as if she already knew the answer and shouldn't have asked it.

The other hesitated a moment, then said, "Dead, Princess. Poisoned same night as your father."

"Oh," Tasia said simply, and the numbness deepened. After a moment, she asked, "He was poisoned, then? My father?"

The scowling guard's scowl deepened.

The hesitating guard hesitated again, then answered, "Yes."

"Oh."

The scowling guard unlocked the door to her anteroom *(Joslyn's cot is still in this room, behind the screens,* Tasia thought) and stood aside for her to enter.

"Three guards will stay posted outside your doors at all times," he said gruffly. "Two more guards will be stationed in the courtyard beneath your window. No one will be permitted in." He paused for effect. "Or out. Except for your trial, which begins tomorrow after the noontide meal."

"What of kitchen staff?" Tasia asked. "How do I get my meals?"

"Food will first be tested by a member of the palace guard," he said. "Then transported to you."

"Alright," Tasia said.

She waited until the door closed and locked behind her, then made her way to the table by the window, the table where she and Mylla used to share their meals. Mylla who had betrayed her. The thought was as numb and wooden as all the others.

Tasia sat, folding her hands on the table for a moment, then stood again and walked to the window. She looked down. Two more palace guards stood below, just as her scowling escort had promised. They talked quietly between themselves, waiting for something to happen. Waiting to make sure Tasia didn't attempt an escape out her window before her trial or her inevitable beheading.

#

The noontide meal the next day came early for Tasia. She ate it mechanically, in silence, with the same numbness she had moved through everything else since the moment of Joslyn's defeat.

The knock on her bedchamber door came not long after she finished. Before she could say "Enter," Wise Man Evrart let himself in, accompanied by a guard.

"Princess Natasia," he said formally, "I've come to escort you to the council room for your trial."

"Very well," said Tasia, rising from the table by the window. She'd done nothing to prepare for the trial — she hadn't dressed for it, hadn't thought of what she might say when it was her turn to question those who spoke against her, hadn't considered how she might turn the council's suspicions in the direction of Norix. She hadn't even brushed her hair this morning; it remained with the same combs it had in it when she had gone to bed the night before. At least she was dressed somewhat appropriately. She'd put on a simple green dress that morning, one that was formal enough for the trial but still humble. It occurred to her in passing that she had accidentally made one good decision.

Evrart spoke to the guard in a low voice, and the man nodded and left the room, closing the door between the bedchamber and anteroom behind him.

"Princess?" said Evrart.

Her eyes found his, but she didn't answer.

"Don't you think you might wish to brush your hair out and re-pin it before the trial?"

"Why?" she said. "Will well-pinned hair make it less likely that the executioner's blade will separate my head from the rest of me?"

"Yes, actually," Evrart said. The smile he gave her was undeniably kind, with no trace of the mocking she'd expected to find in it. He reached into his grey robes. "You know better than most do that appearances matter. And speaking of which, I also brought you this." He produced a black lace armband, extending it towards her. "Would you like me to help you with it?"

She looked at the black band of mourning, then at the genuine compassion in the Wise Man's eyes. "Yes, please."

He took a step closer, took her arm with cool, soft fingers. "Have you given any thought to your defense?"

"No." She watched him tie the armband in place. "I was considering confessing. Just to get it done with sooner."

His dark brows furrowed. "Now why would you confess to a crime you had nothing to do with?"

He'd finished tying off the band, but still held her arm in a firm grip. He locked eyes with her and stared at her intently.

"What game are you playing at, Wise Man?" Tasia asked. "If you know I am not guilty of any crime, then I assume you know your own master is the spider at the center of this web. Would you betray him to save me?"

Evrart cocked an eyebrow. "And what makes you think dusty old Norix is still clever enough to orchestrate a web such as this?"

His question hung in the air between them — an admission that he knew something about the conspiracy to kill her father and his bodyguard. There was something crafty in Evrart's expression as he gazed at her. Tasia had never thought of Evrart as being crafty, but there it was — a gleam in his eye that was both a hint and an admonishment. But then the look disappeared so quickly that she wondered if she had simply imagined it.

"Princess, we really must go," he said. "We can't have you being late to your trial."

#

The council room was sweltering. Nobles, ambassadors, their Wise Men, their heirs took up every available seat, and where the seats ran out, they stood in uncomfortable rows at the back of the room. Palace guards lined the walls, most armed with standard imperial short swords, but some with long spears. Tasia had never seen so many people in the room before, and the fact that it was a warm spring day certainly didn't help the heat.

There was a sizable gap between the front row of chairs and the dais where her father and his close advisors normally sat, and in the gap was a single, high-backed upholstered chair. Tasia recognized it from her father's office, and its relocation to the council room broke through her shell of numbness long enough to send a stab of pain into her heart.

It was to that chair that Evrart and the two palace guards guided her.

The room's buzz of low conversation fell quiet when Tasia walked into it. Under normal circumstances, commoners and nobles alike rose when a member of House Dorsa entered the room, but no one rose for the Princess now. She would have found it unnerving, if not for the fact that her heart remained an empty shell inside her chest.

She sat down and stared straight ahead, vaguely aware that Evrart and the guards had melted away to their own places. Despite the high back of her chair, she could feel the eyes of practically every noble in the Four Realms drilling into her from behind.

Norix sat in her father's place at the dais, of course. He was flanked by Adela on one side, whose eyes were wide and frightened, and a young nobleman on the other.

Tasia studied the nobleman for a moment, trying to remember his name. He was a distant cousin, a minor lordling of House Farrimont — a second or third cousin. Theodorus. That was it. Theo for short. She'd had trouble recognizing him at first because she hadn't seen him since he was a little boy. Now he was an adolescent, probably fourteen or fifteen, a couple of years older than Adela. A spray of acne covered his forehead and chin, but he was well-dressed, well-groomed, with his black hair held back in a neat pony tail, and he tried to show that he was well-composed. But his hands gave him away on that last part. He had them clasped on the table before him, but his thumbs couldn't stay still, fidgeting back and forth.

Tasia stared at him while he looked at anything but her. What in the name of all the gods was Theo of House Farrimont doing here? And why would he sit beside Norix?

Mother Moon, Tasia thought, realization dawning on her. Her box of emotions cracked open for the first time since Joslyn's death. *They're going to marry him to Adela!*

The last pieces of the puzzle snapped into place. Norix, the House Farrimont, and the House Harthing had played the perfect game of Castles and Knights.

House Farrimont had long since stopped supporting the war in the East and had demanded that the Emperor put an end to it. But Emperor Andreth did not listen, and the war continued to drain the Empire's resources. So Norix, who doubtless believed he was acting in the Empire's best interest, and Tasia's grandfather, Lord Hermant of House Farrimont, had conspired together to wrest control from the Emperor.

Perhaps they hadn't planned on killing him at first; they thought they could just pressure him into bowing to their wishes. Rather than attack him directly, they attacked his eldest child, planning to use Tasia's death as a lever to move the Emperor. And to do that, they would need someone close to the Princess, someone who could inform them of her movements. Enter Mylla, whose ambitious father could be recruited for the price of a better marriage prospect for his daughter. Umfrey was too closely related to Tasia and Adela to marry them, so he became Mylla's grand prize in exchange for her valuable cooperation.

But they hadn't counted on Tasia surviving the attack. Or on her being named her father's heir. Then someone — probably Norix — realized they could twist her ascendency to their advantage. Who better to blame than a greedy and impatient heir for the Emperor's death? Tasia had made it easy for them to frame her for the murder; she'd acquired a reputation for being impulsive, reckless, and spoiled long ago. She was the perfect scapegoat.

And speaking of perfect, there was still Adela. Young, carefree Adela, who was sweet and innocent and pliable. By keeping Adela around but marrying her to a member of House Farrimont, everyone would get what they wanted. Norix would get to try his hand at ruling by playing the part of Regent until Adela came of age. Lord Hermant would see a great nephew ascend to the role of Emperor. And although Theo would officially be adopted into House Dorsa, the true balance of power would shift into House Farrimont's hands. While Lord Hermant still lived, he would effectively be Emperor of the Four Realms.

Yes. It had all been very neatly done.

The shell of numbness surrounding Tasia splintered and shattered, replaced a fierce surge of anger at her accusers and protectiveness towards her little sister.

No. They will not do this to Adela, she thought, gripping the arms of the chair with such force that it was a wonder they did not break off in her hands. *They will not take her entire family away and make her prisoner to their machinations. I am Natasia, daughter of Emperor Andreth the Just, rightful heir to his crown, and I will not stand for this.*

"Princess Natasia," Norix began, cunning smile drawing back his thin old man's lips and twitching his white beard, "you stand accused of conspiring to kill your father, the Emperor Andreth of House Dorsa, and the head of his palace guard, Commander Cole of Easthook, distinguished veteran of the Imperial Army. Your accomplices in this matter have already confessed to their crimes and have been hanged. You also — "

A cold ball of anger and fear formed in Tasia's stomach. "Whom did you hang, Norix?"

Norix frowned, pursing his lips. "You will demonstrate courtesy before this council and refer to me as 'Wise Man' or 'Regent.'"

"Very well, *Regent* Norix," Tasia said. "Whom did you hang, *Regent?*"

Most members of the council wouldn't notice it, Tasia knew, but she saw in his twitching mustache his profound discomfort.

"Two cooks and your father's errand boy were hanged yesterday."

Tasia's heart sank. She wondered which members of the kitchen staff had lost friends or family members yesterday, and which of the errand boys it had been.

Common people don't matter, she remembered Joslyn

saying.

Norix's wolf's grin returned to his face as he seemed to think of a way to turn Tasia's defiant interruption to his advantage. "Why do you ask, Princess? Are there names of other conspirators you wish to give to the council?"

"Yes," she said. She paused for effect, listening to the low murmur of surprise ripple through the council room behind her.

Norix's discomfort became more apparent. He opened his mouth to speak, but she beat him to it.

"I name *you* as a conspirator," Tasia said, her voice loud and clear. "Along with my grandfather, Lord Hermant of House Farrimont, my former handmaid, Lady Mylla of House Harthing, and Lady Mylla's father, Lord Galen of House Harthing. I accuse you each of conspiring to murder the Emperor Andreth of House Dorsa, Commander Cole of Easthook, as well as treason to overthrow the crown and seize it for yourselves."

The low murmur behind Tasia became a louder ocean wave of clashing voices.

Beside Norix, Adela's eyes welled with tears. She was caught between her sister and her father's closest advisor. Adela had been too young to remember her mother's death, and was still very small when Nik died. The Emperor's death and the accusation that her sister had played a part in it was the first time her world had been ripped apart. She probably didn't know what to think, whom to believe. But Tasia would mend that later.

"It is typical," Norix said loudly, but the wave of

conversation was too loud for him to be heard, so he waited for it to die down before he continued. "It is typical for an accused party to attempt to divert attention from themselves by accusing another." He nodded to himself, relaxing into his familiar tutor's role. "History has many examples of this. Just think of Empress Farana the Mad, who murdered her husband, the Emperor Baden, in his sleep. She falsely accused her lover, a great lord of the East, of convincing her to do the evil deed. Therefore," he said, and his gaze traveled over Tasia's head, addressing the council members as his receptive pupils, "the council should not be surprised to hear the Princess Natasia attempt to lay the blame at the feet of the innocent."

Tasia gritted her teeth at the word *innocent*, wanting to shout at her former teacher for his blatant hypocrisy.

But no.

Her first outburst had the effect she'd wanted it to; she had suggested to the members of the council that there was an alternative narrative to the one they had been fed, and this new narrative would plant a small seed of doubt in their minds. She could nourish that seed as the trial progressed, watering it and growing it. But a second outburst would have no benefit. It would merely confirm Norix's portrayal of her — that of the greedy, murderous, mentally unstable princess he wanted them to see.

So Tasia bit her tongue — literally — while he finished reading the charges against her. Treason. Attempted coup. Lying to council members. Abuse of highborn status. The irony was bitter fruit to swallow; Norix was guilty of everything he accused her of and more. Tasia bit her tongue with such force that it began to bleed.

She would find a way out of this. And she would avenge her father's death.

44

"Princess Natasia spoke to me often about how much she hated her father," Mylla told the council from the dais, her eyes red-rimmed from tears. "She said she wished he were dead, that she couldn't wait until he died so that she could become the Empress."

Tasia gritted her teeth. She stared directly at her former handmaid, but Mylla wouldn't meet her eye.

"And on how many occasions did she say this?" Norix asked gently, patting the girl's arm with a show of grandfatherly support.

"Oh, many times, Wise Man, sir," Mylla said. "It was a topic she came back to often."

Mylla was the third witness who had been called to speak against Tasia. The first two were palace kitchen staff, who nervously stated they'd overheard Tasia inquiring with the recently hanged about poisoning the Emperor's food. Tasia had seen fear in both women's faces; she had no doubt that either they or their families had been threatened with harm should they refuse to cooperate with Norix's "investigation."

Commoners were relatively easy to manipulate in a situation such as this. A threat, a bribe — both were easier to leverage against common people who did not have the resources or status to fight those in power. Commoners knew that they would always find themselves stuck in the middle of the nobility's fights, and they chose the side that seemed most likely to let them live. But the council knew this, too, and so did Norix, which was why he had saved his high-status witnesses for the end of the trial. The testimony of the highborn, even by young women such Lady Mylla, was considered to be automatically more trustworthy than that of a commoner's.

"It isn't unusual for a teenage girl to hate her father," said Norix. A few scattered sounds of amusement came from the councilmen behind Tasia. "I'm sure you've felt that way yourself from time to time, haven't you, dear?"

Mylla looked down at her lap, hesitating. "I suppose, Wise Man."

"But I doubted you ever considered plotting to *kill* your father," Norix continued. "Correct?"

Mylla gave him a weak nod without looking up.

Tasia wondered if it was actually difficult for Mylla to betray her, or if this was all a stage play to her. The Princess and her handmaid had snuck into Port Lorsin several times per year to watch some of the bawdier plays performed by traveling acting troops, and Mylla had admired the lifestyle of the troopers — traveling town to town, never tied to land, to family obligations, to titles.

Maybe Mylla had finally found a way to troop while keeping the privilege of lands and titles.

"I know this question may be difficult to answer, Lady Mylla," said Norix, "but did Princess Natasia ever discuss killing her father?"

Mylla started to shake her head, then stopped herself.

"Go on," Norix prompted.

"I don't know that I should say, Wise Man," Mylla said softly. "It wasn't recent... and I never thought that the Princess meant it seriously."

"I understand," said Norix. "But tell the council anyway. Just in case it may prove relevant."

"Well... there was a time, many years ago..." Mylla trailed off, looked up at Norix with wide doe eyes.

"We're listening," he said.

Tasia rolled her eyes at his false encouragement. The council wouldn't be able to see it, but Norix and Mylla would. She wanted them to know what she thought of their elaborate drama. Mylla deserved accolades for her performance, which had the council practically holding their breath.

But neither of them would look at her, of course.

"The Princess's brother Nikhost had just died in a tragic hunting accident," Mylla said.

The fight went out of Tasia for a moment at the mention of Nik. Mylla might as well have punched her in the stomach and knocked the wind out of her.

"And the Princess put on a show of grief to outsiders," the former handmaid continued, "but privately... just to me... she said that with Nik dead, she might be able to become the Empress one day. She knew it was unusual for a Princess to become an heir, but she said that she would be able to convince her father that she was worthy."

"Remind the council how old Princess Natasia was at that time?" said Norix.

"Fifteen, sir."

"And you were…?"

"Not quite fourteen," Mylla answered.

"Lady Mylla…" Norix said carefully, "I know this may be a sensitive topic for you, especially since you are recently married, but… wasn't it also at the time of Prince Nikhost's untimely death that Princess Natasia began to request certain… *favors* of you?"

A murmur rippled through the council behind Tasia. She gripped the arms of the chair even more tightly.

Look at me, she thought fiercely at Mylla. *Look at me while you tell them that I was the one who initiated what we shared. Look at me while you tell them that it meant nothing to you, that it was all my manipulation.*

And as if Mylla had heard her somehow, she ventured the briefest of glances in Tasia's direction. But she couldn't keep her gaze there for longer than a moment.

"Yes," Mylla said quietly, and Tasia wondered if she was quiet due to the burden of telling the lie, or quiet because it was all part of her ruse. "That was when it started."

"Started," Norix repeated. "But those… *favors* didn't end then, did they?"

"No," said Mylla, still subdued with her gaze downcast. "I… shared Princess Natasia's bedchamber for many years after the Prince's death. I knew it was unnatural, but she threatened to ruin my reputation should I not comply. And if that were to happen, I worried that I would no longer be marriageable."

Ah, yes. That would arouse the sympathy of the council. Every lord in the room assumed that the greatest fear of all highborn girls was failing to marry well — and in many cases, they were not wrong. In fact, Tasia's stalwart refusal to marry had been the cause of suspicion and confusion for more than one lord.

The Princess who would not marry. The Princess who bedded her handmaid. The Princess who killed her father. Tasia comprehended well the portrait Norix was painstakingly painting for the councilmen.

Norix continued questioning Mylla for a few more minutes, but Tasia stopped listening. He had made his point, and the council would eat it up. The Princess's handmaid, a highborn woman close to the Princess's own age and who knew her better than probably anyone else, had corroborated the Wise Man's accusations. And then he went a step further to bring out the scandalous details of their relationship.

As hard as it was to listen to Mylla testify against her, Tasia could almost forgive her. Almost. The Princess knew that whatever plot was afoot to murder her father and pin it on her had almost certainly not been Mylla's idea. Even Mylla's cooperation had probably not been her idea. She was a puppet, her strings pulled by a puppet master who was probably her father, Lord Galen. And if not Lord Galen, then Norix. Or more likely, both.

But the next highborn called to speak to the council was

much harder for Tasia to hear, because the damning part of his testimony was completely her own fault.

"The next person to address the council will be Mace of House Gifford," Norix announced once Mylla was escorted from the room. "Most of you have probably not heard this news yet, as it has been overshadowed by our great Emperor's tragic death," Norix said as Mace made his way to the dais, "but in the days before he died, the Emperor accepted a marriage proposal from Mace on behalf of the Princess Natasia. Strictly speaking, they are engaged." More whispered conversation from the council as Mace took his seat. It all made for good theater.

Mace folded his hands on the table. Unlike Mylla, he didn't seem afraid to meet Tasia's eye. The look he gave her was both sympathetic and apologetic.

"You understand, Mace," Norix said to the young nobleman, "that it is incumbent upon your honor to answer my questions as honestly and completely as you can? I recognize that you may be asked to tell uncomfortable truths about your betrothed, but unfortunately we have no choice but to accuse her of regicide, patricide, and treason — and there are no more serious crimes than that."

"I understand what you require perfectly, Regent," said Mace, and Tasia thought she heard a certain bitterness in his tone.

"Very well, then we shall begin." Norix paused, glanced down at the sheet of parchment before him. "I understand that the Princess Natasia accepted your proposition of marriage after refusing many other suitors.

Do you have any idea why she accepted you and rejected so many who came before you?"

"My charm and dashing good looks, most likely," Mace said.

A rumble of chuckles moved through the council room, and Tasia felt her grip upon the arms of the chair relax slightly. Here, at last, was someone who seemed in no rush to implicate her in the death of her father.

"Mace," Norix said sternly, as if chastising a child. "Please remember that you just agreed to be forthright and honest. I ask you again: Why did the Princess accept you as a suitor while she rejected so many others?"

Mace let out a breath, obviously reluctant. "Before I met Princess Natasia, it was made clear to me by the Emperor's representatives that I would be adopted into the House of Dorsa but that I would not be molded to wear the crown. The Princess would be the Emperor's true heir."

"You say that the Emperor's representatives were the ones who told you this," Norix said. "Did the Princess also speak to you of this matter?"

"Yes."

"And what did she say?"

Mace hesitated. "Some of what she told me might have implications for the Empire's greater security," he said. "I'm not sure that I should reveal it."

Norix gave a firm shake of his head. "This is the council. What impacts the security of the Empire directly impacts them. State it plainly."

"In private conversation, the Princess revealed that an

attempt had been made on her life not long before we met,"
Mace said, stealing a quick glance in Tasia's direction.

The council broke into surprised mutters and low
exclamations behind the Princess. So most of them hadn't
heard about the assassination attempt. At least the palace
had managed to keep one secret. Tasia wondered where
Norix was going with his line of questioning. How would
he make an attempt on her life work to *his* advantage?

She kept her face carefully blank, hiding the smile that
wanted to emerge. In this elaborate game of Castles and
Knights, it seemed that her tutor had finally presented her
with an opening.

"She said her father worried that someone was trying to
destabilize the House of Dorsa and therefore the Empire,"
Mace continued, "and that he had decided he could only
trust his own blood. That was why she would be heir to the
throne."

"Did she express an eagerness to become the Empress
of the Four Realms?"

Mace glanced at Tasia, then shrugged. "She didn't
seem particularly interested or disinterested in it. She
stated it simply as fact."

Thank you, she thought at him silently. She had been
right before to feel that she could trust him.

"Careful, young lord," Norix said. "Remember that
you swore not to lie to the council. Are you certain that the
Princess did not express any eagerness to become
Empress?"

"I told you," Mace said. "She didn't seem especially

interested *or* disinterested."

"Tell us specifically what she said," Norix instructed.

"It was a conversation some months ago, Regent."

"Then tell us what she told you about your position as Emperor, given she was to be the true power in the realm," Norix said. "Certainly you must remember that. Young men with a chance to be Emperor do not forget such things."

Mace barely suppressed an eye roll. "Princess Natasia made clear to me that I should not pursue her hand in marriage if my ambition was to be the true ruler of the Four Realms."

"So she asserted that the crown would be hers," Norix said.

"I suppose you could put it that way."

"Yes, but what way did *she* put it?" Norix pressed. "Do not lie to a Wise Man, Mace."

Mace looked helplessly at Tasia. "She said I would be as powerless as a hound without teeth," he said. "And she said that she would be like the Empress Adela."

Norix barely managed to suppress a surprised snort. "Princess Natasia compared herself to the Empress Adela? That was rather… bold, don't you think?"

"She said it in jest, Regent," Mace said testily.

"Thank you, Mace," said the Wise Man, smiling like a fox who'd stolen a chicken. "You are dismissed."

"From Mace of House Gifford," Norix said once Tasia's fiancé left the room, "the council has learned that there was an attempt on the Princess Natasia's life. The Emperor sought to keep this assassination attempt a secret until he could determine the party responsible. It was also this assassination attempt that, out of his paranoia, led him to declare Princess Natasia as his future heir." Norix paused for effect, glancing around the council room. *Where was he going with this?* Tasia wondered. "The palace Wise Men now know who arranged for the attack on the Princess's life. It was the same person who arranged for the attack on the Princess's caravan as it traveled east — the attack that took General Remington's life and nearly took my own." He waited again, letting the tension mount. "The person responsible was the Princess herself."

Conversation in the room behind Tasia escalated, all but drowning out Norix's next words. He had to start, stop, and repeat himself twice before the council members settled down enough to listen.

"The next few individuals who will testify to the council all have certain knowledge of the Princess's arrangements to fake attempts on her own life not once but twice."

In rapid succession, the next two hours were filled with supposed "witnesses" who claimed to have overheard or to have been party to the Princess's fake assassination attempts. Four men and one woman were all brought before the council to speak against Tasia, ending with a rather battered-looking mercenary captain who said he had been paid directly by Tasia to stage the raid on her caravan.

The sun was falling as Norix ended the special council meeting with his concluding argument.

"I have known Princess Natasia since she was a girl," Norix said. "Which I say to remind you that it brings me no joy to reveal these rather unseemly facts about her character and her determination to steal her father's crown. But..." He turned his palms up on the table in a helpless posture. "Knowing her so intimately for so long means that I am also well-acquainted with what the Princess is capable of. From tutoring her, I know that she is clever. But I also know that she is capable of infantile tirades, of jealousy, of manipulative behavior, and of vindictive action. I was shocked when I heard of the Emperor's passing while in the East. But when I stepped back from my emotions and considered the situation dispassionately, with wisdom... it was clear to see that one person in this Empire had more reason to wish the Emperor Andreth dead than any other. One person who stood to benefit the most from his death. One person who stood to become the most powerful individual in all Four Realms upon the occasion of his death. And that same person has steadily refused suitors since she came of age to marry over a year and a half ago, because she did not want to share the power she so greedily coveted. That one person is Princess Natasia."

He waited for a long, dramatic moment for his argument to sink in. Tasia wished she could see the faces of the men behind her. She wished she knew which ones were convinced by his argument, which ones weren't, which ones were still wavering. Then she would have a better sense of how to present her defense the next day.

"Gentlemen, we are a just people, and we follow the

laws formalized by the Wise Men of generations past," he said. "Therefore, we shall still allow the Princess to present a counterargument in her own defense tomorrow at this same time. But do keep in mind that the accused will say anything to escape the consequences of their actions. And this particular accused is, sadly, more conniving than most. Good eve to you all, gentlemen."

With that, Norix stood from his spot at the dais, and the rest of the room hastily stood out of respect. He was the Regent, after all, which made him the current ruling power in the Empire.

It took Tasia a moment longer than most to stand. But she stood anyway, waiting in silence until two members of the palace guard escorted her to her rooms.

45

Tasia spent at least an hour after the evening meal pacing in her bedchamber before she settled down to work. Norix had played his game of Castles and Knights well — she'd half-believed she was guilty of treason herself by the end of his closing statement. But it didn't mean he hadn't left her any openings.

At last she found a stack of parchment, a fresh pen, and a full ink bottle. She sat down at the table and began writing letters. Hopefully each party could be reached in time and make it to the trial.

She stopped writing once to relieve a cramp in her hand, and a second time to light the lamps once the room became too dark to see what she was writing.

Then, finally finished, she folded each sheaf of parchment, dripped wax on it, and stamped onto each hot blob the seal of the House of Dorsa. Tasia handed the stack to one of the guards outside her antechamber.

"Would you see that these are delivered to their recipients?" she said. The guard didn't reply right away, but glanced questioningly at his companion for guidance.

The other guard was the one who replied. "I'm sorry, Your Highness, but we are not supposed to allow anything or anyone in or out of your room that is not approved first by the Regent."

Tasia bristled, opening her mouth to educate the guard on the laws that governed royal trials.

But a voice from somewhere down the hall beat her to it. "I will ensure that they are delivered, Princess."

Tasia and the two guards both turned their heads in the direction of the voice.

Evrart.

The younger Wise Man strode up to the guard with the parchments and took them from him, taking them out of the guard's hands before he had a chance to object.

The guards exchanged a glance.

"In all royal trials," Evrart told the guards, "the accused royal is permitted to present a defense against the accusation. The royal person may request any person they see fit to attend the trial for questioning." He looked at Tasia. "I assume that these are letters summoning your witnesses?"

Tasia nodded. Evrart smiled back at her, and she sensed it was a sign of his approval.

The guards looked at one another, looked at Wise Man Evrart.

"Very well, sir," one of them said. "You know the law better than we do."

"So I do," the Wise Man agreed. He addressed Tasia. "I shall see you tomorrow after the noontide meal to escort you to the council room again."

"Thank you, Evrart," Tasia said sincerely. She closed the door to the anteroom and headed back to her bedchamber, but paused at the folding screens that marked off Joslyn's space from the rest of the room.

Emotion flooded Tasia all at once. Before her shell of numbness had broken, forgetting the guard had been easy. Forgetting the dark, solemn eyes that were capable of communicating so much with a single glance had been easy. Forgetting the lines of her profile, the way her lithe muscles moved while wielding a sword, the way she breathed heavily when Tasia had touched her in the most secret of places...

Forgetting had been easy while Tasia's heart remained wooden. But now that the shell had shattered, agonizing pain seared her. It was a physical thing, the pain. Like a hand in a hot steel glove clenching hard inside her chest.

Tasia walked around the corner of the screen and came to her knees before the footlocker at the end of Joslyn's bed. She hesitated a moment, then opened it.

She'd always assumed the guard's possessions would be simple; now her assumptions were proven to be correct. Inside the box, neatly folded, was a spare guard's uniform, along with clean linen undergarments and a roll of cloth that Tasia guessed Joslyn used to bind her breasts. Beneath these was a poncho of apa-apa wool, similar to the one Joslyn had worn on their outing to the Speckled Dog. It was worn but clean.

Tasia picked up the poncho, pressed it to her face. She inhaled deeply, trying to smell past the wool and the soap to get to the fainter scent of Joslyn's skin beneath. It was there, if only just a hint. The smell of leather and desert spices, of hard sun and steel. The smell of safety. The smell of Joslyn.

A lump formed in Tasia's throat. She set the apa-apa poncho aside, planning to keep it for herself. Even if she only had a few more days to live, she would have a few days to live close to the poncho.

Beneath the poncho was a short sword inside a frayed leather scabbard. The sword's pommel bore the imperial crest of the House of Dorsa, but the emblem was worn almost completely away. Gingerly, Tasia lifted the sword from the bottom of the footlocker and pulled it from the scabbard.

All the weapons she'd ever seen Joslyn handle were in immaculate condition. They were spotlessly clean, well-oiled, sharp enough to shave one's legs with if one were so inclined. But this sword was different. It was tarnished, notched all over, as if someone had used it to chop wood, and dull. So dull that even to Tasia's unpracticed touch, she knew it would be worthless in a fight. What was it doing here?

For the briefest of moments, she made a plan to ask Joslyn about it the next time she saw her... then remembered that there would be no next time. Not for her and not for anyone. Joslyn of Terinto, perhaps the best sword master in the Imperial Army, was dead, killed by men who should have been her allies.

Tears threatened as Tasia placed the sword back at the bottom of the trunk. Something caught her eye. Pushing aside the spare undergarments, Tasia uncovered a folded sheet of parchment paper. She opened it. Across the top was Tasia's own handwriting — the alphabet of the common tongue. Beneath was Joslyn's attempt to copy each letter in uncertain charcoal scratches.

Tasia's eyes wandered further down the page, then she sucked in a short breath. At the bottom of the parchment, Joslyn had attempted to write the Princess's name. "Natasia," followed by "Tasia" was written several times, but she'd spelled it T-A-Z-S-H-Y-A.

When had she written it? Tasia wondered. And if Joslyn had been able to write Tasia an entire message, what would it have said?

The Princess would never know now. The thought made the smoldering ember of her grief blaze into anger. How dare Norix do this to her. How dare Norix, Lord Galen, Mylla, her grandfather — all of them. How dare they use her as a crowbar to pry open the door to power.

Tomorrow. She clenched her fists, feeling nails bite palms. Tomorrow she would reveal the truth to the council, and she would begin the long process of vengeance.

#

"State your name and position for the members of the council," Tasia instructed from her spot at the center of the dais.

"My name is Macklin of Port Lorsin, son of Gilbert of Port Lorsin," the man said, eyes darting nervously from face to highborn face. "Most people just call me Mack."

"And your position?" Tasia prompted.

"I'm a night watchman for the Port Lorsin City Guard — deputy shift chief, actually. Just got promoted."

"And before today, have you met anyone in this room?"

Mack nodded. "You, your Most Excellent... Princess Lady. And..." His eyes scanned the room. "The Ambassador Aaron," he said, pointing. "He spoke to the city guard once at a meeting."

"Anyone else?" Tasia asked.

"The, uh, Wise Man Regent next to you," said Mack, nodding at Norix on Tasia's other side. "And the palace guard there." He gestured at a guard standing at the ready at the far end of the dais.

"You met Ambassador Aaron at a meeting," Tasia said. "That's normal enough for a guardsman. But what about myself, the Regent, and the member of the palace guard? How did you come to meet us?"

"I met your Highness and the guard the night the Wise Man tried to kill you, Princess," Mack said. He sounded a bit confused, as if wondering why Tasia had asked a question with such an obvious answer.

A few members of the council exchanged curious glances and raised eyebrows. Good. Tasia had their attention.

"Most of the people in this room only heard of the attack you stopped yesterday afternoon," Tasia said, sweeping her arm out to indicate the council members. "Would you mind explaining to them what you saw and what you did?"

Mack shifted uncomfortably in his seat, but then sat straighter. He and Dawkin had been the heroes that night, after all, and since they'd been heavily bribed — and threatened — not to speak of the incident by Cole, he'd probably itched for a chance to tell his story for some time. The chance to tell it before a highborn audience — that just made the story even sweeter, didn't it?

"Well," he said slowly. Then he cleared his throat, warming up to his task. "Me 'n my patrol partner, Dawkin, we was eating our fish 'n ale at the guard station in the northeast sector of the Ambassador Quarter when we heard a lady scream. We run out to see what's happening, and that's when we saw the Wise Man knocking you down to the ground. I says to Dawkin, 'I think that Wise Man's trying to kill that girl,' and so we hoofed it over across the street fast as we could. Dawk — we call him 'Dawk' for short sometimes — he's a big guy. He whacked the Wise Man pretty hard with the butt of his sword, knocked him clean out before he could stab you."

Mack smiled when he finished, clearly pleased with himself.

"So the attacker was a Wise Man?" Tasia asked.

The council exchanged glances and whispers at this new fact.

"Yes, Majesty."

"And after the attack? How did I seem to you?" Tasia asked. "How was my manner?"

Mack thought for a moment. "You seemed confused — you'd hit your head pretty hard. And if you don't mind me saying so, Princess, you seemed awfully scared."

"Scared and confused," Tasia repeated. "So what you're saying is that I *didn't* seem like I'd expected the attack?"

The city guardsman blinked at Tasia as if surprised by the question. "'Course you didn't expect it. You was running for your life before the Wise Man knocked you to the ground."

"Thank you for telling the council what you saw, guardsman," Tasia said. "You're dismissed."

He bowed awkwardly and left the room.

Good, Tasia thought. Mack had done well.

Norix claimed that Tasia had staged the assassination attempt herself, but he had offered no witnesses to back up his claim. He'd relied only on defaming Tasia's character and then implying from there that her arrangement of the assassination attempt was obvious, with no need for further evidence. Now Tasia had established through an eye witness that she had been shaken and even injured by the attack. She hadn't reacted like someone who had expected it. Mack was a commoner, and a rough one at that, but he was also a member of the city guard, giving his testimony a bit more credibility. If she could bolster his testimony with that of even more credible witnesses, she could dispel the first false notion that Norix had given the council — the assassination attempt that led to her being named heir was her own doing.

Tasia called Evrart next. He'd already demonstrated himself to be Tasia's ally, and as the Wise Man second-in-command to Norix, he had high credibility.

She had Evrart describe to the council the questioning process of the man who'd attempted to kill her. He confirmed that the man was either a Wise Man or had been well-trained by Wise Men, that he had been able to resist the truth serum, and that an odd iron knife had been found on his person — the kind of knife that Cult of Culo members had used before they had been eliminated from the Empire.

"The man who tried to kill me died suddenly while confined to the palace dungeons, isn't that correct?" Tasia said.

"Yes, Princess," Evrart answered.

"And how did he die?"

"He was poisoned," said the Wise Man.

"I remember when Wise Man Norix reported his death before my father's other advisors," Tasia said. "If memory serves correctly, he said that the poison was extremely rare. Something only a very skilled poisoner was capable of making."

"That's correct," Evrart said, nodding.

"How many people do you know capable of making such a poison?"

Evrart thought a few moments. "I am capable of making it. The Regent, Wise Man Norix, is capable of making it. Other than that... perhaps a few of the master instructors within the House of Wisdom."

"And the poison that killed my father and Commander Cole of Easthook — what kind of poison was that?"

It was a risky question to ask because Tasia didn't know the answer to it, and her father had always taught her that she should never ask a question in public if she didn't already know its answer. But she had a strong guess about the answer, and Evrart had indicated that he was on her side.

Evrart hesitated, chancing a glance beyond Tasia to Norix. For a moment, Tasia's confidence faltered. She hoped her risk hadn't been foolhardy.

"I don't know what kind of poison it was," said Evrart, "because no autopsy was performed. The Regent sent a message from the East that both bodies remain unmolested, so that they would be whole for the royal cremation ceremony."

Tasia's heart sank. She'd been counting on Evrart to draw a direct connection between the poison that killed her assassin and the poison that killed her father. From there, she could have come back to the point that the poison was such a complex one that only a few people in the whole Empire could have created it — and Norix was one of those people. For someone who'd made clear that he was on her side, Evrart's ambivalent answer wasn't helping.

But then an alternative line of questioning occurred to her. "The absence of an autopsy… to whose benefit would that be?"

"The poisoner's benefit, without doubt," Evrart said immediately. "Without identifying the exact poison, identifying the poison's origin would be next to impossible."

"You witnessed my father's death. And the Commander's," said Tasia, gaining confidence in her new tact. "How did those present know that they'd both been poisoned?"

"They both died during the evening meal, within seconds of one another," Evrart said. "And their symptoms were the same — their lips, then the rest of their faces, turned a sickly shade of greenish-blue. They acted as if they were choking, and died of asphyxiation."

The description of her father's final moments formed a twisted knot in Tasia's stomach, but she pushed past it. "Those symptoms," she said, "were they consistent with the same symptoms the man who tried to assassinate me displayed in his last moments?"

"They were," Evrart said, and a ripple of whispers moved through the council room.

"And in your opinion as a Wise Man, someone skilled in logic, philosophy, and the sciences, do you believe it likely that the same poison used on my would-be assassin was the poison used on my father?"

"That is exactly what I believe," said Evrart.

"And I just want to confirm, Wise Man Evrart," Tasia said, her heart beating harder. "You said earlier that the poison used on the would-be assassin was so complex that only you, your mentor Wise Man Norix, and a few other Wise Men scattered throughout the Empire would have been capable of creating it?"

"Correct."

"Of the people capable of creating that poison — and

again, I ask you as a Wise Man skilled in logic — would you not agree that Wise Man Norix, who has become the Regent and therefore ruler of the Empire in the wake of my father's death, had the greatest motivation not only to kill my father, but also to frame me for his death?"

The whispering in the council room increased, growing loud enough that Tasia took her eyes off Evrart to study the crowd.

The expressions on the faces of the lords and ambassadors ranged from shocked to concerned to outraged. She supposed there were those amongst them who were part of the conspiracy to behead her, along with those who had never been pleased by the prospect of a woman inheriting the crown. Those would be the outraged faces, the lords she couldn't hope to win over. But she also hoped there were those lords and ambassadors who were neutral or even favorably disposed towards her. All she needed was one vote greater than half the room to clear her name.

She sought out Lord Galen's face. It was a carefully composed mask of neutrality. He held her eye for a moment, arms crossed against his chest, while the lord of another Western house whispered something in his ear. Then he looked away.

"You go too far, Princess!" Norix shouted above the din. "Everyone here knows that *you* were the one who stood to benefit the most from your father's death! *You* faked the attempt on your life to get him to name you heir; *you* arranged for the poisoning of the one man who could implicate you; *you* arranged for the poisoning of your father while you were located conveniently far from the palace!"

Inwardly, Tasia smiled. She had been hoping for this kind of outburst. Instead of facing Norix, she faced the council. "Council members, please take note of Wise Man Norix's defensive posture. As he notes, it could be argued that I had motivation to kill my father. Yet as the recently named Regent, so did he. And I was 'conveniently' away from the palace during my father's death, but so was the Wise Man." She paused, giving the council a moment to process her counterargument. "Unlike myself, the Wise Man was one of the only people in the Empire who had the capability to create the poison to kill the only man who could have named his co-conspirators. That same poison was likely the substance used to kill my father and Commander Cole. Yet we will never know for sure because no autopsy was performed — which itself was highly unusual. When foul play is suspected in the death of a highborn, an autopsy is always performed — those are the Wise Men's own rules, not the crown's. And in this case, the highborn death caused by foul play was none other than the Emperor himself. Why was an autopsy not performed?" Tasia waited, then answered her own question, her kill stroke: "Perhaps because the poison that would have been discovered could have been traced back to the Regent himself."

She watched with pleasure while more of the council members exchanged urgent whispers.

Norix's composure faltered, and Tasia thought she saw his typical arrogance replaced by fear, if only for a moment. "The council should remember that Princess Natasia — "

"It is not your turn to address the council," Tasia said sharply, cutting him off. "I interrupted you once yesterday, and so I tolerated your earlier outburst. But now you will abide by the rule of law and hold your tongue, Regent!"

She spat the word *Regent* at him, hoping the two syllables would sting as well as a slap across the face. Not every member of the council knew what Norix had done, but he did. And Tasia did. And apparently Wise Man Evrart did. Let him taste his own poison now as his case against her began to fall apart.

"Wise Man Evrart," Tasia said calmly, turning her back on Norix. "I have one final question for you. Regent Norix states that he has known me since girlhood and has concluded that I am avaricious, impulsive, and chasing the throne. You have also known me since girlhood. Please tell the council, is your opinion of me the same as the Regent's?"

Evrart was silent for so long that Tasia's heart began to race. Had she just made a horrible misjudgment?

The younger Wise Man leaned forward on the table. He looked out at the council, his eyes moving from face to face. "No," he said at last.

Tasia let out a breath she didn't realize she'd been holding.

But Evrart wasn't done. "I do not believe that Princess

Natasia is guilty of what Wise Man Norix accuses her of," he said, speaking straight to the council. "Furthermore, I believe it is entirely possible that her theory of the Regent's involvement in Emperor Andreth's death is correct. However, if Wise Man Norix was involved, he was but one piece of a larger conspiracy."

Tasia watched as Wise Man Evrart seemed to lock eyes with someone in the audience. But by the time she looked to see who it was, he'd already looked away.

Lord Galen, perhaps?

46

The final hours of the trial went by swiftly, with no more outbursts from Norix. Tasia brought forth several of the men she'd slept with, including the ambassador's son, Markas, and a rather embarrassed Lord Simon, to challenge Norix and Mylla's assertion that she had "unnatural" tastes for young women in her bedchamber. She then questioned Mylla herself, focusing not on unraveling her handmaid's previous testimony, but on the fact that House Harthing had little by way of dowry to offer for her marriage to Umfrey of House Farrimont. Hopefully, the council would draw the same conclusion that Tasia had — that House Farrimont had offered the very marriageable Umfrey to House Harthing as a reward for the access to the Princess Mylla had provided.

Finally, Tasia brought her own grandfather to the dais, the hard Lord Hermant of House Farrimont. She forced him to admit his strong disagreements with the Emperor regarding the war in the East, and the tense conversation in which he'd all but threatened the Emperor with open rebellion if House Farrimont was asked for one more copper penny to finance that war.

By the time the sun was low on the horizon and the orange light of late afternoon filtered into the council room,

Tasia was exhausted. She had spent more than four hours performing feats of mental acrobatics as she defended herself before the council. She questioned men and women who supported her, those who were hostile towards her, those who had their own agendas and their own vendettas. As she finally reached her concluding statements, her throat was raw from talking and a light sheen of perspiration covered her brow and her palms.

This was it. Her last chance to convince the council of her innocence. Her last chance to save her own life.

"Men of the Emperor's council," she said after Lord Hermant left the dais, "you have now had a chance to hear both the Wise Man Norix's argument against me as well as my defense of myself. He leveled accusations against me and I responded in kind. But the truth is..." Tasia let out a long breath as she looked from face to face. "The truth is that I don't know exactly who killed my father, or why. The only thing I know for sure is that I did not. I can promise you, though, that if you allow me to take my rightful place as Empress of the Four Realms, as my father intended, the first thing I will do is investigate the Emperor's death and bring those who plotted against him to justice."

The Princess paused, gaging the reactions of her audience. Some nodded their heads; some maintained blank or hostile faces.

"I admit that I have not been a perfect princess," she continued. "At times I was willful and insubordinate towards my father. But as Wise Man Norix himself pointed out yesterday, such behavior is not particularly unusual for a person of my age." As she'd hoped, the statement earned a few low chuckles from the men assembled in the room. "I further admit that I had private relations with several young men outside the protective boundaries of marriage, and that such relations were rather unbecoming for a woman of my station. You have heard from some of these men this afternoon. However, my minor rebellions against my father's rule and my lack of decorum as a princess do not make me a killer."

Tasia turned her head, looking past Norix to meet Adela's eye on his other side. Tasia had avoided her sister's gaze for the whole afternoon, not wanting to become distracted by Adela's distress. But now the Princess studied the younger girl's face. Her poor sister. Adela had been manipulated by Norix into agreeing to a marriage that she probably did not want, and she had most likely been half-convinced by the Wise Man that her older sister, the closest thing she'd ever had to a mother, was responsible for the death of their father. She'd been forced to watch while Norix ripped Tasia's character apart in an attempt to have the Princess beheaded. Today, she'd had to hear Tasia fire back, casting aspersions on Norix and several others, including their grandfather.

If I survive this, Tasia told herself, *I will make sure I never neglect her again.*

"I loved my father," Tasia said, still holding Adela's gaze a few seconds longer. Then she turned to address the council once more. "I never wanted harm to come to him, no more than I wanted my mother to die when I was seven, or my brother to die when I was fifteen. Each death has been a deep wound that remains unhealed. Those of you who have lost mothers, brothers, and fathers will certainly understand. You will now vote according to your conscience, but no matter how you vote, know this: I am not responsible for the poisoning of the Emperor Andreth or Commander Cole. Nor have I ever committed treason against my family, the royal House of Dorsa." She waited a long moment, hoping her words would impact the councilmen. "That is all I have to say."

Tasia barely heard Norix as he gave instructions for the vote. Instead, she tried to read the faces of the council as the white and black marbles were passed out through the room. About fifteen minutes passed between the time the marbles were passed out and the time they were collected by two palace guards, one holding the chalice in which the marbles were placed, one watching to ensure that each man voted and voted only once. The marbles clinked inside the chalice one after the other, each one bringing Tasia closer to her fate.

The two guards brought the chalice full of marbles back to the dais, waiting for instructions before Norix.

"Normally, the palace's senior Wise Man would be the one to count the votes. However," he said, an indulgent half-smile on his face, "since I have been *implicated* by the Princess in the Emperor's death, it might be considered improper by some for me to do the counting. Therefore, I call on Wise Man Evrart and Wise Man Crestin to count."

The two Wise Men, who had been waiting at the side of the room, crossed to stand in front of the dais. One by one, Evrart removed the black marbles that indicated guilt; Crestin removed the white ones. The two Wise Men counted silently as they transferred their marbles to separate containers held by guards standing on their other sides. Once the marbles had been separated, each Wise Man counted a second time.

Tasia held her breath while the marbles were counted. There were eighty-one noble households throughout the Emperor, each of whom were represented at the trial either by the lord, the lord's heir, or the chief Wise Man. And at any given time, each lord had between two and four ambassadors serving in his district to represent the wishes of the common people. Each ambassador also had a vote. If Tasia's count of the ambassadors was correct, that meant there were currently two hundred and forty-three of them, but not all of them were present. Judging by the size of the assembly, she estimated there were two hundred council members voting altogether.

That made for quite a few marbles to count.

Evrart finished counting a few seconds before Crestin, which gave Tasia a flash of hope. Maybe he finished sooner because there were fewer black marbles than white ones.

"Well?" said Norix when both Wise Men had finished counting. Tasia could tell he was trying to keep the anxiety from his voice, which she supposed was a minor victory. "Do we have a final count?"

"Yes, Regent," said Evrart. He looked at Crestin, who nodded.

"Wise Man Evrart," Norix said formally, "how many members of the council voted to find Princess Natasia of House Dorsa guilty of regicide, patricide, homicide, and treason?"

"One hundred and five, Regent," Evrart answered.

"And Wise Man Crestin, how many of the council voted to find Princess Natasia innocent of those charges?"

"One hundred and four, Regent," said Crestin.

Tasia's stomach seemed to drop a foot. They'd decided her guilty of killing her father, Commander Cole, and conspiring against the Empire. The room began to spin.

"Ah. Quite close then," said Norix, and this time there was no mistaking his discomfort. Obviously he expected the vote against her to be larger. The narrowness of his victory meant that his hold on the room was far more tenuous than he'd anticipated.

"I would like to exercise my right to see the votes recounted," Tasia said. She hoped she sounded bold and strong, not like a girl who was seconds away from fainting.

Evrart and Crestin both nodded and approached her. One by one, they counted the marbles in front of her, laying them onto the table one by one. The room was perfectly silent and still except for the click of marbles against the wooden table.

It must have taken another five full minutes for the votes to be counted in front of Tasia's scrutinizing gaze, but in the end, all she could do was nod weakly.

"Let it be noted," Norix announced to the room, "the Princess had the votes recounted and it was confirmed to be one hundred five votes to one hundred four. According to the laws that have governed the Empire since the advent of the House of Wisdom, the Princess Natasia of House Dorsa is hereby declared guilty. She will face death by beheading tomorrow before the eventide meal within the Courtyard of Justice here in the palace. All highborn personages and ambassadors are invited to attend as witnesses, but attendance is not mandatory. Following the execution, the ceremony of ascendancy will take place here in the council room, officially passing rulership of the Empire to me, Wise Man Norix of the House of Wisdom, senior counselor of the late Emperor, to hold until such a time that the Princess Adela and her betrothed, Theodorus of House Farrimont, come of age to jointly rule the Empire. Good evening to all of you."

Having said this, Norix rose from his seat and swiftly exited through the rear door of the council room, the door that led directly into the Emperor's private offices.

The rest of the council seemed dazed, and rose from their places slowly, almost languidly, as if waking from a deep sleep.

The Princess did not rise at all. She stayed seated until the rough hands of palace guardsmen hoisted her to her feet.

"Come on, then," one of them said, not bothering with the formality of *"Princess"* or *"Your Highness."* "Time to go back to your rooms."

Tasia walked beside him on leaden feet.

So. That was what it would all amount to. A fine but short life, sometimes sorrowful, sometimes joyful, to be concluded with her head rolling off the executioner's block.

Mother, she thought. *Nik. Father. I will see you soon.*

Perhaps death would not be so bad. Perhaps she would find Joslyn there, and the two of them could be together without complication.

47

How should a person with clear faculties and sound body pass the hours when they know the time of their own death is upon them?

Should they write letters to everyone they have loved, along with everyone they have hated, to give their final statements?   And what should those statements include? Sentiments of affection, recollections of times spent together, apologies for mistakes made?

Promises of vengeance from beyond the grave?

Or should the man or woman who faces his or her own mortality write no letters at all, and instead sit quietly, perhaps in prayer or meditation?   But perhaps it would be better to eschew quietude for one last display of life-affirming joy, dancing naked and singing with abandon.

What of the inevitable fear?   Should they anesthetize themselves through some drug, drink, or food?   Is it better to experience the fear, since at least fear marks them as still living?

Princess Natasia of House Dorsa could not decide what to do with her last hours, and so she ended up doing almost nothing at all.   She sat at her table and gazed out the window, dimly hoping she might spot one of her mother's white songbirds.   If she saw a bird, she told herself, it would be a sign of some sort — a sign that her mother was still with her, still holding her hand even during this grim hour.

She kept Joslyn's apa-apa poncho in her lap while she sat, occasionally pressing it to her face to smell what was left of the guard. The scent nourished the hope that maybe the Wise Men were all wrong, and death was not mere oblivion. Maybe the commoners who still believed in the old gods were right, and she would be ushered into the Hall of Rest once her head was separated from the rest of her, and there she would find her precious guard.

Soon it grew too dark to watch for birds. The courtyard emptied of traffic; members of the household staff came out to light the four lanterns in the courtyard's corners. Still Tasia continued to stare at nothing. She allowed herself to remember her girlhood, standing on tiptoes before this same window, watching below for the passage of her mother, her father, the birds. She allowed herself to remember the joy she used to feel when she spotted Mylla crossing the courtyard, heading for the stairwell that would take her to Tasia's quarters. She allowed herself to remember the time that the great cats were there, caged and harmless but still frightening, and the times that traveling minstrels performed there for the amusement of the palace inhabitants.

Even after she ran out of memories, even when it was too dark to see much at all, still Tasia gazed out the window. She realized she'd never sat still long enough to notice the full encroachment of night, the way the shadows grew longer, then thicker, and how they finally swallowed up the last little fragments of light one by one, then tightened their nooses around the circles of lantern light.

Tasia was so engrossed in the scene of shadows playing in the courtyard below that she didn't hear the man who walked up quietly behind her. She didn't see his reflection in the glass, nor notice the way he'd stopped a respectful distance away from her.

The first sign she had of his presence was when he said her name.

"Tasia."

She didn't jump or start. What is there left to be frightened by when one knows that one's own death is only hours away? She simply turned in her seat, dully curious at who might have snuck into her room at this late hour.

It was Wise Man Evrart, and he studied her without saying anything to explain his sudden appearance behind her.

"Yes?" Tasia asked. It occurred to her that she was numb again. The fire she'd summoned to fight for herself during the trial had been spent, and no heat from it remained. Now she merely felt cold and empty inside.

"I would like to ask you a question, and I want you to give me an honest answer," said Evrart.

Her head bobbed with a single nod.

"When you were in the East, you sent one of your men on a quiet mission to befriend the troops and gather information," Evrart said. There was a steel in his voice Tasia hadn't ever heard before. But she didn't care enough about it to wonder at its presence. "He was taken to see the scant few survivors from the battalion that was routed in the mountains. What did he tell you that he saw?"

Tasia didn't answer at first. *Had* she sent a man to befriend the troops in the Imperial Army's camp? The memory belonged to another lifetime. Gradually, the Tasia of that lifetime rose from the deep, fighting through the numbness to focus on Evrart's question.

It had been Alric, the rough but kind army veteran who was probably dead by now. Dead because of her, like too many others. Alric.

"A sergeant. Alric. He told me..." Tasia began, struggling to take her mind back to a time that seemed so distant now. "He told me about men whose hands would sometimes transform into flames, who would sometimes snarl like animals. When Joslyn heard about it..." She stopped herself, letting out a sigh at the name of her dead guard. "When Joslyn heard about it, it was like she already knew. She wasn't the same after the fight with the *undatai.*"

"*Undatai...*" Evrart repeated. It was an answer he didn't seem to be expecting. "A small man word," he said, talking to himself more than to the Princess. "'*Unda*' is one of their many words for cave, or for the heart of a mountain. 'Depths of the mountain' might be a better translation. '*Tai*'... '*Tai*' is a word for fire. A living fire. Sometimes a person with a hot temper is nicknamed '*Tai.*' A man or a woman made of fire. *Undatai.*" He pieced it together. "A living fire in the depths of the mountain."

Evrart stopped, his gaze hardening. "What *exactly* was it that you say your guard fought, Princess?"

"A... I don't know how to describe it," Tasia said. With all that had happened, she'd practically forgotten about the *undatai*. It had become a bad dream, a nightmare which had faded with time and daylight. And it seemed the very least of her concerns. What did an *undatai* matter, given that the heroine who had defeated it was dead? Given that her father was dead? Given that she herself would face an axe the next day? "It was a monster in the truest sense of the word," she told Evrart with a half-hearted, disinterested shrug. "Black skin with fire beneath it. Ram's horns. Sometimes it would change from beast to flame, as if it had no true form."

"Princess," Evrart said slowly, "I want to ask you one more question, and I want your answer to be forthright. I will know if you are lying."

"Ask," said Tasia. "What reason would I have to lie at this point?"

"If your life could be spared, and my brothers and I can find a way to put you back onto your father's throne, would you marshal every resource of the Empire to fight and defeat these... *undatai?*"

Tasia snorted. "Did you not witness your master's performance over the past two days? There is nothing that can spare my life."

"Answer the question."

Tasia narrowed her eyes, taking a second look at Evrart as more of her numb shell fell away. Evrart had always been quiet, unassuming, subservient. Of the Wise Men she'd spent the most time around growing up, Tasia had found him to be the least interesting. But there was something in his dark eyes now that she hadn't seen before. A glint of authority, of self-possession and confidence.

"What is the *undatai?*" she asked him.

"As you said: a monster," he replied. "And the only true existential threat to the Empire and the House of Dorsa."

Tasia said nothing for a moment.

"Yes," she said. "If by some rare chance I survive, and if by a rarer chance I manage to gain my father's throne, I will fight and defeat the *undatai.* Now," Tasia said, a measure of royal authority returning to her voice, "tell me what 'brothers' you refer to."

Evrart shifted his grey Wise Man's robes, revealing a knife sheath that had been hidden before. He removed the knife within.

It had a simple leather handle and a pure black, iron blade.

"My name is Evrart," he said. "Some here call me 'Wise Man,' but my allegiance has long been first and foremost to the Brotherhood of Culo."

Tasia stared at him disbelievingly. "The Cult of Culo?" She pointed at the black knife. "Did you... the man who tried to kill me had..."

Evrart gave a single curt nod. "I apologize for sending one of my brothers to eliminate you some months ago. At the time, it seemed the alliance with Norix was the best way to protect the Empire. I regret my mistake; it was foolish to trust him and the others. I offer to repay my debt by ensuring your survival tomorrow."

For a moment, Tasia only stared at him in shocked silence. For all the times she had wondered who had tried to kill her, never had it occurred to her that the quiet, unassuming, and unimpressively bland Wise Man Evrart would have been the one to send the killer.

Then anger burned away her shock.

"You," breathed Tasia. "You sent someone from the Cult of Culo to kill me!"

"Brotherhood of Culo," Evrart corrected calmly. "And yes. I did. But that is in the past. As is the Brotherhood's allegiance with those who killed your father."

"Allegiance with…" Tasia's face darkened. "Evrart, did you kill my father?"

"No. And neither did the Brotherhood. But we feigned cooperation with those who did for self-protection."

"So you could have stopped it," said Tasia. Her voice was frosty.

"Princess… I will gladly tell you everything I know, but right now we are wasting valuable time," Evrart said. "We need to leave the palace and get you to safety as quickly as possible."

"You want me to willingly leave the palace and go gods-knows-where with the same man who tried to have me killed only three months ago," the Princess snapped.

"Would you prefer to stay and meet your executioner tomorrow afternoon?" Evrart countered. "There will be no interfering city guard this time."

Tasia glared at him but said nothing.

"If I intended to do you harm, I could have done it by — "

The Princess cut him off. "Why? Why save me now? Why help me fight the accusations against me before the council, which certainly put you at risk with Norix?" She recalled one of Norix's lessons on statecraft and repeated it to Evrart. "No one ever gives a royal something out of simple generosity. There is always an expectation or at least a hope of receiving something in return. So what is it you want to receive, Evrart?"

"I will explain after we — "

"Don't say 'after' we leave the palace." She crossed her arms against her chest. "There are fates worse than death, and if I must die tomorrow to avoid one of those fates, then so be it. I will not go anywhere with you until you tell me what you want from me."

Wise Man and Princess each stared at the other for a few seconds, engaged in a silent battle of wills. But Tasia had never been one to lose a battle of wills, and finally Evrart spoke.

"You are your father's true heir," he said. "Once we can reveal the real killers to the public, restoring you to the throne will not be difficult. And once you rule the Empire, you can work together with the Brotherhood to destroy the creatures you call the *undatai*. That is all I want from you. I swear it."

Tasia took a long time to reply, long enough that Evrart

glanced over his shoulder at the door behind him.

"Princess," he said, "the guards agreed to let me in for a few minutes, but we truly must — "

"I accept your offer," she said. "Your 'Brotherhood' will help me clear my name, restore me to the throne, and bring my father's killers to justice. Once that happens, I pledge that the Empire will work to eliminate the *undatai* from our lands. You have my word as a member of House Dorsa and as the true heir to Emperor Andreth the Just."

"Good," Evrart said. He reached into his robes and produced a dried bundle of herbs that Tasia didn't recognize, then muttered something unintelligible and blew on them. "Hold this," he instructed, handing the bundle to Tasia. "As long as you hold it, they will not see you. But do not speak. If they hear you, the illusion will be broken. Are you ready?"

"You can't be serious," she scoffed.

"I am."

"A bunch of... what is this that I hold?" she asked, looking down at the herbs.

"Tasia. We don't have time for this," Evrart said, irritated. "Trust me."

The Princess drew in a long breath. Her choice was to believe one of the most superstitious things she had ever heard and face probable discovery as a result, or stay in her rooms and face certain death the next day.

It wasn't really much of a decision. After another moment's hesitation, Tasia chose probable discovery over certain death.

"Let's go," she said.

48

To say that Tasia was "skeptical" that Evrart's trick with the dried herbs would work was a vast understatement. When he first handed them to her, she gave him an incredulous look and nearly tossed them aside as a sign of her displeasure. But something stopped her. It seemed rather pointless for him to make an effort to play an elaborate game with a Princess who was scheduled to die the next day.

So Tasia gave Evrart the benefit of the doubt. She changed into her riding clothes, and as an afterthought, pulled on Joslyn's apa-apa poncho. Then she held the herbs with both hands the way he showed her and followed him from her chambers.

True to Evrart's word, and much to Tasia's surprise, the guards posted outside her apartments did not even glance in her direction.

"Goodnight, gentlemen," Evrart said to them.

"'Night, Wise Man," one of the guards said.

"Was she in good spirits?" asked the other.

The first guard grimaced like he'd smelled something foul. "Selfish little whore. I hope the axeman doesn't get the blade through the first time, and she has to suffer and bleed before she dies."

Tasia opened her mouth to give a sharp retort, then remembered she was meant to be silent and snapped it closed again.

The second guard gave the first a disapproving look. "She's still a princess of the House of Dorsa. You shouldn't talk like that."

"Goodnight," Evrart said pointedly, and headed down the hall without a backward glance. Tasia hurried after him.

The hour was late; the palace was quiet. Questions swirled through Tasia's mind: Where were they going? What had Evrart muttered before he blew onto the herbs, and why did that make the guards unable to see her? Who else was in the Brotherhood of Culo? What did Evrart know about her father's death?

Not speaking was something Tasia had very little practice with, and the requirement to be silent was killing her as surely as the executioner's axe would have.

Tasia followed Evrart down the short set of stairs that led into the atrium courtyard. Given the path he was taking, she surmised he must be heading towards the Sunfall Gate exit. It made sense; the Princess had friends amongst the guards there. Perhaps Evrart did, as well.

Once they'd entered the atrium, surrounded by fig trees, broad palms, and overhanging trellises heavy with ripening grapes, Evrart slowed and waited for Tasia to come up beside him.

"Don't reply aloud. It will still break the illusion, even though we are alone," he said softly. "I'm taking you out the western gate. From there, we will take a boat down the Royal Canal to the pier, then catch another ship to Paratheen."

Tasia nodded to show she understood. He turned right down a narrow side path, and Tasia followed close behind him.

Paratheen was one of Terinto's two big port cities, and it was one of the many places in the Empire she had never been. But the difference between Paratheen and most of the Empire's other big cities was that she knew things about the others — knew the names of their mayors, the noble House whose land they were on, their industries and size. But her father rarely even uttered Paratheen's name, unless it was as part of an annoyed complaint. The only thing Tasia really knew about Paratheen was that it was notoriously full of pirates, smugglers, and magistrates fond of bribes.

Tasia was in the middle of wondering idly if Joslyn had ever been to Paratheen when Evrart stopped short. Tasia rammed into him, dropping the bundle of herbs in the process.

"Crestin," Evrart said, voice tinged with surprise.

Had dropping the herbs broken whatever strange spell Evrart had cast upon her? Tasia wasn't sure, but she scooped up the herbs and stepped off the path anyway, taking what cover she could from a low-to-the-ground palm tree. A few feet beyond the leaf that drooped before her face, Tasia saw the outline of a man sitting on one of the pathway's marble benches. His head and shoulders were obscured by the leaf, but she could see sandaled feet below long grey robes.

"Hello, old friend," said Wise Man Crestin, who sounded equally surprised. "What are you doing here at this hour? Out for a walk after our rather troubling day?"

"Something like that," said Evrart. "But I might ask you the same thing — what are you doing in the atrium in the middle of the night?"

"Same as you, I presume." Crestin gave a long sigh. "I know it makes me a poor Wise Man, but I must admit that my heart is troubled. The council chose the Princess's guilt by only one vote. One. That means an Empire whose nobility is divided. I've been sitting here thinking about the public announcement about Natasia's beheading that our new Regent wants me to write. It is sure to sow strife in some places. It will bring riots in others, if I'm not careful."

"Ah. Yes, I see the problem."

"Which concerns me," Crestin went on, "especially considering... Evrart, is there someone standing behind you?"

Evrart forced a laugh. "I should certainly hope not. One of the palace ghosts the household staff is always going on about, mayhaps."

From her hiding spot, Tasia saw Crestin get to his feet. "No. There's truly someone behind you. Could you have been followed?" He took a few steps in Evrart's direction. "You there! Come out and — "

"Quiet, Crestin," Evrart said, putting a hand on the

other Wise Man's arm. "It's the Princess. And she's with me."

Tasia stepped out from behind the palm tree. "Good evening, Wise Man."

Crestin gaped. He looked from Evrart, to Tasia, back to Evrart again. "You fool!" he hissed. "What do you think you're doing?"

"She did not kill the Emperor, my friend. You know this in your heart to be true," Evrart said in a calming tone, one hand still on Crestin's arm. His other hand moved slowly beneath his robes. "The Regent is one of the guilty parties — you know this to be true, too. The House of Wisdom dictates that we serve wisdom, truth, and reason before we serve any one man."

Crestin looked past Evrart at Tasia. "The Empire is divided," he said again. "House will turn against House soon. If she dodges the axe — " he pointed at the Princess " — then all hell will break loose." He met Evrart's eye. "I am from a village on the Renkart River, just south of the place where the Imperial Army put down the last of the Western Rebellion. I lived through one civil war. I don't want to live to see another. You must take her back."

"All hell has already broken loose, Cres," said Evrart, still speaking gently. "Lord M'Tongliss tried to warn the council of it. Do you remember? There are beasts decimating the East already, and it is only a matter of time before they spread to every corner of the Empire."

Crestin scoffed. "Beasts? M'Tongliss — the cantankerous Terintan barbarian? You're off your nut,

Evrart." He pulled his arm sharply away.

"Crestin, please. You must listen to me," Evrart pleaded.

"You're going to get yourself killed along with her." Crestin cupped his hands around his mouth. "Guard!" he shouted. "Guar — "

But he never had a chance to complete the word a second time. Evrart's black iron knife slashed out, catching Crestin across the throat. Blood sprayed from the wound, dotting Evrart's face and robes. Crestin's hands went to his throat immediately, the whites of his eyes rolling like a frightened horse. He tried to call for help, but only a rasping whisper came out. Before he could attempt a second scream, Evrart spun deftly, like a dancer, and wrapped both arms around Crestin's head. He twisted his hands sharply, and Crestin went limp.

Evrart lowered the dead Wise Man gently to the ground, speaking over him with words too low for Tasia to catch. It sounded like the same strange language he had used with the bundle of herbs that she'd dropped.

From the marble path, where Crestin's blood was rapidly forming a dark red puddle around him, Evrart looked up. His expression was pained and vulnerable, almost like a hurt child. Evrart and Crestin had been friends, Tasia knew. Killing him must have been heartbreaking.

The distant sound of clomping boots and men's voices echoed towards them from one of the corridors that branched off like a spoke from the atrium courtyard.

"The guard is coming," Evrart said. "And you are no longer hidden. Now we run."

He stepped over Crestin's corpse and grabbed Tasia's hand.

They sprinted through the winding atrium pathways, took the short stairs that led out of it on the other side at a single leap, then ran down another dim passageway. They ducked into a shadowy alcove when a message boy emerged from a doorway, both of them panting with effort and adrenaline as they waited for the boy to disappear down the hall. Behind them, they heard the shouts of the palace's night guard.

Evrart leaned forward, peering out from their hiding spot. "The boy's gone," he reported, pulling Tasia back into the hallway. "Come on, we will exit through the water storage room and cross from there to the Sunfall Gate."

Tasia nodded and followed him at a jog. The palace was filled with caches of supplies in various places, just in case they ever found themselves under siege and in need of their stores. As she ran, she noticed the way the floor changed from smooth marble to rougher cobblestones beneath her feet. They were entering the old part of the palace now, the original hill fort that had been built by an Emperor of Dorsa generations before Tasia's father had been born. It was a part of the palace she rarely had occasion to visit, as it was located far beyond the wing where the royal family was housed. Usually this wing was mostly empty, but given that the trial had brought lords and ambassadors from every corner of the Four Realms, it was quite likely that each room opening onto the hallway was occupied with visiting council members and their staff.

The passage sloped down and curved to the left.

"We're almost there," Evrart said over his shoulder. "There's a side passage up ahead that leads to a set of — "

Tasia rounded the corner behind him... and found herself less than ten feet away from Mylla. The Princess stopped short, as did Evrart.

"Tasia?" Mylla said, obviously as shocked to see the Princess as the Princess was to see her.

Without thinking about what she was doing, Tasia rushed her former handmaid and put the girl into an arm lock that Joslyn had taught her during her self-defense lessons. She pushed Mylla roughly against the wall.

"We don't have time for this, Tasia," Evrart said behind her.

"Traitor," Tasia hissed into Mylla's ear. "Liar. How could you?" She pressed the girl harder against the stone wall. "After all we shared together, you would throw my life away so easily? And for what? A better marriage? I should kill you where you stand."

"Tasia... please," Mylla said, words partially muffled by the wall. "Please don't. I think I... I think I'm with child."

Tasia let go and stepped back as if Mylla had burned her. She glanced at her former handmaid's midsection, as if it might offer some clue. "Then it is your unborn son or daughter I'm showing mercy to, not you."

"I had to do as my father told me," Mylla said,

desperation tinging her words. "I had to. You understand what that's like."

Tasia shook her head slowly. "No matter what my father had asked of me, I never would have given him your life. Never."

Mylla took a tentative step towards the Princess. "I love you."

Tasia snorted out a laugh.

From behind, Evrart grabbed her elbow and gave it a tug. "We *must* go. Now."

Footsteps slapped down the corridor in their direction at a rapid pace. All three glanced in the direction of the sound.

"Go," Mylla said. "I will stall them, send them the wrong way."

"How do I know you won't just betray me again?"

Mylla took a breath, hesitating. "Because my father isn't here this time."

Without waiting for an answer, she hitched up the hem of her dress and jogged towards the place where the side corridor met the larger one.

"Guards!" she called. "Guards! I think I saw something." Her voice faded as she ran from Evrart and Tasia.

"Come on," Evrart said, pulling Tasia's arm.

\#

They made it outside the palace without meeting

anyone else, then dashed from shadow to shadow as they made their way to the Sunfall Gate. Behind them, the palace was waking up as the guard's cacophony stirred its residents from slumber. Candles and lanterns twinkled to life in the narrow windows; the kennel dogs on the other side of the building howled in unhappy unison.

A knot formed in Tasia's stomach. After the trial's conclusion, she had given up the hope that she might yet live. But when Evrart appeared in her room and told her he would save her, she'd allowed hope to spark again. Now, with the guard close on their heels and a gate heavily manned ahead of her, hope threatened to extinguish itself once more.

Her encounter with Mylla hadn't helped matters; for all she knew, the girl told the palace guard exactly where to find her and Evrart. But more likely, since they hadn't been discovered yet, the girl had saved them. Tasia didn't know how to feel about that. She preferred the uncomplicated hatred of Mylla that had protected her from feeling the pain of the handmaid's betrayal.

Tasia drew up next to Evrart, who had pressed himself against the wall of the blacksmith's booth, waiting for a wide-eyed young guard with a lantern to pass.

"What next?" Tasia asked him. "How do we make it through the gate without being seen?"

"We don't," he said simply. "I spoke to the night guard earlier. I told them I would be leaving the palace in the middle of the night, and that I might have someone with me. I gave them a rather significant amount of silver in exchange for their discretion."

Tasia nodded her understanding. It had been smart of him to warn the guards that he might not be alone, just in case something had gone wrong with the charm he'd cast on the bundle of herbs.

"But you didn't tell them the person you would be with was accused of killing their Emperor. And their beloved Commander Cole," Tasia said, finishing her thought aloud.

"No," he answered. "But you have long had a good relationship with the night guard of the Sunfall Gate. That is what I am counting on to get us through the door." He gave her an assessing look. "Will they let you pass?"

The knot in Tasia's stomach twisted and tightened. Sure, she had exchanged bawdy jokes with the guards and occasionally bribed them with copper and silver pennies to let both her and Mylla in and out of the gate without mentioning it to her father or Cole, but that wasn't the same as allowing a convicted murderer through the gate.

Her father had always taught her that in the game of Castles and Knights, one never made a move without knowing its consequences. To know the consequences, one had to know the rules of the game, the opponent's responding options, and how the move would impact all future moves. Most importantly, one had to know one's opponent — their playing style, their personality, their tolerance for risk.

But sometimes Tasia didn't heed her father's advice on Castles and Knights, as she didn't heed his advice in many arenas. Sometimes, Tasia moved boldly, so boldly that her opponents would be taken by surprise and not know how to respond. Sometimes the strategy didn't work, and she lost. But oftentimes, she found that an aggressive risk at the right moment caught the other player off guard and led to a decisive victory.

"There's only one way to know for certain what they will do," Tasia said to Evrart. She pushed away from their hiding place against the smithy's booth, straightened her shoulders, and strode towards the circle of lamplight that marked the Sunfall Gate.

49

"Who goes there?" called a familiar voice, hoisting his lantern higher.

Tasia didn't stop walking until she was inside the circle of light. Evrart stayed just a few feet behind.

"The Princess Natasia," she said. "Rightful heir to Emperor Andreth the Just, future Empress of the Four Realms. Accompanied by the Wise Man Evrart, my senior counsel."

A murmur spilled through the half-dozen or guards who stood in a semi-circular formation around the gate. Tasia heard a sword being drawn, but she didn't look towards the sound. Instead, she kept her eyes on the man with the lantern. Grizzle. The long-time captain of the night guard at this gate, a man she had known since the early years of her adolescence, when she first began to explore the palace grounds at night.

Grizzle glanced left and right at his men, then back to the Princess. His face was troubled. He looked at Evrart when he said, "I take it this is the one you said might be with you?"

"Yes," Evrart said. "Will you let us pass?"

There was a long, uncomfortable silence as Grizzle studied first Evrart, then the Princess. Tasia forced herself not to fidget. The kennel dogs had stopped howling, and now several were barking. For the second time in the past few weeks, someone had set hounds upon her trail. She opened her mouth, prepared to plead her case to the captain of the gate's night guard, but someone else beat her to it.

"She didn't do it, Griz," said a man not much older than a boy to her right. She glanced in his direction. It was Tedric, the guard who'd accompanied her to her father's office the night that Evrart's Wise Man tried to kill her. "It weren't Princess Natasia. It was that bastard who calls himself 'Regent' now. Everyone knows it."

"No, it wasn't," said another young guard on Tasia's other side. "She *did* do it. Crazy bitch wanted to wear the crown, thought she could rule the Empire as well as a man." He spat in Tasia's direction. "Just one more woman who doesn't know her place, that's what I say."

"You'd do well not to say *nothing*, Rob," Tedric shot back.

The other four guards all began speaking at once, some of them arguing for Tasia's innocence, some for her execution.

"Quiet, the lot of ya!" Grizzle said.

The men fell silent. The barking grew louder.

Evrart glanced over his shoulder. "Grizzle, please. If we don't leave the palace now, it'll be too late."

Some hundred yards away, three guardsmen and a dog rounded the corner. A lamp bobbed up and down in the hand of one of them. Even from this distance, Tasia could see they had their swords drawn.

"You, there — Sunfall Gate! Check in!" shouted the lead guardsman.

"Grant of Badenton, palace guard second class," Grizzle called back. He hesitated. "All's well."

The three guards slowed to a trot. The one with the lantern shone the light in Tasia's direction. "An' who's that with you, Grant?"

"No one — a Wise Man and his niece, is all," Grizzle said.

"Very well," said the lead guardsman, tugging the dog's leather leash to turn him the other way.

"It's not just any Wise Man!" Rob yelled at the guardsmen. "It's Wise Man Evrart, and he's got the Princess with him! They're trying to sneak out of the — "

But before he could finish his sentence, Tedric punched him square in the mouth.

Chaos erupted. The guards with the dog charged the gate at a sprint, drawing swords as they went. The dog handler unhooked the leash, sending the dog bounding ahead, snarling and barking. Meanwhile, the guards of the gate drew weapons and threw fists as they fought guard against guard. Swords clanged; men shouted curses; bones crunched and blood spilled.

One of the gate guards rushed Tasia, but before she had a chance to react, Evrart drew his iron knife and punched it through the leather armor and into the man's belly. The guard collapsed forward, nearly knocking over Evrart, who still had hold of his knife's hilt, in the process. He was so preoccupied with trying to dislodge his knife that he didn't see the guard with the black club approaching from his left.

"Evrart, behind you!" Tasia yelled.

But her warning came too late — the Wise Man turned in time to see the club, but not fast enough to step out of its way. He threw his arms up defensively, and the club hit one forearm with a sickening *CRACK*. Evrart cried out in pain, stumbling backward over the body of the fallen guard as he clutched his injured arm.

"Fighting is not about who is stronger or who is bigger," Joslyn said in Tasia's memory. *"It's about who has the advantage in any given moment, and who can keep or steal that advantage. What can you do to take the advantage back?"*

Tasia ran at the guard with the club and shoved him hard from behind. Not expecting it, the guard lunged forward, tripping over the same fallen guardsman Evrart had stumbled on a moment before. Unlike Evrart, however, he wasn't able to regain his footing. He fell face-first into the dirt with a grunt, dropping his club in the process.

Tasia picked up the club and drew a dagger from the guardsman's belt at the same time. He rolled over and made a grab for her, but she hopped back out of his way.

She recognized him. He was one of the guards typically posted outside her father's offices.

"Yield to the true heir of the Emperor," she said. "Or die."

The man hesitated, then sagged. "I yield."

"Good," said Tasia. "I didn't want to kill you."

Evrart got to his feet, still holding his hurt arm. Even in the dim light, Tasia could see that his face had grown considerably paler.

The Princess glanced over her shoulder. In the distance, she saw the silhouettes of men and dogs running towards the battle.

"Let's get going," she said to Evrart. "While we still have the chance."

"Princess! This way!"

It was Grizzle, waving his arm to get their attention. His temple was smeared with blood, but Tasia had the feeling it wasn't his. She nodded and ran to him, pulling Evrart behind her.

Grizzle unlocked the small door beside the gate and ushered the Princess and the Wise Man through it.

"Good luck," he said simply, and slammed the door closed behind them.

They emerged into the flat, graveled area just outside the Sunfall Gate.

"We're heading to the Royal Canal, right?" Tasia asked.

Again, Evrart nodded without a word.

"Are you alright?" said Tasia.

"I murdered one of my dearest friends tonight," said Evrart. "And I think my arm is broken."

"I'm sorry this happened," Tasia said. "And all on my behalf."

"It's not your fault," he said. "It's mine. I never should have cast my lot with Norix. I made things right by sparing you from the axe, but the gods still see fit to punish me for my mistakes."

Tasia gave him a long look, not sure if he was speaking facetiously. "Come on," she said at last. "They'll figure out how we slipped away if we dally."

The two of them took off at a jog for the canal, Evrart grunting in pain every few steps.

"There," he panted when they reached the water. He lifted his good arm, pointed to a black shape on the canal. It was a flat-bottomed canal boat, a single lantern hanging from its prow.

"Who goes there?" a deep voice called.

"A brother, who guards the realm against the night," Evrart answered.

"May the Brotherhood sustain the Empire for another five thousand years," came the gruff reply. A plank fell from the boat to the canal's edge. "Get in, then," said the voice. "It seems like you didn't leave as quietly as planned, which means we need to shove off."

The mystery speaker was right: The sounds of the battle at the Sunfall Gate echoed from beyond the walls of the palace behind them.

Evrart walked down the plank and onto the boat, sitting on a bench. Tasia followed him, and the lantern's soft glow revealed a burly man with a thick bird's nest of a beard.

"Hullo, there, Princess," the man said after pulling the plank back into the boat. He stuck out a meaty, calloused hand. Tasia gave him hers, expecting him to drop to a knee and kiss the ring with the crest of Dorsa upon her finger, but instead he shook her hand heartily, the way commoners greeted one another. "Welcome aboard. M'name's Alvin, but most people call me Cappy."

"Pleased to meet your acquaintance... Cappy."

He smiled good-naturedly. "And I yours." He looked her up and down, then picked up a long pole and shoved it deep into the dark canal waters. The boat swung around smoothly. He pushed down on the pole again, and the boat began to glide south, downriver towards the pier at the south end of the Ambassador's Quarter. "So. You're the one who's s'posed to save us all from the mess we're in, eh? Pardon me for sayin' so, Highness, but ya don't look much the part of savior."

"And you don't look much the part of boat captain," Tasia shot back. "I thought sailors were meant to be skinnier."

Cappy chuckled. "Aye. That they are," he said. He shoved the boat further down the canal, each mighty push of his pole sending them a good hundred yards.

The sound of iron grinding against iron announced the opening of the Sunfall Gate up the hill at the palace.

"Well," Cappy said, amusement lacing the word, "that'll be them figuring out ya ain't in their blessed palace anymore. Hope you're not 'fraid of the dark." He reached over Evrart's head and extinguished the lantern.

"You can still navigate in the dark?" Tasia asked.

"Not really, but it will have to do," he said nonchalantly. "We'll be needin' silence now, Princess, leastways 'til we get to the harbor."

Tasia nodded, realizing only after she did it that he

wouldn't be able to see her assent in the moonless black night. She watched the palace lights grow distant, and she wondered if she would live long enough to see her home again. The palace had always seemed a curse before, a burden she'd been saddled with. Now that she was its exile, she felt a strange ache of nostalgia blossoming in her chest.

Goodbye, she told it silently. *May we meet again on better terms.*

Epilogue

Three and a half weeks earlier

Joslyn swam in and out of consciousness. She lay on the floor of the hut, the bodies of Imperial soldiers around her. She was wounded, mortally wounded, and she knew she wasn't going to regain enough consciousness to tell Tasia what she wanted to say. Despite her delirium, despite knowing she had only minutes left to live, what Joslyn wanted to say was organized neatly in her mind under three headers: an apology, an encouragement, and a declaration.

The apology would be for failing the Princess. Joslyn hadn't intended to fall asleep the night before, but she was weary. So weary. Although she hadn't told Tasia, the truth was that the guard hadn't had a full night of sleep in over a week, not since the night the small man took them to the *undatai*. After Tasia made love to her, the deepest, sweetest sleep she'd had in a long time took her away without permission. And now she had paid for that mistake with her life.

The encouragement would be to tell the Princess to keep fighting. Tasia had been told her whole life that she was nothing but a shallow, vain, and spoiled princess, and so she'd come to believe it. More, she'd come to act the part. But Joslyn had met someone once who had scraped off her own outer tarnish to reveal the pure steel underneath, and lately, Tasia's own tarnish had been rubbing off more and more. She was a warrior at heart, not a mere princess, and she was so close to knowing this truth for herself. Joslyn believed Tasia could still find a way out of her predicament; all she had to do was to keep fighting.

The third thing Joslyn wanted to say, the declaration, would be harder than the other two, because it was the only thing the guard could think of, other than the *undatai*, that truly scared her. She'd managed to say it the night before, and if she'd lived longer, she would've made a point of overcoming her fear and saying it each and every day for as long as Tasia would have her.

I love you, she would tell the Princess if she could manage to claw her way back into consciousness. *I think I have loved you since the day you defended me against Mylla, since the night you stitched up the cut in my side after the Speckled Dog, since the night you begged me to come back to you after I sent the* undatai *back to its own world. And I promise you — I swear in the name of Coyote and Eiren and Eirenna — that my love will always be as unfailing as the path of the sun across the sky, as bountiful as the stars that fill a clear night in the desert, as steady as the rhythm of waves on a stormless sea. Even if I must love you from a distance while you share your bed with others, still I will love you. Still I will protect you, and serve you all the days of my life.*

But there were no days of life left for Joslyn. There

were not even hours left. And so the three things would go unsaid.

The world was grey and spinning, a dull thing whose sounds and images blended and swirled like water headed down a drain. Joslyn was being sucked towards that drain, too, and she knew it was a battle that she could not win.

I'm sorry, she said inside her head, and this time the apology was not directed at Tasia, but at her ku-sai. He would be disappointed if he knew how her life had finally ended.

Careless, he would have chastised. *Rash.*

He'd never wanted her to join the Imperial Army in the first place. He'd tried to stop her. But Joslyn had always been headstrong.

She had a vague sense that the other occupants of the hut were leaving, and at some point after that (was it seconds later? Minutes? Hours?) she sensed that she was alone.

Joslyn was tired. And if her Princess had left, then there was no point in battling the need to rest any longer.

She allowed her mind to drift away, feeling it float like an autumn leaf caught by the breeze. Absently, she wondered where her mind would go. To another place, doubtless.

She just didn't know what that place would be.

#

Blackness.

There was no more drifting. There was only the black.

Then, from the blackness, a voice. No — not a voice, exactly. Joslyn knew there was no sound, but somehow she heard the words inside her head. Like a thought that belonged to someone else.

So, said the voice, and it sounded like rocks and mountains and crackling fire. *You've come back to me.*

Joslyn knew the voice-that-was-not-a-voice well, because it was the same one she'd been hearing in her dreams for the past week and a half, the voice she heard each night since her fight against the *undatai* while the Princess slept soundly beside her.

No, Joslyn said, panicking. *I cannot come back to you. Not yet. My task is not done.*

But it appears you are *done,* said the voice, amused. It spoke to Joslyn the way an adult might temporarily humor the stubbornness of a child. *You are at the edge of worlds. And closer to my world than your own.*

I am not ready to be in your world yet, Joslyn said. *The Princess still isn't safe. You told me I could go back, so I could protect her. She isn't safe yet.*

Joslyn of Terinto, daughter of Salif and A'eshan, the voice said, its amusement disappearing, *we have already made one bargain. Do not test my patience by asking for a second.*

Please, Joslyn said, and in her own voice-that-was-not-a-voice, there was a hint of desperation. A hint of the kind of begging she used to do when she was a slave, the kind of begging she promised herself she'd never do again once she gained her freedom. But everyone was sometimes a slave to someone. Or to something. *Please. I need more time,* she repeated.

No. You have already promised me passage from this realm into your own, said the voice of fire and mountains. *You have nothing else to give that interests me.*

Joslyn thought, searching for something she had or something she knew that the creature would accept as payment. *There are others like you, are there not?* she said after a moment.

The voice did not respond at first. *Yes,* it said at last. *You know there are.*

The voice probably guessed what Joslyn would say next.

Joslyn knew that what she was doing — the bargain she had already struck, along with the one she was about to suggest — was foolish in the extreme. But, as her *ku-sai* might have said once, fight today's battle today. Save tomorrow's battle for tomorrow.

Yet she knew her *ku-sai* would not approve of the battle her bargaining would create. *Careless,* he would have said. *Rash.* Joslyn heard his voice in her head, too, but it did not create in her the same urgency.

Then I offer passage for another, she said. *A second of your brethren.*

And how do you propose to do that? asked the voice suspiciously. *You have but one body to offer as passage.*

I know, Joslyn said, and she hesitated only a moment before adding, *but I will bring you another. I swear it on the name of my true father.*

The voice laughed, and it was a sound like molten rock bubbling from the Earth's darkest places, a sound like a cave collapsing, a sound like villagers screaming while they watched their homes burn.

It was a laugh that frightened Joslyn to her core. And there was very little that frightened the sword master.

Very well, the voice said. All laughter was gone, and it was deadly serious now. *You may have more time in your realm. But the next time you come to mine, you stay. And you bring another with you.*

Are those your terms? You grant me more time in exchange for me bringing you a second body for passage into my world? Joslyn asked, making certain she knew what she was agreeing to.

Those are my terms.

And how much time do you grant me?

There was a pause. Then the voice said, *One year from today.*

Say your terms exactly, Joslyn pressed.

I offer you one more year from this day in your own world, said the voice. *At the end of that time, you will offer your body and the body of one other from your world as passage for myself and one other. We will take your bodies while you remain here, in our world. These are my terms exactly.*

Very well. In this strange place-that-was-not-a-place, Joslyn could not let out a heavy breath — she was not sure that she breathed at all. But if she could, she would let out the long sigh that belongs only to the defeated. Reluctantly, she said to the voice: *I accept your terms.*

The moment she spoke-without-speaking her acceptance, cold air rushed into her lungs and she gasped. The gasp became a coughing fit, and she blinked and coughed and blinked and coughed while the world spun back into focus.

She had been washed down the drain, but the drain had spat her back up.

Joslyn still laid on her back on the floor of the hut, but now color bled back into the world. She stared up at a blue sky, watched as the sun backlit a hawk lazily traversing the clear expanse. In her peripheral vision, she could see the top edge of the hut's walls, charred black from fire.

She hauled herself to her feet, wincing as she did. The place where the sword had pierced her was sore but healing rapidly. She reached out a hand, steadying herself against a wall for a moment before straightening.

One year. One year to ensure that the woman she loved would be as safe as possible for as long as possible.

And then? Well, tomorrow she would fight tomorrow's battles.

She would have to make the most of what time she had. Joslyn sheathed her sword and stepped through the doorway of the hut.

* * *

End of The Chronicles of Dorsa, Book 1: Princess of Dorsa

* * *

Thanks for reading.

Support independent authors — leave a review at Amazon.com.

Kind-hearted readers, thank you for making it all the way to the end of this book.

I set out to write an epic fantasy novel that starred queer women, with the goal of appealing not only to members of my LGBTQ+ audience who happen to love fantasy, but also to mainstream fantasy lovers who happen to be open-minded enough to enjoy a story in which the romance subplots happen to be queer. No matter which type of reader you are, I truly hope you enjoyed the final result.

And if you did enjoy it, I want to ask for just one more minute of your time — literally just one more minute — to leave a review of this book on Amazon.

I'm not sure if you realize how much reviews matter to independent authors like me. We're the "little guys" of the publishing world, trying to get our books noticed despite not having the same resources as big-name authors with big-name publishing houses. Reviews are one of the things that make a difference. People *read* them. People make purchasing decisions based on them. Online reviews are one of the only tools independent authors have to get their books to stand out in a crowded field of competition.

So would you mind leaving a review? One minute, really. That's all I ask.

Get a chance to read the next two books for free.

What you've just read is intended to be the first in a series of three books: *Princess of Dorsa, Soldier of Dorsa,* and *Empress of Dorsa.* Don't ask me when the next book is coming out; my best guess is June 2019, but that's only a rough estimate. *Princess* took longer to write than expected; it's entirely possible the next two will take longer to write, too.

The one thing I can promise is that it's not going to be *Winds of Winter* slow to release. Honestly. I wouldn't do that to you.

When the new books do come out, members of my Readers' Club will get a chance to read them for free. I pick a random selection of readers who say they are interested in the book to get advanced reader copies (ARCs) before the final version goes live.

If you want to be one of those readers and get a chance to read the next two parts of this story for free, you can sign up here: http://authorelizaandrews.com/readersclub

At the same time, I'll give you the free short story I

give all the new members of my Readers' Club. The short story is the first piece of lesbian fiction I ever wrote, published in an anthology of lesbian erotica that has long since gone out of print.

But maybe some of you reading this are more fantasy fans than you are fans of lesbian fiction. In which case: Would you like two free young adult contemporary fantasy / sci-fi novels? I have a series of five books in the YA fantasy / sci-fi genre under my other pen name, R. A. Marshall, and you can get the first two of these books for free by joining the other Readers' Club here: http://ninja-writer.com/free-books/

My Readers' Club is the best way to connect with me. It's where I share snippets of my works in progress, let you know about any sales or events I'm having, give you opportunities to get my new books for free, and highlight discounts from other lesfic authors. I totally do *not* spam you, and if you like lesfic and/or my work, you'll appreciate being on my mailing list. Honest.

WHAT?! No concluding essay?

If you've read my other Eliza Andrews books before, you'll know that this is the point at which I normally conclude with a personal essay. I'm sorry to disappoint you, but... there's not one this time. (There is one brewing for my next book, which should be out in January /

February 2019). Instead, I'll refer you to my blog, where my other random thoughts and personal essays wind up. You can find it here: http://authorelizaandrews.com/blog

Made in the USA
Coppell, TX
03 July 2020